Andy Remic is a young British writer and teacher from Greater Manchester. During his teaching career he developed an interest in martial arts and is now expert in unarmed combat. He can kill a man with a single blow, but prefers writing and hacking computer systems. SPIRAL is his first novel.

Find out more about Andy Remic by visiting the Orbit website at www.orbitbooks.co.uk

D1115915

By Andy Remic

SPIRAL

SPIRAL

ANDY REMIC

www.orbitbooks.co.uk

An *Orbit* Book

First published in Great Britain by Orbit 2003

Copyright © 2003 by Andy Remic

The moral right of the author has been asserted.

The author gratefully acknowledges permission to quote from the following:

Purity
Words and Music by Justin Sullivan
© 1990 Attack Attack Music Ltd
Intersong Music Ltd, London W6 8BS
Reproduced by permission of International Music Publications Ltd
All Rights Reserved

Forgotten Sons
Lyric by Derek W Dick (Fish)
© Copyright Charisma Music / EMI Music Publishing Ltd
All rights Reserved

Get It
Words and Music by Clawfinger
© Copyright control by Clawfinger
All Rights Reserved

A CIP catalogue record for this book
is available from the British Library.

ISBN 1 84149 147 0

Typeset in Plantin by M Rules
Printed and bound in Great Britain by Mackays of Chatham Ltd, Kent

Orbit
An imprint of
Time Warner Books UK
Brettenham House
Lancaster Place
London WC2E 7EN

This book is dedicated with love to my wife Sonia, our liccle baby boy, Joseph, and my mother and father – Sarah and Nikolas.

CONTENTS

PART TWO
TO LOOK OUT WITH COPPER EYES

ACKNOWLEDGEMENTS

Thank you to Jake Crowley for his comradeship, cycling adventures and essential and eternal proof reading; to Dorothy Lumley, my agent, for her belief and kindness – right from the beginning; to Simon Kavanagh, for his insight, need for perfection, and for working me like a bitch – even when I was sulking; and to my wife, Sonia, for her encouragement and understanding over the years. I owe you all many beers!

My personal thanks also go to Justin Sullivan of New Model Army, Zak Tell of Clawfinger, and Derek W. Dick (Fish), for kind permission to quote their lyrics in this novel. Very much appreciated.

SPIRAL

REDUCTION

Demo114: Bolivia

The ancient house sat astride the cliff's rugged shoulders. Sections of rendering had fallen away into the tangled vegetation far below, revealing thick stone slabs underneath: toothless gaps – the dark smile of an old bearded gunrunner, the oblivion kiss of a whisky-drunk Brazilian whore. The house was four storeys tall and had almost been reclaimed by the jungle; this ornate Churrigueresque fortress had been smashed and peppered for centuries by tropical elements intent on a gradual stripping away of its baroque stone carvings.

Something – a *shadow* – slid from the jungle. A figure shrouded by darkness, protected by the night and its moon-suffocating clouds. It climbed easily, fluidly up cliff and carved stone and landed lightly on the walkway's tiles, mosaics that shone dully in what little light penetrated the gloom.

The figure emerged from the shadows and moved lightly across the tiles. Then it paused, listening, a static outline against the night, before sliding again into darkness and vanishing: a ghost; mist; a grey dream.

A deep oppressive silence filled the corridor, at one end of which squatted a riveted steel door, the single portal for the protected sanctum.

Seated, two heavy-set bearded guards, deeply tanned, their hair grease-smeared and lank, were armed with 9mm Glocks and shoulder-slung AK47s. They were playing cards across a small unvarnished table by the warm light of an oil-burning lantern, their brutal scarred features softened by the amber glow, a bottle of cheap vodka their only shared release from the boredom of duty.

There was a soft clatter, muffled, from back along the shadowed corridor and the two men's bloodshot gazes met over the smeared bottle. One man, the larger of the two, removed the bedraggled hand-rolled cigarette from his lips and discarded it in an overflowing ashtray knife-cut from a beer can.

'Your turn, *hombre*.'

The smaller of the two men shook his head. 'It'll be a fucking monkey again. They climb in, looking for food.'

'Not up here. They don't like the climate – or the bullets. Go on, you dirty drunken *mestizo*, go check who's there.' He grinned, baring crooked coffee-stained teeth. 'Anyway, we're safe. If they'd got this far they would have triggered the alarms. *And* there are the *special men* in there with the *hombre* himself,' he sneered. 'We have nothing to fear.'

Cursing, the other man stood and checked his pistol and AK. The magazines were both full and he flicked the safety off. 'I used to enjoy shooting fucking monkeys,' he muttered, and, with his bloodworm eyes as alert as they

2

could ever be in the gloom, dissolved from the friendly perimeter glow of the lamp.

The other Bolivian guard sat, shuffling the cards with the expert hands of a man practised in sentry duty. His eyes shifted left to the digital display on the wall, its plastic casing and LED warnings out of place against the smoke-stained plaster. It registered zero. Nothing. No intruder. No worries. But the fancy electronics made him uneasy. He was a guard trained with traditional weapons: guns and bullets. He did not rate so called hi-tech gadgets . . .

There was a distant sound – almost inaudible. Like—
A hiss.

The seated man frowned, his brow furrowed, his eyes moving from the LED display to the gloom of the corridor. 'Kaltzon, you there, my man?' His words echoed, lonely, a stark contrast with the soft backdrop noise of distant buzzing insects.

He got to his feet and placed the Glock on the table, making a soft *clack*; with his AK switched to automatic he moved with a smooth military precision that indicated a history of violence. Despite his sleazy appearance, sobriety and stark professionalism kicked in; he crept forward, close to the wall, suddenly alert, all senses buzzing with a sudden rush of adrenalin. He reached the corridor junction and glanced tentatively to the right, gun muzzle tracing an imaginary arc of fire. The half-open distant patio doors showed only a beam of faint moonlight breaking briefly through the clouds and spilling over the veranda. There was no sign of Kaltzon.

The guard turned back – and was slammed off his feet, flung against the wall, a bolt of black steel protruding from his forehead. His AK47 clattered deafeningly on the floor tiles. Blood sprayed down his chin, ruining his cheap Hawaiian shirt. His eyes, open and lifeless, stared at the ceiling as his left leg twitched, while a long string of saliva and blood pooled from his slack jaws and formed a slowly growing viscous puddle on the floor.

Demol14: an elite combat squad, supremely proficient and lethally effective in the violent twin worlds of protection and destruction. This was to be an easy gig. Protection: close quarters, waiting for one of Spiral's many top-class analysts to arrive in order to verify certain documents carried – *stolen* – by Sacha Bora.

Bora, Cuban-born, lately of Los Angeles, USA, and before that involved with some nefarious desert activity in Southern Rub al'Khali. He was a man with a unique profession. In the corner of the fortified sleeping quarters sat a pilot's case containing the tools of his trade. The leather was of finest hide, imported from North Africa and handcrafted to a very individual and precise design: the case had been created for the sole purpose of smuggling. Bora's payload was a sheaf of encoded metal documents that, he knew, Spiral would pay well to get their hands on.

The safe room in this lonely fortress had been designed, appropriately enough, first and foremost for the safety of its occupants. The two windows were shuttered with a high-grade steel that was unusual and expensive in this part of the world. The walls were stone, two feet thick, the ceiling and floors solid concrete, the door heavy steel in a frame of the same metal and controlled by digital locks.

The occupant, obviously, was paranoid.

Sacha Bora slept on his back, snoring, a sweat-stained silk pillow beneath his long greasy black hair. The sheets

4

had been thrown free due to the oppressive heat seeping in from the jungle and an air-con unit clattered softly in a corner of the room – its casing armoured, the machinery itself painfully inefficient.

A *click* sounded. Sacha's eyes flickered open, drops of sweat beading on his lashes.

He stared at the ceiling for a while, his breathing even. Then he scanned the room, glad that he was no longer subject to the palpitations that had recently haunted him. Outside sat his two most trusted guards, and the three members of Demol14 were there in the room with him, awaiting Spiral's expert analyst and the money that she would bring with her. Bora relaxed a little more as he watched the DemolSquad; they were rated among the finest and Sacha Bora had had dealings with them on several occasions over the last four years. They were good. No, he thought, they were the best.

Jax was cleaning his S687 shotgun, while Dazna sat with her head resting against the wall as she rubbed at her eyes. Evoss, huge Evoss, was on his feet by the shuttered window. The big man tilted his head sideways, and there was a cracking sound of released tension as his neck vertebrae realigned.

From outside there came a distant muffled roar of engines struggling up the rough mountain roads. Jax and Dazna exchanged meaningful glances. 'What is it?' said Sacha Bora, suddenly – crazily – nervous. He sat up in bed, staring at where his own personal – and concealed – shotgun nestled under an ornately carved wooden chest: the *last line* in protection should Demol14 and the guards outside fail.

Evoss moved towards him, black-clad, menacing and yet, to Bora, reassuring. He pumped his own shotgun to load it and grinned through a mouthful of broken teeth.

'Don't worry, Bora,' he rumbled. 'We are here. You'll be fine.' He reached out to pat Bora's sweat-streaked arm.

A whine cut through the air. There was a metallic *clack*.

The digital locks failed.

The security door smashed open.

'I wouldn't be so sure about that,' came a soft voice.

The figure was of average height and build and dressed in a single-piece dark grey body-hugging garment. The face was hidden by a tight grey balaclava that revealed only the eyes, which were copper, bright and soft.

The voice was lilting, almost beautiful, nearly female but – not quite.

And the grey-clad figure carried no visible weapon.

Everybody froze . . .

'Who the fuck—'

'Demol14, I am here to kill you.'

The figure moved with awesome speed as the three members of the Demolition Squad opened fire. Rounds screamed across the room as the grey-clad figure leaped into the air, somersaulted, twisted, and connected, booted feet first, with the huge bulk of Evoss. The big man fell, and a small gleaming knife had appeared in his chest before he crashed to the ground.

The grey-masked figure looked up – a quick, insect-like motion.

Evoss's gun was lifted gently from the floor.

'You *bastard*!' hissed Dazna, her pretty mouth open in shock. She charged, her gun spitting fire, bullet casings ejecting, but the grey figure was—

Gone.

The gun muzzle caressed Dazna's temple gently. There was a *whump whump whump* as three stray bullets ate plaster before Jax got his weapon trained on the grey-clad figure from across the room. But too late—

'No,' Jax mouthed silently.

The grey intruder squeezed the pistol trigger and, even as Dazna's brains were mushrooming from the side of her head, kicked off from her falling corpse, curled into a ball, somehow avoiding the screaming 7.62mm rounds from Jax's weapon, hit the ground and rolled towards a low wooden chest. From nowhere a shotgun appeared and there was a heavy bass *boom*. Jax was plucked from his feet and blown across the room. He left a huge smear of blood against the plaster, then toppled onto his face and lay unmoving.

Suddenly everything was still, awesomely silent. The flickering damaged light illuminated the kneeling, hunched figure of Sacha Bora. He looked up slowly, glanced around, and let out a long-drawn shuddering sigh. He understood: understood that he was lucky to be alive, understood that he was lucky not to be a corpse sprawling beside the three broken carcasses on the floor.

The grey-clad figure was standing with the shotgun in his – her? – hands.

'I . . . you came just in time,' wheezed Sacha Bora through cracked lips.

The figure said nothing. It made no move – no sound.

Sacha squirmed uncomfortably as trickles of sweat crawled down his face and body.

'I can't believe you killed three members of a DemolSquad,' he croaked. The figure did not move: it made no physical or oral response. '*How* did you move so fucking fast? And are you here for what I think you're here for? I've got it – don't worry, it's safe, I was bringing it to . . . him.'

The shotgun's barrel swung up and with twin snarls smashed Sacha Bora across the room and into a twisted heap in the corner. There was a clatter as the shotgun fell to the ground and lay in a pool of blood. Soft black boots left crimson imprints across the floor while footsteps pounded down the corridor towards the scene of carnage. Men's voices were snarling, shouting orders. The grey-clad assassin threw a switch and the room's shutters began their clattering ascent.

The figure approached the finely carved leather case, hurled aside in the recent confusion. Hands moved swiftly, revealing a further concealed section below the secret compartment. There was a glint as a sheaf of metal sheets was withdrawn and stowed away inside the tight grey clothing.

The assassin leaped up onto the balcony and glanced down at the jungle far below. Fresh morning sunlight bathed the scene and for a few moments the copper eyes seemed to glow like molten metal.

And then the figure was gone, leaving only bloody footprints on the parapet.

There was a distant rattle of machine-gun fire.

The guards who had been examining the room and the four corpses exchanged worried glances.

'How did he open the digital locks? I thought they were foolproof. A billion fucking combinations or something.'

'Hey, look here.'

They lumbered towards the gaping window, saw the footprints in congealed blood and glanced down into the sprawling jungle . . .

Within the damp, dripping cellar deep beneath and *within* the clifftop house, something barely visible dropped to a crouch. There was a scrape – of metal on stone. Then a single red light came on, glowing faintly, an omen of death and destruction.

The bomb detonated.

Fire and hell-fury screamed white-hot through the building, wrenching it apart with the force of unleashed chemical savagery.

In the jungle below, there was a pattering of pebbles, followed by heavy thuds as chunks of stone and plaster described their individual arcs through the foliage and tropical morning mist.

Black smoke rolled up towards the sky, blocking out the newly risen sun.

Demo177: United Kingdom

The wind howled violently across the North Sea's heaving, beating waves towards a dark rearing metal structure, unlit and unloved, pounded and abused by the elements.

The oil rig was old, a cast-off from one of the world's largest petroleum companies. The rusting machinery no longer drilled and pumped, the derrick was a tangle of fused rusting steel being gradually eaten away by sea spray, and the huge engines no longer thundered and beat with life. The rig was a cast-off – discarded, abused, raped, bled, drawn, fucked and forgotten.

The rig was a steel ghost, deserted.

Almost . . .

A figure glided out into the blackness from some pit in the bowels of the machine, wearing a tight-fitting black garment and a rolled-up balaclava. Gloved hands grasped a rusting rail and the man lifted his face, gasping as the wind rocked him, pulled him into a tight embrace and promised him—

Death.

He grinned, revelling in the violent wild-ride feeling, pulled out a cigarette and shouldered his Sterling sub-machine gun as he searched for his Zippo.

'You'll never light that out here.'

'Aye.'

Pulling free the lighter, he cupped the cigarette in a valiant attempt to defeat the gale. Miraculously, the ciga-rette glowed, a bright spark against the gloom. Smoke plumed around the man's face and he inhaled, closing his eyes and enjoying the nicotine rush.

'Scott, this is a fucking shite gig, man.'

Scott merely nodded, turning his back on the wide-shouldered man with the pock-marked complexion and staring out into the black churning waters. 'Get us some coffee, eh, lad? And check on our Chechen friend while you're at it.'

Grumbling, the big man – newly recruited to Demol77 – thudded his way down the riveted iron steps and into the stairwell below.

Scott took his time enjoying the cigarette, gazing out over the rolling waves that hid the Skene Fields. He wondered idly what it would be like, working on a rig, living off the black gold from deep beneath the surface. His mind drifted; he pictured blueprints – of the rig, the seabed pipelines, the outrigged tankers – and thought about the locations of the huge mooring anchors, pontoons and columns that kept this piece of shit squatting like a drunkard in a gutter.

And he thought about himself: Scott; eighteen-year Spiral veteran; fucked up the arse by his superiors and given one of the lamest protection gigs ever devised by the shadowy Spiral planners. To protect Vladimir Kachenyav,

10

Chechen rebel sympathiser and member of VKW, an underground Grozny action group. Vladimir was a hunted man. Scott was merely tired; and he wanted to go home. Wanted to be out of the game. Wanted – that elusive word he never, ever thought he would stoop to consider – *retirement*.

Scott laughed to himself, and leaned out over the rail. It creaked, the noise lost in the wind as he gazed down into that black water. His fear made manifest, close at hand . . .

Scott licked his salt-dry lips and finished the cigarette. He flicked the butt out over the water and the glow disappeared in an instant.

Retirement.

I thought only old men got tired, his inner voice taunted him.

I thought you were a soldier. A fighter. A warrior.

He had seen enough after the Siege of Qingdao to last a man a hundred lifetimes.

Toffee was right, he thought as he moved to the stairwell and caught his breath away from the wild wind. This *is* a shite gig; a full eight-man team locked away on this desolate piece of junk for a whole two weeks with Vladimir, a slightly crazy Russian.

Scott shook his head and spat into the howling wind.

He stomped down the stairs, rigged with emergency lighting that hung untidily from low ceilings, and strode on towards the canteen, his boots hammering the metal, his torso twisting and turning to fit through the narrow doorways with their heavy bastard rims and gunmetal-grey decor.

'You get that coffee on?' Scott grinned as he stepped into the canteen. The smile was wiped instantly from his face. Bodies were strewn across the floor, blood pooling on the grey metal. Blood was spattered up the walls, across the stainless-steel worktops, dripping from the tables and benches. Toffee was sprawled on his back, mouth slack, dead eyes staring as the flickering fluorescent tube above him strobed over his corpse.

Scott did not move; slowly, very slowly, he unslung the Sterling and flicked off its safety. His gaze moved to the right. His teeth clamped tightly and he tasted blood in his mouth.

Fuck, screamed his brain.

Fuck.

Powell was dead, trailing backwards off a bench, blood-speckled fingers clasping the cord of his SA80. Holloway lay face down against the iron-studded flooring. And Worm, arms outstretched, face twisted in abject agony, a huge hole smashed through his throat, looked sightlessly up at the ceiling, blank eyes pleading with the God who had abandoned him.

Focus. *Think* . . .

There had been no sound of gunfire; the assassin – or assassins – had used silenced weapons. The poor fuckers – Toffee and the others – hadn't even known what had hit them. And that meant the assassins were—

Fast.

A blur raced across the edge of Scott's vision and he kicked himself backwards purely from reflex. Bullets sprayed up the iron wall, splashing bright firework sparks that burnt his face. Scott hit the deck hard, rolled onto his front and squeezed the trigger of his own weapon. The base of the stairwell was filled with a deafening roar of gunfire, and ricochets peppered the canteen with hot bright metal flashes as Scott scrambled up and sprinted for his life.

His booted feet pounded along the corridor and the blueprints for the rig flickered back into his brain: corridors,

12

ramps, cranes, derrick – all now seemed a blur and Scott halted, slowed his breathing, and took a quick glance behind him. He stepped sideways into a doorway and waited, his breathing suddenly calm, his professionalism kicking him into—

Reality.

Nothing, no sounds of pursuit, and—

The figure glided into view, its attention focused up ahead, and sensed rather than saw Scott by its side. The head, mere inches from the levelled sub-machine gun, snapped left – and Scott found himself staring into bright copper eyes . . .

He squeezed the trigger.

The world seemed to explode as the Sterling hammered in the confines of the corridor. The assassin was smashed up against the wall and drilled with a whole magazine of bullets whose impacts held the body upright, dancing and twitching, until the 'dead man's click' reverberated in Scott's skull and brought the world to a sudden echoing silence. Scott fumbled for a fresh magazine with gore-slippery gloves, trying not to look at the pulped brains that covered his arms, trying not to choke on the cordite reek that filled his nose and throat.

The corpse slithered to the deck and lay in a slick crimson pool of its own blood.

The fresh magazine clicked firmly into place, and Scott – breathing slowly and heavily through blood-speckled lips – looked left and right. His ears were ringing from the deafening roar in the narrow metal corridor.

What the *fuck* is going on? he thought.

He stepped gingerly over the corpse, then headed towards the steep stairs ahead. Warily, clasping the rail, he climbed towards the night. Rain was pounding, driven by the wind, a sudden heavy downpour. Above, Scott could see nothing but darkness riddled with diagonal slashes of sheeting rain.

Carefully, and with all his senses on full alert, he pulled free his ECube and, with a twist, initiated the emergency call-up. But instead of the usual flicker of lights the ECube failed to respond. Scott stared at the device in disbelief. In all his years as a Spiral operative an ECube had never failed him.

'Fucker.'

He licked his lips again. *Calm*, whispered his raging mind. Focus.

Vladimir: Scott knew that he had to reach the Russian. Had to protect him; save him. Get them both off this desolate rusting graveyard.

The only escape craft that the squad had were boats, moored at a pontoon floater on the other side of the rig. But the most important question now was:

How many killers?

One? Five?

They had killed seven members of a DemolSquad. It had to be more than one. *Had* to be. Which meant—

The game was not yet over.

Scott peered over the edge; the platform, at eye level, was a riveted monstrosity, slippery like black glass, stretching away into apparent infinity. Scott peered along the platform, towards the ramp at the end that seemed to descend into nothing.

Not far.

But not far is always *too far* when bullets are clipping your heels.

What to do? Run or wait?

Scott crept up until he was crouching on the platform; the rain needles drove into him and the wind howled though his jangling brain finding a way into his

14

tight military clothing and caressing him with fingers of ice. His eyes followed every contour that the weak natural light could reveal. He searched for every possible sniping position. He tried to think where best to lay an ambush—

If he could sneak down the left flank of the rig, Vladimir's chamber was nearby; a few easy steps and – hopefully – the fucker would be there, waiting, ready to sprint to the safety of the boats . . . Scott nodded to himself. He craved the nicotine buzz of a cigarette.

It was instinct, more than anything else, that made him freeze.

And then it was there, his worst nightmare.

Cold metal, pressing against the back of his skull.

'No,' he whispered.

He started to turn, but a warning jab halted him. Slowly, he crouched and placed his sub-machine gun on the deck.

'Move.'

Scott started to walk . . . everything ahead of him was blurring and he realised that he was crying – not from fear, fear was no longer an option, but from sheer rancid frustration. Of all the fucking ways to be caught, of all the fucking ways to die—

The *crack* echoed dully against the howling wind.

A limp figure toppled from the railings and disappeared in the boiling black sea below.

Copper eyes watched coldly as it fell.

And, an instant later, the Nex had gone.

DemolS-4: sniper squad: Australia

Rain swept across Sydney Harbour Bay, deluging from towering iron-coloured cumulonimbuses into the churning, raging waters. Rivulets poured down the slick black contours of the bullet-pocked, shrapnel-scarred Harbour bridge, dripping into the chasm below as the lights of distant buildings glittered through the darkness. One half of the Sydney Opera House shimmered, ghostlike, looking almost silver through the sheets of wind-blown rain, its orange-segment sails raised as if in defiance against the elements themselves. But the crumbling, recently bomb-blasted section was open to the storm – the Opera House was wounded, torn, betrayed. To the people of Australia it was a symbol of their world gone mad.

Rex squatted, rain pounding his Gore-Tex wetproof; he listened to the radio and glanced at the ECube in his hand. Digits flickered blue. A voice in his ear said, 'They're on the move.'

Rex edged forward, then glanced down, checking the magazine of the Bergmann 7.65mm sniper rifle. He raised himself, peering from the top of the forward segment of the Opera House. The bridge was hazy in the gloom of the storm, the harbour spread out before him like some majestic oil painting. Rex reached out and steadied himself on the narrow galvanised walkway – he felt like the King of the World up here, wind and driving rain buffeting him. He felt *alive*. He lifted the rifle and touched the ECube to the side of the electronic sight; there was a tiny click, and a buzz as the ECube integrated with the advanced sniper weapon. For a second Rex watched the scope rotate and focus; then he placed his eye against it and the world seemed to spring into clarity.

The bridge was daylight-clear, bathed in a gentle purple tint; he zoomed the scope quickly forward, until he could see each rivet in the steel sections, each bullet hole and shrapnel scar. Then he pulled back and swept left and right, searching for the vans that he knew were coming—

'You OK, Rex?' said a sultry voice in his ear.

'Sure thing, sugar,' Rex said softly, picturing Amber's beautiful lashes fluttering at him over the lip of the telescopic sight on her own weapon. He shifted his weight, sighting on the distant tower block and the position that he knew Amber had secured. She waved, and he returned the signal. 'Is Scope set up?'

Scope grunted over the communication link. He rarely spoke, and Rex's comment was obviously below derision.

Rex moved his own sniper sight back to focus on the bridge, the top of the huge arch. Scope was there, all in black, ready and steady. He had picked the most dangerous positioning of the three, on the Sydney Harbour r itself, and despite being clipped securely in place himself Rex shivered involuntarily. But then, he thought, Scope was a wild fucker, untamed. Some said he was insane; Rex decided that the man probably was.

'Game on.'

The words came from the supporting ground soldiers, Australian Anti-Terrorist Special Forces led by a huge ex-marine named Callum, who were waiting in the wings as the scene unfolded. They were monitoring the suspected terrorist vehicles from the ground. The Spiral DemolSquad was positioned as sniper support.

'Tracking two vehicles: black Ford vans, six occupants. ETA four minutes. Over.'

Rex waited.

There was little else that he could do . . .

Amber went over her drill for the tenth time, checking her weapon, scope, ECube integration, body armour, hair and nails. 'Damn fucking rain,' she muttered, and shifted her weight slightly to ease the cramping in her calf muscles. The crumbling bullet-marked parapet was low, but

17

not quite low enough, meaning that she had to support her weight at an odd angle. After an hour, cramps were inevitable.

Amber swept the scene with her scope. Through the audio link she was listening to the ground soldiers tailing the suspect vans.

The tip-off had come from an extremely reliable source: an ex-KGB agent turned arms dealer who was about to be tried for numerous crimes. He had given them reams of information on terrorist activity – as one of the main weapons suppliers to the Middle East and South America he was in a good position to do so. So far everything had checked out fine and the Australian government had high hopes for this gig. Six Egyptian terrorists were going to blow up Sydney Harbour bridge. They had schematics for the structure and knew exactly where to place the charges.

'Fucking terrorists,' snorted Amber, and swept the site once more.

No vans.

Come to think of it, no ground troops.

'GF 10 through 30, call in. Over.'

No response.

'GF 10 through 30, call in. Over!'

Again, no response.

'You hear me, Rex?'

'I'm here.'

'You see anything?'

'Not a donkey.'

'There's something wrong,' came the sibilant whisper that was Scope's rarely heard voice; both Amber and Rex felt a chill course through their souls. And yet on ChannelJ they could still hear the tail – the *pursuit* – of the vans. *'Heading east away from the Circle Bay area, down Alfred Street, heading towards—'*

Amber swept the area once more. There was a movement of air beside her, a mere parting of the rain – and then the garrotte was around her throat before she knew what was happening. Her gloved hand slammed up beneath the cheese-cutter wire as her eyes suddenly widened and pain sliced into both sides of her throat – she felt blood sluice down her neck and over her breasts beneath her armour as her rifle clattered to the parapet.

Amber was lifted into the air, her legs kicking. She slammed her head backwards, once, twice, three times, hearing a crunch every time. The grip slackened but did not let go. 'Rex!' she managed to scream into the ECube, then slammed her elbow back into the breastbone of her assailant with all her strength. The garrotte slackened and Amber stumbled to her knees, coughing, scrabbling at the wire that was biting into her flesh—

Rex sighted on the parapet at the summit of the dimly lit building. He could see Amber struggling, but her attacker was too close for a clear shot and the rain was falling, obscuring his aim. Then Amber struck back. The assailant stumbled in the gloom and Rex squeezed off a shot into the night, then three more in quick succession. He grinned nastily just as the silenced pistol touched the back of his head and blew his brains and face all over the fine stonework of the Sydney Opera house.

Amber heard the hiss of the bullets as they flew past her. She whirled, crouching low as she drew her Beretta 9mm pistol. The figure flew at her, a kick smashing the handgun from her grip and out over the parapet. Confusion spread through her brain – she had heard twin thuds behind her, *knew* that Rex's bullets had smashed home. *Kevlar?* The question flashed through her mind as reflexes too over. One kick, two – she blocked with her forearms, then smashed a straight right that the figure dodged as it circled. Amber met the stare of her assailant – the eyes were copper, bright – and she hammered out a front kick, connecting. The figure twisted, rolled, and kicked Amber's legs from under her. She hit the ground with sudden shock, the back of her head cracking against the parapet. Stars of concussion flooded her vision – she swung out blindly, but hit nothing. She felt suddenly weightless – and realised with horror that she had been lifted from the ground again. 'No!' she yelled, her arms and legs flailing. But wind rushed up past her as her eyes widened and she screamed in terror and despair. Then she hit the ground and the scene, the act and the play were finally over.

Scope was considered a reptile by those who worked with him. He had no friends and was – or seemed to be – emotionless. He was dedicated, professional – and damn near the finest sniper in the whole of Spiral. Rumour had it that he could clip the tip from a mouse's dick at ten thousand paces and could thread cotton through a needle's eye with an aimed bullet.

He was appalled that he had not seen them coming. Four figures in black had climbed the war-torn bridge below him without being seen. *Impossible!* screamed his mind as they closed in for the kill. He swung the Bergmann and shot the first figure in the face – there was a hiss, a spray of blood and teeth, and it fell back limply and bounced its way down through the bridge's structures into the gloom below.

Lightning crackled across the sky. In the glow, Scope grinned nastily.

The three figures pulled silenced pistols in fluid movements and everybody started shooting at the same time. Flashes flickered atop the Sydney Harbour bridge, an accompaniment to the lightning. Another dark-clad shape fell, hurled backwards like a rag doll, and pitched towards the narrow strip of tarmac below. Then a bullet hit Scope in the shoulder, spinning him round as a second smashed into his groin and a third into his throat. Blood spewed from his crimson slick lips. He groaned 'Fuckers' as he started to topple, but the security harness that held him whirled him round and he jerked to a halt on the line where he slowly rotated. Blood dripped from his limp corpse. The two remaining dark figures crept closer and put five more bullets into Scope's body. Copper-eyed stares met for the briefest of instants. Then the shadowy beings sprinted away across the dizzying heights of the bridge.

The truck screeched to a halt, its headlights slicing through the heavy downpour. Callum stared hard past the thumping wipers, then barked 'Out.' Ten men leaped from the cab and the truck's tailgate. They spread out, SA80s covering each other's arcs of fire. Callum crept back and crouched by the body of the dead soldier. His throat had been cut. Callum swallowed hard, glancing around at the other six bodies. Not a bullet had been fired. 'They hit them hard and fast, boys. Let's spread out, see what the score is. Albert, you got that fucking comms up and running yet?'

'The whole net's dead, sir.'

Callum nodded, then motioned for the men to move out.

They moved purposefully through the downpour. Lightning flickered overhead, and Callum strained to see the sniper atop the bridge. He could see something, some sort of movement briefly illuminated – but then it was gone to be replaced by a haze of rain and confusion.

And Callum knew. Could feel it.

They had been fucked, hard and proper – but to what purpose? Had the terrorists planted the explosives? Was the bridge about to go the same was as the Opera House?

Twenty minutes later, Callum was leaning against the bridge, a soggy cigarette between his lips, smoke pluming around his face. At his feet, on a stretcher, lay the very dead body of Scope. The sniper's face was a mess, his head shot to pieces, most of the rear of his skull missing. Callum stared at the dead eyes and shuddered.

Albert approached. 'Comms are back on-line; the other two snipers are dead as well. No sign of any assailants – except for the fucking bullet casings, of course. Boss, I just don't get what the fuck went on here.'

'Decoy,' said Callum softly from around the bedraggled cigarette.

'Decoy? What about the bridge?'

'This wasn't about the bridge,' said Callum. Reluctantly, he took the cigarette from between his lips and tossed it over the railings, into the black, oily bay below. He faced Albert and their stares met. 'Somebody wanted those snipers dead.'

'So this was a hit?'

Callum nodded. 'Oh yes, my friend. And of one thing I am certain: whoever did this, whoever killed this Demolition Squad – I'm sure as hell glad they're not looking for me.'

'How do you know they're not looking for you?' whispered Albert.

Callum shrugged. 'I'd already be dead,' he said simply.

CLASSIFIED VK12/084/SPECIAL INVESTIGATIONS UNIT
Hacked ECube Interception
Date: August 2XXX

In the undercover world they are called Demolition Squads and work for Spiral. They have no official name and do not 'exist'. They are an urban myth. They are ghosts. These clandestine 'non-existent' groups have more extensive knowledge, training and experience than the British SAS, the American CIA and the former Soviet KGB. They are considered more covert than any global government organisation or secret police network. To all world powers and agencies who even suspect their existence, they are the elite of the elite.

One member of a DemolSquad, code-named Purity, has made herself known to us. We have verified suspected links with the secretive organisation known as Spiral. Purity claims that Spiral, in its battle to crush terrorists, stabilise governments and smash evil and corruption wherever they are found, has developed a prototype CPU to assist their mission. This information is highly classified.

Just before Purity's assassination she claimed that something was wrong with Spiral and with the DemolSquads. In her words: a traitor. Purity mentioned a word: Nex [context: *the* Nex, or *our* Nex] that we suspect indicates an assassin/hunter of some skill.

The woman/code subject vb12Purity was fished from the Danube, SW of Bolgrad, earlier this month. The subject had had her throat cut.

SIU Transcript 2

CLASSIFIED TFG1776/250/SPECIAL INVESTIGATIONS UNIT
Hacked ECube interception
Date: September 2XXX

Transcript of digMail:

'The breakthrough in processor development has escalated beyond all comprehension; the code-core RI nano-gates are writing themselves, and the tech processes used are something we would never have dreamed possible. In initial benchmark tests the speed has physically killed all current military hardware – this processor is at least 50,000 times faster than any other currently in development. The MIP ratings are truly incredible and this chip will revolutionise computing in the 21st Century. It will have groundbreaking effects on all aspects of computing, from military applications to world economics.

'Enclosed are the encoded data files on cellular cube structure, together with schematics for the etching processes needed in creating the QIII cubic processor – #TYGUgfuyd . . .'

###TRANSFER FORCIBLY TERMINATED//HACKER INVOLVEMENT SUSPECTED###

Scanning Terminals . . .

Intrusion detected . . .

Scanning HUT ports . . .

Locked.

PART ONE

THE SEARCH FOR AN UNREAL GOD

we've seen the **restless children**
at the head of the columns
come to **purify** the future
with the arrogance of youth
nothing is as **cruel** as the
righteousness of innocents
with **automatic weapons**
and a gospel of the truth

Purity
New Model Army

CHAPTER 1

ALONE

Carter watched the woman wheelspin the BMW 740i up the snowbound lane, park at a curious and somewhat precarious angle, climb from the warmth and comfort of the car and kick the waxed and polished wing three times. She glanced up towards him, towards his shield of glass. He waved, but she did not see him through the thickly falling snow.

Carter moved across the heavy rugs, luxuriating in the feel of the fur and wool under his bare feet. He threw another log on the fire and Samson, his chocolate Labrador, looked up from his luxurious basket and tilted his head slightly. The dog gave a little whine. Carter smiled. 'She loves me really,' he said and winked. Samson's head dropped and the dog grunted, closing his large eyes.

Carter flipped open the front door with an IR and collapsed into a deep sofa with a glass of red wine.

He heard her, stamping snow from her boots and cursing the climate, the location and, most of all, him. He smiled wryly, swirling the wine and peering into its velvety depths as the woman climbed the stone steps to the front door.

'Are you in?'

Carter raised his arm, and peered over the back of the sofa. 'Guilty, Nats. How's life?'

'It's Natasha, you arse, not Nats.'

'Hmm, tetchy. Wine?'

'What sort?'

'Red. Some kind of Italian stuff, I think. Does it matter?'

'It matters, Carter. Why the fuck did you move out here?'

'I like it out here.'

'It's in the middle of nowhere!'

'That's what I like about it. The cities are full of the military. And after the London Riots they've moved in Justice Troops – JT8s.' Carter shook his head. 'It's not what I call a pleasant environment conducive to relaxation and long life.'

Natasha gave a short laugh, her gaze moving around the room. 'And I can't believe you haven't even got a fucking car.'

'What would I need a car for?' Carter frowned. 'I have everything I *need* right here.'

Natasha stopped, took a deep breath and counted silently as she summoned patience. She removed her scarf and gloves, closed her eyes for a moment and threw her Berghaus fleece over a nearby leather chair.

'I hate Scotland,' she said.

'It's where I was brought up,' said Carter softly. He drained the glass in one. 'Where I was born. It has character and strength and solitude. Sure you won't try some wine, you bad-tempered little temptress?'

'Maybe a whisky.'

As Carter found the Lagavulin decanter and poured two generous measures, he watched Natasha's slim and athletic form. He licked his lips and thought back to better times – long nights and longer days, making love on this very floor, laughing, talking, drinking . . .

He handed her the glass. She ran a hand through her short black snow-damp hair, leaving it spiked – the way that he knew she knew he liked it. He smiled in anticipation, downed the single malt and threw the crystal glass into the fire where it shattered; for a moment the flames grew bright.

'You always were over-dramatic,' said Natasha sombrely, staring down into her whisky. She had moved to sit in front of the fire and she twirled her glass gently, seemingly lost in thought.

'What do you want?' he said finally when he realised that she would not break the silence without prompting.

Flames crackled for a while and Carter wondered if she had heard him.

'How do you know I want anything?'

'It's been over a year,' sighed Carter. 'You still working for that slave-driver Spiral?'

'Of course. Our role grows more important with every passing day.' She smiled softly. 'We have a job for you.'

'Ah.' Carter sighed, climbed to his feet and walked to stand in front of the window. The snow was falling thick and fast and he could see, dim through the swirling flakes, the lofty peaks of Ben Macdui, blue-grey and sheer – exhilarating. The wind howled in the distance and Carter shivered, despite the fire's heat in the room. He felt a twinge of disappointment that he could not see the frozen lake.

'Is it a solo, or a joint assignment with a DemolSquad?'

'Solo. A protection issue.'

'I am finished with Spiral,' Carter whispered softly, turning and watching Natasha through heavy half-lowered eyelids – internal movie screens flashing images of events he would rather forget, nightmares he would rather not relive. She stood, a fluid and graceful action, and moved to him, draped her arms across his shoulders and ducked a little, looked up into his eyes.

'I know you've turned down the last four gigs – as with all Spiral jobs that is your prerogative. But this has come from the top. Real important.'

'It always is,' said Carter bitterly.

'Things are getting worse,' whispered Natasha. 'The world is changing, Carter, and you're fucking *hiding* up here . . .'

She tailed off as she saw the look on his face and cursed herself inwardly. That had been unfair; Carter was good. No, he was the best. And after the Battle of Cairo7 . . . he had the right to live and rest any way he pleased . . .

Natasha took a deep breath.

'Look, *I* want you to do this,' she said. She moved forward slowly. Her lips touched his and he allowed her to kiss him for a few moments. Her breath was sweet, her lips soft and inviting.

'Why?'

'I empathise with this girl's situation. She is young, alone, afraid. And you are the best, Carter.'

'Bull – shit.' He kissed her again, anyway, tasting Lagavulin on her lips. When he pulled away, he was frowning. 'What about Jax? Or Scott? Or Evoss?'

There was a long pause. Natasha averted her gaze and looked over at the fire as though debating with herself. Carter caught a glimpse of something then, in her face, in her eyes. There was something that Natasha knew, a secret she did not wish to share.

32

Carter smiled tightly and reached up, stroking her cheek. She turned back to him, licking her dry lips.

'I recommended *you*, Carter,' she said softly. 'Don't turn me down. Don't let *her* down.'

'Who is she? Why should I care?'

'Maria Balashev. She's nineteen. The niece of Count Feuchter.'

Carter pulled away for a moment. Reflected flames danced in Natasha's deep brown eyes. He searched her face for – he shook his head, unsure of the unspoken signs he sought.

'Feuchter? Where the hell am I going?'

'You shouldn't let me manipulate you,' said Natasha, turning and walking away from him.

Carter watched the hypnotic sway of her hips. He swallowed – hard. How long have I been a hermit? he thought. How long without lips to kiss, soft skin to nibble, a flat stomach to taste . . .

'I can't help myself, Nats.' His voice was hoarse. 'Where am I going?'

'Schwalenberg, Germany, in the Weser River Valley. My homeland, Carter, near the place I was born.'

'Weser? Isn't that where the Pied Piper enticed the rats to their deaths?'

'Could be,' said Natasha, 'although I'm no student of history.'

'Nor literature, I see.'

'Feuchter is based at Spiral_Q, in Saudi Arabia – he's come over to Germany to give a series of lectures to Spiral operatives, and for a celebration of his achievements working on several breakthroughs in processor development. Many of those working on the project have been based in Germany for – shall we say, security reasons . . .

33

Carter sighed and shrugged. He rubbed at his suddenly weary eyes, then met Natasha's gaze. 'Will you stay?'

There was a pause. Natasha put her hands in her pockets and looked at Carter steadily. She tilted her head, her lips pursed, her beautiful brown eyes unreadable. Carter realised that she had aged – matured – wonderfully in the year since he had last seen her. And he realised too that he wanted her more than anything in the world . . . more than *anything*.

'*And you turned her down,*' mocked Kade, a distant whisper in his head. '*You dick. You sent her away.*'

Carter gritted his teeth and battled to ignore the acid sly observations of the ever-unwelcome voice within his mind. Fuck off and die, Kade, he thought.

Then he forced a smile to his face and looked up to see the kindness in Nats's expression.

'Not tonight,' she whispered. She smiled. 'But we'll make a date. When you get back, maybe.'

'You mean in another year when Spiral has another job for me and decides that a cheap kiss is enough to purchase my skilled services?'

Natasha moved forward and placed a finger against his lips. 'When you get back from Germany. We'll meet then.'

'Promise?'

'I promise. Here.'

She tossed Carter a small cube. It was soft under his fingers, and he turned it slowly; similar in size to a matchbox, the dull matt black alloy shone as the cube fitted neatly into the palm of his hand. 'New model?'

'Version 4.2. ECubes have moved on since you last worked for us.'

'Really? Same basic functions?'

'Yeah.'

An ECube was an electronic communications device, standard Spiral issue. Running the V4.2 ICARUS operating system, it sported a 12GHz RISC processor and 256 gigabytes of static RAM. It was solid-state – no moving parts – and quite robust; it had voice – and fingerprint-recognition facilities; it could act as an advanced GPS – could navigate across the whole of the world, relaying data straight back to Spiral mainframes and thus allowing Spiral to keep a tab on its finest operatives. It also had a few hidden and very ingenious little tricks within its alloy casing.

Natasha turned to leave, gathering her fleece coat and gloves and moving to the door and the steep steps beyond. 'When are you coming back to the real world, Carter? It misses you, y'know?'

'I enjoy the seclusion.'

'That wasn't the question.'

'Then, "when I have a reason to" would be the answer.'

She held his gaze for a long time, then turned and left. He listened to her departure, then moved to the window and watched the plumes from the 740's exhaust. Wheels spinning dangerously, the BMW cut a swathe through the fresh snowfall and was soon gone, tail lights flickering into nothing.

Carter felt suddenly, terribly alone.

For a while he watched the snow, then stared down at the ECube nestling in his palm like a tiny Chinese puzzle box. He squeezed it, and it came to life. Small blue digits flickered across its alloy face. He looked from the ECube to the roaring fire – and for a moment was undecided . . .

He could destroy it. Walk away.

He had sworn that he was through with Spiral.

Because . . .

When he was through with Spiral, then he was through with Kade.

Carter shivered, staring into the flames.

Spiral did not know about Kade. But then, *nobody* knew about *Kade*. Kade was a ghost that Carter would rather forget: a dark and psychopathic slice of his personality that had found itself a voice; a dark and menacing angel squatting in his mind. A demon ready to feed, to prove itself again as it had in Egypt and China and Poland . . .

Carter sighed.

He turned from the flames and slumped into the embrace of the deep and comfortable sofa. Samson climbed to his feet ponderously, for the dog was large for a Labrador – hence his fitting and none too subtle name – yawned, padded over to Carter, climbed up slowly next to the man and placed his wide head on Carter's lap. Samson gave a huge dog sigh and Carter rubbed gently at his velvety ears.

Protection, Natasha had said. Carter's mouth was dry and he realised that she – and Spiral itself – understood him perfectly. No more killing. No more demolition. No more destruction . . . Those days were over. Gone. Dissolved into dust, just like Cairo.

Protection.

The protection of the niece of a senior Spiral weapons researcher.

No killing . . . no bombs . . . no cool collective violence . . .

'Talk to me,' he said to the ECube. Instantly it locked onto his voice pattern and linked with a *click* to the Spiral mainframe . . .

CLASSIFIED FFUCH/111/SPECIAL INVESTIGATIONS UNIT
Data Request 117554#887

Count Feuchter; German professor, born in Schwalenberg, educated in Munich, London and Prague. Great-grandfather killed by the Nazis during World War II after being tortured somewhere on the German/Austrian border. Mother and two sons fled to Italy, then to England for protection after the war was over; Feuchter comes from this bloodline.

Expert in computing systems, specialising in processor function and artificial intelligence. Currently pioneering military processor after setting up Spiral_Q, with co-programmer and system developer, Durell. Spiral_Q – currently based in Rub al'Khali, Saudi Arabia, also named The Great Sandy Desert. The technologically advanced research station has been set up with the knowledge of the Saudi government in what is a largely completely unexplored region of desert; the Saudi government has been bribed with technology and information to turn a blind eye on the operations there, and no satellite locks have been discovered: the station is, therefore, invisible to most of the snooping eyes of the world.

QIII Military Proc - classified; Level Z
access required. <Lock>

Caution activation: Feuchter has been the
victim of various death threats; suspect
terrorist activity, probably Middle Eastern
influences with sights set on the 'rumoured'
processor which is in development. German
Special Forces are involved with protecting
Feuchter on home ground. One weak link could
be his niece, daughter of his murdered
brother; she travels with him everywhere and
could be a target for kidnapping, even
murder in order to blackmail Feuchter or
garner information on the QIII.

Keyword SEARCH>>DURELL, QIII [lvlz], NEX
[lvlz] SPIRAL_Q

Carter peered out through the smoked glass as the
engines whined. He grinned like a young boy – unable to
contain himself – as he felt the power of the machine
beneath him wind up like a turbine.

The Sikorsky RAH-66 Comanche eased up from the
snow, suspension bobbing as it was released from the aircraft's dead weight, and Carter watched the Scottish
mountains drop away beneath him. Exhilaration was his
mistress and he licked his lips nervously – he hated flying,
and yet drew some perverse pleasure from the stimulation
such machines gave him. The pilot was ensconced in his
HIDSS – a Helmet Integrated Display Sighting System –
and looked somewhat alien as he eased forward and the
twin 1380 shaft-horsepower LHTec turboshaft engines
moaned like huge ferocious animals in pain.

'Hey, Langan, you hear me in that ugly thing?'

'I hear you, Carter.'

'I thought these choppers weren't in production yet?'

'They're not. Especially ones like *this*. It's a MkIV. *Very* advanced.'

'Is it fast?'

Carter was slammed back, heart in his mouth.

Stupid question, thought Carter as the engines finally returned to their 'normal' speed. His stomach churned and he regretted his fried breakfast. He made a mental note to keep his irrepressibly foolish questions to himself in the future.

'You want to go over land, via the coastline or straight across the sea?'

'Does it matter?' said Carter.

'Not to me.'

'Down the coast, then.'

Carter settled back as the Comanche hummed, settled into stealth mode and cruised down the coastline of England. He ran through the ECube's instructions once more: protection in support of German Special Forces agents. Not even a full job. A support job. Break him in gently; ease him back into the Spiral fold . . . and then he would feel Kade's wings curl around him to obscure the light and the killing would begin . . .

He shivered.

He remembered the probing of the little ECube machine with some annoyance. Spiral testing him: physical and mental responses. Check he was still the same. Check he hadn't lost his magic touch.

'I should have retired,' he mused, settling deeper into the uncomfortable seat; it was structured for combat, not sleep. 'In fact, I thought I already had.'

Carter managed to nod off as they flew low down the

east coast of England, the cold dark waters of the North Sea below them as the Comanche weaved like a reigned-in predator between radar pulses and deflected the probings of other more sophisticated detection equipment. They left the southern coast of England, avoiding both Dover and Boulogne by flying straight down the centre of the English Channel as Carter remembered older, harder days, training in the mountains, running, sweating under packs, carrying logs, wading through snow, navigating blizzards . . . He smiled amiably as the memories drifted through his mind. He had felt so heroic; at the peak of his physical and mental fitness. And yet it had been the beginning.

The beginning of a new career with Spiral . . .

'Can I smoke?'

'No.'

He slept, and dreamed only a little; it was a bad dream. It was a dream about Kade.

'Why won't you leave me alone?' he muttered as he came awake to the sound of rain and the buffeting of wind.

'You OK?' asked Langan.

Carter sighed. 'Yeah. Sort of. Has this thing got a cigarette lighter?'

'Like I said, no smoking, pal.'

'Where are we?'

'Just crossing the Ardennes. We won't be long; touchdown will be just east of Siegen. Nice little pad we've got hidden away in the hills. A car will meet you and rush you off to whatever secret and heroic mission you're destined to enjoy.'

'Langan?'

'Hmm?'

'Shut the fuck up.'

'OK, boss.' The pilot grinned, flicked a switch and the Comanche swooped down from the sky towards the flatlands beyond the mountain range. Carter watched the landscape flicker below him in the approaching gloom like some ridiculous computer-game simulation – and thanked God that this unwanted adrenalin-injected journey was nearly over.

'I'd like to thank you for a smooth flight, but I won't.'

'Any time, pal,' Langan chuckled.

Carter watched the Comanche leap into the air, bank sideways and hurtle into the distance. He shook his head, lit a cigarette and inhaled. His boots crunched stone as he walked to the black Mercedes and climbed in. In minutes the hills were moving past on either side and the car soon drove into the gloomy sanctuary of a pine forest.

Carter wound down the window and breathed in the pleasant scent. Rain spat through the gap and he revelled in the shocking coolness on his face. He saw himself imposed over the image of the speeding forest: Carter, reflected in glass – short brown hair, heavy stubble, pale blue eyes. A broad boxer's nose that had taken one too many punches. A strong chin – he thrust it forward, then grinned weakly at his reflection.

Ugly bastard, he mused, and lit another cigarette, reminding himself that he really should quit.

The hotel was basic. Low-key. Cheap.

Carter unpacked, then spent a half-hour familiarising himself with the room and then with the hotel. He walked around, smoking, checking out entrances and exits. He sat for a while in the lobby, watching the people coming and going, and being eyed himself by the two hotel guards armed with 7.62mm AK49s. A waiter approached and asked him if he required a drink. In fluent German he asked for a bottle of whisky to be sent to his room and then shook his head, telling himself off.

You've one day left, he mused. The last thing you need is a hangover.

Ignoring his own advice, he went back to his room to listen to the rain, drink, and pray that Kade would leave him alone.

'You're drunk,' whispered the voice of Kade in his mind.

Carter ignored the words and poured himself another whisky. It was a cheap blend and tasted burning, sour – evil, almost – on his tongue and in his throat.

'Let me look at her. Just one more look at her.'

'No,' said Carter softly. His fist clenched the glass tightly and he looked across the room at the mirror. He always expected to see something – he wasn't sure what. Maybe a spirit drifting over his head. Maybe a ghost standing behind his shoulder. But it was always the same . . . nothing. Nothing there – no ghosts, no haunting, no floating spirits. He was alone – alone in body but not in soul . . .

Am I going crazy?

The same question. The same question a million times.

He laughed, and downed the whisky. He felt Kade leave him and was thankful – thankful for the peace and solitude. Kade came to him much less these days and that was the way he liked it. But again the thought nagged at him, would not relinquish its alcohol-fuelled grip: crazy man, mad man, insanity . . . Schizophrenia? Severe mental disorder? A fucked-up mind fried on the toxins of three wars and a thousand battles—

Insane . . .

'You're fucking insane,' Roxi had shouted at him from across the room, fear in her face, in her eyes, in her stance. He could see her fingers trembling, could see the enticing pulse beating rapidly in her neck.

And he could still feel the bulky grip of the 9mm in his hand as he pointed it at her, a full 13-round clip in its magazine. And Kade: there in the back of his mind. *'Kill her. She will betray you – betray us. And we shall be nothing. We shall be ashes and dust. Do it – or, if you're such a fucking coward, let me do it . . .'*

He had walked from the room, to the lake, and thrown the weapon into the cold waters.

He had let Roxi leave. Without a farewell.

But at least with her life.

She had known there was a problem – a needle in his mind, a splinter through his soul – and she had begged him to tell her. But he could not. How could he describe Kade in mere words? How could he define his torture, his misery – and, ironically, his *saviour* – in simple sentences?

Yeah, Kade – his Saviour. His fucking *God*.

Carter laughed drunkenly at that and refilled his glass, spilling whisky over his hand. He could remember the shame: like a brand scarring his brain and soul. He had almost let Kade have her; had almost given in to the raging fucked-up beast-demon-murderer roaming his soul . . .

Shit, he realised, sometimes he had even welcomed that merciless unbidden intruder – at first: when he had discovered what Kade was capable of. He admitted to himself that without his dark twin he would now be dead, dead many times in bunkers, bullets in his skull, his corpse rotting on river beds and in sewers and lying in pieces on distant forgotten battlefields. Kade had saved his life, had pushed him on and murdered when

Carter felt weakness and Kade was untroubled by fear or compassion or doubt or consequences and had *maimed* and *slain* and *slaughtered* on his fucking behalf and yet . . .

Carter couldn't help wondering if he would rather be dead.

What is it like to be normal?

How would my life have been?

How would I have turned out?

He slept uneasily, images of the people that he – *Kade* – had murdered floating up from the depths of his mind. They accused him, fingers pointing, silent dead mouths open and screaming at him.

Spiral Memo1
Transcript of recent news incident
CodeRed_Z;
unorthodox incident scan 545834

Outbreak of malicious computing activity across the globe/a malicious virus Kleq5 - so far undetected on even the most powerful computing systems - has hit global networks in quick succession, striking 15,000,000 machines within 30 seconds.

Not a single country in the world has remained unaffected - from America to France, from Africa to the Czech Republic. According to IT experts, the suspected virus detects sectors where operating systems reside and writes random blocks of data in short bursts, rendering any infected machine unusable.

Because of its highly contagious nature, the virus and sample hard disks are being rigorously examined by leading anti-virus software companies. It is estimated that this Kleq5 virus has caused upwards of US$4.3 billion damage.

Computing experts are fearful of a second payload which is expected shortly.>>#

CHAPTER 2

INFIL

The Mercedes swept past three burned-out BMWs, through the heavy iron gates and up the gravel drive to park beside the black iron fountain. Carter pulled free his ECube, weighed it in his palm, then accessed five codes; the ECube flickered at him with blue digits. Carter smiled – the tiny technical wonder would make sure he was not overheard; it would jam or scramble any listening devices in range.

Carter got out, battered boots crunching on gravel, and lit a cigarette. He looked up at the home of Count Feuchter – Castle Schwalenberg, a magnificent structure of old stone dominated by a central tower with a grey-tiled spire. The windows were small, set back into the stone walls and flanked with traditional wooden shutters. Miraculously, the building seemed unharmed by the recent conflicts that had ravaged not just Germany but the whole of Europe. A few stray bullets from long-range rifles had peppered the shutters but no major damage had been done.

The sun was out, glinting from the glass. Carter walked

across the gravel and was stopped beside a crumbling stone arch by a German Special Forces agent.

'You the *special* man? The one who was at the Siege of Qingdao?' the surly German snarled down at Carter, who flashed his ID as his gaze took in the grounds beyond.

'That's me.' Carter took a heavy pull on his cigarette and smoke plumed around him. He coughed. 'Must remember to try and give up.'

'We don't need you here; we do just fine without you, *special* man.'

Carter held up his hand. 'Hey, I'm just here to observe, my friend. Now, I'd appreciate it if you got the fuck out of my way before I start to lose my temper.' He smiled and blew smoke into the guard's face.

Holding eye contact, the agent used a comm to confirm Carter's identity and allowed him to pass. Carter noted the sniper in the bushes as he moved towards the entrance.

His stomach groaned at him – the bad whisky was haunting him. He reached the door. Ten men in the grounds, he thought. Good. He wasn't meant to have seen five of them: *even better*.

He lifted the huge iron knocker and allowed it to fall. It made a sound like rolling thunder.

Carter watched Maria Balashev enter the richly decorated room. Her beauty stunned him. She wore her black hair long, to her waist, a softly shimmering silken fan; she moved with elegance and grace, and a light smile danced across her face when she saw Carter. She crossed to him without a sound, walking over the deep red carpets, and Carter felt himself swallowing hard as he gazed into those oval, beautiful, sorrowful eyes.

'You know why I am here?' he said softly.

'I do, Mr Carter,' she replied in smooth German. 'And I am very grateful for your intervention. Natasha did not do you justice when she described you.'

Her voice was like the gentle flowing of a river. Carter stood, smiled, and without speaking motioned to her ear-rings, bracelet and rings. She cocked her head questioningly and Carter made gestures for her to remove the jewellery. He walked around her, finger-testing the buckles at the back of her short red dress. Taking the items from her, he placed them on a low rosewood table inlaid with ivory, and then motioned for Maria to take off her shoes and follow him outside.

She obeyed, and Carter led her barefoot out into the grounds. The sun was high, the smell of the gardens fresh after the heavy rains of the previous night.

'Where are we going?'

'Indulge me for a moment, Miss Balashev. Round here, through the arch.'

She laughed then, and Carter heard the crack in the laughter; the fear was there, well hidden – especially considering the girl was only nineteen years old – but still there.

They walked, Maria a step behind Carter.

He stopped suddenly and turned. He took her hand.

'Your uncle has received death threats and he considers them to be very real – not a hoax, but linked to the development of a powerful ground-breaking processor with which he is intimately involved. Your uncle fears that those making these threats may attack you, as a soft alternative target, while both of you are visiting Germany, either to kidnap you or to . . . well, I am sure you understand the situation as well as I do. Now, there are many agents here whose job is to protect you – I am here merely to back them up. To be your personal bodyguard, shall we say. But I would like you to agree to something.'

Maria had gone white. Carter could feel her fingers, cool and smooth, against his own.

'Yes, Mr Carter?'

'I want you to do everything I ask. I want you to trust me implicitly. I am beyond being bought – I am a multi-millionaire in my own right and money means nothing to me. But I need to know that you will do what I ask, when I ask – if you want to stay alive. Will you do this?'

She paused, then smiled softly. 'Yes. I will do what you ask. But I too have a question.'

'Hmm?' Carter was looking around the garden.

'Why did you make me remove my jewellery and shoes?'

'Bugged. By the guys here – only doing their job but I wanted a bit of privacy. The ECube is notoriously efficient at blocking and jamming, but I hate surprises. I trust myself a whole lot more than I trust technology. Better cautious than *dead*.' He savoured the word.

'I see.'

'Tell me, why do *you* think you have been threatened?'

'My uncle, who treated me like his own child after my own father . . . well, died . . . my uncle is devoted to his work. He is a genius. All I know is that we suspect a terrorist organisation wants him to stop.'

'Why are you here?' asked Carter. 'Your uncle knows that you are the soft target – his niece and only close family . . . the daughter he never had. You should be somewhere safe, away from the possibility of danger.'

Maria turned away, then stooped and picked a small flower. She held the white petals to her nose and, her eyes lowered, said softly, 'My uncle is a man of iron principles and I admire him for that. He will stand by what he believes. He did not want me here; but I will not have my life dictated by what might or might not happen. I am my own person, Mr Carter.' She met his gaze then. 'I will do what I wish. And let us be honest – if they can get to me here, then they can get to me wherever I chose to ... *hide.*' She spoke the word with contempt.

Carter nodded slowly. 'I want you to know that I have never lost a protection,' he said. He reached out and tilted her chin up. 'So you do what I say and we might get through this alive. OK?'

'Yes.' Maria smiled, a beautiful smile. 'Here, a present.'

Carter took the flower, sniffing it gently as he followed the girl back towards the house. He watched the agents in the bushes and, as clouds gathered overhead with the threat of yet more drenching rain, did not envy them. He chuckled to himself – and remembered Kade from the night before. The smile fell from his face.

He walked across the drive.

'Count Feuchter.'

Carter stood up and watched the older man approaching him. He was well built, with black hair, iron-grey sideburns and a grey-flecked beard. His eyes were harsh and intelligent, his dress smart. Carter shook the offered hand – a powerful grip.

'A drink?'

'Water,' said Carter.

'It was good of you to agree to this. I understand that you are virtually retired but you come, shall we say, very highly recommended.'

'Lots of experience.' Carter smiled wryly. He took the glass and watched Feuchter slump into a wide upholstered chair and light a cigar. The man fixed his gaze on Carter who sat back down and glanced over at Maria, who was seated at a small oak bureau.

'Do you think we are in a lot of danger?' asked Count Feuchter.

Carter shrugged. 'From the reports I have read and the other info, I would say yes. You have been working for Spiral_Q, if I understand this correctly. It would seem your work has gained you many enemies.'

'They are frightened of the future, Mr Carter. Cowards often are.'

'Can I ask you about this new processor? The QIII Proto, I think it's tagged?'

'Even for you, that would be classified,' said Feuchter softly. 'All I can say is that, as you know, Spiral exists to wipe out the terrorist threat wherever it may be found and the QIII will be of tremendous help in that task – it is incredibly powerful and will be able to crack encryptions in the blink of an eye, locate terrorist cells globally, and terminate the military networks, command centres and control systems of rogue states . . . ahhh,' he sighed, relaxing slightly, the look of excitement in his eyes fading to a more guarded, unreadable expression. 'But I get ahead of myself. As you said earlier, this is the Proto – it is not quite ready.'

'It must be powerful technology indeed to evoke such interest . . . and threat to life?' said Carter softly. 'Maybe some people want it never to be completed?'

Feuchter merely nodded, smiling, and sipped at his brandy.

'This threat to your niece – you realise it could be a double bluff? *You* could be the target,' said Carter.

'That possibility had occurred to me. But I can handle myself, Mr Carter. I used to be an operative very much like yourself. It is my niece who needs protection now – I cannot watch her twenty-four hours a day. What with the party tomorrow and her streak of stubbornness, well . . .'

'Once again, I advise you to cancel.'

'I will *not* cancel,' said Feuchter, his face hardening. 'The agents say they will draft in more men. And you are here.'

He smiled without humour, showing tombstone teeth. 'Maria will be safe. She can stay out of the proceedings . . .'

Maria turned to face them from where she sat writing. Her eyes were bright. 'No, uncle. I will not hide.' She sounded indignant.

'So be it.'

Carter rose and left the room. Rain was falling again and he pulled free the ECube and stroked the surface, as if caressing a lover's skin. He linked to the German Special Forces, FG2. He checked the digits. All the agents had signed in, as they had to do every fifteen minutes.

Carter cursed Feuchter's stubbornness. A party! For work colleagues to celebrate a 'breakthrough'.

'Shit, Feuchter. You should have stayed in Rub al'Khali.'

Carter had to admit to himself that he was deeply annoyed. He hadn't realised that he had been drafted in to work on what he thought of as 'Spiral home ground'. Feuchter was a top dog – a Spiral researcher and military developer – and Carter knew that he would therefore have *very* powerful enemies. That meant the game was more important than Carter had at first realised; more important than Natasha had led him to believe.

Carter moved through the house, checking security points, agents and his own small ammo stashes.

'*You lied,*' said Kade. '*You lied, my beautiful brother.*'

'Leave me alone.'

Carter could hear the joy in Kade's words: the excitement, the danger and the promise of killing.

Stick around, thought Carter soberly, checking the last window. I might need you on this one.

The four black Toyota Land Cruiser 70s rumbled to a halt by the roadside, 6164cc diesel engines idling with a promise of power and almost infinite torque. Moonlight glinted from the smoked-glass windows and in the heavy woods to either side a serene silence reigned.

The police car that had been following, a white BMW 525 sporting thick green border stripes, slowed to a crawl as it passed the Land Cruisers before moving on, tail lights glowing. It disappeared around a corner up ahead and was lost in the tangle of dense woodland.

Still the Land Cruisers sat with their engines idling.

Clouds covered the moon; rain began to fall, softly at first but increasing in ferocity until it pounded against the smoked glass of the Toyotas' windows and sent streams running down the narrow strip of tarmac.

In the gloom up ahead, headlights glittered through the downpour. Then the blue lights atop the BMW flickered into life and the large car returned to halt beside the four Toyotas. Windscreen wipers thumped, sending splashes of rain dancing onto the slick road. One of the police car's doors opened, and a large man wearing a thick overcoat climbed out. He flashed a heavy-duty torch at the lead Land Cruiser, then walked warily forward, his hand on his holstered pistol. Behind him, his companion remained standing by the BMW, wedged between the door and the car's body, eyes alert above a heavily moustached sneer.

'*Verlassen Sie das Auto!*' shouted the lead policeman.

Nothing moved; the lead Toyota sat, engine rumbling, the rain running in rivulets down the dark windscreen and bonnet. The police officer tried to peer through the glass but could see nothing inside.

'*Ich sagte, verlassen Sie das Auto!*'

Slowly, the driver's window hissed down on smooth electrics; the police officer took a step closer, his flashlight coming up to reveal—

The muzzle of a silenced pistol.

There was a *pop*.

The officer was hurled backwards, the flashlight's beam swinging up to illuminate rain falling in diagonal sheets. Through the gloom came a shout – '*Nein!*' – as the second officer pulled his gun and began to fire. Two bullets slammed against the wing of the Toyota before a stream of automatic gunfire picked him up, spun him round and left him lifeless and bleeding on the tarmac.

The Toyota Land Cruisers reversed, then drove past the BMW. One ran over the body of the first police officer to have been killed, leaving wide tyre tracks across and *through* his chest.

They roared off into the night, leaving a ghostly scene of horror stroboscopically lit by the flashing blue lights of the abandoned police car.

Carter watched the convoy of expensive vehicles sweep up the drive. Seated on a wide bench outside Maria's room as she dressed, his attention was divided between the room's solid wooden door and the small window out of which he gazed. Rain fell heavily from towering clouds, and a heavy gloom had settled over the world.

Carter could hear two types of music, intertwining, an insanity mix: thumping beats rising up the wide sweeping stairs at the end of the plushly carpeted corridor and coming from the huge ballroom – and the gentle lure of Beethoven from Maria's room. Carter pulled free his Browning 9mm HiPower. He checked the thirteen rounds in the clip, then checked the other five clips he carried about his body. Seventy-eight rounds in total. Carter liked to be prepared. As he had often told Roxi: 'I don't want to die because I ran out of fucking bullets.'

The door opened. Maria appeared – stunning in a

white dress that showed off her pale complexion and dark hair.

'You ready?' asked Carter kindly, sensing her fear.

Maria took a deep breath. She knew – as well as he did, as well as the many agents positioned around the house and grounds – that tonight was a golden opportunity for assassins. If they were for real and not just a hollow blackmail attempt. An empty threat. A *hoax* . . .

'Do not leave me tonight. Not for one moment.'

'So you'll accompany me to the toilet?' she laughed.

'Yes.'

'Really?'

Carter smiled. 'Yes. Prime location for attack – it is the one moment when, shall we say, a person's guard is truly down.'

They went down the luxurious wide staircase, with its thick carpets and carved oak banisters. The walls were richly decorated with plaster frescoes inlaid with gold. Q Division obviously paid well.

Carter had instructed Maria Balashev earlier that evening: no leaving the house, no alcohol, and no picking up young – or old – men. If Maria wanted to live through this potential threat then she had to minimise complications.

Fucking parties, thought Carter.

Fucking Feuchter! Stubborn bastard – stupid bastard!

A hundred and thirty guests. Carter had almost shot Feuchter himself when Hans Jesmar, head of the German security operation, had handed him the slip of paper.

People mingled. Servants with trays of drinks circulated and Carter's gaze swept across the large, gaudily decorated suite. Rich velvet curtains hung to the floor, obscuring the view of any outside observers – and of any long-range snipers.

Carter stayed close to Maria. She knew many of the people who had arrived and Carter allowed the conversations to flow over him. If anybody approached or spoke to him he was curt to the point of rudeness. He did not want conversation – it distracted him.

He watched. Maria socialised and, like a good girl, stayed off the champagne.

Feuchter, obviously suffering a little from stress, was drunk and being loud and abusive in a corner. Carter checked the squad monitor. Everything was OK.

The woodland surrounding Castle Schwalenberg – swathes of deciduous and conifer trees that rose and fell, following the slopes and dramatic contours of the land – spread out for miles. Several rough narrow trails, littered with fallen trees and branches, criss-crossed forest, but on this dark and rain-filled night nothing seemed to move except thick branches swaying in the wind, and rain running in violent rivulets down the knobbled bark of trees.

A deep rumble cut through the gloom, and four black vehicles crept smoothly across the forest floor. Heavy wheels crushed branches and negotiated fallen trees with 4X4 ease . . . slowly the Land Cruisers came to a halt, strung out in a line.

Engines died.

Silence crept back.

Doors opened, and dark figures climbed swiftly free of their metal confines. They moved stealthily forward and crouched, peering through the trees towards Castle Schwalenberg, its lights glittering with promise in the distance.

The line of shadows bristled with weapons.

There were various *clicks* as magazines were slotted home.

Copper-eyed stares met; silent commands were exchanged; and slowly, with an infinite and precise care, the column of armed killers moved off through the undergrowth, untroubled by the rain and the threat of death to come.

Friedrich squatted beside the bush, listening to the commands issued by Jesmar. He hoisted the rifle, the weight burning into his arm and shoulder now that the hour was getting late, and glanced up at the rolling clouds obscured by the driving rain.

'Fucking weather,' he muttered. 'Sent to torture a man!'

He sighted down the Ruger M77 MkII VLE's scope, and swept the grounds in front of him, rotating the rifle on the smooth-action Harris bipod. He could see nothing through the rain, even on IR and UIR. Friedrich rolled back his shoulders and craved a cigarette and a cup of hot coffee. With five sugars. Yes, he could almost taste the steaming brew . . .

His mouth watering, something made Friedrich glance behind him. Despite knowing that other agents were posted at the rear, protecting his back from infiltration, Friedrich nevertheless felt something subtly out of place. He scratched at his rough-stubbled chin and frowned, eyes trying to pick out movement in the gloom. Then he brought round the Ruger and sighted down the scope on IR. There – he saw . . . something . . . A figure slipping behind a tree? Or the taunt of dancing branches fuelled by the desire for nicotine and caffeine?

He shifted the scope slightly, but could make out nothing more between the trees' wide boles and tangled foliage. He shifted uncomfortably in the rain, feeling trickles run into places he had once thought secure.

'Bitch.'

Friedrich lowered the rifle for an instant to wipe a trace of rain from his forehead – and heard the hiss an instant before the black bolt slammed through his hand and into his forehead and brain beyond, pinning his hand to his skull in a final salute to the Goddess of Death. Gore ran down either side of his nose and he slumped slowly backwards, his free arm falling limply to his side, speckles of blood tracing smears across the stock of the Ruger M77 rifle.

There was a pad of soft footsteps; three figures crouched by his corpse. They lifted the weapon from the ground and black-gloved fingers trailed water down the scope.

'Leave it. We do not need it.' The words were low, soft, gentle.

The weapon bounced on the soft forest floor and the figures disappeared into the night.

Two hours had passed. Carter could feel himself growing weary and, motioning to Maria, he followed her into the relative calm and cool of the hallway before the wide sweeping stairs. He took a small leather case from his pocket, opened it and removed a small phial. He stuck the needle into his thigh and replaced the empty phial in the case.

'What was that?' asked Maria.

'A stimulant. Allows me to stay awake and alert. I'll pay tomorrow.'

Maria smiled, and shivered. 'It's chilly.'

Carter looked at her, then turned, his gaze moving up the stairs. 'You feel that draught?'

Maria nodded.

'It wasn't there before.'

'Probably just an open window,' said Maria, as Carter discreetly withdrew the bulky Browning and with his free hand waved Maria behind him. He pulled free his comm. 'Jesmar?'

'Yes?'

'Can you come to the foot of the stairs? I think we have a situation.'

'OK.'

Jesmar was there within fifteen seconds, a small black pistol in his hand. 'Watch Maria for a few minutes,' said Carter. 'I have a bad feeling about this . . .'

'Wait, I'll send some men with you.'

'No time.'

Carter followed the draught, his boots silent on the carpet. He felt adrenalin and the recently injected drugs kick his system and with his spinal column wrapped in the stimulant's fist he climbed to the top of the first flight of stairs. The music drifted into the distance, a ghostly ambience. He checked the squad monitor – five minutes since all members had signed in. Carter tutted to himself. A lot could happen in five minutes.

He moved to a nearby window at the top of the staircase and, crouching low, peered into the darkness. He couldn't see any of the positioned snipers – but that did not mean they weren't there.

He moved across the wide landing, listening, outstretched hand following the gentle hint of a breeze.

He stopped in front of a broad sturdy door. He rested his hand against the wood.

Carter licked his lips.

'*You need me*,' came the whisper of Kade's voice.

I need nothing, Carter thought bitterly.

He pushed gently and stepped aside; the door swung free. Carter peered, then with outstretched weapon slid in. The room was dark and he swiftly switched on the light . . .

Empty.

Carter moved towards the window, which was open – a three-inch gap. He looked out, then down, saw a small strip of mud caught against the wooden sill – and suddenly realised that he was a clean target against the window . . . He moved fast, as a .22 calibre sniper round smashed through the glass of embed itself in the plaster of the ceiling.

Carter rolled on the carpet, was up and running—

He screamed into his comm, 'We have a breach, red floor, sectors 15 to 20 . . . I repeat, we have a *fucking* breach . . .'

He spun out of the doorway and into the path of a surprised black-clad figure; the Browning 9mm slammed twice in his hand and the intruder was kicked from his feet, scrabbling at the holes in his throat as he went down hard.

Carter looked left and right. From somewhere in the house came the sound of distant screams and cries for help. He ran to the top of the stairs and a stream of silenced bullets spat wood from the rail. He dived, rolling against the wall with a bone-jarring *thud*. His gaze fixed on the bullets in the rail, the chewed wood and splinters – he judged the angle, popped his head round and fired off five rounds. Then, scrambling to his feet, he ran for the head of the stairs.

The silenced machine gun ate the wall behind him as Carter leaped, clearing the top flight in a single bound; his Browning slammed in his hand once more, six rounds that picked up the assassin and sent him spinning down the remaining stairs where he sprawled at the foot, blood soaking the plush pile, his chest caved in and slick with gore.

No guests . . . no guests in the hall . . .

Fuck, screamed Carter's brain.

He crept down the stairs and crouched next to the corpse, creating a smaller target. The comm vibrated in his hand. 'Carter, Jesmar. I have Maria in the kitchens. Yellow, sector 34. There are six of them in the ballroom – they've herded the guests together. They are all heavily armed.'

'I've taken out two,' said Carter softly as he replaced the clip in his gun. 'You stay there, I'll come to you.'

The guests were silent in the lounge. Carter slowly eased his head around the corner; a black-clad assassin stood sentry with a silenced Uzi-K2. Carter fired three rounds and ran in the opposite direction towards the kitchen. As he spun through the door bullets tore the wood behind him and he sprawled across the tiles, sliding between stainless-steel cabinets on his belly. His boot kicked backwards, slamming the door shut.

'Jesmar?' he bellowed.

'Over here,' came the shout from one of the adjoining rooms.

Carter peered over the stainless-steel cabinets, strewn with bubbling pans and half-prepared dishes; discarded knives and chopped vegetables littered the worktops. There were no cooks visible. He moved carefully around the room and towards the adjoining chamber. Hairs prickled across the back of his neck.

'I'm coming in – hold your fire.'

He stepped into the dimly lit room. It was a storage chamber filled with sacks and crates with stencilled lettering in German. He saw Jesmar, standing beside an ashen-faced Maria.

Carter met Jesmar's stare and he knew—

Knew that something was wrong—

The gun rose and pointed at Carter.

'I am sorry, my friend. It is your time to die.'

Carter nodded gently. 'I think . . .' His Browning lifted, a blur, and smashed a bullet into Jesmar's face; the bullet entered through the man's nose and exploded the back of his head across a sack of vegetables. Jesmar toppled in a heap. '. . . somebody is playing a game with me,' Carter finished.

'Carter,' sobbed Maria. She ran to him and fell into his arms. He hugged her quickly, then closed the door behind him – sealing them in this kitchen tomb. He moved to Jesmar's blood-drenched body and checked through his clothing. He took the dead man's Glock, pushing it down the front of his trousers and collecting the spare magazines.

'What's happening?' said Maria.

'Bad shit,' said Carter with a snarl. 'How the fuck did they infiltrate Special Forces? Either big money is changing hands, or something is at play here. Something I don't understand.'

'Where is my uncle?'

'I think we have a hostage situation. There are six of them . . .' Jesmar's words came to him again. Was it a set-up? Something was too neat – too mechanical.

Like grappling with a disjointed puzzle, Carter's brain wrestled with the implications.

'Come on, we've got to get out of here. Out of the house.'

The comm vibrated. 'Yeah?'

'This is Snell. Three of our snipers are dead. Where's Jesmar?'

'Dead,' said Carter. 'There are at least six assassins in here. I've killed two. Fuck knows how many more there are. What do you suggest?'

'Where are you?'

'Yellow, sector 18 near the rear porch.'

'Is Maria with you?'

'Yes.'

'Come out, the rest of us are here. We need to get Maria away.'

'We'll come to the inside door and await your escort. Out.'

Carter logged off the comm; he looked at Maria. 'We are in big trouble. You need to follow my every order if you want both of us to survive. Understand?'

'Hmm?'

Carter held her arms and shook her, hard. 'You understand girl?'

'Yes, yes. Ow, you're hurting.'

Carter released his grip. 'This is what we will do. They think we're coming out of the back; they don't realise that I killed Jesmar. I—'

There was a sound. Carter moved smoothly to the door and opened it – fast, the Browning's deadly eye moving, focusing—

'Shit,' hissed Carter, removing his finger from the trigger.

Count Feuchter had been beaten. Blood dripped from his broken nose and his smashed lips. He tottered forward, the stench of alcohol surrounding him like a perverse perfume. Carter helped him into the room and checked the corridor; he could see the door sensor flickering and he checked his ECube once more. He activated a function: anybody else entering the kitchen would trigger the silent alarm.

'Uncle!' Maria ran to Feuchter, hugged him, helped him to sit down as he grunted with pain. His blood dripped on the floor as he stared in horror at the imploded face of Jesmar.

'You killed him?'

'He turned out to be less than honest.'

Carter, the Browning still in his grip, crouched in front of Feuchter. 'What's happening out there?'

'There are six of them. They have herded the guests together. They have sent me to negotiate with you . . .'

'*Me*? But they think—'

Carter halted. The only way they could know that Hans Jesmar was dead was if they had access to the comm network; that meant the whole of the German Special Forces protection squad were in on the assassination. But why wait until the party? Why not just take out Maria with a sniper's bullet?

The alarm sounded, the comm vibrating.

Carter moved swiftly to the doorway; his Browning peered around the door and sent a warning shot through the door leading from the kitchen to the corridor. There was no return fire and no more movement.

Carter turned.

Feuchter, still down on the floor – but now on his knees – held a gun pointing straight at Carter. Carter's stare met that of the older man. There was no emotion in his eyes – just the hardness that Carter had previously witnessed. The hardness of cold steel. The hardness of a killer.

'What do you want?' said Carter softly.

'You fucked it all up,' hissed Feuchter in a spray of spittle and blood. 'Drop your weapon – now!'

Carter glanced at Maria; and something had changed, a change that plucked Carter's heart in its iron grasp and crushed him without mercy. Maria's tears had dried. She was standing, a small silver gun in her hands. The gun was pointing at him.

'I don't understand,' growled Carter. 'I thought you were Spiral?'

'I said drop your fucking weapon!' screamed Feuchter, the pain of his beating lacing his words with an edge of panic.

Something went cold, and dead, in Carter's soul.

Maria smiled at him. She gave a little shrug.

'Don't act so surprised, Carter. It's not as if you're one of the family.'

Carter knew then: knew that he would die. There were two targets, both bearing guns and he could not possibly drop them both in the blink of an eye . . . He *would* die, in that stinking cramped mouldy storage room at the back of a bastard's country castle. Murdered and betrayed by . . . by who? And for what? What game was being played here? And who was the *real* target?

'*You,*' whispered Kade in a voice of cemetery stone. '*Come on, Carter, it'll be just like old times . . . just like the Battle of Cairo7 . . . let me take them . . .*'

Feuchter had staggered to his feet. His fingers dabbed at his lip and came away flecked with blood. He waved his Glock, his face an animal snarl. 'I said drop your fucking weapon now!'

Carter began to stoop, as if to place his Browning on the ground.

'*Let me,*' soothed Kade, his voice hypnotic in Carter's fevered mind. Carter blinked in lazy-time slow-motion as the world descended from colour into a mercury downward spiral . . .

Do it, he thought sourly.

And, slowly, Kade opened his eyes.

CHAPTER 3

BLACK & WHITE

The panoramic scene was colourless, bleached, a picture in black and white. He smiled at the blood-smeared Feuchter; the Browning felt good in his hand, stocky, reassuring, an old friend, a returned lover, a part of his body and essence and soul. It was held low as he stooped, at an angle. All it took was a twitch—

Kade flicked his wrist – faster than thought – and pulled the trigger.

Feuchter was blown backwards, folding in half with a grunt of expelled air, and he slumped, sprawling to the ground with a look of sudden horror on his face. He dropped his gun. He looked down to where his hands clutched a widening patch of red at his belly. Kade, in the same movement, spun on his heel, the Browning flashing up sideways and, again, he pulled the trigger – the bullet smashed into Maria's shoulder, spinning her back to rebound from the wall. She hit the ground hard, moaning, saliva drooling to the cold stone, her small pretty gun forgotten. 'Never trust a fucking woman,' snarled Kade, and moved forward to kneel swiftly beside Feuchter.

'It takes a long time to die from a stomach wound,' he growled. 'And I believe it hurts. A lot.' He pulled back his gun and smashed the butt into Feuchter's face, hammering the already broken nose. Feuchter screamed – and another three heavy blows silenced him, reducing his scream to a gurgle.

Kade moved to the door. He flicked rapidly through the channels on the ECube – and confusion wrenched his face as he realised it was dead. No scans. No location motions. Nothing . . .

Kade searched the open archive of Carter's mind – it took the blink of an eye – then, opening the door, he ran across the kitchen, vaulting the stainless-steel worktop and towards a low serving hatch. He pushed his way into the hole, kicked through the thin boards below, and allowed himself to drop—

Machine-gun fire sounded above.

Kade landed softly and looked around. The cellar. He moved past various cars covered with protective sheets. He halted, looking sideways at a gleaming red motorbike – a Ducati 1296 SPS MkV – the colour registering in Kade's vision as a bright shade of grey. Then he ran forward to the ramp and the wide wooden doors leading from the cellar. He peered through the crack into the darkness. Kade palmed Carter's ECube, rotated it gently and as if by magic a hint of a glow emanated from the hub. On the surface grooves Kade traced a pattern and a pin spat from the core of the ECube. Reaching down, he slid the pin into the lock and within a few seconds there was a *click*. Silently, he eased open the heavy door a fraction—

Running back to the bike, he kicked it free of its stand. He used the butt of the Browning to smash a hole in the top fairing, then reached through and felt for the ignition wiring. A few cuts. A few twists to bypass the immobiliser. Kade grinned and gunned the engine, clutch in, kick down to first, screw the throttle up to 13,000 revs—

Kade ducked his head and popped the clutch.

The Ducati wheelied up the ramp and smashed through the doors. Machine guns turned on Kade as the motorcycle shot like a bullet down the gravel drive, 221 b.h.p. kicking the bike up the arse with the Browning thumping in Kade's left hand. Skidding around the fountain, Kade blew a man's chest open with the slam of three bullets. He dropped a gear and the back wheel spun gravel, dug into dirt and shot him down the drive's straight and away from the figures who ran from Schwalenberg's main entrance with their machine guns blazing.

Bullets screamed past Kade's head and he ducked even lower over the broad tank as the machine hit 224 m.p.h. He clung to the bike like a limpet, an incredible grin hijacking his face, the Browning forgotten in the joy and concentration of controlling this screaming insanity engine as the needle flickered on the redline.

Behind him, a swathe of perhaps twenty black-masked figures swarmed forward, then suddenly halted. Copper eyes watched the Ducati disappear to a red blip. Men were shouting – they jumped into cars and the black-clad assassins leaped apart as the vehicles roared past in pursuit.

On the Ducati, Kade was screaming and laughing in glee, face upturned into the wind, the bike howling between his legs. Hearing the roar of cars behind made him laugh even louder as the motorcycle smashed down an unlit lane surrounded by thick woodland. He suddenly slowed, front end diving low under harsh braking, and flicked off the machine's lights with his thumb as the

Ducati's engine throttled back and the rev needle flickered as he kicked down a couple of gears—

The roaring of car engines approached at speed. The Browning boomed in Kade's hand as he emptied a full clip into the windscreen of the lead vehicle. The BMW veered right and hammered into a tree: a figure was flung, a pulped carcass, through the windscreen and Kade screwed the Ducati's throttle once more and watched the rev counter dance. The front wheel lifted and Kade clamped himself to the fuel tank; as he hit 100 m.p.h. again he flicked on the lights and leaned low into a right-hand bend as the front wheel finally touched down, and his knee skimmed the rough tarmac an instant before the foot-peg showered the ground with sparks. Opening the throttle more, his grin broadened and the chase was forgotten as the Ducati was pushed to the twitching 240 m.p.h.+ limits of the screaming motor's ability.

'I just fucking love bikes,' whispered Kade into the howl of the wind.

Far behind, forgotten, Castle Schwalenberg blazed briefly with a glowing bud of explosion; fire roared, ate, consumed – billowed up into the night sky, causing Kade to lock the Ducati's wheels and weave in a long skid, finally to halt and look back with an intense frown.

The HighJ explosives roared up into the night, a purple blossom opening to receive the moonlight.

Kade put his head down, opened the throttle to full and redlined the bike down the road, leaving a streak of burned rubber. He disappeared into the blackness of the German forest.

Carter sat in the woods, listening to the gurgling of a small waterfall that tumbled into a circular rock basin. Huge rings surrounded his eyes and nearby, badly disguised, was the scraped, bashed, scratched and mud-coated Ducati under a pile of branches and leaves.

Carter wearily toyed with the ECube. Blue digits flickered under his gentle caress. He activated the emergency homer, and felt the ECube vibrate a little as the powerful transmitter gave out short bursts.

Resting his head back against the grassy embankment, Carter felt the sounds of running water having a soothing effect on his soul. But too many questions jostled his brain – too many memories haunted his past.

It was obvious now. It had been a set-up. For him.

Carter shivered; somebody had wanted him dead, somebody had wanted him dead real fast. But why the elaborate protection scam? Of course – to separate him from Spiral . . . to get him out there on his own. If he was *supporting* German Special Forces then he would not be consigned to a DemolSquad . . .

And Maria—

Carter shook his head. She had fooled him; and now she was wounded, with a bullet in her shoulder, possibly dead and buried, and all for what? To kill *him*?

Feuchter and Maria. They were both Spiral . . . and they had both tried to kill him. And it would seem that some of the German Special Forces had been in on the betrayal . . . and the final explosion. What the fuck had happened there? What the fuck had been going down?

After Kade had taken control of him, events were nothing but a dull dream, without colour, and the— hell, he thought, say the word. The *possession* left a bad taste in Carter's mouth, whisky piss of the worst blend. Kade's joy left a sour feeling in his belly, and Kade's fury left an empty void in his soul.

Carter stared at the small white flower in his fingers. It had withered a little since Maria Balashev had given it to him in the garden. Kade had said to him, *'You lied.'* For once Kade had been right and Carter cursed the demon in his soul.

'I have never lost a protection.'

A lie of reassurance. Oh, the comedy of the situation! He had been protecting his own would-be assassin . . . and now? Was she dead? Lying with Feuchter in the cold grave of their ancestors?

'I should have killed them.'

'I still can't believe you shot her,' said Carter softly.

'Yeah, I'm going fucking soft, or something, I should have placed the bullet in her fucking face. Never leave an enemy behind – it's your fault, Carter, you poison my blood, you weaken my resolve, you piss in my mind . . .'

'I poison . . . get the fuck out of my brain, Kade.'

Carter felt Kade depart; his arrogance, hatred and anger a bleak red streak at the back of his mind, burning, but dissipating as the dark twin left him to his own sour thoughts.

Carter threw the dead flower aside and stood, stretching his back and rolling his neck, which cracked with a release of tension.

Why hadn't they killed him earlier?

Carter pondered. Maybe the explosion had been intended – not just for him, but for the guests as well? But something had gone wrong and Carter had fucked it all up, and so it had been left to Feuchter and Maria to finish off the kill. Maybe.

Carter spun the ECube in his palm, then sent the report to Spiral.

What the fuck, he thought. Let them figure it out! Maybe they could discover what had happened to the ECube as well . . .

A low drone reached his ears, pounding over the forest.

71

Carter waited patiently as the Comanche leaped into view, spun around low over the trees and touched down. The *whump whump* of the rotors sent branches and trees swaying and Carter ran to the cockpit and the serious face of Langan.

'Hurry up,' he shouted. 'We've got company.'

'Company?'

Langan nodded as Carter ascended and belted himself into the cockpit. 'Put on the spare HIDSS 'cos I might need your help. Whatever the fuck you've been up to down here, you've certainly stirred up a hornets' nest. Ever used a holographic Bi-Ocular FOV in a real-time combat situation?'

'*What?*'

'Just get in.'

The Comanche RAH-66 twin LHTec engines screamed and the attack helicopter launched into the fast-approaching darkness.

CHAPTER 4

STATE OF PLAY

The Russian Ballistic Missile Submarine 941 Typhoon Class, *Moscow16*, thrummed through the dark waters 130° and a hundred miles south of the Gelz Ice Shelf. Slowly, the seven-bladed perch propellers spun down and the vessel sat squat and dark in the dim cool glow, immobile, predatory and frightening in its bulky, matt black presence.

Juri Kolgar, Captain First Rank of the 19th Submarine Division, drummed his fingers on the desk and stared at the readings on the screen before him. He glanced up at Seaman Bharzova and the worried expression on the young man's neatly shaved face. Kolgar smiled warmly, and dismissed the man.

For the past four months the Russians had been working with Spiral in an attempt to quash a new internal problem – a spate of mass rioting that had been brought on due to a Mafia-peddled designer drug, which had taken the poverty-stricken working classes by the balls and sent them spinning down the cobbled road to narcotic Hell. This drug, Lemon Vodka as it had been nicknamed, had made the Mafia-led clans even more rich and powerful, but was costing the government dear – financially, politically and, of course, socially. Spiral had been called in as a last resort to try and help stamp out the illegal importing of Lemon Vodka.

A day earlier, the *Moscow16* had been tracking an unnamed surface vessel that was under suspicion of drug trafficking; the vessel was the size of a battleship, of unknown origins, and had been making slow progress to the north-east, close to Russia's Arctic coast.

Now, however, the vessel had gone.

Kolgar had sent out Tykes, tiny aquatic machine scouts no larger than a tennis ball. A hundred had surged from the sub, humming quietly and darkly into the deep cold waters in search of the mysterious vessel that had – impossibly – evaded their most high-tech searches.

Now they were playing the waiting game.

Kolgar sighed, opened the drawer to his right and looked longingly at the bottle of crystal-clear liquid nestling within. He shook his head, rubbed a hand over the bristles on his chin, and closed the drawer again.

Standing, he left the room and walked slowly to the Control Centre, which was situated above the batteries where energy from the 2x600 mwt nuclear reactors were stored in order to give the huge craft its propulsion.

Seamen snapped to attention as Kolgar entered. He saluted his men, and took his seat on the bridge. 'Anything on the sonar?'

'Negative, Captain. Not even on the I/J band surface-target detection. But she was there, as real as a bear in the woods. She isn't there any longer.'

Kolgar cursed.

'What about the Tykes?'

74

'Nothing yet, Captain. They've spread out, and are heading away in a globe formation. If there's *anything* around us, they will find it and report it.' Their gazes met. 'You know, Captain, as well as I that they have never missed a target.'

Kolgar nodded, rubbing wearily at his temples. 'Have you informed Spiral Tac of this?'

'Not yet, Captain.'

'Do so. Their intelligence may have some records or information on this vessel. What did we find out before it . . . it . . .'

'Vanished?'

'Yes.'

'Vague dimensions estimated by the BattleSubTec computers. Nothing more. An estimation of possible weapons capabilities. And the fact that it moved much, much faster than any seagoing vehicle had a right to move.'

They waited, watching the Tyke scanners. A tense silence surrounded them, filled with the glittering glow of computer read-outs and submarine-control displays. Red light scattered like rubies across Kolgar's heavily bearded face, and his eyes narrowed as they fixed on one of the Tyke ScannerReps.

He pointed. 'What's that?'

There was an instant of blackness, and the light went out.

'What does the TerminationDisplay read?' asked Kolgar slowly.

'Zero, Captain.'

'That's impossible! No last-nanosecond read-outs? No transmissions on what was around the Tyke when it was destroyed?'

'Nothing, Captain.'

The two men stared at each other, frowning. And then, like a scene from some digital firework display across the control wall, the Tyke-linked scanners arrayed before them – each signal linked to individual Tyke scouts spinning through the voids of dark ocean all around – seemed to *explode* in front of their very eyes . . . the red lights scattered, spun through shades of attack report from green and blue to yellow – and then, like a visual tidal wave, the lights were swept out and into darkness and *death*.

Kolgar stared, numbed, at the scanners. All were black. Every single Tyke had been simultaneously destroyed.

'Reports?' he asked, his voice a dry croak.

'None,' came the soft, disbelieving reply.

A hundred scouts had been destroyed; and not a single transmission to give the submarine a clue to their attackers had been registered; not a single warning given. Nothing.

Kolgar could taste sweet vodka on his tongue and he longed for a drink.

Later, barked his intelligence.

'Contact Spiral Tac. Tell them we have an *emergency*.'

'Transmitting.'

They waited ten seconds – a long ten seconds of tense wondering filled with uneasy sweat and thoughts of death as every seaman in the Control Centre waited for a reply, looking around and *up* into the imaginary dark waters around their sub, imagining dark enemies with incredibly superior technology – the sort of technology that could make a massive warship disappear, the sort of technology that could evade their most sophisticated scanning equipment, and the sort of technology that could annihilate a hundred scattered scouts without giving away any indication of method or weapons.

There came the *blip* of reply.

'Three TacSquad officers will be with us in just over two hours from the nearby stationed British destroyer *Castle*. They are deploying as we speak in an underwater Shark Attack Craft, very, very fast. They recommend that we sit still and do nothing – merely report if our situation changes.'

Kolgar nodded, and wiped the sweat from his forehead on the back of his sleeve.

The scanners remained dark, quiet; this was no help when you suddenly believed the enemy to be *invisible*.

The *Moscow16* received the Shark Attack Craft into its huge belly like a subterranean Leviathan swallowing its prey. Decompression chambers hissed, pumps whined, and within a few minutes the ramps engaged and two military-suited women and a man walked down the ramp and saluted Juri Kolgar.

'I believe you have a problem,' said the tall, red-haired female. She had cold blue eyes and high cheekbones that highlighted rather than diminished her incredible beauty. Her hand moved slowly, confidently, to Kolgar's and they shook. 'Commanding Officer Reyana Treban at your disposal. I am an expert in aquatic machinery and covert tracking systems, and was part of the design team that invented the Tyke Tracking Systems.'

Kolgar nodded. 'I have heard of you, Lady Treban.'

'You may address me as Reyana. I have no time for rank when we need to work together in an emergency situation. This is Alice Metrass, bio-weapons expert, and James Rothwell, who has an incredibly detailed working knowledge of practically every submarine utilised by most world governments.'

Formalities were speedily dispensed with, and Kolgar led the trio straight to the Command Centre.

'We have your reports, as issued by our connective ECubes; they inform us that a *hundred* Tykes were destroyed within a few seconds of one another, and not a single scout reported back anything as to their situation?'

Kolgar nodded.

Reyana seated herself at a console, and began to type; she integrated with the sub's computers and for a while all was silent as data flashed across the screen. Eventually, she stroked her cheek, eyes distant. 'I think we are in grave danger.'

'You found something?'

Reyana nodded. 'It was hidden in a data structure; you did receive the reports, but they were *scrambled* so that the sub computers would not recognise the codes.'

'What destroyed them?' asked Kolgar slowly.

'I don't know. But you were tracking a huge ship, is that correct? A surface vessel?'

'Yes.'

'Now it is tracking you. And it is closing fast.'

'Weapons?' asked Kolgar.

'Break out every fucking gun you've got.'

The *Moscow16* glided through silent dark waters. Fish darted from its path as engines roared, all need for stealth thrown off as the machine surged forward towards the protection of the nearest Spiral naval outpost. A distance of two hundred and thirty miles.

As the submarine increased its speed, so it increased its depth; nose dipped, it powered down deep below the surface, cutting through shoals of silver glittering fish, deep deep into the abyss of darkness that was the Tremanan Valley, scraping into the deep trench of scythed-out rock filled with stagnant dead water from a million years past.

Unidentified debris floated past in the depths, several of these huge metal casks thumping against the sub's hull with distant echoing *booms* that made all the inhabitants shiver – even though scanners confirmed that these objects were not *mines*. On Reyana's instruction they slowed their speed and once more she analysed the sub's scanners, calling for Rothwell's help in disassembling navigational data.

Suddenly, a siren sounded and data started flashing across all the screens in the Control Centre simultaneously; Kolgar leaped forward as Lieutenant-Captain Lyagarin burst in and the sonar operator turned to him.

'Active sonar acquiring! The bastards have locked on!' came the panicked voice of the det-ops seaman.

'It's above us!' hissed Lyagarin.

'That's impossible!' snapped Kolgar. The 941 Typhoon Class was fitted with active/passive sonar, surface target detection, ESM, radar and direction-finding systems, and a contemporary combat-control interface. The *Moscow16* was supposed to surprise the enemy – the enemy was not supposed to surprise *it*.

'Arm and lock-on the VA-111's!' snapped Reyana as the Command Centre exploded with activity. Every man and woman present knew their jobs and knew them well; this was war, and they all had a job to play.

'There it is,' snapped Kolgar.

Suddenly, as if uncloaking, the huge warship became visible. It was directly above them. It had them locked in its sights, ensnared in its net; caught in its trap.

The submarine rocked; there was a distant *boom*, a scream of steel and a rumbling like distant thunder. The whole submarine started to shake, vibrating, and Kolgar looked helplessly down at his hands as they trembled before his very face.

'The pressure hull,' he croaked, suddenly white-faced as he met the stare of Lyagarin. Reyana and Rothwell were screaming orders to the seamen, and understanding passed between them all, and their faces were bleached, with shock and horror, at the terrible implications.

Some form of advanced depth charge or torpedo had cracked the supposedly 'unbreakable' parallel pressure hulls. You could have as many SLBMs or torpedoes as you could carry, but the pressure hulls were the only substance between life and the terrible, crushing sea which surrounded the deep-sea vessel.

The 941 was going down . . .

More than that, it was being crushed by the sea.

The rumbling increased in volume. Men charged across the Control Centre, panic their master, but Kolgar and Lyagarin just stood staring at one another. They were deep; far too deep. They both knew; they both understood. They were dead men savouring their last breaths.

Reyana grasped Kolgar's arm. 'The attack craft; we can still escape!'

Kolgar shook his head sadly. He had been at sea far too long; he knew the dangers, accepted the dangers; only a miracle would even allow you to reach the belly of the sub, and the chances of escaping . . .

Reyana, closely followed by the other TacSquad officers, fled the Control Centre, boots stomping metal grilles, pushing past panicked seamen who were also torn between fleeing and saying their last goodbyes to their gods.

The submarine suddenly tilted, and the crew were thrown like dolls across the Centre; bodies smashed into screens and sparks showered the riveted steel decking. Kolgar hit the wall with bone-jarring force and lay still, staring at the lifeless eyes of Lyagarin. The man had broken his neck and his limbs lay splayed in some bizarre horror contortion.

Water poured in; sirens wailed; red lights were flashing in the back of his brain but all Kolgar could think about were his wife Sonya and their baby girl Olivia. Short blonde hair, a beautiful smile, 'Papa' she called him as he carried her in his arms and she nestled close to his chest, softest of soft blonde hair tickling his unshaven chin, her tiny fingers grasping his huge hands.

The water was cold around his legs, a heavy and suddenly powerful swirling, remorseless. Men were screaming. Sparks showered him but he did not flinch. And then the power died: there was a distant groan, a shudder, and the lights went off.

More groans began, as if the Ballistic Missile Submarine 941 Typhoon Class was an animal suffering from an incredible wound; the groans rose in pitch and Kolgar could *feel* the pressure forcing in on them, could *sense* the sea – powerful and without remorse – crushing them in her fist. Steel and alloy screamed. Rivets spat from stanchions like machine-gun bullets. Stairways buckled and folded in on themselves as the might of the sea compressed and *crushed* the life from the submarine.

Those last moments, in the pitch black, with ice-cold water shocking his system into a rigid spasm – those last moments were the most intense moments of Kolgar's life; he dreamed of what Olivia would grow up to be, and how Sonya would mourn at his grave. Tears ran down his cheeks. How did they miss that ship? he thought. How did they fucking miss it?

Reyana strapped herself in at the controls of the Shark Attack Craft; both Rothwell and Metrass were dead.

Rothwell had been crushed by a split steel stanchion, the huge slab of metal screaming down to cut him in half at the waist as his entire system of blood flushed from his torn flesh in a scant few seconds. Metrass had been thrown violently down a steep stairwell as the sub rolled, Reyana hanging grimly onto the rails, legs dangling over an abyss as she watched her friend and comrade for the last eight years vanish under a surge of freezing dark waters and fail to reappear. It was a miracle that she had reached the belly of the sub, an even bigger miracle that the compression controls were still active.

As the submarine groaned like an animal in the final throes of death, the fast nuclear-powered Shark Attack Craft spat from its belly and spun between deep rock formations, bubbles spewing from its exhausts. Reyana, tasting blood from the wound to her forehead, watched in horror on the ECube-linked monitors as the submarine broke in two and sank in the deep ravine of the Tremanan Valley. Tears rolled down her cheeks, mingling with the blood there, and she armed the Shark's weapons systems with a dry, fear-filled throat.

Something bad was happening.

Something incredibly bad that she did not understand.

She increased the Shark's speed, descending deep into the ravine and navigating using sensors alone; outside the plasti-titanium hull of the tiny Shark the sea was a dense and uncompromising *black*.

She sensed rather than saw the small object spin in front of her; squinting, she realised that it was a black globe, tiny – similar in concept to the Tyke scouts her team had designed several years earlier.

Reyana moved as if to lock her weapons – and realised that there was nothing on her scanners on which to lock. Swallowing hard, she switched to manual and flicked off the safety on the trigger. Beneath the Shark's belly missiles and mini-torps slotted neatly into place. And then, suddenly, the black globe screamed towards her and there was an insane implosion of plasti-titanium and the sea rushed in towards her as she screamed, an intake of breath as the world went suddenly black and cold and the Shark spiralled down down down deep under the ocean, lost and out of control and *dead* . . .

CHAPTER 5

JAM

The busy London traffic sloshed through the rain, horns blaring, engines revving, lights cutting personal slices from the darkness with thin metal skins shimmering under amber light. Snakes of cars wound across the city, past burnt-out husks of buildings standing stark and forlorn, blackened fingers pointing accusingly at the God who had not saved them. Euston Station was nothing more than a crater of war detritus, guarded by five blackened stumps that had once been tanks, fire-torched turrets and twisted guns evidence of disharmony in this major UK city. As the snakes wound on, they would pass buildings smashed by shells, razed by fire, windows gaping tooth-holes and razor glass littering pavements. People treading the pavements did so warily, eyes watching one another with unease, guns hidden badly under coats.

The tall man stood by the kerb, long leather coat pulled tightly about him. His eyes were dark, hooded, his face a half-beard, hair short and spiked by the light rain. He drew on a cigarette and flicked the butt into the gutter where it mingled with the broken bottles and petrol-bomb remnants as a break appeared in the traffic; boots stomped puddles and he weaved his way through the rush-hour jam, picking his way between Porsches, Volvos, Fords and Fiats, interiors dark and gun-laden. He mounted the opposite kerb and halted, momentarily attracted to a shop display showing digital receivers and the latest in computer-guided weapons. The window was guarded by thick razor-mesh, further evidence of a city that was on the brink of internal collapse and war.

The man scratched tiredly at his beard, obsidian eyes reflected in the window. His hand flitted across his hip, then he turned and walked briskly down the street, boots thumping the pavement. He passed a gathering of Justice Troops – JT8s – drafted in after recent civil unrest who eyed him through their evil black masks before he turned right down a narrow alley stinking of long-unemptied bins, rat disease and the pungent aroma of tom-cat piss.

The rain fell, cooling his face, making his long leather coat glossy. As he walked, he undid three buttons down the front and rested his hand lightly on a dark metallic object within.

Jam knew.

Knew that he was being followed.

The footsteps were almost inaudible behind him and he increased his pace. He blinked, raindrops falling from his eyelashes, and reached out as he passed a huge metal waste bin overflowing with stink; the tiniest of clicks revealed his DP – a 'detection plant' that would lock to his ECube and signal him if he was being pursued.

Jam halted, listening, the hairs on his scalp prickling.

He lit a cigarette, hands cupped against wind and rain. Smoke plumed, dragon's breath, and as the lighter was replaced so a silenced machine pistol found its way into his grip, still shrouded by his coat, still hidden by the gloom.

He turned –

A casual glance –

Nothing.

Jam walked on down the alley, under rusting metal fire escapes adorned with graffiti, under heavy drips from a dark and brooding evening sky that looked down upon this decaying city with malevolence. In the distance neon porn invitations glittered in a puddle and Jam felt the vibrating buzz of his ECube, a relayed signal from the DP. Three. Four. Five. Six, he counted. Shit.

Somebody wanted him *bad* . . .

Jam increased his pace yet again, tossing the cigarette aside and switching left, down another narrow alleyway. He brushed past parked cars, many battered and bullet-scarred, and his eyes moved up, checking, scaling, adjusting. He reached a parked Mercedes, long and sleek and black, almost new and standing out from the other battle-wounded vehicles. He crouched behind it, sighting the machine pistol down the glossy machine's flanks, using the coach line to steady his aim.

Six . . .

Shit, thought Jam again. Which group? Which organisation?

Were they a terrorist group? After the URG Bill of 2010 and the closely following Anti-NBC Laws, which carried immediate death penalties, terrorists of every nationality hated Spiral with a fervour.

Or maybe it was just a random gang, heavily armed and out for cash and guns?

Or maybe even the JT8s . . .

Rain fell.

Jam waited . . .

A noise, behind the poised man, alerted him. He turned, eyes still watching the distant entrance to the alley. The noises were too loud to be made by these secret followers. There was no element of stealth . . .

Five huge black men, bedecked in chains and sporting expensive suits, were making their way down the alley, lacquered shoes dodging puddles. Their gazes alighted on Jam, crouched and leaning nonchalantly against their Mercedes SL2i, and their teeth bared in a curious cross between humour and anger.

They halted. Jam threw a glance back down the alley –

'Get off the fucking car, man,' came a heavy drawl reminiscent of a Hollywood gangster movie –

'Where am I, the Bronx?' Jam smiled easily –

as –

machine-gun hell broke loose.

Bullets screamed, slapping at the flanks of the Mercedes, and Jam hit the floor hard, rolled, dodged the body of a black man who was picked up and spat backwards in a series of heavy-calibre punches. There were shouts, the black men produced pistols and a gunfight ensued with the Mercedes taking centre stage—

'Motherfuckers . . .'

Jam backed into a doorway, heeled the heavy door open and spun into darkness –

Screams and the smack of bullets into flesh followed him.

Blood splashed up the back of his long leather coat.

Jam ran, dodging huge cold machines that loomed suddenly from the gloom. The machine pistol did not feel so comfortable now and he switched hands, wiping sweat from his palm. Six followers, the DP had relayed to his ECube – buzzing at him as it logged each pursuer . . .

could he rely on any of these mysterious figures – assassins? – being taken out by the gangstas?

No. Assume the worst; assume six to follow; and all six at least as heavily armed as himself.

He took the stairs in threes, long powerful legs pushing him up into the light. He was in a narrow stairwell that wound its way up as far as Jam could see. He ran on, producing a small dull silver ball from his pocket. A HPG – high-pressure grenade, working on chemical reaction instead of gunpowder detonation. No loud explosion . . . a covert weapon, near-silent and utterly deadly . . .

Jam paused. Listened, head cocked. He pulled the tiny pin and allowed the ball to drop into the gloom below. He ran.

There was a muffled crack, and a hiss.

A wave of pressure rocked Jam from behind and below, a bellow of angry and silently screaming air, rushing past him like the close passage of a train – he didn't wait to see if the HPG had caused a death toll: if nothing else, it would have made his pursuers more cautious. His head snapped left at the sounds of people, chattering, laughter.

He changed direction, opening a door and closing it behind him.

People are good, he thought.

People make good cover . . .

Nasty though that may seem.

He passed through a series of extra doors, through some kind of thin-carpeted sparsely furnished smoke-stinking office with yellow walls and a pyramid of cups sporting tar-brown stains. An untidy pile of discarded beer cans, errant tangles of streamers and distant music intruded on Jam's immediate pain. Office party? Jam stowed away his weapon and broke into the—

Dull light, dancing with cheap strobes and the flicker of amateur coloured disco lights as bad boy-band music crucified the air.

Jam strode through the group, past a stack of beer and decks and thumping speakers. Several office workers gyrated into his path and with the precision of whores on heat, tongues on wet lips, tight leather and glitter-spangled low-cut breast cups spewing tequila pheromones in a call for sweat-stained party sex.

Jam swiftly sidestepped groping hands, glancing behind—

To see the door open. Slow motion. Gaunt-faced men, anonymous in their cold professionalism, appeared: dark-haired and dark-suited—

And followed by—

Jam caught a glimpse of a masked figure, slender, with bright piercing eyes that seemed to connect with him as he stared, lips suddenly dry and the need to be free thumping in his guts.

Which organisation? spat his brain, searching the files and folders of his mind without success. He did not recognise these pursuers; but then, this information was an irrelevant factor . . .

Jam broke into a run, bursting through another door. Bullets tore through the party, chewing plasma monitors and smashing partitions into sprinkler foam; Jam dived to the soundtrack of sudden panic screams, rolled, darted right and checked below. He kicked a hole in a window, wrapped his leather coat around him, and jumped . . .

His boots thudded against the roof of a red double-decker London bus, and he slid for a moment before righting himself. The driver of the bus climbed free of the cab and started shouting up at him: Jam slid to the rain-slippery edge and leaped lightly to the ground below.

Ignoring the insect buzz of the annoying driver as he waved a shotgun, Jam approached a helmeted man sitting astride a large 2000cc Honda off-road motorcycle. Without time for conversation, Jam grabbed the man's collar, hauled him backwards onto the wet tarmac, jumped aboard the machine and, with the clutch in, he kicked down. The Honda screamed, fumes exploding from the exhaust . . . the bike kicked up its front wheel, climbing onto the boot of the Ford in front and Jam ducked his head as bullets howled from the smashed window above him, slamming metal thumps across the queuing traffic as the Honda's rear wheel spun against the chrome bumper, then fought the bike onto the Ford's buckling roof – the bike screamed and lurched, up and down over this impromptu corrugated road of bumper-to-bumper traffic.

Wheels spun across the wet slick roofs and bonnets of waiting queuing cars; Jam slung the bike to the right, dropping from this hastily invented car-road and landing with dipped suspension on the narrow pavement to send cowering late-night pedestrians screaming for cover. The bike surged down the pavement and out over a small park, churning grass and mud and heading for the trees lining the opposite side. He hit the brakes, ending in a long mud-slewn skid, and jumped free at the last moment as the Honda collided with a wide-boled oak. Then, looking left and right, he jogged to a nearby van and climbed nonchalantly into the back.

'Hit it, Nicky.'

Bullets wailed from behind as the transit wheelspun and joined the snake of traffic, smashing holes along its flank. In the back of the van Jam and Slater ducked, scrabbling across the floor as shafts of light with ragged metal edges appeared between the racks of guns, bullets and neatly packaged explosives.

'Holy fuck!' growled Slater and his stare met Jam's.

'Get us out of here!' bellowed Jam, eyes wide, mouth dry with understanding as he eyed the punched metal holes.

Nicky dragged the van right, mounted the kerb and smashed a series of parking meters into oblivion; the van's engine roared and the bullets fell behind.

They sped from the busy streets.

Jam, sweating now, slumped onto a bench and ran a hand through his hair.

'Was I right?' growled Slater.

Jam met the large man's gaze and nodded. 'More than right. They wanted me – *us* – bad. Bad enough to mow down lots of innocent bystanders.'

'What do we do now?' asked Nicky, her sultry tones for once edged with a kind of panic so unlike her usual well-trained stability that it brought a frown to Jam's handsome face.

He shrugged. 'We have to warn the others.'

'We can't use the ECubes – I bet that's how the bastards have been tracking us,' said Slater with a snarl. 'You remember the Battle of Belsen?' He cocked the Heckler & Koch MP5 A3 9mm sub-machine gun in his huge hands and grinned nastily. 'We could try the phone.'

'We've no fucking choice. Get a message to Spiral_H that some fucker has set us up – the cunts were lying in wait. *And* the fuckers messed up my hair *and* my new coat. The *bastards*. Nicky, get us out of this fucking dangerous fucking city. Then we'll ditch this van – it'll be tagged.'

Slater pulled free an ECube. He squeezed the small

91

electronic device and it came to life, blue digits flickering; but as soon as it lived, it died, and the blue digits faded.

Slater frowned. He squeezed again.

''S not working, Jam.'

'Give it here, big guy.'

'I didn't do nothing,' complained Slater.

Jam tutted. 'You're a fucking technology gimp. Remember China? The dam? You were in charge of the fucking det?'

'That was an accident,' moaned Slater.

Jam played with the ECube, and frowned again. 'I thought these things were supposed to be practically unbreakable?'

'They are,' Nicky called back from the front seat. 'I doubt whether Slater's huge fists could have damaged it. I've seen them survive much worse than that.'

Jam tutted again, as Slater took hold of Nicky's battered and bruised ECube. Slater fumbled with the machine for a moment, but it refused to spark into life. He shook his head, growled, 'Where to next?'

'We need to contact Spiral, and we need to pay a visit to an old friend,' said Jam, lighting a cigarette and lying back, staring at the panelled ceiling, the shafts of dull phosphorescence creeping between the torn bullet holes making him feel a tad wary. Explosives and spinning bullets did not marry well. A cold draught whistled in through the holes. Slater started to clean his Heckler & Koch.

Jam closed his eyes, thinking back to Iran and the rebellion.

And the bullets.

And the torture . . .

He shivered. And welcomed his drug-induced sleep as the van rumbled through the rainswept war-spattered streets.

Spiral_Memo2
Transcript of recent news incident
CodeRed_Z;
unorthodox incident scan 554670

Between the hours of 2:00 P.M. and 5:20 P.M.
the entire city of London and the
surrounding Home Counties were left without
electricity.

Millions of homes and businesses, including
schools and hospitals, were left
electrically stranded or relying on
emergency back-up generators. Prior to the
power cuts, monitoring equipment registered
great surges of energy, which are being
blamed for this occurrence, although no real
cause for these freak power surges has been
discovered, and UKLocalPower Corp.
spokespersons are unwilling to make any
comment.>>#

CHAPTER 6

TAG

It felt like a million years later, a million miles away and a different planet. Carter stood in the shower, the hot water flowing over his shoulders and back, easing the tension in his muscles, washing away the speckles of blood. His eyes closed, his face down, he reached out and placed the flats of his palms against the steam-frosted tiles of the cubicle. It had been a long journey and his weariness had consumed him, eaten him whole and spat him out of the other side of oblivion—

He stepped from the cubicle. The towel had been warming for a half-hour, and he dried himself in slow motion – automatic movements, machine movements. Then, naked, he walked through to the bedroom and collapsed on top of the rich duvet, sleep claiming him and leaving no prisoners.

Carter tossed between the sweat-streaked sheets . . .

Maria –

screaming

crying

An explosion; a bullet, slow-motion, spinning from the barrel of Kade's gun, impacting with her flesh—

a scream, saliva drooling from blood-speckled lips
cloth tearing
flesh parting
a metal parasite burrowing into muscle,
kicking aside bone
Feuchter, face stark, smashed with pain

Carter leaped and took the bullet in his own body, felt
the impact and looked up from a thick pool of red, could
see Maria's face staring down at him as he was lowered
into the hole in the ground and they threw flowers on top
of him and started to shovel in the dirt and he wanted to
scream –

scream, I'm not dead yet

I'm not dead . . .

He awoke in the darkness, shivering and remembering the
past. He could feel warmth against his back and, groaning,
he rolled over, hand reaching out to stroke soft fur. There
was a noise, a decline of sound like a reverse turbine. Carter
laughed, and patted the Labrador's head with a sigh.

'You OK, pal?'

Samson panted, tongue flicking out to steal salt from
Carter's cold back.

'Cut it out, you mongrel.'

He rolled from the bed and pulled on grey combats
and a thick jumper, much too large but soft and comfortable and the way he liked it. Samson watched him dress,
then jumped off the bed and followed him out and down
the stairs to the kitchen. Carter fed the Lab as the grey
rays of weak sunshine filtered over the mountains and he
crouched, watching Samson eat.

'You eat like a fucking animal,' he said soberly.

Sam cocked a single beady eye at him, and continued
to shovel.

Leaving the dog, Carter returned to the living room and stretched his spine, then unlocked the door and stepped out onto a narrow balcony. The cold hit him like a brick in the face and he gasped, smiling at the shock. Wind lashed his short hair and he leaned over the balcony, gazing out over the snow. In the distance he could see woodland, snow-laden and picturesque. Roads snaked into the distance, between hills, and beyond it all squatted the mountains, old Grey Gods watching over these Minor Petty Mortals.

'A damn sight better than fucking London,' he muttered. The phone rang. He stepped back inside and picked up the receiver. 'Yeah?'

'Carter, it's Natasha.' She sounded serious.

'Natasha – I need a *fucking serious word* with you, my friend . . . Have you any fucking idea what happened to me in Germany—'

'No time, Carter. Bad shit is hitting the fan. I'm coming up.'

'Here? Now?'

'Yes. I'll be four to six hours. Don't use your ECube. In fact, I don't think you *can* use your ECube.'

'Why—'

'It's the DemolSquads. One of them has been wiped out; fucking *assassinated*. I'll be there as soon as I can.'

The line went dead. Carter scanned the signals on the phone; the line was untraceable and had, by all accounts, never existed. Nats had used an advanced descramble signal only issued to the TacSquads.

She obviously wanted *nobody* to hear the call . . .

Carter scratched at his stubble, her words troubling him. He shrugged to himself, trying to push the worries from his mind. Now: now there was nothing he could do. He could merely await Natasha and wonder at her brisk

96

words – and warning – but it wasn't that simple, it was never that simple. Why hadn't he heard from Spiral? What the fuck was going on?

Realising that he always thought better when exercising, he called, 'Samson, we going for a run?' as wariness and bad images concerning Natasha, the assassinations, and the lack of communications from Spiral flickered in his mind . . .

The dog was there in two seconds, jumping up, tail wagging, eyes bright at the promise of exercise and a few cheap sniffs.

Carter pulled on his running shoes, battered old Nike Airs, and trotted down the steps from the living quarters to the front door – the price of having a house built into the side of a steep hill – and with Samson panting eagerly at his heels, jostling and pushing as if to send him cartwheeling down the steps. With a cursing 'You trying to kill me?' – a traditional pre-run invocation – they spilled out untidily into the snow.

The morning was extremely cold, a frost having made the snow hard and slippery. Carter, with the sniffing Lab at his heels, set off up a gentle incline towards the woods. The silence welcomed Carter into its embrace and he groaned internally at the strain of such early morning exercise—

And yet he felt the need. The need to work, to feel the exhilaration and power that only came with hard exercise; to feel the trail beneath his running shoes, to feel the burn of lactic acid, the strain of muscles, the tearing of strained lungs . . .

Soon, calves burning, he crested the first rise and entered the woods. A frozen stream cracked with a gunshot sound under the immense mass of Samson jumping from the top of a gentle rise. The dog rolled in the cold water, then sprinted around in circles with his tail between his legs before rejoining Carter further up the trail between the sparkling trees.

'What was all that about?'

Samson panted with a wide dog smile.

'Well, come on, tell me what's going on in your dumb canine brain?'

Samson looked up, head tilted. Carter patted him and increased the pace, watching bemusedly as the dog suddenly sprinted off to the left, flashing between the trees, legs heaving, tongue almost on the ground, nose occasionally touching a smell and then veering off at random angles at some stimulus that Carter was – thankfully – immune and blind to.

Carter frowned, his run slowing, his pace faltering. His head snapped to one side, breath pluming in front of him, a spray of sweat stinging his eyes. He halted, breathing deeply, and Samson cantered round and gazed up at his Master.

'You hear it too?'

Samson grinned – a dog grin.

'Come on.'

The distant engine noise indicated a large vehicle. It could just be passing by but Carter had a bad feeling gnawing his stomach – ever since the events in Germany only hours before and the low-flying race back home to Britain . . . The pursuit had ended without event but Carter could still feel weariness, a sense of being drained after those bloody unexpected events at Schwalenberg—

The engine changed pitch. Carter ran along just below the tree line as he heard the vehicle turn up towards his house. He reached the rise and gazed down at the old van, rattling and pumping diesel fumes from an engine that had seen much, much better days.

A van? It had to be . . .

Jam, smiled Carter. 'Come on, Sammy!'

They ran back towards the house and, ever careful, paused to watch the visitors disembark. Jam, Slater and Nicky, all grumbling and stretching after the obvious ill effects of a long journey. Carter checked back down the track – nobody following – then stepped out and jogged slowly down to his three old friends.

'Carter!' yelled Jam, and embraced the sweating man. They clasped hands, patting one another on the back. Slater grinned gormlessly, and Nicky smiled warmly. 'Any chance of a party, my man?'

'You're joking, aren't you? I remember the last one!'

'It wasn't my fault Slater got thrown from the bedroom window!'

'*You* threw him!'

'Hey, just our little tiff! It's good to see you again.'

'Come on in,' said Carter, forcing another grin through his mild depression. 'I'm ready for some breakfast, if I can entice three of my old friends to join me?'

'Slater is hungry,' rumbled Slater, kneeling and wrestling with Samson who began to growl and bark, play-fighting with the large man who pinned the Labrador to the ground and tickled the fur between his pads.

'I seem to remember that you're always hungry, Slater.'

'Aye. I'm a growing lad.'

'You are forty-six years old, Slater.'

'Aye. Like I said, still growing.'

'You don't often pay me a visit, Jam. I assume there is a reason?' Carter's eyes were hooded, his mouth a grim line. Recent events had removed much of his humour, and this unsummoned gathering felt somehow ominous.

'Oh yes,' said Jam softly. He lit a cigarette, rested his head back and rubbed at tired eyes. 'Something bad is going down, old friend. Have you logged on with your ECube? Checked out the coded info on your escapades in Germany?'

Carter shook his head. 'No, not yet, I don't like bad reviews.'

'Something doesn't add up. It doesn't fit. Spiral seem to have no answers on how German Special Forces were infiltrated. And Feuchter – our friendly Spiral_H QIII coordinator – has disappeared and is presumed dead. They pulled the fried corpse of his niece – and the bodies of *all* the guests from the party – from the wreckage after the fire had been brought under control. Dog meat. But, mysteriously, no sign of Mr Feuchter himself. Strange, eh, considering you put a bullet in the cunt? I do find it disconcerting that our faithful employers have no answers for these questions – after all, their surveillance and technology budgets must exceed NASA's.'

Carter shrugged. 'They're not God. They can't know everything.'

'You're dead right,' grunted Slater, busy picking pieces of bacon rind from his remaining teeth. 'Go on, Jam, tell him about the Squads.'

Jam sighed, and Carter caught the resignation in the man. Strange, for sure, because they had survived some tough campaigns together. They had crossed the desert during the Battle of Cairo7, performed TankerRuns after a designer plague – the Grey Death – had wiped out 58 million people and devastated the economies, and of course populations, of Europe, North Africa and North and South America, and fought several pitched battles against the terrorist resurgence after the Anti-NBC Laws were passed.

Jam's face was stern. 'A DemolSquad, number 14, has been wiped out.'

'I know,' said Carter softly. 'But things like this *can* happen. It is a probability in our line of work. Men and women *die*. Life's a bitch, yeah?'

'Yes, but what's even worse is that Spiral have not published the information. I found out by hacking Cuban Special Circumstances computers, stumbled across the information by accident. So, me and Nicky set out to find out a few things, keep a few tabs on several of our other brother Squads, including members of the Core. Two more DemolSquads are missing, 77 and S-4.'

'The sniper squad? Rex, Scope and Amber?'

'Hmm,' nodded Jam, blowing the room full of smoke. 'Coincidence? I thought to myself. Then we get a real bad job in London; the sort that makes you regret ever even thinking about signing that fucking pink form by which you gave up your freedom. And guess what . . .'

'Set-up?'

'Yeah.' Jam finished his cigarette, and immediately lit another. 'They were waiting for us. I went in on foot to scope ahead; bastards almost tagged me. Six of them. Very professional: well armed, hard as fuck, intelligent, swift movers.'

'And you also think I was set up?' said Carter softly.

'Did occur to me, old buddy.'

Carter scratched at his stubble, and accepted a cigarette from Nicky. 'It's funny . . . I had a call from Nats this morning. She's on her way up here. She sounded a little panicked.'

'Be careful with her,' said Slater. 'She's one of the TacSquads, a Tactical Officer. Old School. Crafty as a fucking bitch.'

'I've known her for years. We're good friends . . .'

Jam shrugged and reached across the table, patting Carter's hand. 'Natasha is a bird—' Nicky gasped . . . 'No offence meant, love. You know, Carter, a bit of moist cunt and you always did think with your dick. Trust no fucker, my friend. Not Nats. Not even us. There are DemolSquads dead, others missing. You've been popped at, and we sure as fuck had a lot of high-velocity shots spat our way. Why do you think we came up here in the van? For fucking fun? Our ECubes have been compromised . . . and if ECubes are the pinnacle of encrypted communication, then nothing is safe. You can't fucking *text* me your descramble code and hope it doesn't get compromised when the shit finally hits the very large fan . . . Carter, Spiral know something and they're not telling . . . you sure *this* place is not bugged?'

'I'm, sure. I have my own – shall we say *custom* – scanning equipment.'

'Good lad.'

'I still don't believe Spiral have anything sinister to add to this. After all, they pay our wages. They employ us. I'm sure they have their special reasons for withholding information – I bet there are people on the job right now.'

'Maybe,' said Jam. 'But then, we're employed because we think. Because we trust nobody. Because we do the job ourselves. Don't have blind faith, Carter old buddy. There will be people in Spiral just as corruptible as in the real world . . . as you found out for yourself. Listen, Spiral_H is assembling a strike force to shut down Spiral_Q. Things are getting way out of hand, or so it would appear . . . the apparent betrayal by Feuchter when you had your little lovers' tiff in Germany is being kept quiet so Spiral_Q can be shut down with extreme force and minimum fuss. Don't want to give the fuckers due warning, eh, lad?'

Carter rubbed at his stubble, then his tired eyes. 'Feuchter. That fucker got everything he deserved.'

There was a long, uneasy pause. Outside, snow began to fall once more, small flakes falling straight down to earth through the absence of any breeze. Jam shivered, then grinned over at Nicky. 'You be keeping my bed warm tonight?' He winked broadly, a cheeky grin on his face.

'Only if you pay me, Jam.'

'This can be arranged.'

'I'll bite it off if you even try and wave that fucking maggot near me.'

'Well, I'll look forward to it. But enough of this banter – come on, team, we're fed and have delivered our warning. Time to move on—'

'Where to now?' asked Carter as the group stood, leaving a pile of dirty dishes.

'Can't say,' smiled Jam. 'Classified. Y'know how it is. Remember, don't use your ECube – not yet; I think ours are fucked so it doesn't matter for us. Listen, Carter, I have a bad feeling about this one. A real bad feeling.'

'Your bad feelings always turned out to be sheep instead of rogue enemy soldiers when we were training in the mountains,' said Carter.

Jam shrugged. 'Just advice, brother. Take it or leave it.'

'Let's swap descramble codes. I have a feeling that one day soon we will need secure communication. And ECubes are surely letting us down now, my friend.'

Jam nodded, and they memorised the information. Then Nicky led the Squad down the stairs, Samson jumping at their heels with the apparent motive of murder, and out into the snow and towards the van. They thanked Carter for breakfast and, with Jam's grinning face mouthing the words, 'See ya, Butcher' from the rattling van window, in seconds through thick exhaust fumes they disappeared through the snow.

Carter's face went hard at the name. He spat in the snow, and said, 'Come on, Sam, back to solitary confinement.'

'*You earned it, Butcher,*' said Kade.

'Fuck you,' snapped Carter.

He sat, gazing out at the snow. He toyed with the ECube, but did not activate it. The surface remained black and dead and he tossed it thoughtfully from one hand to the other, as you would with a soft ball.

Samson lay snoring beside his chair, and a low fire burned, crackling occasionally, the glow warming the room and contrasting cosily with the snowy wilderness outside the windows.

Carter stared at the mountains, tracing their contours. On his lap sat a small A4 pad, and his fingers held a small knife-sharpened pencil. He dropped the ECube to the floor, and then chewed the end of the pencil thoughtfully for a moment. He wrote:

```
Problem: DemolSquads missing/ murdered

Problem: Feuchter . . . and Maria's
involvement?

Problem: German Special Forces in on the
betrayal in some way/ percentage not
known/ Bribed? Or other incentive??

Question: Who was the real target?
Carter? Or party guests? Or both?
```

Probable that Carter a target in lieu of
other Squads being wiped out. But why?
And by whom?

Feuchter – expert in computer processor
development – The QIII Proto, developed
under licence for Spiral at specially
built complexes around the world, namely
stations   Spiral_H,   Spiral_M   and
Spiral_Q. The QIII processor: military
chip and surrounding hardware destined
for implementation over the next five
years. Highly classified; many Spiral
members even unaware of its existence.

Who is the enemy?

Spiral? Unlikely.

And where is Feuchter? How did he get
out before the explosion wiped out
Castle Schwalenberg?

Carter stared at the scribbled words on the page. Spiral
knew that he was alive. He had signed in, reported on
events in Germany. They had okayed his return to
Scotland and told him to await further communication. If
they wanted him dead, he was sure as fuck he would
already *be* dead. Unless it was somebody *within* Spiral
operating independently, or *unless* they were awaiting a
certain turn of events . . . like Jam arriving? Or Natasha
making an appearance? Had Jam been tracked?

No. He shook his head. Spiral stood for everything
that was good; they might have their own seemingly

strange reasons, but everything was carried out with precision. There were no mistakes . . . not usually . . .

Carter followed the premise: if Spiral *did* want the Demolition Squads dead, why the elaborate set-ups? Why not just gather them together and murder them in one huge gas chamber? And why could they possibly want their top operatives dead in the first place? Why spend billions of pounds in recruitment, training, faking deaths – only to wipe them out?

Something did not fit.

And where did the QIII Proto fit into this jigsaw? This puzzle? Feuchter was in charge of development, programming and refinement of the military processor; Carter knew very little about the project because it was tightly under wraps, but Natasha had worked some long hours in the early QIII development stages before being reassigned to babysitting the DemolSquads as a Tactical Officer and seeing to their every whim and need. A year ago, when they had shared much more than just sex, she had trusted Carter implicitly; she would talk in the long warm comfortable hours after love-making, her features softened by candlelight, lips ruby and wet; she had spoken, almost aimlessly, feeding his desire for technological knowledge . . . she would tell him about the advanced chip architecture, about the implementation of ProbEqs which were being drafted into CoreCalcs and the CoreClock. And despite his expertise with computing systems the jargon had flown way, way above Carter's head. He still remembered Natasha's bitterness at being pulled from the project, but she had finally taken it with good grace when assigned as a TacSquad officer.

And now. Now?

Carter wrote:

Demolition Squads in trouble? ALL the DemolSquads?

Assassination/ how to assassinate the world's most professional operatives? DemolSquads are perfectly trained killers; the elite of the elite; each chosen for specific skills. DemolSquads are assassins; demolition experts.

How to assassinate the assassins?

And why?

ECubes no longer secure; in Germany the ECube died, only reactivating afterwards, as if affected by some sort of power drain????? Somebody has access to Spiral mainframes????? Internal betrayals?

Feuchter.

Everything revolves around Feuchter; he pulled gun on Carter: therefore he was willing to throw away his position within Spiral. Who would do that? It is rare somebody wants to leave Spiral . . . leave the ultimate organisation - leave the embrace of such a world-active company, who strive for peace, who genuinely set out to fuck the bad guys????

Spiral were being betrayed. Set up.

Who better than the star military-processor development team? Feuchter, obviously . . . but he is more of a puppet; he cannot be the one pulling the strings.

So, who else?

And Natasha . . . Natasha knew Feuchter; Nats set up the protection gig in the first place. Sent Carter to his own assassination. How perfect.

The game is larger than I realise.

Carter rubbed at his tired eyes; it was a fucking circle and he was treading his own footprints, following his own tail. He threw down the pad and sank back into the sofa.

'I don't know,' he said softly, closing his eyes.

Outside, the wind howled and Carter, in almost unconscious response, threw a log on the fire. It was Feuchter who worried him more than anything – the hard look in the man's eyes, the glitter of those cold, cold orbs when the unwavering gun muzzle was pointing straight at Carter . . . something in Feuchter made Carter's soul go cold. There was something different about the man. Something *strange*.

And Natasha . . .

Natasha had set him up with the gig. She had known Feuchter a long time ago, worked closely with him on the QIII early implementation and development drawings.

And if they had wanted *him*, Carter, dead, then—

Then Natasha had to have known.

Carter felt suddenly miserable. Cold inside.

He loved Natasha; and knew deep down that she loved him.

But the facts were staring him in the face.

She was a part of it. Integral. A cog in the machine.

She *had* to be . . .

Carter knew; he would have to be careful. He would have to be prepared. He would have to watch Natasha like a hawk – and if she stepped out of line?

Then Kade would be waiting.

Carter stepped over his snoring Labrador and moved to his study. Entering the book-lined room, he moved to the sixteen feet of desk and the five computers, all open-cased and showing a myriad of circuit boards, processor-fans whirring, monitors showing a colourful spinning collection of humorous screen savers.

He sat down at the master system and initialised the OS. Entering the shell, he switched to his house and land defences, bypassed the encryption, and logged in—

Nothing.

He scanned all monitors for a two-mile radius. Nothing had been tripped or tampered with, the current and voltage meters had not been broken or hacked. He had designed and programmed the system himself, in 68000tz machine code. It had been a challenge and he had enjoyed the steep learning curve, although he still stood by his inherent hatred of mathematics.

He finished the scan.

Nothing. He scratched his chin, and lit a cigarette. The machines purred around him and he flicked through a variety of hidden match-head cameras but could see nothing suspicious.

Just because it doesn't look suspicious, doesn't mean it isn't there.

Carter was tempted for a while to start messing about with the equipment; it had a soothing effect on his soul, the swapping of components, the improving of performance by processor and memory enhancement. He checked his watch. Natasha would be due in a few hours and he would need to be ready.

He walked down the hallway and pulled on his boots, lacing them tightly. Then he moved down the stairs and punched a sequence into a pad; a section of wall slid smoothly back and he stepped into the brightly lit armoury. It smelled slightly of gun oil, and he moved to the locked cabinets and pulled free his Browning HiPower 9mm. He checked all the magazines and strapped them about his body. Then he pulled free an automatic sniper rifle chambered for the .338 Lapua Magnum round and slotted a scope to the weapon with a precise *click*. He checked the magazine, placed a spare one in his pocket, then dropped the rifle into a sacking bag and pulled tight the drawstring. With the gun under his arm, he locked up the room and returned to Samson, tapping the dog with his boot.

'You coming with me, pal?'

Samson grinned his dog grin.

'Safer with me than in here, I think. Come on, I have a real bad feeling about Natasha's impending visit. Let's check she isn't being followed by big perps in suits with machine guns.'

Carter locked the front door and armed the trip meters. Then, breath pluming and snow settling like a shroud across his head and shoulders, he started across the grey-lit fields so free of war and violence in this distant part of Scotland, and up past the edge of the lane towards the sanctuary of the beautiful shaded woods.

Carter was cold.

His hands, protected by gloves, clasped the semi-automatic rifle stock and he sat shrouded by trees and bushes, staring down at the lane. A straight of one mile led away from him and he targeted the scope down the lane, picking out leaves on the trees and the fluttering of snowflakes: and he grinned. The lane made a good killing ground, and was one reason why he had purchased the house. If he was ready for danger, then this made a good spot – for raining fire from Heaven upon the Infidels.

Samson, at his feet, was restless. He'd wandered away for a while, sniffing, but had returned to nuzzle at Carter, to whinge at the man with his whimpers of boredom. 'Shhh,' he soothed, rubbing the dog's ears. 'We shouldn't be long.'

He heard the engines, echoing up from the valley, before the car swung into view. And swing it did, slewing with churning tyres around the bed and smashing into the embankment with a thud, bouncing the back of the vehicle violently onto the uncleared road as the engine howled and tyres spun and the BMW 740i shot towards him—

Carter licked his lips and lifted the scope to his eye.

Natasha was coming – and it appeared she was in trouble.

The BMW accelerated madly down the lane—

A black Mercedes spun around the corner, gripping better due to its tyres' snow chains. It must have been waiting for her, ready to attack the snow; it accelerated down the lane and began to catch the BMW.

Carter sighted smoothly. The cross-hairs crawled up past the Mercedes grille, up the bonnet. He could see five shapes inside the vehicle – large men in dark coats, some with dark glasses. One window was down, allowing snow to blow inside the car – a gun appeared and began firing—

The *cracks* echoed up into the woods.

Carter trained on the driver; the Merc slewed left and right and Carter cursed, the figures inside the car bobbing madly, unsteady targets—

He breathed out. Squeezed the trigger.

The report was deafening to his ears, the stock punched his shoulder with a kick, and he saw the windscreen shatter like a crazy spider's web; the bullet missed the driver and took one of the rear passengers in the chest, merging his body and blood with the Merc's seat. With a scream of gears and engine, the Merc swerved left, smashing into the embankment and then righting itself; the front bumper was torn free, was crushed under the frantically spinning wheels—

The lane – and Carter's killing ground – was running out.

'Fuck it,' snarled Carter.

He flicked the rifle to automatic and squeezed off a four-round burst. Bullets slapped up the bonnet. Another four rounds, and the windscreen caved in and the car veered again—

Carter was not there to see it. He left the rifle in the snow and sprinted for the house and the turning circle in front of the steps. Arms pumping, he heard the Mercedes pass on the roadway below him, engine whining, more gunshots ricocheting. The huge Mercedes flashed from view and Carter ground his teeth, pushing himself through the snow, the Browning HiPower in his hand, sweat stinging his brows—

More gunshots rang out from up ahead.

Carter pounded across the ridge and the world opened up ahead of him, backed by mountains and a picturesque view of falling snow, an idyllic romantic scene punctuated with the harsh full stop of—

Violence.

Natasha had swung the BMW around to form a barricade behind which she crouched, gun out and resting over the raised boot.

As Carter appeared, the Mercedes howled straight towards the BMW; Natasha dived out of the way with a yelp as the two cars collided amidst tearing noises of screaming steel and metallic crunching; the BMW was ploughed into the front of Carter's house, buckled and broken, one of the windows shattering; the Merc's doors were opening even as the collision took place and men tumbled from the vehicle, automatics and sub-machine guns drawn—

Natasha rolled to her feet, firing – in seconds bullets smashed across the space. One of the men was punched from his feet with a bullet in his cheek, ripping his face apart and dropping him in a flurry of blood.

A line of bullets scythed across the trees, drilled across the clearing—

Three smacked into the embankment behind Natasha in quick succession, their impact making dull slaps in earth.

The fourth bullet smashed into Natasha, puncturing her flesh and flipping her backwards, up and over diagonally, legs kicking out. She landed in a crumpled heap, wedged against the embankment, face to the ground, legs propped up and twisted against tree roots and icicles.

'No!' screamed Carter.

CHAPTER 7

DEEP RED

Spiral_H, London.

Headquarters to the Spiral mainframes; a massive, awesome collection of machinery used to coordinate worldwide Spiral affairs, from DemolSquads to financial deals, from the buying and selling of land, weapons and military hardware to the masterminding of Wall Street economics. Battles had been and were commanded from Spiral_H. The Battle of Belsen. The Attack on Poland Ridge. The transport of festering tanker-borne bodies to Siberia after the Grey Death . . .

Those who knew of Spiral, or who worked for Spiral, would often wonder about finance: how had this organisation become so big? And how did it fund such huge worldwide schemes and plans?

There were no simple answers. Spiral had fingers in many pies – Spiral had the controlling shares of a thousand financial institutions, owned a myriad of businesses from rubber plantations to petroleum refineries. If there was money to be made – good money – then Spiral would be in some way involved.

Spiral_H could not be seen from the air; it burrowed under the ground, a massive 500-metre-wide shaft that had been sliced vertically from the rock and layers of the world. Above Spiral_H were rows of shops, houses; normal London streets made less normal after the vicious and bloody London Riots . . . but delving deeper, below the tarmac, below the howling traffic, below the bustling shoppers and camera-touting tourists and gun-bristling JT8s, below the subways and underpasses and below the insanely heavily guarded London Underground . . . Spiral_H *existed* . . .

Deep deep down: an underground base, an underground world.

The entrances were masked; hidden; only the elite few who knew of Spiral knew of the access points. One entrance was a wide rotating glass door leading into an insurance company's single-storey complex. On this particular morning, the door spun slowly to reveal a beautiful young woman. She was smiling as she emerged, her expensive suit crisp and clean and neatly pressed, her security badge masking an extremely high-tech access tool to grant her passage to Spiral's underground HQ.

She glanced up at the gathering clouds, watched by a group of armed policemen at the corner of the street, their eyes admiring her long legs and polished make-up.

Her gloved hand reached up, touched momentarily at her gleaming red lips.

And then she was gone—

Replaced by a ball of gas and flame that roared from below the level of the land, smashed up into the heavens screaming so loud that it was beyond aural appreciation; as in the aftershock of a nuclear explosion, the houses and shops and buildings were disintegrated in an instant, were stomped kicked smashed up and out and down into oblivion. Steel and concrete and glass and disintegrated rooms and furniture and computers were pulped and pulverised and the occupants of the buildings and houses and *below the ground* the heart of Spiral, its core, its soul – all were vaporised in an instant as explosives smashed and fucked and stomped all shape and mass from a wide slice of the world . . .

Dust billowed up in a huge cloud, a clenched atomic fist of concrete dust with a twisted Tube carriage caught and spinning in its centre, a fist that seemed to gather as if summoning strength, a blossom of disintegration, a bloom of detritus – and then exploded and rolled out in a huge booming concussion wave that encompassed the surrounding broken buildings and rain-smeared landscape . . .

The explosion could be heard a hundred miles away.

With the dust came a blanket of silence.

Soon the screams could be heard.

And the aftermath took an eternity.

Feuchter lay on a beach of black sand, dark waves of pain washing over him like the waves of the ocean. In fact, he could hear the sea; struggling, he forced his head to the right and could see crests of gleaming white foam on the black waters. Feuchter groaned, his whole frame shuddering. He forced up his head, gazed down at himself. He was naked – a hole, a crusted bloody eye, marked a bullet entry low down in his belly.

What happened? he thought sombrely.

And then the words; the words drifted to him as if from a million miles away, buzzing insect noises in his brain, merging with the sounds of the sea, hissing and rolling, surging and slithering across the sand—

– He must be in great pain . . .

– We have removed the bullet, but there are still pieces of metal lodged inside; the bullet shattered on entry, bits of metal scything out in all directions. This man should be dead, I am amazed we're looking down at him in a bed and not in a coffin . . .

Feuchter groaned. He closed his eyes.

A cold breeze blew in from the black ocean.

He reached out inside himself, searching his bloodstream, searching his tissue; he found the rogue pieces of metal and despite carrying them in his shell, he knew they were doing him no harm; he could feel his body working, repairing itself, his veins buzzing with blood and *something else*. Feuchter smiled; he could feel the strange chemical within him, nestling in his veins and organs, in his brain, in his spinal column. It took away his pain.

He thought back, Feuchter thought back—

Across the long hard years.

Pain lanced him.

He concentrated again on the wound; he felt the ebb and flow of chemicals in his system. He could feel himself getting stronger; could feel his body repairing the damage wrought by the bullet.

He floated for a while on waves of agony.

He listened to the sea.

Voices.

– Give him another ten mils of morphine; there, that should soothe his suffering for a while; or at least stave off death for another couple of days. Nurse, has he spoken?

– Yes, he cried out in his sleep.

– What did he say?

– He cried out for Maria. Who is Maria?

– The woman who was found dead and burned up in

the castle at Schwalenberg; they brought in her corpse – what a fucking mess. She's bagged up down in the mortuary awaiting an autopsy, although I'm not sure what remaining part of her they would like to fuck with . . . there's not much left.

– Were they close?

– I believe so; it was his niece, but she had lived with him, treated her like a daughter.

Feuchter felt a rage well within him.

He remembered: remembered Carter – remembered the bullet . . . and he remembered the gun, black eye focusing on Maria, blowing her backwards across the chamber, her small silver gun clattering on the floor, her face slapping to the stone, her tooth cracking, blood pooling from her smashed lips . . .

Maria; ahhhh, sweet Maria.

He remembered a time, from years earlier: sitting at the broad untreated-timber farm table. The sun was gleaming outside, casting strips of bright light over the tiled floor. He could smell rosemary, and the trees from the cherry orchard. Maria had only been young then; eight, maybe nine. She sat on his knee, a bowl of cherries on her lap fresh-picked only an hour before – both of them standing precariously on the small ladder and giggling as they reached out, plucking the ripe fruit from the branches. Now Maria ate the harvest of their daring, her fingers and lips stained red with juice, her eyes wide and gleaming and beautiful, her face a picture of delight.

Feuchter closed the door on the memory.

There was a bitter taste in his mouth.

Anger and . . . something more.

Cold and clinical.

He knew; knew he should feel something incredible for Maria; he knew that his emotions should flow thick

118.

and fast, and his anger was there, and a hatred for Carter that spoke of long hours of torture to come . . . but he knew he should be weeping at her death. Weeping uncontrollably. His intelligence told him that much.

But something strange had happened.

Feuchter could not bring himself to cry.

His face turned to a grimace now; the bullet wound was healing and acid ate his flesh as it knitted together; in this dream state it seemed to be happening so quickly, almost instantaneously, strands of skin and muscle joining together, cells growing and repairing and replicating.

It hurt. It burned him *bad*.

Hans: a shame he'd had to kill the man. Feuchter remembered the indecision; and the orders typed on the white sheet before him. To murder his own brother, to murder a man he loved knowing full well that he would leave an orphaned girl with nobody to care for her—

He had carried out the orders. A single shot to the head.

And he had cried afterwards; Maria had come to him, asking what the matter was, and she had cuddled him and sat on his knee and accidentally smeared the speckles of her father's blood on his face in her innocence and ignorance; and Feuchter had cried, cried long and hard and told himself to be strong and then on that dark bloody evening of murder he had risked everything to get Maria away from there, to get her away to safety and save her life—

Things had changed, he realised.

And then, bitterly: *I* have changed.

Now; now there were no tears. And he understood why – he understood the chemical processes that had altered his body but it still haunted him. He had thought that he would be strong; he had thought that he would be able to make the sacrifice for the good of the future; for the good of all things.

I am doing the right thing, he told himself.

The sacrifice *will* be worth it in the end.

The sea crashed against the dark shore; and Feuchter realised that the surf, the rolling sound of the surf and the hiss of the spray were voices once more, distant voices drifting from the infinite dark horizon:

– . . . Will stabilise him in the event of an . . . hey, who are you, you can't come in here, you've—

– Check him; are they using the right drugs? OK, substitute it for Methylperdazone, 15 mils, and make sure you inject it straight into the wound, through the healing tissue.

– Good; and for fuck's sake, put your guns away.

Feuchter awoke. His eyes were gummed shut, and he waited for a while, listening to his own gentle calm breathing. His senses were alert, though; he could hear breathing, from another three men in the room. He could smell sweat, a hint of old aftershave, whisky, and somebody's odorous feet. Feuchter did a system scan on his own body: it felt weak, the muscles tightened, taut with cramps, burned with fatigue. And his stomach: it was now nothing more than a dull throb where the wound had been.

He forced open his eyes, sticky and filled with crusts of sleep; he could see a fire-retardant tiled ceiling in the gloom. Yellow light cast spiral patterns across the tiles, which were quite new; a private ward, then?

Feuchter's hand moved down his body; he felt the fresh scar where the bullet had recently smashed into him; he probed it gently but there was no pain. He smiled to himself, then propped himself up on one elbow.

There were three men; they were all watching him. Two were heavy-set bruisers, carrying Sterling submachine guns concealed badly within their long coats; they were unshaven and looked weary. The third was a tall thin man, with a hawk face and a crooked, hooked nose. His hair was shaved close to the scalp, his hands heavy with rings. He wore a white doctor's coat and a stethoscope. A small case was by his side and Feuchter knew exactly what items were in it.

'It's good to see you, Tremont. How long have I been out?' he asked.

'Three days, sir. A little longer than we expected, but you were nearly dead when we got to you. And you have to appreciate that in controlled laboratory conditions we do not replicate real-world random activities with such precision as when these incidents occur naturally.'

Feuchter nodded. 'Can you get me a coffee? And a cigar? I am gasping – I feel like I've been unconscious for months!'

'That is a side effect of the accelerated processes, sir.' Tremont waved away one of the bruisers, who slid from the room. Outside the self-closing green door Feuchter caught a glimpse of a sterile corridor, with several waiting trolleys and distant lights.

'Does Durell know that I am OK?'

'He does, sir.'

'Am I in a private facility?'

'Yes. We had to work quickly; you had lost a lot of blood and although your body was already regenerating we had to give it a slight boost. This will stay in your system for the next two weeks, or thereabouts.'

'Side effects?'

'Exhaustion; but we have new drugs to combat this also.'

'Good.'

Feuchter sat up. 'There are still bits of metal inside me.'

'Yes, we know; they are benign and can be removed at a later date; Durell said speed of recovery was of the utmost importance because of the developments with the QIII. He said to tell you that we have had advances with the location of the stolen schematics.'

'And . . .' A pause. 'Carter?'

'After the incidents in Germany, he has been traced.'

'Tell me.'

'He evaded several Nex operatives; nearly killed *you*.'

'He's better than I thought – much better. Could almost be a fucking Nex himself!'

There was laughter; cold laughter; it contained little humour.

'Units have been dispatched to remove him.'

Feuchter nodded. The bruiser returned and Feuchter lit his cigar. 'Out of interest, my niece, Maria Balashev: she died, did she not?'

'She did, sir. Nobody seems to know quite what happened in that room . . . we were waiting for you to awake. The Nex got you out just before the explosion designed to remove the QIII development team and mask your disappearance, but Maria . . . well, the bullet had clipped one of her lungs – she choked to death on her own blood. There was nothing they could do for her and didn't have time to make snap decisions . . . you were the priority.'

'Priority?' said Feuchter coldly, a dark intelligent twinkle in his eyes. 'Yes, I suppose I am.'

'One other thing, sir.'

'Yes?' His eyes glittered.

'Spiral_H had set up a task force to remove Spiral_Q from operation.'

'And?'

'It had been successfully dealt with, sir. Spiral_H no longer exists, and many of their operatives and networks are dead.'

'A downward spiral, you could say?' chuckled Feuchter nastily, and closed his dark eyes and allowed the pain to wash over him and take him away to dark obsidian shores.

Natasha lay, broken and torn and smashed on the ground.

'No!' hissed Carter. His own Browning started to bark as he leaped from the ridge, both hands clasping the weapon. The man who had shot Natasha was slammed from his feet, bullets eating him whole like tiny metal parasites, and blood exploded from his mouth, staining his beard and nose in a crimson shower. Carter landed, rolling across the ice, grunting, his Browning on empty and his body sliding against the buckled BMW with a *thud*. He swiftly changed mags – checked inside the Mercedes.

On the ice, two men were still standing, retreating towards the woods; one was dead in the back seat of the vehicle from Carter's sniper round; another had been shot by Natasha, and one lay on the ice with his face blown apart, Carter's bullet in his brain.

Carter popped his head around the car's protective shell; bullets screamed from the edge of the woods, eating into the stone and metal behind him with showers of dust. Carter dropped to his belly and slid along to the edge of the Mercedes which clicked and hissed with the sighs of cooling, stressed steel—

Legs, sticking out from behind a tree.

He opened fire, heard screams, saw blood erupt from feet and shins.

123

One last man—

Carter squinted but could not see the assassin. Where had he gone? He had been by the side of the trees, down near the low stone wall that needed serious repairs which Carter kept putting off until the eternal 'next summer' . . .

Boots thudded on the Mercedes bodywork and Carter looked up – too late – as the man leaped on top of him with a growl. Carter caught a glimpse of tanned features and a bushy black moustache. He smelled garlic before he was grabbed, his Browning knocked easily aside. He brought up his knee, but missed – the large attacker rained down blows on Carter's head and face and he was momentarily stunned, blinded by multiple impacts—

The weight lifted. Carter lay on his back, on the ice, tasting blood and a sliver of tooth. He glanced up—

Into a boot.

Stars flashed across his vision and he was smashed backwards against the Mercedes, grunting, blood flowing down his chin, his nose broken. He might have screamed, he wasn't sure—

His fingers slipped on the ice beneath him as he tried to push himself up.

'Now, I kill you,' came the heavily accented voice.

Carter's eyes flickered open – everything seemed to be in slow motion,

Let me take his fucking soul, whispered Kade.

Carter dodged left as the boot connected where – a split second before – his face had been. Carter's fist smashed a heavy curling hook against the man's groin and then—

The man screamed.

Carter dragged himself to his feet, suddenly aware of the snarling; the man was on the ground, Samson's teeth

124

clamped on and through the attacker's collarbone, tearing at his neck and throat. He was squirming, trying to punch the dog but the compression and snapping and tearing was making him wail, there was a *crack* of collarbone, and the man struggled manically to get away from that awesome crushing bite—

Carter staggered against the Mercedes. He gave a quick glance to Natasha – she was down and out of the game. He scanned for the Browning but could not see the weapon through the blood in his eyes; he felt a warm stream down the back of his throat and he spat stark red against the snow.

He moved forward and met Samson's eyes; they were smiling.

'Good dog. Off.'

Samson retreated, lips up baring evil blood-stained fangs—

Carter kicked the man in the head several times, until he was sure the killer was unconscious. Then he knelt, and slammed the heel of his hand into the man's nose, breaking it in a return favour and making doubly sure the bastard wouldn't get up.

Covered in blood, Carter skidded across the snow and ice to Natasha. Gently, he eased her legs from the embankment and rolled her onto her back. She was breathing, raggedly, her eyes open, her Berghaus soaked in blood. 'Can you feel your fingers?' he asked.

'You look a fucking mess,' she smiled, her voice hoarse.

'You're not so beautiful yourself.'

'I can't move . . .'

Carter lifted Natasha into his arms and staggered, despite her lack of weight. His head was spinning, pounding after the blows from the large man. She was still as light as he remembered . . . from better, happier times . . .

Carter lurched towards the house.

Nat's eyes grew large and her fingers clawed his arm—

Her tongue protruded. Carter cursed, and dropped to his knees in the snow, amongst the droplets of raining blood. Natasha could not breathe . . . the bullet had triggered an adverse reaction inside her, fucking with her central nervous system to inspire anaphylactic shock—

Natasha's windpipe had closed.

Her own body had become the Enemy.

She spasmed, back arching as if in a fit of epilepsy; Carter pinned her down with his own body weight and fumbled in his clothing, searching, hunting—

Natasha squirmed beneath him, as if in some bizarre act of love. She was strong, incredibly so. Carter dug a pen from his pocket, a cheap plastic biro, and, grunting, he held her spasming heaving body in place, clamped her arms under his legs and grabbed her short hair tightly in his fist, pulling her head back swiftly—

He could not look her in the eye, because he knew she could see and feel and hear and understand—

The ballpoint pen looked suddenly so innocent in his fingers. Carter pulled the cap free with his teeth and spat it into the snow. Natasha was going blue, her eyes so wide he thought that they would pop—

He made the stroke with one quick movement.

Down, just above the sternum . . . at the base of her throat—

Punching a hole through her flesh . . .

Through her oesophagus—

There was a sudden *whoosh* of intaken air through the ragged, improvised mouth. Carter withdrew the pen, releasing a tiny squirt of blood that hit him in the face and mingled with his own. Carter stared down into

126

Natasha's eyes, unable to speak, and the unhealthy pallor gradually faded from her flesh as the air flowed into her lungs.

Her eyes closed, blinked. She could not speak.

Carter lifted her, limp now in his arms, and crawled wearily over the bonnet of the smashed BMW which was partly blocking the entrance to his home. He slid across the buckled surface, then kicked open his front door. He climbed the steps, suddenly weary, suddenly aware of a million pains screaming through his battered and bruised body. Stars danced in front of his eyes and he had to pause halfway up the steps, leaning, heaving and panting, against the wall. He continued, and felt elation when he reached the top.

He carried Natasha through to the living room, kicked the leather couch over in front of the open fire and laid her out. Blood had soaked her clothing, seeping through the fabric.

There was a repetitive *blipping* coming from a control panel on the wall: proximity-sensor alerts triggered by the assassins. Carter reached over, disengaged the alarms and welcomed the silence.

Carter threw a few logs on the glowing fire, then moved into the kitchen. He removed his coat, groaning, then his own jumper. Cuts and bruises appeared across his body and shoulders, across his throat and face and when he glanced into the mirror—

A battered shell gazed back. It grinned through damp glistening blood.

Carter ran off a bowl of hot water, grabbed a knife from the cedarwood rack and returned to the living room. He knelt, and carefully cut away Natasha's clothing, her sopping silken shirt and bra. Her flesh was pale under Carter's appraising gaze. He realised that she had, thankfully, taken only a single bullet but he still cursed, leaning over her to analyse the wound. It had entered high through the shoulder – tearing flesh, just missing the lodestone of bone within and exiting in a tight hole from the back of the muscle. An inch lower and it would have caused *serious* damage . . . the hole was slick with fluid nestling like stagnant crimson rainwater in a tiny shell hole.

'Shit.'

Carter limped to his study and grabbed a leather medical case; he returned to Natasha and pulled out a syringe, injecting her intravenously with a morphine-based sedative. He checked her pulse and BP, using the medscan on the ECube. Then he pulled free a sterile solution and cleaned first the front of the wound, and then, rolling her mumbling over onto her belly, the exit wound. Carter cleaned the hole, using a scalpel to shave free friction-burned flesh and cut out alien particles of metal and cloth. Using sterile wire, he finally stitched the fresh sliced skin together.

Stitching the front wound, Carter checked Natasha's pulse and BP once more, then applied a sterile dressing to her tightly stitched flesh and also to the improvised hole in her throat. Then he linked her to a tiny mobile monitor, which checked on heart rate, oxygen-saturation levels and blood compositions. He pulled down her trousers, checking for other wounds he might have missed. He checked her blood group and haemoglobin level, but her Hb was 8g/dl – dangerous, because the oxygen carrying capacity of her blood had been seriously reduced and she was in need of a transfusion. He strapped a tourniquet around her forearm, tightening it gently, then pulled free a cannula and tore off the sterile packaging. He inserted the thin needle into a vein of her hand, then eased it free, leaving the plastic sheath in place. Working quickly, he secured the cannula with a dressing and moved to the kitchen, removing a pint of his emergency store of universal O-negative; he grabbed a small folding metal stand from a low shelf, shaking free the dust, and returned to Natasha. He erected the stand, hung the O-neg from the narrow frame, and from his case removed a sterile blood-giving set. This he connected first to the unit of blood, being careful to prime the line before connecting the other end of the cannula, ready to commence transfusion. He flicked up the dial on the blood-giving set, and watched the drip rate in the chamber for a moment in order to establish a steady flow.

Content with his work so far, Carter considered wrapping her in foil, but decided against it – foil kept the cold in, and Nats was *very* cold. Instead, he merely wrapped her in blankets and piled more logs on the fire, giving her a final injection of antibiotics and another dose of sedative before stumbling to the bathroom himself.

He removed his torn, bloodied clothing, switched on the shower and stepped into the steam, wincing as the water lashed his broken face like a whip. Slowly, he lathered his body, washing free the dirt and sweat and blood – his own and that of others.

His brain hurt, his mind a whirlpool of confusion—

There were too many questions to answer, and a broken nose did nothing to calm his thoughts.

He stepped free and towelled himself gently, his movements lethargic now as the adrenalin left him. He looked at his face in the mirror and cursed. Heavy bruising, cuts and scrapes. His nose was a mess, twisted and deformed. He dragged the medical case over and, with some difficulty, injected himself with diazepam and waited for his

129

flesh and soul to go numb and provide him with that sick-liest of sweet sensations.

He pulled on shorts and a T-shirt, feeling a little groggy as the drugs ate his system resources. Then, taking his nose between his two thumb-heels, he counted to three and wrenched the bone and cartilage back into some sem-blance of position. Everything went black and he screamed, despite the anaesthetic. He vomited into the sink and stood there, leaning over the bowl, drooling and panting.

Carter glanced up.

His nose was straight once more, but buckled, like corrugated iron that had been beaten with a lump hammer. He grinned weakly, brushed gently at his teeth – avoiding the broken one – to remove the sour vomit, and splashed water on his face to carry away his pain-fuelled sweat.

He moved, checking on Natasha who was breathing more regularly now, the colour having returned to her face. He pulled on a heavy coat and gloves, and a set of boots unstained with blood, and trotted down the steps.

'Why didn't you call me?'

'I didn't need you.'

'You could have been killed; I would have wiped them from the face of the fucking earth . . .'

'I didn't do so bad myself.'

'Don't trust Natasha.'

'I don't need your fucking advice, Kade. I never even asked you to come, so fuck off to whatever hell you inhabit and leave me with my thoughts. Life is hard enough without you sticking your spiritual nose into it . . .'

'Ooh. Tetchy. The broken nose hurt, did it?'

'Kade. Go.'

'*I don't want to.*'

'You are driving me mad!'

'*Good, isn't it? I believe I have found my true vocation in life.*'

Kade left, suddenly, and Carter felt even more light-headed at the abrupt – unexpected – withdrawal.

He stepped out into the snow. Flakes were falling, heavier now, from a grey sky that cast silver shadows across the landscape. The world was silent, an oil painting of stillness and serenity: except for the intrusion of Samson who was worrying the corpse of one of the attackers, tearing at the stomach and chest, bloodied strips of flesh in his teeth—

'Whoa. Sam, get the fuck out of here, you dirty little bastard.' He chased the whining dog away, and Samson retired across the turning circle, lying under the trees and rubbing his muzzle between his paws, licking free the remaining blood. Carter located his Browning HiPower 9mm, checked the mag and the state of the weapon, and used a rag to wipe it free of blood and dirt. He checked the unconscious man, and then moved around the battered Mercedes and towards the edge of the woods. There were pools of deep red on the ground where the man whose legs he had shot had been standing; the blood led away and Carter followed for fifty paces until he found the man curled into a ball, dead. Carter checked him, then, taking him by his feet, dragged him deeper into the woods and rolled him down a small embankment into a snow-filled ditch.

He worked slowly, watched by Samson's bright eyes. He pulled the corpse out of the Mercedes, and gathered the other bodies, dragging them all into the woods and laying them to rest in a line like some grisly murder scene from a horror novel. He rinsed the red stains from his hands with snow and returned to the final man, who was making low moaning sounds. Carter rolled him over onto his belly and pulled wire from his pocket, binding the man's hands and feet so tightly that the wire cut deep. Then he dragged the tanned man to the porch, propped him against the foot of the stairs and placed a coat over him.

'Don't want you to die of exposure, my little flower,' he muttered.

Night was falling fast with the snow, the heavy flakes tumbling through the darkness like leaves from some great tree. Carter moved to the cars and stood, hands on his hips, chewing at his lower lip – which began to bleed, forcing him to curse, head lifted into the darkness.

He got into the Mercedes, brushing shattered glass from the leather upholstery. The keys were in the ignition, the dashboard still illuminated. He turned the keys and the engine rattled into life, vibrating the buckled bonnet. A squealing – probably from the fan belt – emerged like the cry of a strangled cat. Carter pushed the automatic gearstick into reverse, shivering at the icy breeze and flakes of snow peppering through the shattered windscreen. He eased the accelerator. There was a groan of buckled steel as the Merc dragged the BMW back and then released it suddenly, leaving a twisted wing in its wake. Carter reversed the battered Mercedes, then turned it around to face the lane exiting from Carter's own little world. He turned off the ignition and dropped the keys into his pocket. The front of the Merc was smashed to oblivion; no headlights, no grille, only an exposed and severely leaking radiator and a buckled shock strut. Carter moved to the BMW, eyes scanning the twisted coach lines. Two side windows had been smashed, a tail light was shattered and bullet holes had peppered the bodywork. The front end was OK, and Carter climbed in and started the engine. The 4.0-litre straight 6 kicked into life and rumbled steadily, fumes pluming from the wide twin-piped exhaust. Carter eased it into first gear – then cruised the BMW away from his house and out onto the snowbound road. The car ran reasonably smoothly, a few rattles and creaks and excessive noise from the shattered windows betraying its recent abuse. Carter turned the vehicle in the entrance to a field, then drove it back to his house, revelling in the still-powerful handling of the damaged motor.

He parked up the car. The central locking had become defunct – probably a stray bullet. He pocketed the keys and, re-entering the Merc, drove the long black car into the woods and out of sight of the road. Then he limped back to the porch and stared down at the would-be assassin; the man was big, much bigger than Carter and quite fearsome-looking. He was dark-skinned, almost Arabic in appearance. He had an oiled black moustache and was squinting up in pain – Carter gazed down at the man's savaged shoulder and his broken nose and the wires biting into his skin. Carter crouched down. 'Who are you?'

The man's lips went tight.

'Are you here to kill Natasha, or me?'

Silence. He looked straight ahead.

Carter's fist slammed into his prisoner's broken nose, and the man screamed, saliva and blood drooling from his mouth. His head hung, and then lifted slowly to stare at Carter. He spat into Carter's face and grinned, deep red globules staining his teeth.

'If that's the way you want it.'

Carter grabbed the man's hair, shouted for Samson, who was sniffing at the edge of the woods, and dragged the man up the stairs, wailing and bumping. He had to stop halfway up when a clump of hair finally came out in his fist, but he wound a larger portion between his fingers and dragged the man up the final steps, across the floor and into the kitchen. Moving to the back of the house he opened a door that led into a stone-floored utility room, mostly bare except for a washing machine and drier. It was terribly cold, and dark. Carter rolled the man down the three steps, and closed the door.

He returned to Natasha and slumped by her side. Her breathing was deep, her colour good. Samson trotted in and jumped into his basket in the corner, curling up and dropping asleep almost instantly.

Carter armed the house defences with the remote IR, placed his head on the sofa beside Natasha and wearily flicked on the TV. Keeping the sound low, he watched without interest as images danced in front of him. Carter hated the TV; the Americans called it the 'dead-eye' and he could understand why. But he acknowledged begrudgingly that it had its uses as he flicked through the news channels, eyes searching, brain working on maximum despite his weary state.

And then he saw it, like some incredibly bad coincidence . . .

The camera swept across the devastation in London, across the huge circle of the explosion zone where once Spiral_H had nestled in its secret enclave. Carter did not listen to the reporter's hysterical monologue because he did not need the commentary, and he did not care what the man had to say; instead his widened eyes watched the amateur camcorder footage, as filmed by a Japanese tourist. The sudden annihilation, the sudden disintegration, the sudden extinction of Spiral_H.

Carter rubbed at his eyes.

What's fucking going on? screamed his confused brain.

He pulled free his ECube; the surface was dead. Not surprising, considering the HQ's mainframes had just been obliterated in a single violent catastrophe of mankind's chemical making.

Carter found that his mouth was dry.

The game was getting bigger.

The game was getting nastier.

'I've fucking had enough of playing by somebody else's rules,' snapped Kade, surging into the forefront of Carter's brain like a black brooding leviathan emerging from the darkest depths of the ocean.

'You're not the only one,' growled back Carter.

For a while he dozed, drifting in uneasy sleep. When he awoke the fire was still glowing warmly, but outside he could see only pitch black, emphasised by small piles of snow caressing the windowsills. Carter looked over at Natasha. She was still sleeping deeply, her breathing regular. He checked the sterile dressings, and replaced them with fresh ones. Carter poured himself a large tumbler of Lagavulin, and retook his seat next to Natasha on the floor, on the rugs, sipping at the mellow fiery drink and staring into her face. She looked so serene in sleep, so beautiful.

And yet soon he would have to wake her; how long would it be before more men came after them? Men with guns, and with murder in mind?

He reached over and pushed some stray hair from her forehead. She murmured in her sleep, shifting slightly, and Carter stroked her cheek, enjoying the warm flushed skin under his fingers, his mood descending into one of melancholy moderated only a little by the bulk of the Browning against his hip.

More will come, he thought.

They will know that they failed, soon enough.

Natasha moaned in her sleep; she turned, sighing, then her face twisted in pain – stitches pulling tight. She coughed, settling back against the cushions. Carter fought his desire to wake her, question her. She had lost a lot of blood, was weak from the ordeal and her injuries, the shock of the GST. She needed to rest . . . but not for long. They had to move; and move soon. How long did they have? Five hours? An hour? Ten minutes? Carter's hand stroked the Browning.

He would be waiting.

And he would fuck them bad . . .

Spiral_Memo3

Transcript of recent news incident

CodeRed_Z;

unorthodox incident scan 554670

The Russian government has fifteen missing nuclear-powered submarines.

These long-range undersea vessels, which are both nuclear-powered and carry nuclear warheads, have been officially confirmed missing in action after they disappeared, one by one, from sonar and other sophisticated ERV scanning and monitoring equipment.

Military-led rescue operations have been circling the areas where the subs were last monitored, and small one-man speed-subs have been diving in search of the missing vessels, but with no success.

Many countries have already been offering
condolences for what could be one of the
greatest ever marine disasters in peacetime.
Reports to follow.>>#

CHAPTER 8

MOBILE

The deck rolled gently beneath his thick grey boots, and looking across to the shore as the wind caressed his long curled hair and thick beard, he could see the darkened mass of the woods, ensconced in the embrace of deepest winter. Where the river poured into the sea, he could see that it had frozen in places and sported huge plates of ice slicing like flat axe blades of silver through the smooth waters. Seagulls flapped and cried like forlorn children, and fought along the edge of the Alaskan shoreline and the woods as dusk embraced this darkened corner of the world.

A wolf howled, distantly, lamenting the full moon, its eyes watching from the woods as the huge black battleship sat rocking gently in the calm icy bay. The wolf turned, and disappeared beneath the trees.

The man reached the door, heavy and black, and it swung open on well-oiled hinges. Giving a final, wistful look back towards the fresh freedom of nature, and the world beyond the sea which now trapped him, he dipped to enter the narrow confines of the ship's corridor. He stepped carefully down the broad iron steps, his walking stick clanging as he felt his way with a precision and caution born of age; his frame was muffled in heavy furs, worn not just to protect him during the brief crossing by boat, but to offset the natural weather of this desolate part of the world.

Despite his age, he was a bear of a man, huge and brown, his head wrapped against the cold and ice by a circular fur hat, his face hidden under a huge shaggy grey-streaked beard.

Moving down the corridor, he paused as he reached a huge door that seemed somehow out of place; he wanted to enter, *needed* to enter, and yet still he paused. He considered knocking, but realised it would be a waste of time. Durell already knew he was there.

He pushed, and the huge door swung inwards.

He stepped forwards, into a darkness lit only by candles. The room was carpeted, and wood-panelled; huge rows of unevenly sized books lined the walls and through a tiny porthole grey light spilled in. The room was awash with shadows and gloom. Against one wall, almost out of place among the wood and old tomes, was a single silver bank of incredibly high-tech equipment; several white lights flickered across the surface, and a black screen reminded the man of a dead portal into another world.

'Durell?'

'I am here, my friend.' A figure stood beside a stack of old, leather-bound books; tall and thin, shrouded in a black robe and wearing a voluminous hood that hid any features within a circle of obsidian darkness. The voice was rich, had melody and strength. 'You may speak – we are alone for the moment.'

'They failed,' said the bear-clad man in Russian. 'He has been a year out of Spiral. We thought him an easy target; retired, lacking the professionalism of the others.'

'Even after the events in Germany with . . . Feuchter?'

'That was luck.'

'Your naivety astounds me. You ranked him so low on the list of priority kills, when in fact he should have been near the top.' The smooth voice came from the folds of the hood and the bearded old man shivered.

'What would you have me do?' came the gravelled voice of the Russian. The voice was cracking under pressure. His stick came up, a swift movement for one who initially appeared so old and frail. The stick touched his shoulder and rested there, as if proffering some small protection against the black-robed figure before him. His fear was a tangible thing, physical, an aura surrounding him like a cloud.

'Send the 5Nex,' came the soft voice.

'The 5Nex are ready?'

'They have been ready for longer than you could possibly imagine; and there are battalions on the move, battalions preparing for war! Soon this ship will be the hub of our activities . . . yes, my friend, you are living through times of change and it is good for you that you are a part of them – integral, shall we say.'

The Russian gazed at the black-robed figure, sensing the smile, the show of teeth, within the darkness. His mouth was a dry line, his eyes seemingly filled with tears. His knuckles were white where they gripped the walking staff.

'You may go,' said Durell softly.

The large man turned, and stepped out from this chamber deep within the heart of the battleship – Durell listened as the walking stick rang down the corridor, the noise finally disappearing into the bowels of the apparently deserted and ghostly vessel.

The battleship rocked gently on eddies of sea current.

Ice caressed her huge prow and black flanks, and glittered like diamonds across the frozen decks and the huge guns, which were silent and motionless.

Seagulls cawed outside the room's porthole as Durell threw back his hood and cold eyes glittered in the mixed silver of candlelight and moonlight. A hand stretched out and patted the candle flames into extinction. Then he moved to the porthole and opened it, allowing the breeze of the wild darkness to invade his sanctuary.

Pain gripped him, but only for a few seconds of savage intensity. As his twisted face returned to calm, he licked his lips – a small red tongue darting out to smear a trail.

'Soon,' came the soft words. 'Soon, Mr Carter.'

In the dream, Carter stood on a mountain plateau, a flat section, a *scoop* carved from the vertical wall of a vast towering black mountain that reared above a world of dark sand. Dust and jagged black rock squatted under his boots, and the sky stretched away for infinity, curled with trails of purple and yellow – a bruised night sky. Kade stood in front of him – with Carter's own face, his own body, but deformed twisted corrupted sporting darker, brooding eyes, a heavier face and stockier set of shoulders. Altogether more—

Intimidating . . .

'Why have you come here?' snapped Kade, standing beside a fire that burned within a small ring of rocks. The wind howled around them, through narrow channels of rocky teeth, and it whipped Carter's coat and caressed his face with a corpse's kiss.

'I didn't want to come here. It just happened,' said Carter slowly, his words soft and without tension.

'Fuck – off,' said Kade harshly. *'This is my place. My world. My mountain.'*

141

Carter grinned without humour, his brow furrowing, and sat down cross-legged beside the wildly whipping flames of the fire. They crackled like tiny bottled demons. 'I think I will stay,' he said. 'After all, many is the time *you* pay *me* unwelcome visits.' This was something that suddenly amused him; an irony, a reversal of fortunes: here was Kade, his poise suddenly gone, his humour and bitterness appearing as melted ice. He was pissed off at Carter's intrusion. 'I never ask for *you* in my dreams,' he said softly.

'*That is different,*' said Kade. '*I help you.*'

'Help me? Or help yourself?'

'*I don't know what you mean.*'

Kade did not move. He remained standing, heavy brows furrowed at this unexpected intrusion. He stared down at Carter with ill-disguised distaste; as if he'd just found a rotting bone in his bed.

'*What do you want?*'

Carter shrugged. 'I want nothing. I did not request or intend to come here. This is only a dream.'

'*A dream to you; reality to me.*'

'As you are a dream in my reality?'

'*Yes. Until you give me life.*'

'What are you, Kade?'

'*I am you, Carter.*'

'But what are you *really*?'

He caught the sly smile, and then it was gone. A fleeting shadow; a cloud passing before the sun. '*I am you,*' he repeated. '*I am the finger on the trigger. I am the power behind the punch. I am the hands pulling on the garrotte. I am the poison in the vial. I am you, Carter. I am your dark side, your bad side, your fucked side, your frustration and your anger and your hatred. Call them what you will. I am you – only you choose to debate my existence and I fear you will never accept me.*'

'You do things I would never dream of,' snapped Carter. 'Do not try to make me out to be some fucked-up schizo freak. You are in my brain and you live your own life. You only say that you are me to try and stop me going fucking insane . . . but I will find you, Kade, one day I will find you and we will fight and I will kill you.'

Kade laughed, a cold chilling sound.

'That would be . . . interesting.'

'It'll be fucking interesting when you're eating worms.'

Kade laughed again. *'I will welcome the day, my friend. My saviour. My lifeblood. It is good to see you still carry such anger – it was that anger which earned you your title. The title which scars your heart, Butcher.'*

'That was not me!' Carter's words were suddenly low, the tone unreadable, dangerous.

'It was your hands that killed so many.'

'That was you!' hissed Carter.

'How could you murder them all?' sneered Kade, his voice mocking.

'It was you, you fucking piece of shit, and you know it! Don't condemn me with your fucking haunted past.'

'I am not haunted,' said Kade calmly. He turned then, glancing over the dark desert at something in the distance that Carter could not see. *'There is a bird called a plover that feeds on the meat caught between the teeth of a crocodile,'* said Kade softly. A smile danced across his lips. *'The crocodile could kill the plover easily – with a snap of his jaws. But he chooses not to do so, because this bird performs a service for him and so he lets the bird live. And by performing the service, this plover helps the crocodile to protect his greatest assets – his teeth, which in turn keep him alive. So by keeping the bird alive, the crocodile extends his own life. They are symbiotic. They feed from one another; entwined, like lovers.'*

'And you think we are like that?' laughed Carter coldly, eyes staring up from shadowed brows, all sense of humour gone to be replaced with a cold hard splinter through his heart.

'Oh yes,' said Kade, smiling. *'But I want you to think carefully. Decide which you are. Are you the crocodile – or are you really the bird?'*

'Carter . . .' A shaking. The world tumbled, dissolved. Carter came awake to find Natasha's hand on his arm. She was looking down into his face, worried. 'We need to talk,' she croaked, her face creased and screwed with pain.

'OK, let's talk,' said Carter thickly, climbing to his feet.

He stirred the coffee slowly, the headache crashing against the shores of his mind and crucifying his soul on a cross fashioned from Kade's bones.

'You OK?' came Natasha's voice, weakened, jagged, almost unheard.

'Yeah.'

Carter carried the sweet hot drink into the room, knelt in front of Natasha and looked up into her eyes. She had sat up on the couch, her face lined, her eyes hooded. Every movement brought a little grimace of pain and Carter sipped his coffee, drums thumping in his head, rippling across his temples, scoring his brain with steel claws.

Carter opened his mouth, and Natasha whispered, 'Shh,' with a finger against her lips. She met Carter's gaze. There were tears in her eyes and she smiled warmly at him.

'I'm sorry for bringing such trouble to your home.'

'They were here for me,' said Carter slowly.

'Both of us, I feel,' said Natasha. Tears rolled down her cheeks, and she brushed them viciously away. 'I thank

144

you for saving my life. I . . . I don't know what I would have done without you.'

'Die,' chuckled Kade in Carter's mind. Carter felt the demon squatting there, at the back of his thumping brain.

Natasha coughed, her face wincing; a finger came up, touched the sterile plaster covering the stitched hole in her throat; she smiled wryly. 'You are a brave and strong man, Carter. I have come here to warn you.' She laughed softly. 'Your life is in danger . . . yeah, I know, a little bit too late, eh?' Her gaze met Carter's.

'Do you know that Spiral_H has been destroyed?'

Natasha's eyes went wide. 'Spiral_H . . . are you sure?'

'It was on the TV; and part of Jam's special message when he came to visit me was about how Spiral_H was assembling some kind of strike force to close down Spiral_Q. How's that for a coincidence? And now the whole place – gone!'

'Completely destroyed?' Her voice was a hushed whisper. 'How?'

'They blew the fuck out of it. Nothing remains. The pictures looked like an atomic wasteland.'

'This is bigger than I could have ever imagined,' she whispered, horror lining her face like battle scars.

The fire crackled. Carter finished his coffee, and Natasha, head bowed, deep in thought, looked up, her face pale, lips trembling. 'Listen, we need to move, Carter . . . we need to get away from here. They will come for us!'

'If we move you now, then you could die.'

'Then I will die. If we stay, we will both die.'

Carter grinned, and it was a nasty grin. 'They will have to send many,' he whispered softly. His hand was against the Browning and bad bad twisted images flittered through his brain.

145

'You're not listening,' said Natasha sadly. Her hand reached out, stroked Carter's cheek. 'They will send the Nex.'

'The Nex?'

'All I know is that they are Spiral's oldest and best-kept secret. They are awesome killers. We thought them all dead – but they are not dead. They have . . . somehow survived the . . . *extermination*.' The word tasted bad on her tongue.

'Why now? Why me?' Carter's voice was cold as dread sank into his mind and he remembered Jam's theory that the DemolSquads were being wiped out. The possibility passed like a chilling breeze over his soul, the certainty walked like dark demons over his grave.

'You remember Count Feuchter? From Schwalenberg?'

'How could I ever forget that cunt?'

'Here goes,' said Natasha softly. 'There is a splinter group within Spiral – a group of individuals who have decided to betray everything that Spiral stands for. You think of me as a Tactical Officer – but I am more, Carter, much more.'

Carter met her gaze.

Natasha licked her lips.

'I am part of a group – we have no name – who work within Spiral to root out and eliminate any who try and use Spiral's power against itself. We look for the enemy within.' She sighed.

'You're the fucking secret police?'

'Something like that,' said Natasha, smiling wearily. 'But the enemy has hit hard and hit fast; we had only just discovered that Feuchter was one of them . . . we did not think they were anywhere near ready to move . . . I sent you on a blind mission to your death – but thank God you survived. Others were not so fortunate.'

146

'And Feuchter?' Carter's voice was as cold as diamond ice.

'Feuchter is one of the splinter group; as is another man, Durell. They've struck now because the QIII is practically ready, and with its awesome power they can use it to secure their stronghold. They can use the QIII to take over military installations, satellites, fuck only knows what else. It is so terribly, terribly powerful, Carter – I can't explain how dangerous this processor could be in the wrong hands.'

'I don't understand why,' said Carter gently. 'Destroy the Demolition Squads? Destroy Spiral_H? It's lunacy! Spiral fights to preserve what civilisation we've got left – I thought Feuchter was a good man?'

'This splinter group, headed by Feuchter and Durell – they believe Spiral is weak: corrupt, like Rome at the end of her empire. They believe Spiral knows too much and does nothing about it; they believe Spiral is in the pay of the Big Boys – financed, controlled, governed. We both know Spiral was never meant to be that – it was alone, untouchable, worldwide and incorruptible! Feuchter and Durell think they can do a better fucking job. They think the NBC Laws and the URG Bill are not enough. And then, after the London Riots and the Siege of Qingdao – well, I think they lost all faith in Spiral. With the QIII processor and the Nex they think they can bring us the ultimate in world peace . . . a new world order . . . but . . .'

'Yeah, "but",' snapped Carter. 'In times of war there are always casualties, yes?'

Natasha nodded.

'We definitely need to get the fuck out of here; they will be coming even as we speak.'

'Yes.'

147

Carter reached up and kissed her softly on her lips. 'There is only one person I can think of, one person who has the resources and the knowledge to help us.'

Natasha pulled back a little, her stare meeting Carter's.

'No,' she said, shaking her head.

'Yes,' said Carter. 'The world is fucking collapsing, Nats. Spiral is being force-fed its own entrails, the DemolSquads are being fucked left, right and centre – Gol used to work with Feuchter, and Durell. If anybody knows what they are up to and where they are, then it is Gol. If we can find the QIII, destroy it, then it will be a level playing field again – and if we can take out Feuchter and Durell on the way, then so be it. Gol is the fucker who will point us to the QIII, and the fuckers who want to abuse their power.'

'We can't go to Gol,' said Natasha.

'But he's your father!' hissed Carter.

'Yes, but he's also a *suspect*. He could well be one of them. He could well be working with Durell – with Feuchter – with the Nex! It would be death to meet him.'

Carter climbed to his feet. He withdrew the sturdy 9mm Browning, checked the clip, and rammed it back home as his eyes lifted and he took a deep breath. 'If Gol is a traitor, then the death will be his,' said Carter with grim finality.

Carter had removed the cannula and Natasha was rubbing softly at her hand. Her face was incredibly pale once more and Carter helped her to dress, wincing with her in her pain as she struggled into fresh clothes.

'Tell me more about this Nex that they will send?'

Natasha shrugged weakly. 'All I know is that the Nex were some kind of project from way back – started in the 1990s, I think, but based on work from much earlier.

There is an assassin who is supposed to be awesome – a 5Nex, I think it was called; it was this killer who wiped out Demol14.'

'Alone?'

'Yes, alone.'

'Without help?'

Natasha nodded. 'So the encrypted files read – just before I fled and came here to warn you, and to ask for your help. This thing has spiralled out of control.'

'The irony,' barked Carter. 'Look, I will go and tool up, check the monitors, throw a few things in a bag and we can get the fuck out of here. Is there anything you need?'

'A bit more blood?'

Carter smiled. 'Yeah, time would have been great.' He turned his back on Natasha and walked towards the door leading to the stairs and the monitoring equipment beyond. He could sense her gaze on his back.

'Carter?'

He stopped. Turned.

'I love you.'

'Really?'

Natasha nodded. 'Really.'

Carter winked. 'Get your shit together. We need to be moving in five.'

Carter glanced with a heavy frown at the PC monitors.

Something was wrong.

Badly wrong.

'She is coming,' said Kade.

'How do you fucking know?'

'I can tell these things,' he said smugly.

'Leave me alone, I can do without your input, *brother*.' Carter's sarcasm was an almost tangible thing, but it had little effect on Kade.

149

'Do you want to know what I think about Natasha? I think she will betray you – us! . . . Are you listening to me, Carter?'

'Shut up. Something's happening.'

'I'm giving you my advice . . .'

'Shut up!' Carter snapped.

There came a silence. Carter watched the screens. A sensor came alive, blinking with a proximity warning. By the south woods. Carter switched to video; darkness and snow welcomed him—

And he felt it—

A ripple of energy sang across the woods, a wave of *nausea* that ripped through the equipment and through his belly, making him want to vomit. The PCs instantly shut down . . . followed a couple of seconds later by the lights. The room was plunged into darkness. The PCs' fans whirred to a halt.

'Shit.' Carter sprinted across the landing and down the stairs.

'What's happened?' asked Natasha.

'All the power's gone. I find this incredible because I'm supposed to be furnished with automatic back-up generators.'

'Give me a gun,' said Natasha.

Carter tossed her a small black pistol, a 9mm Glock from his armoury. Stooping, he drew a narrow knife from a hidden sheath in his boot, then slid it carefully back. Metal was always a reassuring back-up option.

Samson whined from the darkness . . .

'Sam. Here boy!' The Labrador appeared, bright eyes glinting in the gloom.

Carter crouched and whispered something in the dog's ear. Sam whined again, tail down. Carter led Sam to the stairs, down, and to the door where a cold wind howled.

150

Carter opened the portal warily, and Sam disappeared into the snow.

'Go. Go now . . .'

Carter ran back up the steps and moved towards his pack.

'Where have you sent him?'

'Away from this place. It's far too dangerous,' said Carter softly. 'Here.'

Natasha caught the keys with a wince of pain and licked her lips nervously, eyes suddenly bright and fevered in the darkness.

'Your BMW keys. I've turned the car around; I think we might need to leave in a hurry.'

'You believe me now?'

'I believe somebody has a lot of fucking technological help, and anyone who can knock out all my sensors and back-up generator in one go has a head start on us.'

'Did your set-up detect anything?'

'Proximity. In the south woods . . .'

'Don't trust it. The assassin could be closer . . .'

Carter shivered, and flicked off the safety on his HiPower. He moved across the room, picking his way by precise memory . . . a good place to defend, he thought. He knew the contours in the darkness so well – but to leave now? The open road at night?

Dangerous and foolish.

We should have left immediately, he realised.

This few hours could have killed us . . .

He calmed his breathing. He forced his heart rate to reduce. He licked his salted lips slowly and peered out from the window and into the snow—

Nothing.

Entry point? he mused.

Only the front door – unless the assassin is a climber . . .

151

'You need me yet?'

Only when I'm dead, thought Carter.

'Don't be such a bad sport. The assassin is in the house even as we speak.'

Carter was about to reply when a breeze washed across his soul, like a ghost seeping into his bones. His head snapped around. The shadow was a patch of darkness—

His arm shot out. At its end grew—

The Browning.

Five bullets screamed, smashing into the far wall and spitting sparks from the rim of a metal picture frame; Carter dropped to one knee and glanced sideways. Natasha was on her belly – automatic reaction to gunfire.

'That was rather an erratic action,' came a soft, smooth voice. The tone was curiously asexual and Carter blinked sweat from his eyes and tried to track the voice. He moved slowly sideways, the Browning a close extension of his body – until he was crouched beside Natasha.

Gun still outstretched, he reached down with his free hand and took her hand. She still held the BMW keys. He pressed them deep against her palm and she patted an acknowledgement—

They moved together, towards the stairwell that would lead them out into the snow.

A movement—

Carter opened fire.

Bullets howled across the wall, chewed the wood of the door and smashed the glass of a cabinet across the room; Natasha left him; the Browning's firing mechanism came down on a—

Dead man's click.

The figure sprang at him from the darkness and he ducked, twisting to the side; the figure landed lightly and – without time to change mags Carter thrust the

Browning in his pocket at the same time going for the other gun – a Glock – in his belt—

A high kick came from the dark and hammered into his chest with such force that he was picked up and thrown backwards, toppling over the couch and landing in a heap, unable to breathe, eyes wide, pain smashing through his heart—

The figure leaped again with incredible speed and agility—

Carter spun, was on his feet, leaped in a blur to meet the assassin; they collided and Carter's hands grasped clothing and flesh and his head smashed forward, connecting with bone. They both hit the ground and Carter smashed another blow, then a third – there was a deep grunt, they rolled, and the figure was—

Gone.

Carter scrambled up as the boots hit him in the chest, but his arms locked around them as both were punched backwards, stumbling, to the stone steps and—

The darkness below.

They fell, tumbling and bouncing down the stone steps, banging from the walls, both too shocked and stunned by the fall to fight until they bounced five steps from the bottom and in a tangle of limbs connected with the unlocked door, smashing it open.

Carter landed on his back in the snow, tasting blood.

The Nex rolled, coming up in a rigid poised crouch—

A cold wind blew across them, ruffling hair, cooling skin.

Carter coughed, then rolled to his feet and whirled in the moonlight as the figure leaped – Carter blocked, backed away, and shook his head. Blood was running down his face. He grimaced, realising that he had broken a finger and two ribs. He felt the ribs clicking within his chest cavity but he was careful to show no reaction, no indication of injury and location—

The figure circled.

Carter caught the shocked face of Natasha to the right. Get in the fucking BMW, his brain screamed, why don't you get in the fucking car, you fucking stupid bitch? He watched her level the gun and fire off three shots, but even at that distance he could see the shaking of her hand . . .

Snow kicked up and bullets whined.

Carter calmed his breathing. The Browning was still in his pocket, the Glock was lost and he had to *focus*—

The Nex approached. He – or she – was considerably smaller than Carter, clad all in grey and sporting a grey balaclava. Flat tight black boots were on the assailant's feet—

Carter could see no weapons.

The Nex charged – Carter blocked a series of three punches, ducked low and smashed a right hook to the assassin's face; he stepped in close, and was kicked in the throat, sending him scrabbling backwards choking and coughing, hands held out in front of him for protection—

'*The Nex is clearly faster than you,*' said Kade calmly.

The attacker leaped; in a blur Carter ducked, twisted and smashed three blows at the figure sailing over his head. The Nex landed lightly, spun on one heel, and charged—

Blows were smashed left and right. Carter blocked, received another kick to the chest and a series of rapid punches that sent him spinning to the snow. He tasted blood and looked down at the frozen ground, which was suddenly cool and soothing to the bruised and battered flesh of his face. It would be so easy, so easy to lie there and never, ever get up again . . .

Carter tried to get up, but his body screamed at him. Colours flashed a metallic rainbow in his mind.

He pushed, heaved, but finally sagged against the snow, energy fleeing him.

Behind, he heard the assassin approach, soft footsteps on the snow but he could not move, could not bring himself to turn, to roll over, to meet that strange copper gaze of this—

His killer.

He could do nothing . . . was paralysed . . . just like in Egypt . . . and in Belfast when the women were screaming and dying . . .

'*Fight*,' howled Kade in his brain.

'*Fuck you, Carter, don't let me die like this! Fight!*'

But Carter could not move.

CHAPTER 9

SPIRAL_Q

The church was a cold place. The floors were polished wood, buffed to a well-worn shine and displaying decades of well-trodden worship. The walls were panelled in wood, polished oak, and led around domino stacks of pews that were so steeped in antiquity that their surfaces were slightly curved from the presence of praying bodies.

Weak sunlight spilled through the myriad of stained-glass windows; the coloured glass glittered like jewels – sapphire and ruby, emerald and diamond; the displays revealed the Last Supper, Moses and the Burning Bush, Adam and Eve and a hundred other religious displays taken from the Great Book itself.

A cool breeze drifted down the aisles, between the polished pews, between the members of the small congregation who had gathered in silent prayer. There was no Mass on this morning, just a gathering of local worshippers who attended when they felt the need for the company of God.

The Priest knelt by the altar, his hands clasped together

in prayer. He was a huge man, broad-shouldered, wearing casual clothes and a long finely tailored woollen overcoat that reached nearly to his ankles. His wide oval eyes were closed in this act of prayer, his face calm, serene almost, bathed in the light of Jesus and this stained-glass phenomenon. By his side, on the low leather-padded bench on which The Priest knelt, sat his Bible; it was a small, ornately embossed leather-bound edition. The pages were as thin as toilet tissue, and edged in gold. It exuded age; it was The Priest's most prized possession and this man was willing to die for his Book.

The Priest was aware of the people around him and his heart swelled with pride. They were fellow worshippers, all caught in this loving act of prayer, all there to commune with the Lord and to receive His Blessing. The Priest sighed; this was as close to contentment as it could get.

Footsteps.

Something changed the karma at his core; something ate The Priest's serenity like an anthill devouring a rancid corpse.

The footsteps approached slowly, calculated, with care.

The sound struck a discordant note in The Priest's soul.

The Priest kept his head down; he continued to pray; he heard the sound of the other worshippers hurriedly leaving this small rural church and he knew this intruder was the Enemy even before the opening speech or move was made.

'The Lord will protect me,' said The Priest suddenly, his voice loud and booming, crashing around the near-empty church. 'I am one of His flock, and He never deserts His flock. He is the Master, and I am merely His servant. Amen.'

The Priest climbed slowly to his feet. His hand reached down, closed over the small leather Bible, and placed the book in the pocket of his overcoat. Only then did he raise his eyes to look at the intruder who stood in front of him.

The figure was slim, athletic, and wore grey; he, or she, had burning copper eyes that watched The Priest warily, drilling into his brain with the pure intensity of a hatred stare.

The Priest surveyed the figure.

'You are not welcome here,' he said, his words soft, steady. 'This is a place of God; of Worship; of Love.'

'I have come to kill you.' The figure took a step back, spreading its hands out a little more in anticipation. The copper eyes were fixed on The Priest and his brown eyes flecked with gold noted the killer's stance and concealed weapons; the liquid flow of movement.

'What manner of creature are you, who dares to intrude on God's Holy Ground? I would say thou art vermin; I would say thou art an infidel in the Lord's Palace; I would say that you need to leave before God smites you down in a hail of hot death.'

The Priest waited, arms folded across his huge barrel chest.

The Nex attacked.

A police siren wailed through the village. The small Ford J2 hammered down country lanes, flashing through a series of tiny village centres that had once been flowers of the country but that now bore the scars of recent battle. It hammered past startled villagers, past the bloated corpses of bio-smashed cattle surrounded by swarms of flies and farmers with sticks piling animal corpses onto reeking bonfires that belched black smoke to the heavens.

The Ford screeched around corners, tyres squealing, and rattled to a halt with a smell of burning engine outside the tiny village church.

A small group of ladies stood huddled outside behind a man carrying a shotgun. They were all peering at the door as the large, pot-bellied policeman struggled from the Ford and moved towards the group. The sub-machine gun slung over his shoulder looked out of place, alien.

'Come on now, people, stand back, let me through,' barked Sergeant Ralph.

'There was gunfire!' said one frightened lady, her hand to her mouth, her shining handbag reflecting the glint of the sun. Her eyes held a haunted quality – she was living through terrible days.

'I was just about to sort this mess out,' said the old man with the shotgun. He looked relieved that the sergeant had arrived. 'Lucky for him that you got here, constable!'

The sergeant cursed himself. Gunfire! He unslung the machine gun, an Armalite X, and grimaced, looking down at the high-tech weapon. Somehow, it seemed so daunting in his fat-fingered hands. In the training centre he had felt brave: a hero ready to do battle as the country descended into anarchy and chaos. Now he merely felt fear, which dulled his brain and brought dryness to his tongue.

'Are you sure it was gunfire?'

'It sounded like a machine gun,' said one old lady.

The sergeant stepped forward towards the heavy wooden doors, pitted and stained with the passing of centuries. He reached, turning the squeaking rusted iron handle.

He shivered as a cold wind caressed him.

He knew; could feel that Death was waiting for him in the gloom.

With a great act of courage, he stepped through the portal alone, Armalite X clasped in fear-slippery hands.

The Priest stood, arms folded, staring down at the dead Nex. It had been tossed across the church, its spine broken, creating interesting shadows among the pews where the twisted snapped smashed body sprawled. The Nex's small alloy machine gun lay, black and evil, a weapon out of place against the polished wood of the church floor. The stench of cordite hung in the air, gun smoke drifting from the barrel. The Priest nudged the gun with the toe of his boot. Then, stepping carefully forward with a quiet tongue click of annoyance, he reached down and grabbed the limp body. The head rolled slack on a ball-bearing spine but, incredibly, the eyes opened. The mouth moved wordlessly for a little while and The Priest lifted the disabled but miraculously living Nex up to his face.

'Have you found the way of the Lord, my son?' he asked quietly.

'I . . . underestimated . . . you.' The dull copper eyes screamed with inward hatred, and anger, and frustration. 'I will not do so again.'

'You are correct, of course, my son,' said The Priest as kindly as he could. He shook the Nex, and a rattle of pain erupted from crushed lungs. 'Who sent you? And how did you know I was Spiral?'

The Nex's lips formed a compressed line.

He would not speak.

'Come on, lad, tell me. And I can take away the pain.'

'I will tell you nothing.' The soft asexual voice was laced with agony; The Priest sighed again, and holding the body upright in one fist he reached down and pulled out a shining broad-bladed knife. One edge was serrated – it was an evil weapon with only one obvious function: to kill.

'Are you sure now, my son? Are you sure you cannot share this information about these evildoers who sent you? If not, you are betraying the Lord, and as His servant I must punish you with bright tongues of silver fire!'

'Fuck you.'

The Priest lifted the knife. Light gleamed from the blade, cast down by a multi-coloured Jesus; shimmering coloured sunlight glanced from the knife and reflected in the eyes of the Nex.

'Has God shown you the light yet, my son?'

The Nex stared up with hatred.

'Then I must show you the darkness.'

The blade smashed down – a single massive blow. The Nex gurgled and The Priest cleaned the blade on the Nex's clothing before allowing the dead spine-snapped body to topple and lie at his feet.

The Priest's head came up, eyes narrowing. A figure moved into the church, cautiously; The Priest smiled when he saw the rotund figure of Sergeant Ralph, Armalite X shaking in his hands.

'Ah, Sergeant, just in time to save me.'

The large policeman wobbled forward, eyes wide. He stared at the dead body, then up at The Priest. He licked his lips nervously, awe shining in his eyes. 'You killed him?'

'God worked through me, my son,' said The Priest, with a kindly smile. He patted Sergeant Ralph on the shoulder. 'He decided to punish the infidel for destroying His beloved place of holy worship.' The Priest gestured to the bullet marks up the wood panelling, across the stone, and the tiny holes in the stained-glass window where three bullets had allowed shafts of pure sunlight to stream in.

'Shall I . . . shall I . . . shall I call more officers? Or the military?' The sergeant was confused; dazed. The stink of death and cordite was stinging his nostrils. The church – a place of love and worship – had become a charnel house.

'Better let my people deal with it,' said The Priest calmly, and strode out towards the sunlight.

Spiral_Q: sand-blasted stone, steel and dull glass, a massive complex that rose for a single storey above the desert dunes – and for sixteen storeys *below*. A surface scratch; an inverted pyramid; a man-made desert iceberg.

Jessica Rade slumped back in her leather chair, and gazed out over the desert on the monitor before her from within the depths of the underground complex; she watched the wind spin and whip the sand into spiral eddies, shifting and dancing, twisting as if possessed by some great stone amber demon. Saudi Arabia, the Middle East, the Arabian Peninsula: Rub al'Khali – the Great Sandy Desert. How Jessica loved and loathed this vast desolate region of Saudi; how it lived, a dual existence, in her favourite dreams and wormed into her worst nightmares. A place of contrasts; a place of life and death; a place of beauty and a place of great ugliness, hardship and fear.

Rub al'Khali – three hundred *thousand* square miles of mostly unexplored desert. A *vast* rolling landscape of Nature's hostility. A huge plateau of sand and rock, smashed into mercy by Nature and the heat and aridity of the climate.

If Jessica tried, if she closed her eyes and *really* tried, she could smell the Red Sea far off over the mountains past Al Hijaz. It had been too long since she had enjoyed the sea; far, far too long.

Jessica was considered 'bright'. In fact, 'bright' did her little descriptive justice: she had passed her GCSEs at the age of eight; her A levels at the age of ten; age restrictions had kicked in then, but she had subsequently attended the University of Cambridge at the age of sixteen – by which time she had already achieved degree and post-degree success through a variety of private tutorial systems. She graduated in computing, specialising in artificial intelligence and the newly emerging field of RI – *real* intelligence. Artificial intelligence was just that – artificial. Set parameters. Set fields. Sub-routines and instructions and base2 binary linear control following scripted routines that were *scripted* . . . WHAT IFs . . . THEN DOs . . . ANDs and ORs and XORs . . . Jessica Rade had pioneered the new school of thought: the concept of the ability to self-learn, self-teach, self-*program*. The ability for a machine to *learn and truly adapt by altering its own core code*. Ergo, to possess *real* intelligence, instead of a stack of pre-programmed directions.

Spiral_Q had snapped Jessica up after the publication of her third paper. And now, aged twenty-three, Jessica was a rich woman living a life of dreams in a secret location deep within the Great Sandy Desert. She was an incredibly rich woman. A *stupidly* rich woman. And yet it was nothing as vulgar as finance and money and *material possession* that kept her at Spiral_Q – despite the desolation of the land: it was to do with her dreams, her aspirations for the future. She could choose to work anywhere she wished: Mexico, the Seychelles, Florida – all had a particular lure for this young sought-after computer genius. But Spiral_Q was based in Rub al'Khali. And

Spiral_Q was where the important computing shit went down.

Jessica Rade *had* to be at the centre of that importance.

Otherwise, her rise to the pinnacle of her chosen career would have been for nothing.

She sat at the terminal, linked to five servers and harnessing the power of forty minor processors. Her fingers blurred across the keyboard and she paused, adjusting the settings of various programs and sub-routines that were running in the background. She compiled her current project – saw the bug even before the compiler reported it; she adjusted her code, compiled a second time, ran the binaries and sat back as figures flickered across the screen. The optical/digital QuadModems flashed small green lights at her.

Jessica Rade rubbed at her weary eyes, licked at dry lips. She suddenly realised that she was incredibly hungry – and incredibly tired, although she acknowledged these were small discomforts in comparison to what had recently gone down in London.

Spiral_H – detonated.

She shivered, and killed the external view.

Jessica gazed through the thick smoked glass at the offices below her; most of the terminals were empty and it was with surprise that she checked the time. 7 p.m.

'Jesus,' she breathed wearily. She had worked straight through from 8 a.m. without a break, her concentration complete, her focus intense and uninterruptible. Now her system suddenly cried out for sustenance and she sighed to herself, climbing to her feet and stretching her perfectly formed athletic body. Her muscles groaned at her.

I need a fucking beer, she realised. A cold one.

She caught the lift up to her personal quarters – all the

Elite Level programmers and designers were given the most luxurious living quarters near the top of the underground complex. They called it 'Ground Level', but in reality it was just below. This was one of the benefits, one of the perks, one of the *expectations* of working for Spiral_Q. They were offered the best salaries, the best holiday packages, opportunities to work worldwide and the opportunity to work on the most exciting projects with the most powerful computing equipment ever created.

And Jessica Rade was, quite literally, at the top of the pile.

She stepped through the doors of her apt, stripped off her clothing and revelled in the feeling of the air-con on her naked skin. She walked barefoot across the marble tiles and flicked on the shower, stepping under the warm jets and soaping her lightly tanned skin. She massaged conditioner into her long dark curls, washed it free and then stepped out of the glass cubicle and towelled herself dry.

Still naked, she crossed to the fridge and pulled free a bottle of ice-cool Budweiser. She flipped the cap, and took a long, long deserved drink. Then she set about preparing a light salad . . . what with the recent worry and gossip surrounding Spiral and the London HQ's annihilation, satisfying her hunger had not been a priority until just now.

She revelled in the simple task of preparing the salad; she enjoyed the basic simplicity of slicing lettuce and cucumber and arranging it neatly around a plate after the brain-wrenching math calculations of an average day working on the QIII.

Jessica Rade was on her fourth Budweiser when the comm buzzed.

She hit the switch.

'Yeah?'

'We have a problem.'

'Another one?'

'The QIII secondary-source has just de-compiled.'

'Shit. I'll be there in five.'

'Can I just remind you that we only have a week left to hit 98%?'

'Yeah, yeah, I fucking understand. I'll be down shortly.' She killed the comm.

'Shit. Now I'll have to get fucking dressed . . .' she muttered, tossing the empty bottle into the bin where it clashed against its comrades. She disappeared into the bedroom, brain whirring at the possible errors that could have caused such a computing calamity . . . and all the time at the back of Jessica's mind was the nagging doubt about Spiral, and what was happening to the organisation . . .

She did not see the flashing white cursor on her screen.

Jessica Rade loved the small hours.

The early hours of the morning when everything was still; when everyone was sleeping; when the world had *died*.

Jessica had often fantasised as a young girl – and, indeed, had carried the fantasies on into adulthood – had played out intricate scenarios in her mind, imagining what it would be like to be the only woman left alive in the world – the only *person* left standing after some horrific chemical accident, after some amazingly deadly virus that had affected everybody on the planet *except her*.

And now: 4 a.m.

She was awake, lying in her light cotton pyjamas on top of the duvet, staring at the ceiling. She rolled from the bed and stood for a moment. The air-con hissed quietly behind her and she sighed, brain swirling with numbers and calculations and projections for WorldCode. She shook her head, smiled to herself, then wandered, seemingly aimlessly, out from her quarters and towards the lift.

The lift ascended with tiny hydraulic sighs. The doors opened.

Jessica Rade listened, and with a sense of danger stepped pyjama-clad out onto the carpet, her feet luxuriating in the rich pile, her whole being tingling at the audacity, the daring, the temerity of her actions . . . to creep around in her own Spiral_Q at night . . . naughty naughty . . .

She walked the corridors while the majority of the complex slept, and after passing several guards who merely nodded sedately at her presence, she moved stealthily to the unguarded laundry shaft leading to the true ground-level kitchens and boiler rooms. Here there was noise and she had to stay alert. She ran a hand through her curls, stepped lightly over bags of linen and clothing lined up for the washers and driers; but, as usual, she was alone in this vault, alone in this world of her own choosing . . .

She reached the exit at the rear of the ground-level complex. She produced a key and overrode the electronic protection – after all, if one was a computer expert one might as well use that expertise to one's own advantage.

Jessica stepped *outside*—

The cool of the desert night washed over her and she took a few steps, revelling in the feel of the fresh air, the real world, the *danger* of being merely pyjama-clad out in the Rub al'Khali desert surrounded by heavily armed guards . . . guards who sat at their posts with mounted machine guns and other heavy metal to take out aircraft and tanks. Part of her wondered if they could see her, and merely endured her quirkiness, her eccentricity. Another part of her revelled in the feelings of *rebellion*.

Of course, she couldn't go far or else the perimeter guards would certainly and undoubtedly spot her and Feuchter or Johansen or Skelter would moan and whine at her: they were only allowed out from the complex with the strictest supervision. But she could at least *sample*, at least *taste* the freedom of a life in a world completely alone—

She gazed at the stars for a long while, their wan light glinting across her slim figure, and her hand dropped to her flat belly. Jessica didn't work out often, but when she did she gave 200% – and this had provided her with a well-formed athletic figure that was the talk of the programming department.

She patted her belly again.

'Still firm and strong,' she sighed.

She stepped back inside, heaving the thick vaultlike door closed and rerouting the detection systems. Digits flickered across the micro-monitor and Jessica stooped, found the small hidden brush, and carefully flicked sand grains into the corner where they would not be noticed.

If only they knew, she thought.

If only they could catch her!

She shivered; half in delight, half in fear.

Yes; she had been the best programmer and systems analyst – probably in the whole of the UK. But there had been something else; a splinter deep in her soul that led her to *hack* . . .

Her skills had been developed, honed, refined by taking on the largest computing conglomerates and corporations. She cracked their databases for a laugh. She was turned on by smashing their personnel files. She got a heroin high from fucking their finances.

Jessica knew not what drove her; there was something wrong with her soul, but she hated – *loathed* – that part of the world which said, You will know this, you will have access to *this*, but the rest of you . . . well, you can all fuck off.

Data protection? Ha.

Jessica wanted to give the world everything.

Freedom of information.

Freedom of choice as opposed to electronic prisons, math cells, digital locks and keys.

And the QIII Proto?

Jessica smiled mischievously to herself.

Well, the QIII would become her greatest achievement. Spiral could use it to override military systems; hack world data banks; match terrorist identities from satellite scans; redeploy troops on the battlefield from RI hack based on WorldCode probabilities . . .

And WorldCode, again, one of Jessica's finest moments.

The perfect honing of Artificial Intelligence.

Real Intelligence, the ability for a computer to *think*, to possess *emotions and control the fight for civilisation!* It would be the ultimate weapon against evil, and Spiral would be at the forefront of this awesome new technology, Spiral could conquer the growing terror of gun-runners and bomb-makers, assassins, hijackers, drug smugglers . . .

Jessica shivered. She understood that the stakes were high; she had not really understood, never really *considered* before the destruction of the London HQ. But the deaths of so many colleagues had left her chilled to the dark corners of her soul.

Jessica knew; this was no longer a game.

And probably it never had been.

Jessica returned to the lift, and then, on a whim, decided to call on the lab_central, see what the ghostly machines were running at this midnight hour, this graveyard shift. All ops were normally automated during the night and so she had little fear of meeting anybody at this lonely time.

After descending to the lab depths, she padded along the corridor to her own specialised departments. She stopped. She accessed the first of three reinforced glass doors. As the first door closed behind her, leaving her in a cubicle of glass awaiting access to the second door – she saw it.

A figure . . .

Jessica Rade froze.

The figure was motionless, standing near the QIII deck.

Jessica stared for long, long moments. No movement came from the figure and Jessica tried to meet its dark gaze, sure that she had been seen and yet aware that the figure gave no indication of having spotted her.

Was it a guard? A *real* guard, not some doped-up corridor sentry with nothing to do except clench his toes to stave off cramp and share the odd cigarette with other examples of patrolling boredom?

Or was it a sentinel?

A protector?

Jessica sank slowly to the carpet and sat, wondering what to do. She crawled over to the door that had admitted her, and swiped her pass. The door slid open silently and she crawled for it, down the corridor, across the carpets and tiles, then got to her feet and, with a smile at her incredible luck, ran for it—

A few minutes later, she was sitting on the edge of her bed, a glass of brandy in her shaking fingers, sipping it slowly and wondering what the dark figure had been up to; why had it been there?

Her heart was still hammering as she contemplated the figure she had witnessed; clad in grey, wearing some sort of lower face mask and with dull copper eyes. The hair was non-existent – shaved to the skull. The figure had seemed relaxed and yet—

Threatening.

Very, very threatening.

Jessica shivered, and sipped again at her brandy.

Who was the guard?

Must have been some new kind of security drafted in to watch over the QIII in this late stage of development. But weren't all the other security measures good enough? Weren't the electrified fences, the armed guards, the huge concrete walls and steel doors and electronic passes – weren't these enough to protect this revolutionary new processor?

But of course.

Jessica laughed softly, bitterly, to herself, and stared out over the desert through the monitor. Spiral_H had been hit. Detonated. Wiped from the face of the Earth.

Pondering her strange and very near encounter, Jessica took another drink of the brandy, enjoying the hot fire in her throat. A word crept into the corners of her mind; a word she had once overheard, when barging in during a fit of temper, into Count Feuchter's office and an ops meeting between Feuchter, Durell and Adams . . .

'The Nex . . .'

They had stared at her. She had apologised and retreated.

But now; now the word seemed to come unbidden from Jessica's forgotten vaults of memory. It seemed to fit.

171

Nex. A Nex. The Nex? Was Nex the name of a person? A guard? A *killer*?

She shivered, realising that she had drunk a little too much, and then downed the rest of the brandy in one.

She decided she would ask Adams in the morning.

Yes; a good idea; he would explain the Nex.

Maybe.

CHAPTER 10

FLIGHT

Carter hit the snow with Kade screaming in his brain. Kade's words were so anger-filled as to be unfathomable; Kade's hatred was a tangible thing and as his energy fled him so a cold detachment took his soul in its fist and gave him a nasty squeeze . . .

'Fight,' howled Kade in his brain.

'Fuck you, Carter, don't let me die like this! Fight!'

But Carter could not; for the briefest of seconds, he could not; it was as if all the worst moments of his life had been distilled, a potent liquor of horror with the power to drop him instantly. Without knowing it, he changed mags by sense of touch in his pocket as the footsteps came close and his brain seized and the footsteps suddenly increased in pace and—

'Roll!' screamed Kade.

Carter rolled, the Browning out and in his hand and pumping bullets up into the night sky—

A kick sent the weapon spinning into the darkness.

'Let me,' came the soothing voice of Kade.

'Fuck you,' snarled Carter.

173

An engine started – the BMW. The Nex's head snapped left – a sudden-impact movement, so fast that Carter's eyes could not follow. He leaped, clumsily, arms encircling the attacker, and they both hit the ground. Carter slammed both arms down, the heels of his hands smashing into the Nex's head. One blow, two, three, four, five. He felt something break within the mask—

The BMW, pluming smoke, accelerated away from the scene.

Carter staggered up.

The assassin's foot lashed up into Carter's groin and he stumbled back; the scene flashed red, there was a screech of brakes, tyres crunching snow, brakelights illuminating the snow in a soft red glow. Exhaust fumes jettisoned like dragon smoke.

Carter looked up into the Nex's face—

Grey-clad. Unreadable—

But the eyes. The eyes were copper, glowing in the BMW's red lights.

The figure lifted its arms above its head, as if in some martial-art preparatory stance. Carter scrambled up and the figure's stare fixed on him, eyes boring through him, and he grinned, bloodstained teeth bared through thick strings of saliva. 'You fucking surprised, motherfucker?' he snarled.

'We have danced for long enough,' came the soft voice.

From hidden arm-sheaths the assassin drew two short black blades and lowered his head. Carter pulled his own darkened blade from his boot and spat blood into the snow.

'But I like the dance,' said Carter. 'It's just getting interesting. And you want to fight with knives . . . I will cut you so fine, my boy . . .'

174

The BMW revved, plumes spitting. Carter could see Natasha looking back over the seat; the white reverse lights came on and Carter understood . . .

The Nex charged—

They clashed, blades flashing—

Carter came away with blood weeping down his bicep. He felt the pulse of freed muscle within sliced skin and the smile fell from his lips. They circled and Carter edged the Nex closer—

Carter charged – as Natasha floored the BMW's accelerator and the engine screamed high and loud. The assassin slashed left and right, then turned – Carter dived left.

The high boot of the BMW hammered into the assassin; the body was plucked from the air and tossed away in a tangle of limbs to collide with the wall of the house. The knives fell dark and bloody to the snow. The Nex collapsed in a tightly curled broken heap.

Carter – breathing hard – looked slowly to the left at the tyre merely two inches from his nose. He dragged himself to his feet and glared at Natasha through the smashed window.

'You trying to kill me?'

'Get in,' she hissed, pain lancing lines across her face.

'I want my gun. And I want to check our friend there—'

'Get *in*!' screamed Natasha.

Carter turned, and his jaw dropped. The Nex had rolled to his – or her – feet. Those copper eyes met Carter's gaze and he caught a glimpse of black; the Nex sprinted forward, a blur of motion powering across the snow . . . Carter dived, scooping up the battered Browning, then dragged open the door and sprawled full length across the back seat of the BMW as Natasha hit the

175

accelerator. Spitting snow, the car screamed down the track, sliding left and right, bouncing from a fence and then shooting off down the darkened lane with lights suddenly extinguished—

Carter stared out of the back window.

The Nex was close, copper eyes burning into his own. A gloved hand reached out, brushed the boot and Carter swallowed, hard, as the BMW's engine screamed and Natasha's foot floored the accelerator pedal with a harsh stab . . .

The Nex slowed, then halted and stood, arms limp by its sides, copper eyes watching them flee. The would-be assassin was not panting, nor showing any signs of exertion.

'I don't fucking believe that,' said Carter.

'Are you hurt?'

'I'm hurting all right,' he said. 'How about you?'

'I'm bleeding. I think I might . . .'

The car swerved. Carter clambered into the front seat, and helped Natasha guide the car to the side of the road. They swapped positions, and Natasha held a sterile dressing pad to her reopened shoulder wound as Carter, hands slippery with his own blood, gunned the 4-litre vehicle's engine and they sped off into the darkness.

Carter drove at high speed, and after thirty minutes left the snowbound highways behind, tyres gripping tarmac once more, the BMW purring in its natural environment. He found a small side road, and drove into the darkness. Finding a secluded copse beyond a fence and a heavy galvanised gate, he jumped out, leaving the engine running. He unlatched the cold metal, then stared around at the silent dark woods, eerie and watching. The silence made him shiver, and the darkness was so complete that it formed an infinite horizontal void; Carter hurried back to the light and warmth of his mobile sanctuary. He eased the BMW over woodland debris and killed the engine, then the headlights.

'Let's take a look at you.'

Carter helped Natasha onto the back seat and checked the reopened gunshot wound. It had clotted, the bleeding nothing more than a trickle now. Natasha's face was grey with pain.

'I'm sorry, I have no painkillers,' said Carter, brushing a strand of hair from the woman's brow.

'That's OK,' she said, smiling. She coughed, and winced. Carter ran his hand through her hair, then eased his own jacket free with difficulty, his broken finger stabbing anger at his every movement, his ribs grinding and biting him inside, clicking within the cavity of his chest. He checked the knife wound across his bicep; this too had clotted and had almost ceased bleeding. He eased the flesh open – could see a muscle part within. Blood started to seep once more and, ripping a strip from his thick woollen shirt, he tied a makeshift bandage around the wound. Blood soaked it immediately.

'That needs attention,' said Natasha.

'I don't dare risk the hospitals. *They* could be watching.'

'You think so?'

'I know so. Come on, we'll stop at a motorway service station; pick up some provisions. How much cash have you got on you?'

'None. What about plastic?'

'No good. It leaves a trail. I've only got a couple of hundred – it will have to be enough.'

'Why don't we leave a false trail?' said Natasha. 'Draw a shitload of cash out of a machine – let them tag us, tag our location – and then switch directions?'

177

Carter considered this, scratching at his stubble. They would need money, wherever they were going. He nodded, smiling, and, bending down, kissed Natasha on the cheek.

'Thanks for saving my life,' he said. 'Now we're even.'

Natasha's arm came up and pulled his head down to her. They kissed again, tongues dancing, and for a couple of seconds the world spiralled down into nothing more than this intimate moment.

Carter pulled away, his gaze locked to hers.

'Come on. We have to get moving.'

'Can't we rest here? For the night?'

'No. We have to put some serious distance between that meat fucker and us. You understand?'

'Yeah. Can I sleep?'

'With my blessing,' said Carter, smiling. He kissed her again, passed her his coat and then climbed into the front seat. He started the huge engine and turned the heater up. He checked the fuel gauge, then reversed slowly from the copse, tyres crunching twigs, and out onto the lane.

'Where are we going?' said Natasha sleepily, snuggling under coats against the raping wind, which violated the cabin through the recently smashed windows.

'I'll tell you when we get there.'

'Do we have to fly?'

'Yes.'

'I thought you hated flying?'

'I do.'

'Oh.' Natasha snuggled against the rolled-up jacket and closed her eyes. Carter angled the rear-view mirror and watched her sleep as he drove through the darkness; the cool air from the smashed windows made him shiver occasionally as mile after mile of catseyes and the occasional midnight traveller sped by in a blur.

The horn beeped.

Carter blinked. Looked up, over the BMW's steering wheel. Heavy rain pounded the bonnet and roof, spitting through the smashed side windows. The windscreen was awash. Thunder boomed in the dark night sky; he readjusted his mirror and saw the headlights glowing behind him like yellow eyes. The horn blared again.

'OK, OK,' hissed Carter. He flicked on the wipers, eased up on the clutch and took the BMW around the roundabout and off towards the south – towards the Lake District and Lancaster beyond. Glasgow was now a ghost in the night behind him . . .

He drove on bitterly through the rain.

It was an hour after dawn when Carter pulled the BMW into the lay-by. An hour earlier had seen him buying supplies in a service station – everything from crisps and Coke through to travel medical kits containing needles, sterile dressings and emergency airways, T-shirts that weren't stained in blood and some mysterious items which he kept locked away in plastic bags. Now, both bandaged, scrubbed in the service-station toilets, and clad in garish coloured T-shirts, they looked at one another and Natasha ran a hand through her hair. She'd just taken some Ibuprofen – the maximum dose – but was obviously still in quite some pain . . .

'What now?'

'We steal a plane.'

'Steal a . . . you *are* joking?'

'Not at all,' said Carter grimly. 'We can't risk requesting air transport from Spiral, and over the wire, on the other

179

side of these trees, is an MoD airbase. A *special* airbase where they keep some of Spiral's aircraft and other vehicles.'

'Carter,' said Natasha slowly, 'there will be armed guards. Dogs. We've only got one gun between us.'

'One gun is enough. I find in these situations that one gun tends to breed more guns.'

'And you think you can fly a . . . well, whatever it is you want to steal?'

'Of course. It's been a few years, I haven't flown since Egypt. But they're all the fucking same. Joystick. Rudder. Flaps. Landing gear. Hey, come on, liven up – it's not as if we've been betrayed by everything we have come to know and trust and believe in. Why the grim smile?'

'You're mad,' said Natasha slowly. 'And tell me you don't still plan to visit Gol.'

'Yeah, I'm sorry, Nats – but I do. Gol can help us.'

'He will shoot us. Well, you,' she corrected.

'Don't overestimate him. The big oaf had a heart of gold . . .'

'Yes,' said Natasha slowly. 'But remember? Remember when you fucking *shot him* . . . you can't possibly have forgotten?'

Carter shrugged. 'It was for the best – he'll understand,' came the simple reply. 'He's still alive, isn't he?'

Natasha tutted. 'Man, have you got a death wish?' She sighed, and rubbed at her tired pain-filled eyes. 'Where will we find the Big Man? Do you know if he's still playing games on the African continent?'

'I cannot divulge this information,' said Carter with a lop-sided grin.

'You *are* mad,' Natasha repeated with feeling.

'Of course. That's why I work for Spiral.' He coughed. 'Used to work, I mean. You think they'll accept my formal resignation?'

'You don't know that, Carter. You don't know who sent the Nex.'

'You said they were Spiral's best-kept secret? Well, put two and two together.'

'Yeah, they sometimes make seven. If you've still got your ECube we can try and contact—'

'Oh no.' Carter's words were soft. 'No contact. We do it my way; if it *is* Spiral, and the fuckers *are* tracking us, then the ECube will light us up worse than any flare on a winter night.'

'But if they aren't the ones – well, they could help,' said Natasha simply.

'I don't need any fucking help,' said Carter, his humour gone. 'I do it on my own. I always have.'

Natasha shook her head slowly, and ran a hand through her short black hair. 'When are we – ah, I mean *you* – going to accelerate into this mad scheme of theft from the British government?'

'Theft. Ha.' He smiled wryly. 'Am I hearing you right, Nats? I am no thief . . . I am part of the huge machine that is Spiral, and Spiral not only have part-ownership in the MoD but own this very airfield and the equipment therein. Because I belong to Spiral, and they to me, I am merely *taking* what is already rightfully *mine*. You get it?'

'I don't think the armed guards will see it that way.'

'Well, I haven't got the time to sign in fucking triplicate.' Carter pulled the battered Browning from his pocket. He stared lovingly at the dull black surface. 'I am sure I will be able to persuade them with Sergeant 9mm here.' He smiled without humour.

Night fell. With it came more rain.

Carter slammed the BMW's door shut. The hunters would find the vehicle soon enough, he was sure – but then, hopefully, the couple would be far away from this place. Far away from the promise of bullets and pain.

Carter supported Natasha as they crept through the damp woodland. Before long they came to a heavy-duty fence topped by the customary barbed wire. 'This is where we climb,' said Carter softly. 'But don't worry – this is a pretty unimportant base and subsequently the 'high' security is shit. Unless the fucker has been compromised.'

Natasha stared hard at him. 'Compromised?'

Carter nodded. 'Somebody seems to be trying hard to bring Spiral down. There are links. Spiral keeps aircraft here at this base. It's a long shot, but hey, so was that fucking Nex almost killing me back at my home . . .' He shrugged, moved forward, and scaled the rattling fence. Using pocket cutters he snipped through the coils of barbed wire. Then he reached down, hauling a grimacing, groaning Natasha up behind him and they climbed warily over and dropped to the grass, panting, sweat stinging their eyes.

The base squatted mostly in darkness. A few dark buildings, with weak lonely yellow lights, sat over to one side of the compound. Several airstrips criss-crossed the gloom, and beside several more outbuildings sat a collection of damp and darkly glistening aircraft.

'Can you see the markings?' said Carter.

Natasha shook her head.

'My eyesight is getting bad with old age, I fear,' he said. 'Come on.'

They made their way slowly across the grass, and Carter halted. He pointed, to where a low shed obviously housed chained dogs. Making a huge detour, they circled the base and finally scurried through the rain to crouch under the limited shelter of a galvanised roof overhang. Water poured around them from inefficient guttering, splattering and clashing. Carter pointed through the gloom. 'You see her?'

'What is it?'

'A Cessna T206H Turbo5. Fully fuelled and with good range. Fast. We can sling her under radar, keep her low over the hills; she's got excellent navigational equipment but isn't military, and so won't arouse too much suspicion.'

'Are we going far?'

'Far enough,' said Carter. 'You wait here, I'll check her out.' He moved away from Natasha, and was soon a ghost in the rain. His senses sang, and he felt incredibly awake: energy washed through him and no longer did the pain from his strapped finger, his broken ribs, his broken nose, his sliced bicep – no longer did it push him into the borders of angry red teeth-grinding acceptance. Now it flowed away and left him feeling . . . alive.

He halted beside the Cessna, alert, focused, the Browning in his hand and glistening dark in the rain. Just behind the wing he reached up, found the handle and twisted. The door hissed outwards, exposing the dark interior.

Carter reached up and pulled down the steps, which clacked against the tarmac. Then he sprinted as best he could with broken ribs and gestured for Natasha to follow him, aware that his back presented a broad target to the darkness . . . and to any hiding snipers . . .

Natasha crept forward through the rain, hair plastered to her scalp, and soon they were both climbing the steps and into the dry interior of the cramped single-engine plane.

'Where we going, Carter?'

'Africa.'

'Africa! You are joking . . . so I was right . . .'

Carter looked her in the eye. 'Joking? Well, you want to hang around here? Try and reason with that Nex fucker?'

Natasha shook her head and, wiping water from her face, followed Carter to the cockpit.

'Then we'll do it my way. Belt yourself in over there.'

'You sure you know how to fly one of these?'

'As easy as slotting a Nex.' He smiled bitterly.

The silver Mercedes flashed through the night, tyres hissing, squealing across wet tarmac, groaning under pressure as the vehicle hit speeds of over a hundred and fifty m.p.h. The rain smashed down from the tumultuous heavens, and the Mercedes finally pulled to a halt beside a BMW: battered and bruised, victim of a recent hard-core automobile fucking.

Boots splashed down in a puddle. The door slammed shut.

The tight grey garment turned black swiftly under the dark rain. Copper eyes stared through the downpour, through the fence and across the apparently deserted airfield. A Cessna taxied along the airstrip and, engine growling, shot up into the sky and disappeared, tail light blinking like the tiny red eye of a retreating monster. Almost immediately, alarms squealed shrilly through the rain, a tortured sound, like an animal in pain. Red lights danced across black tarmac, flashing, spiralling.

The copper eyes stared into the darkness, glinting with reflected flashing red lights for a long while after the Cessna had droned out of view. They stared, unblinking, unmoving. Then as dogs barked and the harsh sounds of military voices spread out through the rain, the figure moved, fluidly, swiftly, climbed back into the Merc and picked up the comm.

'He's gone,' came the soft, asexual voice.

'Do we know where?'

'Of course. We know everything.'

'Drive down to 180.770.775.'

'180.770.775. Is he keeping below radar?'

'Confirmed. Out.'

The engine started, tyres hissed, the silver Mercedes disappeared into the darkness with only the barking of dogs following the plumes of exhaust that dispersed into the dark and the rain – and nothing remained to provide evidence of the car's recent passing.

Spiral_Memo4

Transcript of recent news incident

CodeRed_Z;

unorthodox incident scan 554781

Extract from local newspaper, Nanchang, China:

'Several major cities in China were today left in chaos when every automated cash point affiliated to major banks in Shanghai, the newly rebuilt Qingdao, Zhengzhou, Nanchang and Kunming disgorged their entire monetary contents onto the pavements at surprised pedestrians' feet. Panic ensued, and soon scuffles and mild rioting took place as the machines continued to pump out notes like bullets from a machine gun. Riot police were deployed to disperse the crowds, and a spokesperson for the Chinese National Bank, Chow Lien stated, "This was not just the work of a simple bug in software. We are investigating claims of a malicious employee with in-depth computing experience. Our automated machines are well protected with both software and other more traditional methods; to see something like this happen was a travesty. We have top people working on the problem even as we speak."'

No official explanation has been given by the Chinese Government or by the Office for Economics & Industry.

CHAPTER 11

GOL

Jam stood at the top of the hill, his mouth a grim line. Behind stood Nicky, and Slater, both shocked into silence. Before them the road dropped towards – a bomb site. The *crater* where Spiral_H had burrowed under the ground before its savage chemical fucking.

'I don't believe it,' said Jam softly. He reached into his pocket, pulled free a cigarette and lit up. Smoke plumed around his face, swirling in the cold air. He took a deep and heavy draw.

'Those cunts,' said Slater, his face an animal snarl, saliva glistening on his teeth.

'Yeah,' drawled Jam. 'But which cunts, exactly?'

They moved slowly down the hill, boots thumping, crunching on glass; the bustle of activity following the immediate blast had subsided; no longer did rescue vehicles line the destruction zone, hundreds of people picking through the rubble, machines lifting blasted concrete slabs and massive H sections of steel. Most of the debris had already been cleared from around the hole; all of the bodies had been recovered.

'We could have been in that,' said Nicky, her face pale, her stomach churning. 'That was *our* HQ. We could have been inside; we could have died with all the others.'

Jam merely nodded. All strength had flooded from him. All fight had gone.

Tapes had been set up surrounding the crime scene. The group stopped at this false barrier and were eyed suspiciously by several police officers who moved towards them backed up by the heavy military presence of about fifty Justice Troop squads with heavy machine guns.

'Can we help you?'

'No . . . no. Did many people escape?' asked Nicky softly.

'Not a single one,' said the PC gently. His smile was filled with kindness; his eyes glittered with horror stories and pain. He obviously had his own nightmares to contend with.

As the policemen moved away, Jam, Slater and Nicky just stood, dumbstruck, bitterness filling them with vinegar acid; their gaze roved over the mound of remaining rubble, the blackened scarred pavement with its twisted buckled flagstones and melted tarmac. By the edges of the crater stood the relics of life and work: a charred settee here, half a desk there. A battered and flame-eaten filing cabinet. The burned remains of a rubber plant. Business detritus now witness to the most terrible of man-made catastrophes: the bomb.

'We need to catch these fuckers,' said Slater softly.

'Yes,' breathed Nicky.

'We need to make them pay.'

'But that's the problem,' snapped Jam, turning, his stare angry. 'How many people died here? Three, four hundred? Fucking pay for that? You can't; even if you catch the people responsible, the leaders, or the monkeys planting the devices – you can't make them pay for such a loss of life.'

'Ironic, ain't it?' said Nicky bitterly.

'What is?'

'Spiral – experts in demolition and destruction; their own HQ wiped out in true Spiral style. Could have been done by our own people.'

'We don't take life with bombs,' said Jam sourly. 'Ours have always been surgical strikes against terrorist and military targets.'

'Boys and their toys,' sneered Nicky. There were tears on her cheeks. 'Things always go wrong; people always die. It's just the way of the fucking world. But this . . . this . . .' she gestured.

'This,' said Jam, 'this was done to destroy office and investigative personnel. It was to wipe out the fucking mainframes, that's why Spiral_H was targeted.'

'I have an idea,' said Slater.

'Oh yeah?'

'We need to see The Priest. He will have the answers, and he is the only man I would trust right now.'

This statement was met with a moment of stunned silence.

'He's fucking insane,' said Jam, staring into Slater's weary horror-shadowed eyes. The huge man shrugged, turning back to look at the remains of the devastation.

'He is head of the *secret police*. So fucked-up as to be incorruptible.'

'That's if he's still alive,' said Nicky.

'He'll be alive,' said Slater. 'It'd take more than a few assassins to murder The Priest. After all,' he smiled sombrely, 'God is on his side.'

They turned away from the rubble, the stones and

glass glinting in weak sunlight. They walked, rubble crunching underfoot, back up the hill, away from shattered dreams, detonated lives, smashed worlds. The van was waiting; they drove away in silence.

The moor road was cold, winding, and awesomely dark. The van hissed its way through the rain, headlights carving slices of yellow from the absolute black. Jam, Slater and Nicky all huddled together on the vehicle's wide front bench more out of dismay at this hostile environment than from any real need to share heat.

'You sure it's up here?' said Nicky miserably.

'Aye,' said Jam. 'I've been once before. Ain't that right, Slater?' Slater grunted in his sleep and Jam punched him; Slater's snoring altered pitch but he did not wake up. 'You fucking heap of lard.'

Jam guided the van with care; past hordes of huddled sheep, through vast puddles where water had gathered at inadequate drainage channels, and still the rain pounded down and Jam began to wonder if agreeing to this meeting had been the best decision he had ever made.

The van screeched to a halt.

Rain danced in the beams of the headlights.

Nicky stared at the map. 'Should be just up here. On the left.'

'I'm remembering it well,' said Jam sombrely.

He crunched the van into first, and they moved forward; Nicky was right, they found the rutted mud-trail and Jam turned the van onto this slippery ascent. There was a grinding sound as wheels spun, then a modicum of grip was established by tyre rubber and the van lurched forward.

They bounced and wheelspun up the narrow trail, the

van rocking. To either side were steep banks of earth and heather; it made the trio – or the two parts of the trio who were at least awake – feel incredibly confined.

'I can't understand how he can fucking sleep,' said Jam bitterly.

'It must be a talent,' agreed Nicky.

'I mean, you wave a gun near his nose and he's awake faster than a male virgin's first ejaculation. But put him in a non-threatening situation, a mountain could fall on the lumbering bastard and he'd happily snore through the incident.'

'You've got to admit, you're fond of him though.' Nicky grinned, stroking the sleeping man's cheek. 'He's big and dumb, but he has a heart of gold and would die for you.'

'I'm fond of him like I was fond of a particularly bad case of VD. Like Slater, the VD itched a lot – a constant annoyance, and so I was permanently fucking reminded it was there. Like Slater, the VD induced fond memories of distant pleasure – but in the grim reality of grey dawn-light I found the real world a much more grim and painful place. And finally, just like the VD, Slater is a constant pain in the cock.'

'You have such a way with words, Jam. You make me so horny.'

Jam grinned. 'I know, love, I know. Keep calm.'

The steeply ascending lane ended on a ridge and as they bumped over twin ruts a huge quarry opened up ahead of them, gleaming ghostlike in the moonlight that broke through the scattered black clouds. The headlights carved sections from this disused place, this abandoned surface mine: rearing jagged slopes and pyramid piles of debris and rock were everywhere. Jam paused for a moment, gaining his bearings, then they moved away down a wide stone-floored corridor between two dynamite-blasted walls. They passed huge stacks of rock, some neatly square, some shaped randomly from the blasts that had freed them from their thrall. They passed tracks that had been adapted by motor-cross riders in search of excitement, and they came upon a huge, stagnant black pool that filled a rock basin, a lagoon of ancient oil and mud, a dumping ground from the days when the quarry had been operational.

'Here we are.' Jam stopped the van at the side of the murky black lagoon. It gave off a dead stink and, glancing out, Nicky could see a couple of sheep corpses bogged down in the mire. She shivered; what a fucking way to die, she thought.

The rain had lessened and Jam stepped from the van, a pistol in his gloved hand. He stared around, then saw lights and a car creeping towards him. In the van, Slater had slotted a magazine into an SMG and she held the muzzle low, unseen; heavy-artillery back-up.

The car halted, its tyres crunching. It was a huge and battered old Volvo.

'We cool?' shouted Jam.

The Priest climbed ponderously from the vehicle.

'Oh yes, my son,' he said. He looked left and right, and, carrying a Bible in his left hand, walked slowly towards Jam, boots stomping on the hard quarry ground.

'I hate this place,' said Jam miserably. The rain was soaking him; his hair was lank, rat-tails, his face a sheen of water.

'God's weather is to be tolerated, for He is the judge of what needs to grow, what needs to be sown, and what needs to be reaped. He is the Gardener, Jam. He is the Gardener. *Then will I sprinkle clean water upon you, and ye shall be clean: from all your filthiness, and from all your idols,*

192

will I cleanse you; a new heart also will I give you, and a new spirit will I put within you.' The Priest beamed, brown eyes shining.

Jam frowned.

'Yeah. Right, mate. Listen, I assume you got the ECube transcript?'

'I did. The infidels have been busy. They seek to overthrow us.'

'I thought – *think* – that I can trust you, because I know you are one of the main Tactical Officers – one of the main men, the Spiral secret police. Internal affairs, yeah?'

'By your trust, I assume you mean the HK trained on me from the van, by that huge ham-fisted oaf Slater?'

Jam shrugged, grinning. 'Hey, you know how it is.'

'Indeed I do,' said The Priest calmly. 'What is it you seek to do?'

'Things have gone from bad to worse; we've just come from London.'

'The HQ?'

'Yes,' said Jam sombrely.

'We must pray for their souls,' said The Priest, great sadness in his melancholy voice, his huge eyes filled with tears. 'And yet, before prayer, I cannot help but feel that this crime must not go unpunished.'

'We need your help,' said Jam softly. 'You have higher clearances than we have; and, let's be honest, you probably know more about what is going on than we do . . .'

The Priest's eyes glittered. 'Shall we say, there have been . . . *complications*. What is it you have in mind?'

'Find out who the fuck is responsible – gather together all the remaining DemolSquads and fuck the bad guys severely from behind. Shit on them from a very great height.'

'First you need the Source; then you need the Target.'

'That's why I'm here,' said Jam. 'There's nobody else we can trust – and believe me, it was hard deciding even to contact *you*.'

The Priest stood, rain dripping from his huge dark bulk. He thought, long and hard, brow furrowed; finally, as if coming awake from a trance, he smiled down at Jam, then reached out and patted him gently on the shoulder. 'I have had guidance.'

'You have?' Jam looked up, nervously, at the heavens.

The Priest nodded. He placed his hands together, as if in prayer. His huge shaggy brows bunched together as his forehead wrinkled in concentration. 'The Lord will lead us, Jam; the Lord will protect us; and the Lord will guide us.'

'You sure?'

'Yes. The Lord has already placed important information in my possession from a variety of sources; already I am acting upon this information. But I need to make a journey, and I will need help – I was going to call for some back-up but . . . you are here now, my friend. Sent, I think, by the Almighty.'

'What kind of journey?' Jam's voice was suspicious.

'As Tactical Officers, we keep tabs on a variety of people and places around the world; monitor them, shall we say. There has been recent increased activity at a variety of locations and I sent TacSquads to investigate – just before the explosion at the London HQ. I was on my way for one such reconnoitre when I received your garbled transmission.'

'So now we can go with you?'

'Your help would be much appreciated, Brother. This increased activity links conveniently with the troubles in London, and in Spiral as a whole. I have high hopes of there being a very strong connection.'

194

Jam nodded.

The Priest chuckled. 'We will have to meet at Sambray Airfield – first I have a few jobs to take care of.'

'OK. Just name the time.'

'Twelve hours.'

'We'll be there,' said Jam softly.

The engine droned like a bee gathering honey. Natasha woke up, yawned, and watched the sun dancing across the tops of the cotton-wool clouds. She rubbed at her eyes, and enjoyed the view for a few moments; far far below, the sandy landscape, marked with the odd ravine or range of hills and dotted with scattered bushes and trees, reminded her of better days – happier days before the world became such a war-torn fucked-up place . . .

She shifted. Winced as stitches pulled tight.

She glanced across at Carter. 'You OK?'

'Sure am, flower.'

'Where are we?'

'Greece. You see the island down there?'

'Hmm?'

'Zante. I had a good holiday there, once. Our apartment became infested by ants and we had to lead a trail of sugar to our noisy Glaswegian neighbours – ha, soon shut them up – but overall it was a good gig. How are you feeling?'

'Sore.'

'You hungry?'

'Yeah. Can I check your bags now?'

'Sure. The green one is full of food and I apologise in advance for the poor calorific content. I swear, somebody should sue those fucking service stations.'

Natasha rummaged. Found food – or a close approximation thereof. She ate, and fed small tit-bits to Carter who guzzled greedily with hands clamped on the Cessna's controls.

'Why don't you have a break? Eat? Drink?'

'Are you going to fly?'

'Hmmm . . .'

'Well, perhaps not, then. We'll be landing at Cairo to refuel—'

'I thought you were a wanted man in Egypt? Wanted by men with machine guns who want you very, very dead?'

'I am. When I say Cairo, I don't exactly mean Cairo – I kind of mean a secret rendezvous seventy miles out of the city.'

'So there'll be no time for sunbathing or seeing the pyramids at Giza?'

'Not this time, love. I'm sorry. Anyway, the bombing during the Battle of Cairo7 put an end to *that* Wonder of the World. The pyramids are just rubble now.'

'I'd still like to see what's left. It's *historical* rubble, after all.'

They were over the sea now, and the sun glittered across waves and tiny crests of foam. Natasha watched Carter carefully; she could see his fear but he hid it well. He hated flying. She had read it on his file, and seen his nervous sweat first-hand. As he always said, it wasn't the height that bothered him, it was the heavy impact with the unforgiving ground . . .

Hours had passed.

The 'rendezvous', much to Natasha's horror, was a narrow desert strip marked in the sand between two huge rocky outcroppings. Carter brought the Cessna down in a swirl of dust and had a heated conversation with four men in Arab dress who had honking muzzled camels with many tufts tethered to a nearby twisted palm. Natasha watched the tense discussion from the Cessna's cockpit, decidedly on edge and alert for signs of trouble—

She needn't have worried. Carter, all smiles, winked in her direction and she watched the men lead him away to throw back tarpaulins concealing drums of what Natasha assumed was aviation fuel. She did not understand how Carter had made his contacts, nor how he had arranged this little meeting; she decided it was probably best not to ask.

Two hours later, when Carter climbed sweating and sand-flecked into the cockpit, Natasha had been sleeping again. She smiled wearily at the man. 'We full up?'

'It will see us to Mombassa at least. I curse having to deal with dodgy Egyptians. And I curse even more the fact that a Cessna will only fly twelve hundred pissing miles without completely emptying her bladder . . . the cheap whore . . .'

They flew into the sun.

Natasha decided it was quite romantic—

Or it would have been if she hadn't recently been shot and hadn't been running for her very life. What happened? she thought. What happened to my world? It had been going so smoothly—

So smoothly.

Gol sat in the sand, gazing down at the grains that swept scattering across one another, fighting for precedence, fighting for height, fighting to be king. He lifted his head slowly, beard whipping gently in the breeze, and gazed out across the vast landscape before him – a medley of browns and burned orange. The amber light flowed majestically across the landscape like molten honey, breaking across the rocky formations, moulding itself around the trees. Huge protrusions of rock smashed up from the earth and Gol felt the violence of the land within his soul.

The rugged red rock squatted hard beneath the large man, comforting, solid, real, without any give. Gol sat on the mountain and the mountain was his, was a part of him, belonged to him – and he belonged to it; a symbiotic relationship that made Gol smile through his beard. His hand reached down, touched the jagged rock and the sand and the dirt. He sighed.

The sun was sinking, glinting a deep burned red in his dark eyes.

He rose slowly to his feet, pulling himself to his full height and stretching the heavy muscles of his back and shoulders. Moving out from his beautiful vantage point, from his Window of Wonders, he was soon walking through the dust, boots leaving imprints between the scrub bushes. The trail was narrow, winding between large groups of boulders and leading uphill towards the summit of the low mountains that hid the sparkling dance of the sun's sinking rays. Gol walked on, sweating heavily, his grey hair plastered to his heavy-set thick skull, his large and apparently cumbersome rifle slung tightly across his back.

As he pushed on, the ECube pressed against his thigh through the pocket of his beige desert DPM combats. He hated the feel of the device. It had been hacked of course, by his programmers – just because they *could*. A small act of individualism. An act of pride. The ECube had been pulled to bits and reassembled minus certain circuitry and AI core components. Gol kept the small machine close to him at all times; it reminded him of older, better days.

The ECube dug against his leg and he halted for a moment, turning, hands on hips, regaining his breath.

The African scrubland spread out before him, the most awesome of panoramic views he had ever witnessed in his years of travelling the miserable ball of rock called Earth.

Gol loved Africa; that was why he had chosen this place in which to set up and run Spiral_F.

Gol pushed on, cresting the rise and finding himself momentarily dazzled by the sun. A horseshoe of low mountain hills surrounded him, rocky and wild, trails snaking down onto the flatland and the orange-tree orchards filling the valley beyond. This vision of contrasting violent colour splashes filled his perverse mind with calm, soothed the raging beast that burned his soul, selected his neutral gear and allowed him to coast gently downhill.

It must be wrong, he realised.

The hacked ECube must be wrong—

An icicle sliver wormed into his heart.

Carter would never dare come to Africa . . . Gol laughed out loud then, his laughter echoing out over the valley. And if he *was* coming to Africa – and by the ECube codecs and encryptions, it seemed that it was a top priority to find and intercept him – if the fucker *was* coming to Africa, then the chances were that he was coming to find Gol.

'I swore I would kill you.'

Gol's voice was deep, incredibly deep and melodic – almost Shakespearean in its delivery, a rich voice, the voice of an actor, not the voice of a . . .

What are you? he thought.

What have you become?

Spiral had redeployed him. Had sent him from London to work on a special new project. Spiral_F.

He hissed between clenched teeth.

Gol began to walk, boots now stomping rock, leaping from ridge to ridge and then thudding onto a new track. This one led across the summit of the hill, winding like a red dried snake under the sun towards the string of concealed proximity detectors and anti-personnel mines—

Spiral . . .

They had a lot to answer for. A *fucking* lot to answer for . . .

He reached the lower end of the track. Gol glanced back, then set off, entering the cool protection of the trees. The sinking sun still burned hot as it sank quickly towards oblivion.

Gol relaxed the closer he got to his home: the HQ of Spiral_F – a simple white-walled house hiding a billion dollars' worth of technology under the ground in the form of extremely high-tech vaults, weapons systems, hangars for vehicle modification and . . .

Gol's eyes glinted.

And *something else*.

A breeze rustled the branches of the orange trees.

How the world has changed, he thought. How it has descended into a quagmire of guns and wars and violence.

He shivered.

How *I* have changed . . .

He caught a flash of white between the trees, and soon the crumbling dilapidated house came into view. Gol moved cautiously, attempting to catch out King George, a huge black man who stood on guard with his SMG safety catch switched off. The big man spotted him at a good distance and Gol grinned, waving as he approached.

'You OK, boss?' growled King George, his broad face split into a smile.

'Just sneaking up on you,' said Gol.

King George shook his head. 'That never happen, Big Boss. This king too smart; he have too good an eye; that why you buy my services, eh, boy?'

Gol grinned wider. How could somebody call *him* a *boy*? They shook hands, and Gol stepped past the huge sentry, past the man's natural aroma of oil and fruit and into the cool shade of the red-tiled white-walled villa beyond.

Such a nondescript mask, he thought.

A true disguise, hiding technology the world could not even begin to comprehend.

His boots clacked against the polished wooden floor – cracked and warped in places after the dry passing of years. He jogged up a few battered steps and turned right, moving down a wide corridor with its peeling paintwork and past personal artefacts that were there more for show than for any real personal value or nostalgia; Gol was the sort of man who did not harvest history. He carried love and pain in his mind and in his heart.

He stopped by a section of battered wood panelling, peeling and warped. He flipped free a small door and punched digits into an alloy panel that contrasted severely with the dilapidated surroundings. The panelling slid away and Gol descended – down through the rough-hewn narrow rock, circling down and down the tightly curved iron stairwell towards a low-roofed dusty passageway and on towards—

The Vault.

Welcome back to Heaven, Gol thought.

It was evening when Carter flew the Cessna across the shimmering ocean east of Kenya. Sunlight glittered, accelerating over the horizon. Natasha was sitting with her head on Carter's shoulder when a tiny rumble vibrated through the plane's cockpit.

Natasha stirred. She turned, her gaze meeting Carter's. 'What was that?'

The rumble came again, followed by a stutter from the engines as Carter leaned forward, eyes scanning the digital read-outs.

'Tell me we don't have a problem.'

'We have a problem,' said Carter through gritted teeth. 'Fuel pumps. Shit.'

The engine stuttered once more, and Natasha's grip tightened on Carter as fear flashed bright in her eyes. Breathing deeply, he turned the Cessna south. 'We'll have to land.'

Carter knew Africa – especially Kenya – extremely well; he had carried out a variety of overt and covert missions across its rugged dusty ravaged landscape. He hugged the coast ten miles south of Mombassa, and chose a spot where he had previous agreements with a certain landowner of disreputable disposition.

Carter brought the Cessna in low over the sea. Turquoise waves sparkled. White foam danced in huge curving crests. They cleared a long line of beach-hugging palms and a wide sweep of unspoilt white sand. The Cessna approached a wide long lawn within an arena of high walls and touched down smoothly, then bumped along the short grass towards high fences and a dazzling white-walled house. Natasha gazed up at the structure as they rolled to a halt, bushes and trees whipping to either side, the drone of the engines an irritant chirping in this sudden paradise. The house was large, built from wood and stone, the lofty roof supported by huge beams lashed together with thick ropes skilfully woven from huge leaves and dried grass.

Several men ran towards the plane. They carried guns.

'A welcoming party?' asked Natasha.

Carter smiled. 'They know me here. Don't worry.' He killed the engines, which died swiftly, the propellers humming and clattering unevenly to a halt. Carter helped Natasha from the cockpit, down the short steps, and onto the grass—

Where they were hit by the heat.

'Warm,' breathed Natasha huskily. 'Just what an injured woman needs to recuperate while you fix the plane.'

'We're near the equator. What do you expect?'

'Just a shock after *sunny* Scotland,' she said and smiled sardonically.

Carter greeted the men and explained his position in a garbled mishmash of English and Swahili. He and Natasha were escorted back up to the house at gunpoint by an obviously suspicious group.

As they reached the porch a man appeared, wearing a loose-fitting white shirt, which flapped in the strong east-coast breeze, shorts and Adidas trainers. The man had a look of hatred and insanity and unfathomable anger in his dark eyes, and a silenced sub-machine gun in his huge hands.

'Justus, I have a fucking problem.'

The huge man grinned then, a broad grin, breaking the spell of fear, and shouted, 'Papa Carter, you old dog! How the hell are you, Big Man? You a horny old goat who still has the bastard look of eagles about you? Come up here and give old Justus a hug.'

Their stay was short, sweet and very much to the point. One of the twin fuel pumps had worn free of its housing, the matrix-mesh innards clipping the metal base and smashing it up, reducing fuel-pumping capacity. A new pump was needed. Justus said he would do what he could.

With limited medical facilities Carter restitched a couple of Natasha's wounds, applied fresh sterile dressings and gave himself an injection of antibiotics. He strapped up his broken finger and they showered quickly to remove the stench of travel and battle, sweat and blood.

When ready, they waited on the porch of Justus's huge white-walled house as night fell. An engine broke the silence; a huge Toyota Land Cruiser rumbled into view, a little battered and sand-scarred, the bright headlights carving a huge slice from the night pie. The vehicle squeaked to a halt on heavy springs, and Justus leaped out. The large black man, bald and grinning widely, slapped Carter on the back, making him groan in agony.

'For you, and Mama Natasha,' he boomed.

'Mama Natasha?' Nats's hands went to her hips, her stance on the porch changing subtly from submissive to aggressive with barely a change of muscle tone.

'It is a mark of respect,' rumbled Justus, a frown creasing his huge black brow.

'That,' said Carter dryly, 'doesn't look like a Cessna fuel pump to me.'

Justus shrugged. 'I do what I can. This is all I can do; your part take maybe three days to arrive. This is Africa, Carter, not London or New York.'

Carter sighed. 'All I fucking need. A cross-country fucking trek.'

'You look after my baby, Carter. You bring her back to her Papa; she cost me many shillings, understand?'

'Don't worry,' grinned Carter bitterly. 'And anyway, you've got a Cessna out of the deal. More than a fair trade, I'd say.'

Justus shouted to another man, his words fast and smooth in the local Swahili dialect. The man disappeared into the white-walled house, then returned with two rucksacks.

'Supplies. For Mama Natasha.' The huge black man smiled. He ran a hand across his shaved head, where a sheen of sweat could be seen in the light from the Toyota's headlamps. 'Now you be careful out there, Carter. This is not a place for a weak-kneed English white man!'

Carter laughed, patting the man in return, his affection genuine. 'You take care, Justus. And remember: we were never here. And we didn't steal that Cessna on your lawn.'

'Justus always remember for the right price.'

They circled the Toyota – or what had once *been* a Toyota. The paint was peeling, and rust showed through. Parts of the coach-lines were dented and, worryingly, bullet holes rimed with rust peppered one flank. At the rear, a flat-back section had been devised – the rear seats had been ripped out and a huge upside-down U-bar welded into place. Mounted on this was a 106mm recoilless rifle with a small box of ammunition.

'This has seen the wars,' said Natasha softly.

'It's a Technical,' said Carter, helping Natasha into the cab of the customised Toyota. 'What do you expect?' He slung the rucksacks in the back, then climbed up himself and slammed the door, which shut with a dull *clunk* on the fourth attempt.

'A what?'

Carter turned the key. The vehicle rumbled into life, belching smoke from an impromptu welded exhaust. 'A Technical. When a man needs – shall we say – off-the-record protection from the local guardians, he pays for a vehicle and a few armed men. He reclaims this cost on his balance sheet as "technical assistance" – hence Technicals.' Carter wound down the window, which groaned as if in pain. 'Hey, you pack me a compass, Justus? Sometimes this low technology just gives me a hard-on.'

'On the dash, white boy. You see? By all the gods, I hope you look after yourself. This not a tourist safari now! You not have comfy beds to fly back to!'

Carter laughed again, pushed the grinding gears, then hit the accelerator. Wheels spun on loose gravel; the huge engine roared and they shot towards the gates where two men hurriedly pulled the iron barricades open. Carter accelerated down the narrow single-track dirt road, tyres bumping and thudding, and suddenly—

Suddenly the light from the house had gone—

And a terrible, complete darkness closed in.

Natasha shivered. 'Jesus, it's dark out here.'

'No ambient light,' explained Carter. 'No street lights, no house lights . . . just landscape and wild animals. Including lots of monkeys.'

Ahead stretched a perfectly straight dusty trail, lined with huge trees, swaying palms, and screeches from the darkness. The Toyota's lights cut a slice of life from the black, but all around was the promise – the inherent threat – of oblivion . . .

'Relax,' said Carter. 'Get some sleep. I think you're going to need all your energy when we meet Gol.'

The dark trees flashed past, and the two fugitives were swallowed swiftly by the African night.

It was over an hour past dawn. The sun had risen, a bright flash slicing over the horizon. The land changed from a gentle, purple-hazed hue – surrealistic, as if witnessed through frosted glass – to a bright hot furnace of sand and tangled trees. They travelled down a perfectly straight road – single-track, rough-dirt. It stretched ahead, an arrow, a slice of trail carved from the chaos of trees and jungle and scrubland that crowded the road, attempting to usurp its threadlike hold on some semblance of civilisation . . .

The tyres thudded over and into the ruts of the track.

Monkeys screeched and fought in the trees beside the trail, sometimes on the track, scattering with squeals and chatters as the Toyota roared in its aggressive approach.

Natasha moaned tenderly, fingers coming up to touch the sensitive area of her throat that had so very recently been punctured; Carter had claimed it was healing nicely, but to Natasha it still felt on fire . . . a razor sitting in her windpipe and gnawing her flesh.

The sun rose; so did the temperature. Carter wound down the windows, and fresh breeze heavy with tree scents and dust flowed into the cabin. The Toyota's air-con was totally shot and the fuel gauge reported its precious load erratically.

They passed through a village. Most of the houses were huts, built from mud bricks and a random selection of breeze-block, stone, wood and corrugated iron, which had rusted in the rains and now displayed deep orange streaks. Fires burned by the edge of the road, with groups of villagers standing around. Some worked, one old grey-haired man sharpening knives. He paused as they rumbled past, lifted his arm and waved. Natasha, smiling, waved back. A swathe of children ran after the Toyota, hands outstretched.

They left the village, heading inland over rough roads that the Toyota ate with ease.

They drove for an hour, tyres churning the red dust which flew up to coat the entire vehicle in a fine matt veil. When they stopped, to empty their bladders and to stretch their legs, they stood under the baking sun for a moment and eased their backs. The tyres of the Toyota were stained red and, glancing down, Carter saw the fine dust covering his boots – and he felt intimate with the African land, almost welcomed back . . . it covered him, possessed him, called him its own . . . he was a child again . . . The sun was high, a singular piercing eye. It was incredibly hot, almost unbearably so without the coastal breeze to cool their skin. The scrubland seemed to stretch off to infinity.

They rumbled on, stopping at an insanely ambitious outpost to fill up with diesel and buy a few supplies – mainly of the liquid nature. There was even a fridge, with a few out-of-date cans of chilled lager. Carter bought them and half fulfilled Natasha's heat-induced fantasy . . .

Another two hours saw them climbing a rise. Carter licked his lips, and slowed the vehicle to a halt on the summit of the track. Rock reared up to either side, and this seemed to be an entrance – a doorway or marker to a mammoth canyon walled by low red-rock mountains and filled with a wide sweeping splash of orange trees.

'Down there,' he said simply.

'What?'

'One of Spiral's hidden outposts . . . and Gol.'

Natasha stared. 'All I see is trees. I knew there was an outpost out here somewhere – after all, I *am* a Spiral Tactical Officer – but it's fucking well disguised!' Natasha's voice was a little strained, her gaze searching the canyon.

'Someone will come shortly. They'll have sentries. We haven't got this far untagged, I assure you. Let's just hope they don't shoot us on sight, eh, love? But then, that isn't Spiral company policy, is it?' He gave Natasha a sly sideways glance. And she knew; the mistrust was still there. He wasn't sure if she was real or . . . or what? A Spiral spy?

But then, in all the years she had known him, Carter had never trusted anybody. It would have surprised her if he was to change now.

Within a minute an old US army jeep, bearing five black men wearing cut-off combats and little else, arrived. They all sported an array of gleaming weapons and Carter watched them warily, the Browning in his hand held concealed between his legs.

He smiled broadly.

'Hiya, guys. Coupla tourists, out sightseeing, you know how it is.'

'You leave here,' said a large man in a gruff voice. He jumped down from the jeep, bare feet leaving imprints in the red sand. 'This not a good place for you to be visiting.'

'But maybe I'd like to catch up on an old buddy while I'm out playing with the elephants. One happy old Mr Gol. Ring any bells?'

'Nobody here by that name,' said the big man.

Natasha leaned across Carter and saw the man grin, gleaming white teeth turning his face from an intense mask of controlled hatred to a thing of beauty, a visage of soft lines and generosity.

'Tell him that his daughter, Natasha, is here.'

The man stared. He did not blink. Then he nodded to another man, who crossed over from the jeep and climbed into the back of the Toyota. 'Drive straight through the trees. Head for the white-walled house. Try nothing funny or Benjamin here—' he patted the other man's arm '– well, his gun sing a song for him.'

The large man leaped back into the jeep. Carter

gunned the Toyota and rolled slowly over the lip of the ridge. Wheels bumped over a rim of jagged rock and then they were in—

Inside the canyon.

Inside Gol's lair.

The jeep followed, automatic weapons bristling, and Carter eased the Toyota down into the verdant valley, the track soon disappearing to be replaced by soft earth. People were out, mainly women, harvesting and trimming the trees, wicker baskets of fruit on the grass as they worked. Carter guided the Toyota for the full mile through the orange-tree orchards. Sometimes there would be a break in the trees allowing sunlight to stream over the vehicle – but then they were back in the shade and they welcomed the coolness, the protection of these orange trees after their journey through the scrubland. The red walls of the canyon reared to either side; threatening; enclosing; insular. Carter licked his lips nervously, and decided that he did not like this place . . .

Gol was waiting, hands on his hips, eyes staring down at the ground as if deep in thought. Carter halted the Toyota, climbed out and allowed the Browning to be taken from him. Natasha climbed down and stood, gazing up at the sun for a moment before fixing her eyes on her—

'Father?'

Gol's head jerked up. He smiled briefly, then his gaze turned to Carter and the kindly expression fell from his face.

'They call you The Butcher,' he said softly, his deep voice the rumble of the Earth's shifting plates. 'They say you killed men – women – children. Anything that stood in your way. Without remorse.'

Carter said nothing. He made no move. He merely

allowed his gaze to remain fixed on Gol, a silent invisible umbilical of connection – a linking that Natasha did not quite understand.

'The report said that on that day you went insane.'

'No,' said Carter softly.

'I don't understand,' whispered Gol, eyes intense.

'It was . . . messed up. And when I shot you, Gol, it was to keep you alive, not to take away your life.'

There came a long, tense pause.

'You are the legendary Dark Knight of Spiral's history.'

'That title is . . . misplaced,' said Carter gently.

'How so? How can one earn such a name without actions? How can one become so *revered* and *feared* in an organisation like Spiral without action, without destruction – without *demolition*?' The contempt in Gol's voice could not be missed.

'I saved your life,' said Carter slowly. 'I *saved* your life, Gol. I know you have always hated me – because of my links with Natasha, and because of my reputation and because of what happened in Egypt and later at Cairo7 . . . And I know you will have read all the crap printed about me in those little electronic ECube memos . . . but you really, really have it wrong. I know you will find it hard to trust me on this . . . but I swear to you that Spiral did a better job on me than they did on you . . .'

Gol was silent. He lifted his Glock 9mm and examined the barrel.

Carter calmed his fluttering heart; he relaxed his muscles and readied himself – for Gol's body language was the body language of preparation.

Carter's eyes scanned the available weaponry and he realised, realised too late that maybe he had overestimated Gol's . . . humanity – understanding – nature?

And it came to Carter in a flash of profound understanding. Gol was the same. The same as Carter. The same *breed* . . .

'*This is dangerous,*' said Kade.

'Not now.'

'*Let me take him. I can fucking take him.*'

'No!' he hissed inwardly.

Carter closed his eyes as pain lanced through his exhausted mind, through his head, burning bright red and glowing with white edges; he dropped slowly to his knees, panting, and Gol no longer existed and it didn't matter and nothing mattered and the surge of adrenalin was dying and he placed his head in his hands. Pain smashed like a stormy sea against the walls of his memory and his mind. A low moan growled through his lips and Natasha was there, holding Carter in her arms. She stroked his brow free of sweat, rocked with him in the dirt and looked up at Gol – at her father—

'Get him inside. In the cool. Now!'

'What is wrong with him?' came Gol's deep rumble.

'I don't know. He's exhausted . . . Help him, father. Please help him.'

Gol gestured and the large black men approached, lifting Carter easily and helping him to stumble into the house. 'I will help him now, but I cannot guarantee what will come later.'

'You cannot see it?'

'See what?' growled the huge man.

'Can't see the fucking wood for the trees. father – he is you. He is the *same* as you. You call him an assassin; a destroyer. And what the fuck were you under Spiral? What the hell were you doing in Prague, and Egypt, and later Afghanistan, in the first place? You are like brothers . . . and you are a fucking *hypocrite.*'

212

Gol stood for a moment, staring hard at Natasha. She lowered her eyes then, in fear, almost as if reverting to childhood. Distant memories taking over; reflex actions from a lost world. Gol stepped forward, took her in his arms and hugged her, kissing the top of her head. 'I have missed you, girl. Despite everything I said to you back in London . . . and the world has moved on since then, the world has changed . . . savage events have brought us together. The attempted smashing of Spiral has brought you back to me, hasn't it, my girl?'

'Yes.'

Gol lifted Natasha's head. Wiped tears from her cheeks. 'I'm sorry. Can you ever forgive me for the evil words I spoke? That was not me, Natasha. That was not me . . . and . . . I understand what you are trying to say. About Carter. I understand.'

'I forgive you,' she whispered, and hugged the huge man tight. 'I missed you, father. I have been so alone without you.'

Gol held her close as the sunlight played over the two embracing figures among the orange trees.

Spiral_Memo5
Transcript of recent news incident
CodeRed_Z;
unorthodox incident scan 455827

Between 05:00 AM and 05.25 AM (GMT), a variety of high-tech jets and attack helicopters from a range of countries including Germany, Italy, Japan, USA, Norway and Israel crashed in or around their respective countries within a few minutes of one another.

All jets were modern fighters, including MIG24s and newly revealed Comanche NV prototypes. All air vehicles were on practice manoeuvres and all pilots are reported dead.

Prior to crashes, no pilot reported adverse conditions, technical failures or any suspicious factors.

A spokesperson for the US military made this comment: 'The US is working closely with all other countries who have suffered recent similar tragic events. We are comparing logistical data including weather reports and are also combining retrieval efforts in order to examine black-box recordings. We hope to have answers within the next few days. Terrorist activity has not been ruled out.'>>#

CHAPTER 12

NEX

The Boeing 747 flashed through the sunlight, engines whining in deceleration. Mountains reared all around, peaks soaring skywards. The Boeing banked and came smoothly down to land amid and seemingly *within* the mountains, suspension dipping as the tyres met with the sand-blown runway, an incredible feat of skill by the pilot.

The plane taxied to a halt and the single emergency vehicle at the rough rocky edges of the runway sat watching lethargically in the heat. A huge black Land Rover rumbled across the hard-packed dust as rusting makeshift steps were laboriously hauled by two heavy-set men and attached to the large plane's exit hatchway.

The 747's singular passenger stepped out, shielding his eyes from the sunlight. He was a large man, his dark hair flecked with grey. His greying beard was neatly trimmed and combed, and he wore an expensive German suit and the finest handcrafted Italian shoes. He carried a small bag in one large hand, and descended the steps with measured care, apparently unaffected by the blast wall of heat that contrasted so dramatically with the coolness of the recently pressurised aeroplane cabin.

'Count Feuchter, welcome.' The voice was heavily accented, and Feuchter nodded at the man garbed in desert-combat gear. Feuchter seemed unconcerned that his host carried a black sub-machine gun, its matt surface dull in the sunlight.

The driver of the black Land Rover opened the door and Feuchter climbed into the cool interior. The door clicked solidly shut, shading the occupant from further harassment by the sun. The military-clad man climbed in the opposite side, and within minutes the heavy-duty off-road vehicle was purring and bumping along the primitive runway and out of the tiny desert airport carved from the mountains.

They drove in silence. At first the roads were narrow, dusty, unused. They drove for several hours, down narrow passes and around sharp bends, along roads little more than tracks and crowded by scrub bushes and wild hardy trees, and through explosive-blasted rock canyons. They reached the flatlands, the Land Rover's heavy tyres humming and bumping, and eventually came to a city. All the while Feuchter sat, perfectly composed, eyes closed, mindset calm.

They passed large tenement blocks, some crumbling and run-down, surrounded by fencing and barbed wire. Children dressed in rags scattered from their path; and then the Land Rover moved out from the suburbs, out into a stretch of dusty rural land that was poorly irrigated, populated by obviously poverty-stricken workers who glanced up as this ridiculously luxurious vehicle – so out of place in this area of Saudi – cruised past. Feuchter forced himself to smile at the contrast. The thought pleased him.

They had to stop once, where a cattle herder had his herd milling in the road. With a wave of apology, the man slowly – painfully slowly – herded the ragged collection of goats and worse-for-wear cows out of the vehicle's path and Feuchter was on his way without any emotion flickering even for an instant on his neatly barbered face. His dark eyes stared straight ahead.

The Land Rover passed through the suburbs of a tiny town. The low, sand-blown sun-bleached houses were fashioned of brick and stone and breeze-block, many only half-built; chickens skittered, clucking madly, from the vehicle's path and people turned to stare, shading their eyes from the harshness of the sun.

Feuchter watched, his intelligent eyes twinkling as a man failed miserably to control his three camels and had to sprint after them into the sand and scrub, past rickety rusting corrugated fences and ramshackle boarded huts.

Feuchter finally settled back—

Closed his eyes—

And slept.

They drove for hours.

They passed no more settlements.

The Land Rover rumbled and bumped into the desert on an unnamed road, its destination the middle of nowhere, its purpose unguessable.

Feuchter did not dream. Feuchter never dreamed. To Feuchter, sleep was a pure form of regeneration so close to death that it shared the same stable. And dreams: dreams were something that happened to other people.

'Sir.'

Feuchter rubbed at his eyes. He felt refreshed. The air-con worked reasonably well. 'Are we there?'

'Yes, sir.'

The Land Rover halted at a high electrified fence. Passes were flashed and armed guards peered into the vehicle's interior. Then they were allowed through. The Land Rover swept down a long winding concrete road, between two hills of sand and scrub and into a circular depression in the landscape, which housed the single visible storey of the stone, glass and steel complex of Spiral Section Q.

The car was met by a squad of semi-military personnel, heavily armed. Feuchter stepped from the Land Rover and the men saluted him. He smiled in acknowledgement and, with a small entourage, walked through the steel doors that hissed open in response to the group's proximity.

The interior was cool; controlled. Marble floors stretched away in a huge reception hall; it was almost like a hotel, with low couches and tall potted plants at strategic intervals. A huge reception desk stretched along one wall and glass elevators in clear shafts went down to the carefully temperature- and humidity-controlled depths where the bulk of chip and other hardware production and research was carried out.

Feuchter shook hands with Adams, the Head of Developments.

'How are you, sir?'

'Well, considering I was shot recently.'

'I heard about that, sir. We were all glad to hear of your swift recovery. Was it true that it was an assassination attempt? On you, or your niece?'

Feuchter stared hard at the man, who suddenly went white.

'I . . . I . . . meant . . .'

'You will never mention my niece again,' he said softly.

'Yes, yes, of course, Count Feuchter.'

'Explain to me what the communications situation is with our companion Sections.'

'Since the explosion in London nobody seems to know what is going on. Communications are suspended between many Sections – we tried to find out if you were in London at the time of the explosion, but this information was withheld from us. And considering that the Hub had been destroyed . . .'

Feuchter merely nodded, then asked, 'How successful has the Accelerated Group Phase been?'

'We have garnered 95% reaction factors.'

'It needs to be 98%.'

'Yes, sir.'

'Within the next two days.'

'Yes, sir.'

'Is there any news on the QIII Proto Schematics?'

'No, sir. This is still a mystery to us. Mr Durell has called several times, and wants to speak with you upon your return.'

Feuchter left the entourage behind and stepped into the elevator and the welcoming silence. The tube hissed away and carried him down to the lower floor that he occupied alone. He kicked off his shoes, draped his jacket over the back of a low couch and walked past a variety of carvings and statues towards his twenty-foot-long ebony desk. He pulled a fine Cuban cigar – a Vega Robaina Dos Alejandros – from a carved rosewood box, then poured himself a brandy and sat back in his plush leather chair. The comm buzzed.

Feuchter took a long draw from the cigar, enjoying the flavour, which filled his senses with its richness, then hit the button. 'Yes?'

'Several things, Feuchter. How long will you need to fully implement the cubic math events?'

'Two days. It just needs tweaking.'

'And we will start to see these probability equations emerging?'

'Yes. I am promised they will work at a 98% rate.'

'And the world data factors have been implemented? The WorldCode?'

'I am assured, by my top people, of success. The WorldCode will be able to predict the future, in a fashion. The prediction algorithms have all been implemented.'

'Good. How are you feeling after tasting the bullet?'

'I have felt better.' Feuchter smiled nastily. He stubbed out the cigar, took a sip of brandy and twirled his seat to stare at an extravagant oil-painting representation of the desert of the Empty Quarter; he loved this place, loved the serenity, loved the feeling of culture and history. He could still imagine the ancient armies of Alexander marching over the sand, thirst-dying Macedonian soldiers battling the massive expanses of the Great Sandy Desert and meeting with other armies . . . armies clashing, battle cries, the clangour of swords, the screams of the dying . . .

'I have some good news for you. This Carter man – he has been located. Tracked. He is presently in Africa – in Kenya, to the south, near the borders of Tanzania. Despite Carter's best attempts to evade us it would seem that your QIII-based implantations have worked. We tracked him, but his destinations are quite obvious – he would seek to contact Gol, at that fucked-up Spiral outpost I wish I could forget about.'

'Gol,' said Feuchter through an exhalation of smoke. 'There is a name I have not heard for a long time.'

'I had hoped he had died,' came the soft voice at the other end of the comm. 'But then, Carter is almost doing us a favour. They have discovered the location of the schematics. Yes, by an amazing coincidence, it would seem Gol is the man who seeks to create his own version of the QIII processor.'

'The fool,' snorted Feuchter. 'It would take him years!'

'Yes,' said Durell, 'but the fact still remains that he has working knowledge, available technology, and copies of how the QIII operated at a basic machine level. We need those plans – we must either retrieve or destroy them. We can kill two birds with one stone.'

'How many Nex will you send?'

'I will send enough,' said the voice of Durell softly. 'There cannot be that much resistance; after all, they are only human.' He laughed softly. 'The Nex will wipe them out.'

'Good.'

'Our time is coming, Feuchter. Can you taste it? Our fucking time is coming and when we have complete control, we will not abuse our power, we will not squander our resources like Spiral has done and let evil men rule the world. We will be just and fair . . . not weak and spineless . . . but to get that far, first there must be mayhem . . .'

Dark eyes glittered and there came a pause. A long and thoughtful pause. 'I have a request,' said Feuchter eventually. He was still facing the large oil painting that dominated the wall, but something was changing within him, something strange, something acid. Somehow the colours were disappointing to him now; what he craved was reality.

'And what is that?' asked Durell.

'Carter: I want a guarantee. I want that cunt dead.'

'I'll see what I can do,' said Durell.

Night had fallen over the desert.

Outside, the temperature had plummeted and the sky was perfectly clear, stars twinkling like jewels cascading

221

across the finest of black skin. Feuchter still sat in his chair, now in darkness, only the glow of a cigar in his hand evidence that he remained in the deep underground office, awake, alert, dark eyes glittering. He scratched at the scar on his belly self-consciously.

He stared at images of the black desert on a monitor. Nothing stirred; there were no lights, no movement, no intrusions. This place was an emptiness; this place was a void. Spiral_Q was invisible; a non-place; a desert within a desert.

Feuchter smiled softly to himself.

Around him, in the silence, he could almost feel the hive of activity. Thousands of workers: programmers, hardware designers, hackers, the world's finest computing minds working together like a well-oiled machine on the finest of computational designs ever created –

The QIII Proto. The first-ever cubic processor.

The first-ever *cellular* processor.

The prototype of an electronic *mind*.

A *brain*.

And combined with WorldCode, it could predict actions, reactions, military instructions: it could almost *predict the future*. It would be the perfect weapon. It would make him, and Durell, and the *others* . . . it would make them rich, it would make them powerful but – more importantly . . .

It would make them God.

Feuchter sighed, blowing a cloud of silver smoke into the darkness. There came a tiny *click* from the lift and a small pool of light invaded the black. A figure stepped free, the door closed behind it and soft footsteps approached.

He gazed up at the Nex, naked now, body perfectly toned, perfectly formed; muscular and taut. Feuchter licked his lips and met the copper-eyed gaze of the Nex. This was a female – a scout, smaller than the warrior caste, less deadly but much more athletic, much better at feats of endurance and stamina. A slim, tough little fucker.

Feuchter's gaze travelled down, and then back up again across the perfectly formed thighs, hips, stomach, chest – and to the face. The pale-skinned face with its burning copper eyes.

The face was beautiful.

Cold and beautiful.

And only a little deformed.

Feuchter smiled, a strange twisted smile.

'Come here,' he said, spreading his arms as he felt desire and lust smash through his body. And the Nex stepped forward, opened her legs and silently obeyed.

CHAPTER 13

AFRICA

Carter knew it was a dream, and yet that somehow made it worse. In waking life he had some element of control; in the dream he was merely a spectator and he already knew the events, knew what happened, knew about the world's pain and the shocking after-effects of the Grey Death ... and yet, again and again he could relive those moments with curses and anger and hatred – but without control.

He stood, his boots planted firmly on the oil-slippery deck of the tanker, a huge 200,000-tonne vessel that cruised through the dark black waters like an ebony iceberg on its descent from the Arctic. Carter's eyes were dark, deeply ringed, and his black uniform ruffled in the cold sea-breeze as his gloved hands clasped the Kalashnikov AK582 with its sub-needle clip and 10-round bomb-burst.

The Grey Death.

It left a bad taste in Carter's brain, like a poisonous dose of cocaine.

A mutated biological weapon, the Grey Death had

spread like Godsfire through Europe, North Africa and the Middle East, and had touched upon Russia. Paris had been wiped clean – ironic. Berlin had suffered a human enema. Rome had been annihilated, bloated corpses filling the streets, the dead outweighing the living by a thousand to one. The Grey Death had rioted through both North and South America without prejudice, and was only finally tamed after slaughtering fifty-eight million people worldwide.

Fifty-eight fucking million.

At first, Carter had not been able to quantify the amount. Ten, fifty, yes – he could visualise that. But fifty-eight million? Just numbers. Stupid numbers. Until he stood on the decks of the tankers – corpse tankers – during the TankerRuns where he and most of Spiral had been posted as Anti-terrorist.

The tankers, some nearly a mile long, had been stripped of most of their deck plates, leaving massive criss-crosses of girders through which the bloated corpses were dumped. Hundreds. Thousands. Millions.

At first Carter had been unable to watch, unable to look upon so many millions dead. The Grey Death, man-made and devastating, had done the job it had been created to do. Only it had done it too well. Too fucking well.

Carter stood on the deck, oil glossing his boots, submachine gun cold. Jam waved, moved towards him, and their bleak gazes met over the staring faces of a million grey stinking bodies.

'There's activity,' said Jam coldly.

On their way to Siberia, there had been several threats from TJF, a Japanese terrorist group linked to murders in the Western world carried out against a blame-filled decadent society. The threat here was that TJF claimed the poison of the Grey Death had been created in the West – and should stay there. They planned to turn back the TankerRuns . . . or sink the huge vessels if they refused.

Machine guns roared.

Carter and Jam sprang into action, along with a hundred other Spiral operatives and soldiers from the crumbling special forces of a crumbling world.

Helicopters roared overhead, and the tanker's guns picked many flaming from the sky to scream, blazing fire and spitting bullets, into the sea. Japanese TJF soldiers abseiled from the helicopters, machine guns blazing, and Carter and Jam sprinted forward with Kalashnikovs juddering in their grips, faces grim, giving covering arcs of fire for one another as they crouched, bullets ricocheting from the steel girders under their boots.

Carter spun and put a bullet in a Japanese terrorist's face . . . but, almost by reflex, the TJF man's gun was firing, pumping bullets—

One caught Carter high in the chest, clipping his armour and entering under his collarbone. With a gasp he was lifted, punched backwards with a fist of iron and the air flew cold around him as he fell, fell, fell into the tanker hold filled with a million grey corpses . . .

He landed and felt pus-filled bodies sag beneath him. He screamed as he sank a little. Arms brushed against his ears, his head, his arms and back. He started to struggle, started to sink. He felt flesh part. Reeking fluid surrounding him in a lake of filth. Limbs were all around him now. Their stink, tallow-sprayed from above, intruded past his protective armour and filled Carter's nostrils, filled his mouth, filled his throat. He gagged, spewing down his armour to mix vomit with his own pooling blood.

The corpses were above him. He was sinking.

He screamed again, struck out.

But the bodies pulled him down.

They burst like old refuse sacks.

Their rancid fluids filled his screaming mouth, ran like battery acid down his gagging throat and he punched out but all he could hear was the roar of laughter from a million bodies intent on revenge for a bio-weapon that had betrayed humanity . . .

'Fuck!'

Night had fallen. Carter awoke, a terrible pain crucifying the centre of his brain. He could smell burning wood and he sat up quickly as the bitter cold horrifying events flooded his mind—

'Shhh.'

Natasha was there, kneeling by the side of his bed. Her hands were cool and she laid him back down, comfied his pillows, pulled the single sheet up over his naked body. Carter's eyes focused and he realised that the room was dimly lit by a single candle. The noise of insects spiralled in through wooden shutters, and it amazed Carter to think that below, *below them* was a hive of technological advancement – a Spiral base disguised by a simplistic mask. Distantly, he heard the crackling of a fire and the subdued voices of the armed guards.

Carter rubbed at his head. 'Any painkillers?'

Natasha handed him tablets and a glass of water. 'You dreaming about the tankers again?'

He nodded. 'Yeah, that and Kade.'

'Kade?'

'Don't worry about it.' He took the painkillers and washed them down with mineral water.

'They've reset your finger, X-rayed your ribs, checked all the minor cuts and gashes on your body. You'll live, but the doctor who examined you was unsure why you became so incredibly weak out there under the trees.'

'Just a headache,' said Carter lamely.

'They gave you an intensive scan, your body and brain. They could come up with nothing.' Natasha smiled softly. 'The doctor commended your work on me. The stitching, everything that you did. He confirmed what I already knew – that you saved my life.' Suddenly, Natasha stood and slipped from her T-shirt and shorts. Moonlight glinted on her taut, athletic body; on her flat stomach, high pert breasts, smooth unblemished skin. She climbed into bed beside Carter and lay on her side, pressing herself against his warmth—

Suddenly, Carter's headache had gone. A new pain invaded him; the pain of fear; the pain of panic; the pain of a dangerous and all-consuming lust . . .

'Natasha . . .' he whispered.

Her finger touched his lips and stayed there. She leaned forward, her lips brushing against his neck. He groaned, mouth opening, his teeth taking Natasha's finger and biting gently. Her free hand came up and stroked his hair. He turned, rolling towards her – the feeling of her soft skin, soft breasts, firm shapely legs all pressed against him and he was fired into instant readiness and he allowed himself to press against her as he gazed into her eyes and they were silent for long, long moments. They kissed, nothing more than a touching of tongues. Carter's hand came up and rested on Natasha's hip and she groaned, voice husky, scent invading Carter's mind and consuming his brain; she parted her legs a little, allowing him to press further against her, further into her, further through her and towards the silver paradise beyond—

They kissed harder, with more passion. Carter's hand ran up her ribs and she giggled, then he traced a spiral

228

down her back and rested his hand on her firm buttocks. She reached down, taking his penis in her hand and squeezing gently, feeling him pulse and harden in her tight strong unforgiving grip—

'You seem mightily excited, Mr Carter—'

'Not me, my sweetness.'

'But you must admit that your body seems rather pleased to see me.'

'Nah. This is just . . .' he licked his lips, eyes glowing mischievously in the gloom '. . . moderate appreciation.'

'Well,' Natasha pouted, 'I would hate to see rampant hard-core lust!'

'Now I'm sure *that* can be arranged.'

Natasha giggled; Carter kissed her neck, her breasts, her belly, then her lips. Carter's fist gripped Natasha's hair and she groaned—

Suddenly he pushed her down to the bed, hard – then allowed his tongue to leave a trail down her breasts, and belly – her legs parted and she moaned as he tasted her cunt. His tongue darted, in and out, a gentle teasing. Her legs came up, encircling his neck as both her hands grasped him, nails digging in as Carter's teeth nipped at the soft flesh of her vulva, then pushed in, pushed deeper, he kissed her moist lips and tasted her, sucked at her roughly, his tongue probing hard and soft, deep and shallow, teasing and tantalising as her moans filled his ears and she dragged him around into a symbiotic dual-feeding – to take him in her mouth – It was Carter's turn to groan. He breathed deeply the musky mind-spinning need-inducing scent of her sex. For long moments he was lost to the softness of her lips and tongue, her oral caresses, the promise of danger delivered by her neat teeth. Her hand cupped his testicles, tickled him, squeezed hard the taut muscle of his buttocks and he began to work eagerly on her, his tongue finding her clitoris, toying, probing, his face buried until—

Natasha moved, suddenly, unexpectedly. Carter was flung onto his back, a startled 'O' passing his moist shining lips. She grabbed both his hands and pinned them above his head. He gazed up at her – at the perspiration bathing her body, her wide, wild eyes, her sweat-streaked hair. He watched a drop roll down her nose and hang – then drop to her breasts, which swayed in a drunken dance above him.

She lowered her mouth to his, then pulled teasingly away. She lifted her leg, straddled him, hips raised so that the tip of his penis was a hair's breadth from her. She could feel his eager twitching and, with a smile, lowered herself – a single centimetre – held it – another centimetre – held it longer—

Carter groaned.

She dropped herself onto him with a sudden rush of violence and her hips heaved forward, ramming him deep into her, her breasts brushing against his face, her teeth dropping to bite savagely at his neck – Carter's back arched. He thrust himself hard up within her, the world a spinning lost dark spiral of blood-red lust and black velvet pleasure and they fucked, fucked hard and slid in one another's sweat, lips touching caressing biting tearing, hips thrusting and fucking . . . Carter was groaning and Natasha was screaming as the explosion came – with Nat's muscles taut above Carter's arched and thrumming body – and then they went limp, collapsed against and into one another in a warm sanctuary, and eternity slid into another languid eternity and they lay—

They lay entwined.

Panting.

Together.

Gradually their heat left them and the cool air soothed them.

They wriggled beneath the solitary sheet, holding one another. They kissed softly, enjoying each other's heat, each other's gentleness after the violence of their love-making.

'You just get better as you get older, Mr Carter.'

Carter grinned. He couldn't help himself, despite the deep throbbing in his ribs which had returned to haunt him.

'You get wilder.'

'I try to please,' she said softly and smiled, nibbling his chin.

'How did you stop Gol from shooting me?'

Natasha pouted. 'Carter, how can you ask such a question when we've just been fucking?'

'I need to know.' He propped himself on one elbow and looked down at her. His free hand traced twirls in the sweat on her breasts and he reached down, took a nipple between his teeth, bit mischievously.

She squeaked in mock pain.

'I didn't stop him. *You* stopped him. Your words, your actions.'

'What actions?'

'The battle. Inside you. It was on your face—'

'Battle?' Carter closed his mouth, his teeth shutting with a sudden *clack*. Then he sighed.

'I don't understand what goes on inside you,' she said.

'It's complicated.'

'Try me. *Trust* me. I'm an intelligent girl. Something was tearing you apart; something was burning you up and you were –' Natasha grappled to describe what she had witnessed '– you were like two different people. One side of you wanted to attack Gol; one side of you wanted to roll over and give in. I saw it, Carter. I saw it on your face; I heard it in your voice.'

'Do you believe in possession?' he said suddenly.

'Like in *The Exorcist* – possessing a child sort of shit?'

'Sort of. You see,' he paused, uncertain. Natasha squeezed him reassuringly. 'I am haunted,' he said. 'Something haunts my mind – talks to me. Feeds voices into my head, tries to take control of me.'

'And that's why you've asked me about schizophrenia, in the past?'

'Yeah. But this is different – it talks with me, argues with me – tries to take control but I have to let him . . .'

'Him?'

Carter met Natasha's stare then, and she could see it: the fear. The fear that she would think him – mad.

'Tell me,' she said softly.

'His name is Kade.'

'Can you talk to him now?'

'No. He comes when he smells the promise of a fight . . . if I allow him to take over he gets the job done. Gets the killing done. It was Kade who had control – too much control – when I earned myself the title of The Butcher . . . but that wasn't me, Natasha, I swear it, you've got to believe me . . .'

Natasha was silent for a long time. She hugged Carter tight.

'It sounds like a guilt complex.'

'I know exactly what it sounds like. I understand what I would be thinking if this was reversed and *you* were telling *me* this pile of shit. That's why I don't speak of Kade; that's why he lives alone, burning in my soul, and I rarely set him free . . .'

'But you do? You do set him free?'

'If I give up hope. If I resign myself to death . . . and

that's the sad thing. Take Schwalenberg in Germany – I was as sure as fucking dead. Betrayed by those I thought I was there to protect. I lost my mind, literally and physically. I no longer cared and I gave myself to Kade . . . he revelled in the killing and bought me my life for another few days. You understand?'

'This is too weird,' said Natasha.

'Don't be frightened. I have complete control . . .'

'I am not frightened. And I believe you,' whispered Natasha. She kissed Carter's ear and held him for a long time until she felt his breathing become regular and he was sleeping. Her fingers traced gentle patterns on his spine – and time after time she returned to a spiral. A spiral against his flesh. A spiral leading—

Down.

Carter awoke in the gloom. Natasha slept in his arms, a sticky warm embrace. Carter disentangled himself with care, then, pulling on his trousers and stealing Nat's cigarettes and lighter, he crossed the room and stepped outside.

There was an armed guard outside their room, a man named Marcus, sporting dreadlocks to his waist. His chest was heavily scarred. The huge black man grinned the sort of sheepish knowledge-filled grin that said, 'You sure don't know how to keep the noise down.' Carter returned the grin, padded down the hall and went outside.

A cool breeze whispered across his skin. He lit a cigarette, sat down on the wooden steps and gazed out across the dark silver-gleaming orange-tree orchards. The stars were bright against a dark canopy and Carter tilted his head back to allow a soft plume of smoke to escape his lips and rise into the infinity of the warm night sky. The nicotine buzzed through his brain, the harsh tobacco burning his lungs, and he blinked dreamily as a soft call echoed across the orchard.

'How are you feeling, Mr Carter?'

Carter turned and smiled up at Gol who was standing with his hands on his hips, breathing in the night air and the rich scents deeply – a love affair with the ambience. His eyes were unreadable, his grey-flecked beard – actually more grey than black now, Carter noticed – was neatly combed and oiled. Carter caught the distant scent of coconut oil.

'Much better.'

'Would you care to walk with me?'

'It's a fine night. That would be good.'

The two men stepped from the porch of the white-walled house and the sandy soil felt soft, comfortable under Carter's feet. They moved beneath the trees, inhaling their fragrance, moving through the gloom a little uncomfortably at first: untrusting. As they walked, Carter offered Gol a cigarette. They both lit up and stopped within a small circle of trees, lifting their faces in an attempt to attract the slightest of breezes to evaporate their sweat.

'This is a warm place to choose to live,' said Carter eventually.

'Yes,' rumbled Gol uneasily. The cigarette seemed tiny in his huge hand. 'But we don't always have a choice in these matters. Spiral is a harsh mistress. She commands, and we mere mortals obey.' He smiled a smile without humour, bloodless in the moonlight.

There was a pause. Something called through the darkness. The breeze whispered between the trees.

'I think I am following in your footsteps,' said Carter.

'Yes. I have just researched your recent – ah, shall we say *exploits* in both Germany and Scotland. Natasha has,

234

of course, filled me in on some of the details. It would seem that you are a wanted man Mr Carter.'

'Well, I'm wanted *dead*, if that's what you mean.'

'Hmmm. That would be one eventuality; a thought which does leap to mind is that you have been used. Set up. A tracker with the function of leading somebody to me. After all, the other DemolSquads were wiped out by three Nex – and yet they only sent one after you. Strange, don't you think?'

'Yes.'

'And further moves have been placed across that great gaming board we call the Earth.'

'Such as?'

'Another Spiral base has been destroyed.'

There was a long, long silence. Gol enjoyed his cigarette. 'Forty minutes ago, Spiral_M was also wiped from the face of the Earth. It's now just a pile of rubble surrounded by emergency services and brave people trying their hardest to find survivors.'

'Fuck.'

'My sentiments exactly,' said Gol softly.

'But . . .'

'Carter, I *know* for a fact that Spiral do not want you dead. We have bigger problems . . . And the assassin, the Nex who came for you, I fear these killers are not used by Spiral any longer – not for many, many years – even though it was Spiral's loins from whence they sprang.'

'Who sent them?' asked Carter, voice hard, humour vaporised.

'I don't know,' sighed Gol, rubbing at his beard. He ground his cigarette stub into the earth. 'Although I have a few suspicions.'

'I have a few fucking suspicions of my own,' snapped Carter. 'Now, I know you want me dead Gol – and I can't really say I blame you after what we went through: I thought I had misjudged you when we arrived here.'

'You had,' said Gol softly.

Gol faced Carter, who looked up at the huge man. Gol rubbed at the scar on his leg self-consciously and Carter noted the movement, remembered in mild embarrassment that it had been his own bullet that had wounded Gol's flesh.

'You are Carter, Spiral's most resourceful man – or you used to be. No longer do you seek assassination contracts; you have become withdrawn, hidden away in the Scottish mountains with your dog and your own company and knowledge. And yet you possess the most awesome skills in tracking people down – and in killing them . . . Now, I had thought I would kill you,' said Gol gently. 'Here, now, in Africa . . . but I have a greater use for you than that.'

Carter lit another cigarette. Offered the packet. Gol held up his hand in refusal.

'Oh yeah?'

'My anger has gone. You love Natasha. And because of your love for her, I forgive you; I will put aside our differences in this hour of need . . . Natasha needs you, and Spiral needs you. Carter, somebody is trying to wipe out Spiral – why? Because Spiral is what stands in the way of chaos. Spiral is the final firewall; Spiral is the bullet in the firing chamber of the world; Spiral is death to those who oppose all that stands for good.'

Carter frowned. Gol was one of the strongest, most fanatical men he had ever met. There was no streak of weakness – Gol had shot sleeping men, wounded men, dying men. Carter would have been little problem . . . and this reinforced the notion that Spiral was in a world of shit.

'What is happening here?' asked Carter softly, turning his eyes away from Gol, scanning the orange trees rimed with moonlight. 'Who is using heavy HighJ detonation to wipe us out? Where do your *suspicions* lie?'

Gol shrugged, but looked away. Carter caught a hint of something; something unsaid, something he almost grasped but missed in the darkness. Gol was hiding something. Hiding something bad.

'Two mammoth Spiral divisions have been destroyed,' he rumbled, rubbing wearily at his beard. 'But more – nearly thirty DemolSquads have been wiped out in the last forty-eight hours alone.' Gol turned to look into Carter's eyes. Carter's mouth had opened in a silent 'O' of shock.

'Thirty?' he whispered, awed.

'Yes, thirty. And our little friends are looking for something – something retrieved by Natasha, and passed on to me for safe keeping. A possibility arises, Carter – the possibility that you were *chased* here. This base is highly classified . . . Natasha knew of its whereabouts, but you sure as fuck should not have done. This is outside the boundaries of normal Spiral influence.'

Carter nodded, smoke pluming from his nostrils. He scratched at his forehead with his thumb.

'You think it is that black and white? I lead the bad guys here, because they know you have something and they know that I know where you are? Are you fucking crazy?'

'Why did you come here, Carter?'

'For answers.'

'And because you had nowhere else to go. Nowhere else to take Natasha. Where better than to her father, despite your earlier *differences*?'

Carter dropped the cigarette. Ground it underfoot.

He turned to meet Gol's impenetrable gaze and their stares locked.

Carter smiled bitterly. 'What is it you have?'

'Schematics,' said Gol softly.

'For what?'

Gol waved his hand dismissively. 'I believe you will find out soon enough, my inquisitive friend. For tonight, I advise you to get some sleep. I have many things to show you.'

'I am confused. You know who is behind this.'

It was not a question.

'I know,' said Gol, smiling – and his smile held no humour. It was the smile of a shark cornering a little fish. The smile of a tiger sinking its claws into the flanks of a lamb. The smile of the natural predator.

The wind blew. The trees shivered.

'This Nex assassin has followed me here, then. To Africa?'

'Not one, but many. The schematics I have in my possession are, shall we say, integral to the demise of Spiral. They need them, or else it is a chink in their armour; their *Achilles Heel*. They cannot let them go unretrieved, and they therefore cannot let me live. I hold their secret in my hands, like a God holding a newly born sun.' Carter shivered as Gol's words caressed him like a stench-breeze of corpse smoke.

'They will come. And they will come soon.'

Carter frowned, lit another cigarette and blew a plume of smoke into the air. He knew that Gol was holding out on him, and it sat bad with him, like an act of incest.

'We'll fucking see,' he said quietly.

Gol stood in the shadows of a tree, thankful that Carter had gone. The man made him uneasy, put him on edge. Gol did not trust him; his eyes held too much the look of a killer.

He watched closely as one of his guard groups exchanged duty. They disappeared into the gloom, moving like ghosts, and he took a long, deep breath, staring up at the vast vaults of the night sky. A cool breeze at last caressed his skin. He rubbed at his beard. He closed his eyes—

But images haunted him.

From a million years ago.

From a different world.

Dark stone walls, damp with water and slime. A voice, crying in the darkness, a woman's voice, shouting out, the language Austrian, the embedded emotion that of raw terror. He moved down the steps, boots thudding dully on the heavy ancient stone. In addition to his knowledge of where he was, he could *feel* that he was deep underground; could *feel* the weight of earth and stone above him leading up.

A face. Pale and drawn.

'Feuchter.'

'Come in, Gol. We've been waiting.'

Gol stepped forward. There was a heavy solid *click* as the door closed neatly behind him. He nodded to Durell, who nodded with a *crackling* sound in return – but Gol could not meet the man's gaze; he felt himself shivering, and he looked instead at Feuchter, forcing himself not to turn and stare at Durell, at his deformities, at his terrible *wounds* . . .

The images drifted.

Dissipated like smoke.

Gol opened his eyes, stared again at the night sky.

'What did we do?' he murmured wearily. 'What in God's name did we do?'

Slater stared up at the Boeing Apache AH64A, resplendent in desert camouflage colours, with its squat powerful wings carrying clusters of Hellfire missiles and 70mm rocket groups, flanks scarred and battered from battle encounters, a crack in the windshield and one flat tyre. Slater turned back to Jam, who was leaning against the old van, enjoying a cigarette.

'You say you can fly this thing?'

Jam nodded.

'You sure?'

Jam nodded again.

'It looks a little bit . . . battered?'

'Meet *Sally* – apparently Mongrel flew her during the Second Great Gulf War. Took out about thirty-five tanks single-handedly in that baby, and still brought her home for tea and doughnuts.'

'But . . .' said Slater.

'What?'

'It's damaged!'

'Damaged? Merely superficial.' Jam smiled through gritted teeth. 'Anyway, what did you expect? Us to waltz in here and requisition a brand new one? Now, when I give the order, I need you and Nicky to climb in – you see the release for the cockpit there? Good. Climb in – insert this key, turn it twice clockwise and hit the five green buttons on the dash. You got that?'

Slater frowned. 'I thought you cleared this, Jam? And I thought we were waiting for The Priest?'

'I did, I did, I cleared it with Mongrel. Those are the keys, and I have the ignition sequences stored up here.' He tapped his head. Blowing smoke through a cheeky smile, Jam slapped Slater on the back. The huge man did not budge. 'And as for The Priest? Well, he's a little bit late and we can't hang on for the insane fucker.'

'Late?' rumbled Slater. 'Don't you mean that *we* are early?'

'Depends on your perspective,' said Jam. 'Look, Slater, Spiral are being shafted left, right and centre – we need to find out, and find out fast, what is actually going on. This was the nearest base with access to this sort of technology.'

Slater looked around, his face carrying the weight of guilt. Across the almost deserted airfield other aircraft sat unattended, mainly Cessna single-propeller planes, a few Lear Jets and two clusters of ex-war Apaches like *Sally*. Jeeps hovered in the distance. Activity seemed centred on a huge hangar, originally used during World War II to house fighter planes but now owned by Spiral for its private fleet of air-going traffic.

Slater looked up at the sky. Heavy clouds rolled, and wind whipped at him with the promise of rain.

'I didn't know you could fly a helicopter,' said Slater suspiciously.

'I am a man of many talents. Where the fuck has Nicky got to? If she's not quick The Priest might arrive early. And we don't fucking want *that*.'

Nicky appeared, jogging across the expanse of tarmac. She carried packs and, panting heavily, dropped them at Slater's feet. 'They were happy to give me supplies; everything's in a bit of a panic. Some of the Spiral navigation systems have gone down; the loss of Spiral_H hasn't helped things either. Once they clocked my ID and ECube – wham bam.' She smiled, then looked at Slater's dubious expression. 'What's the matter?'

Slater pointed. 'Did you know this cunt could fly?'

Nicky shook her head. 'No. So what?'

'I don't trust him.'

'You don't have to trust him, sweet-pea. Just let him get us out of here; it's beginning to feel a little threatening, what with those masked fuckers killing our guys and taking out the HQ.'

'Come on,' said Jam, dropping the butt of his cigarette. Smoke trailed from his nostrils. He ground the remains of the cigarette under his boot and wrapped his long leather coat around him. 'Let's do it.'

Slater and Nicky moved swiftly to the Apache, Slater opened the cockpit door and they climbed in. Jam moved around the war-bruised machine, poking here and there; he kicked away the blocks from under the tyres and climbed up, squeezing into the position of control. He fired up the ignition, then the twin-turbine engine. The engine whined, then roared and Jam smiled like a small child discovering a new toy he thought was lost.

Rain began to fall from the dark broiling skies.

'I hope he knows what he's doing,' said Slater, as the Apache bobbed and the engine noise increased.

'I'm sure he does,' smiled Nicky, a touch uncertainly.

'Here we go! Let's see what this baby can do. Kamus-5 . . . here we come!'

Out of the gloom, doing perhaps a hundred and twenty m.p.h. across the rugged concrete airfield hammered The Priest's battered old Volvo; oil smoke plumed like a dragon's breath from the wide tailpipe, and the car slewed around, wheels locked, skidding to a halt in front of the Apache in a scythe of water.

The Priest stepped free of the car, crossed swiftly to the helicopter with his Bible in one hand, long heavy coat flapping, and climbed up to be greeted by three blank stares.

'Well done, my children, for convening so early. It is good to see the servants of God so willing to carry out His work.'

'Yeah,' said Jam, casting glances at Nicky and Slater. 'We're just warming up her engines.'

'And *are* they warm?' asked The Priest softly.

'They are now.'

'Praise be – then what are we waiting for? Onward, Christians! Let us discover the source of this scourge.'

The Apache, engines roaring with power, lurched up from the airstrip, rotated through two full circles, then shot straight upwards with a caterwaul of engine; it halted, hovering, rotated again through about 270 degrees, then, with its short squat nose dipped, hammered forward into the heavy falling rain.

Jam grinned sheepishly. 'Sorry! I'll get the hang in a minute—'

'Or twenty,' muttered Slater.

'I fucking *heard that*!'

The rotors thumped through the downpour.

Nicky found herself staring out and down at the bleak landscape below. They passed a town, grey and huddled, its roofs slick with water; cars moved warily, like predators hunting through the streets, and occasional shoppers cowered under huge umbrellas. The streets were laid out like some huge brick-walled game, and a feeling of melancholy fell over Nicky as she watched these tiny people in their tiny houses with their tiny lives.

'I know what you are thinking,' said Slater.

'What's that?'

'You're looking at the people – secure in their ignorance, not aware of the world events unfolding around them. They watch the news, believe the media and propaganda – like sheep. They have no real concept of what is really going on, of what the stakes are.'

'That's quite profound for you, Slater.'

The huge man smiled, revealing his missing teeth. 'Slater not think too well sometimes, but he hold a gun well and know what he believe in. You laugh at Slater sometime, but really I is good and I smash the bad men.'

Nicky patted his huge bicep. 'I know, I know. When we're laughing, we're just fucking with you. We love you really; we know you'd give your life for us.'

Slater nodded, a big smile across his face.

The Apache banked, heading towards the coast; below, cliffs sailed into the distance and they were flying low over cold churning grey seas. Jam and The Priest seemed to be arguing.

'We're not going lower,' said Jam through gritted teeth.

'The wave formations will mask us against radar,' said The Priest softly, eyes bright with the light of conviction.

'Yeah, and then drag us down and wrap us in Neptune's cold fishlike embrace. You can go to fuck, you insane religious bastard.'

'God will protect us.'

'God will laugh at us!'

'You do not know God's will as I do.'

'What, so you're in contact with the man himself?'

'Let me just say that I have seen the light.'

The Apache dropped closer to the waves; sea spray rattled against the glass and Nicky and Slater stared out warily, watching the churning water, the crests of white foam against the rolling liquid slate-grey.

'Do you know anything about this Kamus?' asked Nicky, after long moments of thought.

'A little,' said Slater slowly, his eyes hooded. 'It used to be an operational Spiral base. A military centre, a place from which we could mount operations in middle and eastern Europe.'

'What happened? Why did they close it?'

'Several reasons.' Slater's voice was cool, his eyes moving to stare out over the sea once more. 'Things kept going wrong; people started dying. The Kamus is built *into* the side of a mountain, high up on a ridge. There are only two ways to reach the place – by air, or by a single cable car. Kamus was a fortress; almost impregnable. Tunnels inside travel across and *down, deep down* – access shafts, huge stores, research centres – all carved from within the rock. In the end, Kamus-5 was beaten by an enemy – not an external physical enemy, but an internal psychological one.'

'It was haunted?' asked Nicky softly.

'Not haunted, more *cursed*.'

Nicky shivered.

Slater continued, his gaze still distant. 'I remember the last days; the huge transporters leaving the platform; much heavy equipment was abandoned there, they said it was not cost-effective to move. Hah.'

'What else?'

Slater looked at her. Met her gaze. 'It was said, those who worked deep within the research centres – something down there turned them mad. There was some kind of massacre, in the living quarters – thirty or so people, including wives, children, all were involved in some kind of shooting. Lots of bad death. Deaths of innocent people.' Slater rubbed at his temples. 'It was covered up well. I be honest, Nicky – Slater not really want to go back.'

'We don't have much choice.'

'Only a mad man would set up camp in the Kamus.'

'Or a fanatic,' said Nicky sombrely.

Slater nodded.

They remained in silence for the rest of the journey.

Spiral_Memo6
Transcript of recent news incident
CodeRed_Z;
unorthodox incident scan 556126

A Russian nuclear-weapons depot was completely deactivated this morning. The deactivation sequence lasted for 180 seconds. Both reactors and fission services were left stranded and without power and cooling.

The reactivation occurred as an automated sequence that left technicians and scientists without answers concerning the nature of this apparent security breach. When reactivation occurred, all passwords and security measures were instigated without authority intervention.

This would suggest either a complex bug in software, or it could hint at hacker/sub-terrorist involvement.

The Russian Minister for Technology, Sergei Kessolov, was unavailable for comment.>>#

CHAPTER 14

THE CALM

Carter and Natasha had a simple breakfast of fruit and bread and cheese brought to their room by Marcus, and washed it down with thick black coffee containing lots of sugar. Carter gestured for Marcus to stay, and the large black man sat on the end of the bed, making the aged and rusting springs creak. He poured himself a coffee and grinned over at Carter.

'They say you a bad boy.'

Carter shrugged. 'You look quite a bad boy yourself.'

Marcus shook his head, long dreads swaying. 'I here, man, because I am mathematician and I am good mathematician. I help repair the Spiral mainframe codes.' He beamed, and sipped at his coffee. 'I let Gol tell you about that; he may not want me to speak.'

'And there's me thinking you were merely a beefy bouncer. Nats, don't he look like a bouncer?'

Nats nodded, taking a bite of melon. 'Sorry to stereotype you, but it's the muscles.'

'A man must work out,' said Marcus. 'You not want to turn to fat; to grow old and fat and weak and plump. I

247

stay trim; I run and I fight. They say you are a fighter, Carter – this true, man?'

'I used to box, once. In the army.'

'Maybe one day we spar?'

Carter shook his head. 'Don't know about that.' He reached over; felt Marcus's huge bicep. 'Hmm. Maybe another time, Marcus – you understand? – I've got a broken rib at the moment . . .' The last bit was spoken in the voice of an injured squeaking schoolboy.

Marcus grinned. 'Look forward to it. Gotta go, man, or Gol will cut off my dreads.' He stood, hoisted his AK47 and stepped from the room. He peeped back in. 'Thanks for the coffee.'

'Our pleasure,' said Nats, smiling as the door closed. 'A mathematician, eh? I wonder just what the hell my illustrious father is up to down here in Kenya under the Spiral umbrella?'

'I'm sure its not legal,' said Carter.

'With Gol, it never was.'

They dressed and, stepping outside into the early-morning sunshine, saw Gol sitting on the porch steps. He turned, smiling up at the couple and stroking his greying beard. 'Looks like we've been lucky,' he said.

Carter stood, stretching his back. He lit a cigarette and inhaled deeply. 'Lucky?'

'No signals have been triggered; we've scanned the ECubes via our hacked satellite links. There are reports of you – both of you – fleeing the UK but there is no mention of your destination, no traffic referring to Africa. If your enemies – *our* enemies – are coming here for us, then they are extremely quiet about it.'

Carter snorted. 'Don't get lazy, Gol. Just because you can't see them, doesn't mean they are not there.'

Gol frowned, his face hardening. 'I know that, boy.

And we have been making preparations. This operation is far bigger than you – or anybody – suspects. It would appear we are safe from discovery, for now; and you, therefore, can help *us*.'

'Help you? How?'

Gol smiled down at Natasha. 'I know for a start that you are a little hacking genius; you worked on the QIII Proto at its integral stages, and you know the Spiral mainframes like the back of your own hand. We have a little problem decoding information that we could use your assistance with . . .'

'Just what the fuck is it that you are doing here?' asked Carter. He sat down on the steps, looking out over the orange trees, which swayed gently in the caress of some warm breeze.

'This is Spiral_F,' said Gol. 'We are the secret police of Spiral. The secret within the secret. The central layers of the onion, surrounded by outer layers and outer layers and outer layers. Spiral watches Spiral, who watches Spiral – we are a central mechanism to stop *bad* things happening.'

'Hmm.' Carter rubbed at the back of his neck, easing the tension, 'I knew there was a secret police,' he gave Natasha a long sideways glance, 'but I didn't realise you were involved.'

'Not many people do. Our cover is that of a research centre; and yes, we do research in the name of Spiral. But we are so much more than that . . . ironically, we are the people who are supposed to have all the answers, and yet there are things happening here and we're at a loss to discover the real reasons. This QIII, this military processor – something is out of place, a discordant note, and I'm not sure how deep it goes. You want to know what we do here, Carter? We solve problems. Pure and simple. And then we hunt.'

'Hunt?'

'Oh yes,' said Gol, dark eyes gleaming. 'We hunt.'

It was night.

Gol had spent some of the day showing Natasha and Carter around his private world within the rocky canyon; the orchards flourished with the loving care of a small group of village women who travelled in by foot to tend the trees and harvest the fruit.

Now they were seated outside, around the side of the house, where a small fire had been built. Carter sat with his back to the wall of the house, Natasha beside him. Gol was seated across the fire, large chunks of meat on a skewer before him sizzling fat into the flames. Also present – some of them meeting Carter for the first time – were a few other members of this Spiral_F operation whom Gol slowly introduced.

'This is Marcus; I think you have already met.'

Marcus grinned, reached over, and shook Carter's hand, his dreads swinging near to the flames.

'Careful, mate, or your hair will fry.'

''S all right, Mr Carter. It happened before.'

'This is Shanaz; our resident computer expert and presently on the hack with the newly updated Spiral mainframes – or she was, until the HQ was stomped into chemical oblivion. She learned her computing trade at BUET – the Bangladesh University of Engineering and Technology in Dhaka.'

Shanaz smiled, a wide beautiful smile; of Bangladeshi descent, she wore her hair long, a silken web that descended to her waist and which she plaited and decorated with interwoven wooden beads. Her lips were a deep red, shining in the glow of the flames.

She reached over to shake Carter's and Natasha's

hands; Carter's gaze met the intelligent bright look of the woman and he licked his lips; there was wildness there, true animal wildness that promised nothing less than a true roller-coaster thrill.

When she spoke, her words were a soft purr, a luxury sound, the husky growl of a hunting animal. 'I have heard many things about you, Mr Carter. Gol speaks with – shall we say, passion – about your exploits.'

'I am sure he does.'

'Are you everything he promises you to be?'

Carter was entranced by that beautiful gaze and that throaty, husky, magical voice. He realised that their hands were still touching, her skin warm against his, the fingers stroking his hand with gentle pressure.

'I . . . I am not sure.'

'Come, do not be modest, Mr Carter.' Shanaz licked her gleaming red lips. She turned, winked at Gol, then back to Carter. 'He says that you really are an *animal*.'

The men chuckled; Natasha glared, first at Shanaz, then at the side of Carter's head.

Shanaz broke the handshake. She licked her fingers. Carter swallowed.

'And this is Jahmal; another professional computer hacker. He used to be wanted by the FBI, no less, until he taught them a few things about data protection; bought his freedom and their respect.'

'Yo, man,' said Jahmal, grinning. He was a slim black man, his head completely round and shaved as close to the scalp as the clippers could go; his whole face seemed to be one huge grin. He shook Carter's hand energetically.

'Nice to meet you,' said Carter.

'And you, and you; ignore Shanaz, she's a weird bitch. It's nice to have some new faces round here, we're stuck down in that dump and we hardly ever get some new blood to tell us stories around the fire and liven up the evenings . . .'

'Jahmal!' snapped Gol, frowning.

'Sorry!' he said. 'They don't know?'

'Not yet. I am saving it,' said Gol. He smiled at Nats and Carter over the flames; the heady scent from the orange trees flowed down and around the group. 'Our struggle – it is the struggle to keep Spiral from becoming what it aims to destroy. Within any corporation there is always corruption; it comes from a myriad of different sources. You can never know from where. We are here to try and stop that; we have been specially vetted; we are about as pure as you can get.' Gol laughed at that. 'Fucking funny, hey? Spiral_F is a collection of people who have been brought together for that special purpose. To keep the good good. To keep Spiral pure. We operate external to Spiral policy. We are the hidden camera behind the grille and it spreads much further than this little gathering you see here . . . I am merely a small cog in a huge machine that watches another huge machine.' Gol held his arms wide and grinned. When he spoke again, his voice was low, eyes staring into the fire where fat dripped sizzling and spitting to be consumed and spat out as black smoke. 'Spiral operates as cells; individual cells so that no one person can be in total control. But that system is breaking down . . . one or maybe more of the cells have turned against Spiral. And they are powerful.'

There was silence. The flames crackled. Gol stared into the fire, melancholy descending on him.

'I never fucking thought it could happen so fast, or so bad,' he said. 'Two bases wiped out; the DemolSquads being tagged left, right and centre. We've sent out warnings but it is too little too late. And there are other, wider implications. Strange events have been happening all over the world – you may have seen them on the news. A malicious new computer virus, nuclear submarines going missing, power cuts, jet fighters crashing, gas plants powering down, the deactivation of a Russian weapons depot, financial institutions losing millions of dollars, digital interference in the stock exchanges . . . all sorts of shit, being blamed on software bugs and human error – but this is not the case. We are linking many of the cases, chasing them back to their source, but the paths are not clear. But there is one thing we *are* sure about – all these world events, all these fuck-ups on a global scale – they are not fuck-ups, they are a test of some sort, an initiation – and they all stem from the same source.'

'The QIII,' whispered Carter.

'Yes.'

'They are testing it before it becomes fully operational?'

'Yes.' Gol nodded. 'It is flexing its muscles; running internal diagnostics; seeing how far it can go. But it is little things, the odd submarine here, a power station there, wipe the computers in a bank in London – and then replace the data in a "freak occurrence" . . . when the final push comes, it will come in a sudden rush. Everything will happen at once, and this fucking processor can do it.'

'Why haven't they done it yet?'

'A couple of reasons,' said Gol softly. 'One, we know about them, this Spiral splinter group, and we have agents searching for them as we speak. Two, the QIII isn't quite finished – it's working, and is running its own diagnostics but it isn't quite complete. A premature attack might fail. And finally, we have the schematics. We understand how it works. And we can stop it.'

Carter looked from Natasha to Gol. 'You have the

schematics for the fucking QIII processor? How the fuck did you get them?'

Natasha smiled bitterly. 'It was a long, hard fight, Carter.'

Carter shook his head, rubbing at his tired eyes as Natasha moved over to Gol and placed her hand on his shoulder. 'Are you all right, father?'

Gol looked up and smiled weakly. 'Yes, but soon you must leave this place. The reports are coming in. They will be here in the early morning; a force of Nex with heavy armour support. It would seem that they want what they think is rightly theirs.'

'We will not leave,' said Natasha.

'We will fight,' growled Carter. 'You say the Nex are coming? Well, we have fucking run for long enough. We will not flee any more – there are only a few of us, but we can make a difference. Shouldn't we be working now?'

'I have a hundred people working on this thing – we can do no more than we are already doing,' said Gol softly. 'But that is for later. Now, now we must relax, we must drink, and then – then we will prepare. We cannot evacuate this place because there is nowhere to run . . . and our research cannot be moved without many days of labour. We must defend ourselves against these infidels . . .' He rubbed at his beard thoughtfully, his stare fixed on Carter. 'You say you are ready to fight with us, Mr Carter . . . but I wonder?'

'What?'

'Is your soul ready for Heaven?'

'If not,' Carter growled, 'then I'll see you fucked up in Hell.'

Carter groaned as he was shaken awake. His sticky eyelids opened and he could picture the jug – the jug of sweet

254

golden liquid that he had enjoyed so thoroughly the night before. Images of flames crossed his mind; good food; good drink; humorous bantering company. The glistening face of Shanaz . . .

He groaned again and stared hard at Gol.

'Yeah?'

'Get Nats up. Meet me outside in five.'

'You got some cigarettes?'

'I have,' rumbled Gol. 'Come on, move yourself. It's almost dawn. We have little time left. The Nex are coming.'

The sun was just rising, a weak grey pre-dawn light gently caressing the horizon. Natasha followed Carter, grumbling about their lack of sleep and touching tenderly at the healing wound in her throat, and then at her shoulder. 'Gol's painkillers are working, but not well enough.'

'You still bad?'

Natasha gave a weak smile. 'I'll survive, I'm sure.'

She moved across the porch, linked arms with her father. 'What can I do for you, daddy? You taking us out on safari?'

'I wish we could have such fun,' rumbled the large greying man. He rubbed Natasha's hair. 'It's good having you here, girl; it's good having you around me again. It makes me feel younger!'

'Me too,' smiled Natasha. 'You make me feel like a child again.'

'You're certainly not that,' he said softly, glancing over at Carter who was leaning against a wooden support and smoking heavily. 'Hey, Carter, come on. I have something to show you.'

'Does that something include a bed?'

'No. But it has something to do with the Nex.'

Gol led them around the back of the battered, run-down white-walled house with its peeling paint and dilapidated appearance: a clever mask, a wonderful disguise. He led them a little way into the trees, and then out across scrubland and through another stand of orange trees until they came to a rusting iron hatchway half concealed by vegetation, small scrub bushes, fallen leaves and branches. 'This is no longer classified,' said Gol, 'because our security has already been breached by the impending Nex visit. We must prepare. We must be ready.' He was serious, deadly serious, standing above that rusted iron covering. 'While I commend your skills in searching me out, you really, really have no idea what you are dealing with . . . you really do not understand what you are *fucking* with here . . . you see an old house, but it goes much, much deeper . . .'

He spun the rusted iron wheel, which moved with surprising ease. There was a hiss as the iron hatch was released. Gol heaved up the hatch to reveal a small section of silver alloy with a slot for a key. Gol removed the key from a chain around his neck; he inserted the key and turned it. Then he retreated a pace or two, saying, 'Step back.'

Carter and Natasha obeyed.

There came a distant hiss, followed by a deep rumbling – and the earth began to shake. Natasha grabbed hold of Carter's arm, and they glanced all around. Suddenly, the ground folded in on itself and – like a huge metallic puzzle – it folded in and down, and then spun up in a huge spiral of metallic slivers that hissed and spun out like knives in a huge fan to reveal—

A massive circle in the ground, metallic-walled, a huge riveted alloy ramp leading down.

From the darkness below the ground lights shone dazzlingly. There came a roar of engines, more rumbling, and Gol, Carter and Nats all jumped back. From the

256

depths of the earth came a desert-camouflaged six-wheeled vehicle, a huge armour-plated wagon with steel welded over the windows and machine guns poking from dark rectangular slits.

The wheels, each nearly as large as Carter was tall, pounded the alloy ramp and ate into the sand. There were clangs as the massive machine hammered by, motor roaring and wheels churning as the vehicle sped past the group and to the front of the dilapidated white-walled house where it stopped, engine rumbling, fumes belching from a huge plated exhaust. 'We call them Pigs,' shouted Gol over the roar. More lights dazzled. Another armoured car approached, wheels thundering up the ramp – and then Pigs positively *spewed* from this hole in the ground, one after the other, a seemingly never-ending stream of armour and guns until thirty weapon-bristling behemoths sat in a huge circle around Gol's small house, growling, coughing, waiting.

Carter licked his lips as he surveyed the firepower.

'Fuck me,' he said. 'I didn't realise you had such . . . *resources*.'

Gol smiled wanly.

'If only they were enough.'

'When you said the Nex were coming . . . exactly *how many* did you mean?'

Gol's dark-eyed stare met Carter's. 'The schematics . . . they want them bad, Carter.'

'How many?'

'Hundreds,' said Gol softly.

'Show me where the weapons are,' said Carter grimly, and Gol led Carter and Natasha down the alloy ramp and into the darkness of Spiral_F below the hot ground of Africa.

CHAPTER 15

BATTLE

Carter reached the bottom of the wide alloy ramp and moved warily into a huge chamber hewn from the rock. Panels of computer banks glittered across one wall, a contrast to the rough harshness of the environment.

'Controls for the anti-aircraft guns. We even have some missiles.' Gol gestured at the walls.

'*Missiles?*' said Carter softly. 'It would seem that Spiral have infinite resources, do they not? Fuck me.'

'Come on, I will take you to the armoury. The other Spiral_F members are ready; it was a shame that you decided to sleep in so late.'

'A battle is one thing,' said Carter, 'but I didn't realise we were preparing for a fucking *war*.'

Gol explained quickly as they walked, gesticulating passionately with his hands, his eyes wide and focused; they came to many turns in the underground passage-ways – sometimes they branched in three or four directions. Always Gol would take a tunnel – seemingly at random – his boots treading the dust as he led the couple through the correct sequence of the—

'Maze?' asked Carter.

'Sort of. That was not its primary intention, but it has become so. We have been busy boys down here under the rock.' He grinned a broad square-toothed grin.

'So I see,' said Carter softly, brushing his way through thick cobwebs.

'Where to begin?' said Gol in his deep melodic voice. 'You want answers? You sounded surprised when I mentioned missiles. The Spiral you know and love own fifty-eight drilling rigs at a variety of locations around the world. Spiral own about a million square miles of ocean with oil and minerals and precious metals beneath the waves. Spiral own millions of acres of forestland in Scandinavia and in Russia, and thousands more miles of desert in Nevada, as well as here in Africa and in a variety of locations scattered across the Middle East . . . secretly, and under the guise of major business concerns. Spiral also owns many of the world's major computing organisations, ranging from the development of software, games and operating systems through to hardware – processors, communications, fucking DVD writers and the latest digi-optical scanners, memory cubes, blue-laser peripherals, Qglass-storage, you name it . . . Spiral's finances are beyond your comprehension. And beyond mine,' he added wistfully. 'They have a finger in every pie; if you can make money out of it, Spiral does. Gold, precious jewels, oil, construction, computers. Spiral is one of the richest organisations in the world – and also the best-kept secret. And it works for the good of mankind, but—'

'There is always a but,' said Carter softly.

'The splinter group we talked of last night: they seek to master the QIII – with it, they plan world domination.'

'I knew the QIII was rumoured to be incredibly powerful, but—'

'But nothing. Tell him, Nats.'

Nats, who had gone pale, said, 'The QIII is the most powerful military processor in the world – bar none. It is years ahead of its time, but the biggest breakthroughs are in two areas; it uses RI – real intelligence, it is a *superior* brain, not an artificial program following scripted moves. It can think. It can fucking think, Carter. But more importantly, it has what is called WorldCode. It can predict the future . . .'

'Predict the—'

'To within a certain percentage rate. It is not perfect – nothing ever is. But it follows new probability equations that it helped to create; its intelligence is astounding.'

They came to the end of a corridor, blanked by an alloy door. Gol punched in digits. The door slid open to reveal—

A huge chamber, full of guns and armour. Banks of guns, racks of body armour. The bunker was hewn from the orange rock, the walls rough and coarse, grained and grooved by the tools used to create this underground network.

'Take your pick,' said Gol softly. 'But be quick, we have less than twenty minutes.' His deviant ECube rattled. 'Yeah? OK. Arm the air defences.'

'They here?' Carter's eyes were bright.

'Soon. There are more than we thought.'

Carter frowned. 'And?'

Gol swallowed softly. 'The good news is that they have come over land, as we expected. Our air defences are too formidable; their planes or copters would be merely shot from the sky.'

'The bad news?'

'They have brought tanks. Lots of tanks. Had them airlifted in from a Spiral depot in Egypt.'

'What the fuck are we going to use to fight tanks?'

'Down at the bottom, over there,' said Gol, his humourless grin bloodless in the white lights. 'Grenade launchers. After all, these tanks are only *Tjorny Arylo* – Russian Black Eagles weighing in at 50 tonnes apiece and sporting 125mm-calibre cannons. I've sent a message to Langan who was flying air support over Nigeria to come and give us some fucking heavy air weaponry in that bitch of a Comanche he uses . . . but he might not get here in time. If you have to shoot one of these Black Eagles, Carter, don't aim for the turret because there are no crew there; aim for the hull at the front.' Gol spat. 'Bastards are heavily protected. *And* they have automatic loading systems; every shell doesn't have to be manually loaded.'

'But why?' asked Natasha, confused.

Gol grinned again. 'To speed up the rate of fire,' he said bitterly.

'This is not my fucking day,' said Carter.

'*It never is, Brother,*' whispered Kade in his mind.

'So you are back?'

'*You don't think I would miss this for the world, do you?*'

'I thought you might have died in a hole, lonely and unloved.'

'*Such bitter words stab me through the heart. Now, be a good lad and take me to the guns. Big guns, and some bombs – it's a while since I've seen people burn.*'

'You have no soul,' thought Carter bitterly.

'*On the contrary,*' said Kade. '*I am part of yours.*'

Sunlight rolled into the valley, red tendrils dancing through the disturbed dust. It glanced and spilled from and through the orange-tree orchards. Occasionally, a monkey chattered.

The men and women of Spiral_F waited.

261

They waited for the Nex.

They waited for the signal.

Carter stood beside a huge six-wheeled Pig, a Sterling sub-machine gun in his hands. He hefted the automatic weapon thoughtfully, for it had been many years since he had used such heavy hardware, always relying more on his Browning, or at least a Glock or Walther PPK. Carter didn't like machine guns; he didn't agree with the principle of mass destruction. It went against his morals, such as they were.

Gol tossed a bottle of Coke to Natasha, then another to Carter. They cracked open the bottles and drank, Natasha keeping her eyes fixed on the small plasma screen that had been set up on a small stand. It showed the entrance to the canyon, the sweeping African vista beyond and the images relayed from one of the sentries' headsets.

Natasha sported DPM desert combats and boots. She held her sub-machine gun awkwardly, and Carter's gaze swept along the line at the nervous groups of men and women, many lounging around and against the protective armoured Pigs. He could read their faces, the fear, the apprehension, the realisation that their comfortable – top secret but comfortable – existence had suddenly been shattered.

'I hope they don't come,' said Natasha softly.

She moved to Carter and slumped down beside him, stretching her legs out. The scene was strange, alien, disjointed. Orange trees, a white-walled house with crawling plants and a bed of prettily coloured flowers, their hues radiant in the sunshine . . . and heavily armoured vehicles, rifles, machine guns, men and women in boots and combat clothing—

'They'll come,' he said, passing her his cigarette.

She shook her head. 'I'm giving up.'

'How are your wounds? Hell, girl, you were like a pin-cushion back in Scotland.'

'OK.' She smiled, but the smile was a mask for her nerves. 'The shoulder one gives me the most trouble. Like some bastard sticking a knife in me every time I move my arm. How about you?'

'Ribs still grinding together.' Carter grinned. He held up his neighbour-strapped fingers. 'At least these don't stop me pulling a trigger and I have a horrible feeling that that skill will be needed real soon . . .'

They waited.

'How long?' asked Carter.

Gol shrugged. 'Ten minutes, maybe less.'

Carter checked his ammo and licked his dry lips. 'I fucking hate these situations; I prefer to work alone.'

'We know,' said Nats, glancing up. 'This time we have little choice.'

Shanaz appeared from the alloy entrance leading underground; she carried a small optical disk in one hand and was smiling broadly. She tossed the disk to Gol.

'There you go, boss.'

'All data transferred?'

'Yeah – it'd make Feuchter weep.'

Carter's head snapped around at the sound of the name, his eyes bright. 'Feuchter? I left that motherfucker to die in Germany.'

'He is not dead; far from it, Carter. Spiral_F has had its eye on Feuchter for quite some time; he's wrapped up in this Spiral QIII charade tighter than a first-time whore's legs around a sailor's back. He's head of Operations and operates out of Rub al'Khali, in Saudi Arabia – but, again, we are grasping at straws when we try to discover how his game is implemented. We suspect that he has links to the Spiral splinter group, but there is nothing solid. He is too good – he evades watchers, the fucker is almost untouchable. And since our fucking HQ was blown away it's pretty hard to check out such facts now. The whole comm SP1Network is screwed. Spiral has been fucked up; and, sadly, I believe this situation can only get worse.'

Carter rubbed at the stubble on his chin. 'Feuchter,' he said softly. 'That fucker is definitely a player in this game, I can sense it in my bones. He was ready to kill me back in Germany. He has obviously become more reckless . . .'

'Nobody had time to act on your report,' said Natasha.

Carter nodded, his eyes becoming hooded.

Natasha's gaze returned to the plasma screen.

'What do you know about Spiral_Q?' A gleam had appeared in Carter's eyes; Feuchter brought back bad memories and he knew that one day – one day – he would meet the man again. They would have a little chat. They would dance together. They would remember the good old times in a symbiotic embrace . . .

Gol frowned. 'The QIII is under development in Rub al'Khali under the banner of the Spiral_Q Division, rumoured to be located just south of Ash Shu'aybah in Saudi Arabia. Some of the design specifications were leaked recently over the Net and there have been some very pissed-off people . . . especially since we also acquired the schematics for this extremely dangerous processor.' Gol laughed bitterly. 'After the Nex have paid us a visit, we could do with nipping over to say hello to Feuchter and the other QIII developers. I'm sure they would have something interesting to contribute to our research. But considering the game they are playing, that place must be wired up tighter than a virgin's—'

'Yes, daddy,' pouted Natasha smartly. 'Remember that there are ladies present.'

'Yeah, ladies armed with guns and quite capable of dropping dangerous men and women without regard for where their brains and bones scatter . . .'

Natasha made a rude noise before turning back to the monitor.

'Shit,' hissed Gol, sitting up suddenly. 'Something is wrong.' His gaze flickered to the plasma screen – but there was nothing, nothing visible, no Nex sweeping down, no armies of tanks lumbering over the horizon.

'We're still safe,' said Natasha uncertainly.

'No, no, it's this. A PB: panic burst.' Gol pulled free a small black device on which a red light was glowing. Gol licked his lips, his stare coming up to Carter and Natasha. 'We only use this for a breach . . . The fuckers must have out-wired our electronics . . . but how? Fuck, fuck! Look, if anything should happen we have a rendezvous point for emergencies. The coordinates are 551.222.222.340; the ECube can patch them through, but remember that ECube security has been breached – you could be transmitting to the enemy.'

Carter pulled free his Browning and hoisted the SMG . . .

His mouth was suddenly a desert canyon floor.

He felt a stirring deep within his brain; like a lizard uncurling from a century of sleep around a rock.

Bullets screamed, a line of them smashing an inch above Carter's head and denting holes along the flank of an armoured vehicle. There was a *slap slap* of impacts in flesh and a soldier sitting atop a Pig, smoking and nursing his gun, was cut in half in a violent spray of blood. The top half of his body was punched out of sight behind the huge vehicle as his legs dropped, twitching and drooling trails of crimson to the ground.

'Down!' screamed Carter as gunfire erupted all

265

around – and he suddenly *knew*, remembered the digital avoidance of his own network back in Scotland, how a single Nex had evaded all his home-made electronic traps . . . and the bastards had done the same here – they'd bypassed the security networks and were now—

Inside the canyon.

Why use tanks when subterfuge could carry the game off more smoothly?

And Carter knew: the tanks were a bluff. To draw their attention. After all, who *wouldn't* hear a fucking tank coming?

Carter hit the dirt hard, Natasha beside him.

Gol slammed against a Pig as engines roared all around and machine-gun bursts echoed and screamed among the fumes. Carter glanced left and his eyes bulged like marbles from their sockets. A swarm of about a hundred Nex emerged from the trees and sped with incredible agility across the killing ground between the line of Pigs and the orchards—

Machine guns thundered.

'Aim for their heads!' bellowed Gol and, ducking low, charged behind a Pig and towards the wall of the white house. Carter rolled onto his belly, took aim with the SMG, and fired a burst. A Nex was picked up and slammed into the earth with a hole where the face had been. Carter chewed his lip grimly. To one side a Pig revved and charged at the Nex, guns blasting from behind the slits in the windows. The hefty front iron bumper smashed into two Nex and heavy wheels ploughed them into the ground, crushing their limbs and torsos. There was a *click*, followed by a concussive *boom*. The Pig was picked up and tossed spinning into the air to skid onto its side, slamming into a tree. Fire licked from the insides. Black smoke rolled skyward.

266

Carter could hear men screaming.

Insanity followed. The Nex came from everywhere, charging at the Pigs with guns roaring. More detonations sounded and Carter and Natasha backed towards the white-walled house that they had originally thought was Gol's home. Both were firing, SMGs clattering in their grips. Carter sent bullets scything across a line of Nex – but they did not go down. Their attention was diverted his way and chips of stone and plaster were chewed from the walls behind him.

'Fuck,' he screamed, dropping to his knees and fumbling with the Sterling's magazine. The Nex charged – but were cut off by a rumbling Pig that ploughed into them, scattering bodies, tossing them high in the air like limp rag dolls.

They hit the ground hard.

Most rolled to their feet.

'I'm here!' came Kade's sudden triumphant crow.

'You are not needed!' snapped Carter within the asylum of his mind. He wiped more sweat from his eyes, wiped his hands on his shorts and fired another four-round burst into the Nex, who were shooting from the edges of the trees – many had been forced back by the sheer volume of projectiles spewing from the Pigs.

'You need me Carter; let me, let me do what I do best—'

'Get the fuck out of my brain, Kade!'

Carter blinked.

Something dark and ominous crept like a nuclear winter across his soul: superimposed across the beauty before him was a dark shroud like nothing he had ever seen before and his senses flowed, time slowed, everything went—

Black and white—

'We have to get back, get back inside the house . . .' he hissed.

Natasha nodded, gun clasped tight.

They started to creep along the wall. Bullets were coming from all directions, and several Pigs were churning about in front of the house, their guns thundering. The bodies of men and women littered the ground. A Pig wreck billowed thick black smoke.

'What is it?'

'The tanks are coming,' said Carter bitterly.

Suddenly, distant gunshots ceased. Machine-gun fire rattled to a halt. They heard the distant roaring of engines; an explosion boomed down the canyon, deep and rumbling, reverberating from the valley walls.

There came more exchanges of gunfire.

The sun beat down. Carter wiped sweat from his brow. His mouth was dry – too dry – and his ribs and several other minor cuts were nagging at him. Worst of all was his nose – broken one too many times, it impeded his breathing and the pain annoyed him.

There was a *boom* of heavy-calibre.

A Pig had been positioned between the trees – suddenly it was gone, disintegrated, a thousand panels of twisted steel spat up and out like a giant exploded grenade . . . a black flaming mechanical carcass sat where the vehicle had been, three wheels attached to a fire-raped dented chassis. Carter shook his head, dropped his SMG and made a grab for Natasha's hand.

'This is fucking insane – we have to leave.'

'Where's my father?'

'It's too fucking late for that! Come *on*!'

'I don't want to die like this,' said Natasha.

'I don't want to die at all,' said Carter.

They sprinted for the door. Carter ducked as a *phat phat phat* smacked against the tiles above him, describing a diagonal down the wall. There was a scream to his left

268

as a woman was punched flailing from her feet, scrabbling at her throat, blood pumping between useless grappling fingers, her gun and this war suddenly forgotten in her bright hot agony. She squirmed for a moment and Carter leaped up and emptied a full magazine into the charging mass, which spread out as if welcoming his bullets—

Natasha screamed.

Carter whirled – but too late, a figure was upon him . . . Natasha's gun rattled in her hands and gunfire echoed inside Carter's head and all around . . . he slapped hard against the dirt, and for a second thought he was dead. Carter kicked out, heaved the dead body from him, rolled to see madness exploding around him. The Nex had charged again, and the men and women of Spiral_F were being slaughtered.

Carter pulled free the trapped SMG and shot the Nex – which had cornered Natasha – in the back of the head, watching the brains emerge in a spray and the figure toppling to reveal Natasha's shocked visage staring dumbly at him. He reached forward, grabbed her, screamed, 'Where the fuck is Gol?'

Natasha did not speak—

'Are you hurt? I said, *are you fucking hurt?*'

A figure ran at them – Natasha whimpered – the SMG in the figure's hands lifted a fraction and Carter could see the finger on the trigger, sensed the applied pressure, pushed Natasha away and squeezed his own SMG's trigger at the same time as he dived—

Bullets skimmed past Carter's face, so close that he felt the breeze of their passing; a line of bullets caught the figure and slammed it into the air where it spun for a moment, then landed twisted and dead.

'Come on.' Carter snatched Natasha's hand and dragged her after him. To one side he could see a small

269

group of men kicking at a Nex on the ground; two Nex leaped to its aid and there was a short and very bloody exchange. Carter sprinted to the house and stopped suddenly in the doorway. He checked behind him—

He wasn't sure how many were still alive – how many of Spiral_F, or how many of the enemy – as he glanced down at Natasha, who had been dragged along behind him in his mad flight for temporary safety away from the gun battle. There were spots of blood on her face, and Carter could feel her hands shaking. He looked into her eyes and said slowly, 'Don't panic, Nats. Come on – I need you focused. We are not going to die – I promise you I will protect you—'

'How can . . .'

'Shh.' He put his finger against her lips. Then he leaned forward and kissed her softly, whispering again, 'I promise you I will protect you—'

'Liar . . .'

Carter heaved Kade away with such a blast of mental anger and hatred and violence that he felt Kade spat into a dark infinity – and calmness settled on his mind, an insane sort of calmness which he had only rarely experienced before in highly dangerous combat situations—

His brain ran to codes, to numbers—

Everything was clear—

Black and white—

Logical.

No emotion no panic no fear—

It was what had marked him out for the Demolition Squads in the first place.

'Follow me.'

Carter led the way swiftly, Natasha close behind him. They entered the house through a narrow bullet-chewed doorway; behind them rattles of gunfire still burst through the orchards, decimating the trees. But the noises of violence were growing less. Spiral_F had been overrun.

Carter gripped his Browning tightly with his free hand and inched forward down the corridor towards the bright light on the other side of the room. He wasn't even sure where the SMG had gone, which episode of the insanity had removed the weapon from him.

His hands were slippery with blood. Was it his own? Or that of a Nex?

Nex, spat his mind.

What the fuck had happened to the world?

Carter paused. Something in his soul howled into his consciousness, a warning as—

Three Nex came smashing through a huge patio-type window in a sudden flurry of movement that shattered the stillness. Their masked heads were down as a shower of glass vomited into the room directly in Carter's path, scattering across the floor like diamonds tossed at his feet. As their boots hit the tiled floor and their SMGs lifted, Carter's Browning snapped up and he squeezed the trigger – bullets ripped across the short space—

Carter leaped towards the figures. Two were smashed immediately from their feet, clawing at bullets in their faces. The third leaped at him as—

The Browning clicked on empty.

The dead man's click.

The kiss of death.

A fist slammed forward, an inch from Carter's nose and he twisted, left elbow coming around with incredible velocity to crack against the Nex's head, hammering the killer's head down onto his rising knee which connected with bone-jarring force.

But the figure still managed to slam a fist into Carter's chest.

He was lifted vertically, pain smashing through his entire body, vomit splashing from his lips. He seemed to halt in mid-air, then fell suddenly and hit the ground hard with a dull *thud*, groaning in agony. The Nex stepped over him, moving towards Natasha—

Carter rolled over, foetal, disabled . . .

—A punch to the heart . . . an induced heart attack—

Natasha cowered in front of the masked figure that was poised, ready to strike, a cobra with a fixed stare. The Nex stopped, swiftly bent to retrieve an SMG and pointed the dark emotionless eye at Natasha's face—

Carter, unable to breathe, almost unable to move, fumbled in a time-vacuum to slot a fresh mag into his gun; then he dragged the Browning into his line of sight. He felt his hand, wavering, felt his vision warp for a split second and nausea screamed through him and he pointed the Browning and time had slowed and his calmness and his serenity had gone and this was Natasha, Natasha his love and she was going to die with hot metal in her brain and it would be all his fault and he had promised—

Promised to protect her—

Promised to keep her alive—

Seven bullets hissed past the Nex's ear.

The figure whirled – but Carter kept on firing and the figure was suddenly jerked and kicked up and back, holed and smashed and bleeding, to twist and flip and land in a heap on top of Natasha. She screamed, a long low animal sound. Carter felt the Browning click on empty and he crawled to his knees—

'*Behind* . . .' came Kade's warning.

Carter rolled, fast, faster than any human had a right to move. A line of bullets tore a strip of smashed tiles into the air in a cloud of brittle dust. Carter's eyes fixed on the swaying figure of a Nex, chest torn open, a slick glossy organ visible through the scorched cloth, blood soaking the grey clothing and falling in heavy slow drips to the remaining tiles. The Nex's cheek hung as a loose flap of skin.

Carter spun to his feet, and leaped.

The SMG barked once – and was silenced.

Carter took the bullet; it sliced across his side just below his ribs, a twisted trajectory tearing a path through flesh and leaving a line of red that spewed blood to soak Carter's clothing. The force of the blow punched and slammed him around, spinning him and sending his face crashing forward to hit the ground.

There was no pain.

That's fucking bad, he thought.

No pain is bad.

Enemy . . .

Got to kill—

Where are you, Kade? Where the fuck are you when I need you?

Don't want to die . . .

Pain . . .

Don't want to die . . .

He tried to rise, but only managed to turn his head as he slumped forward. He lifted his hand in front of his face and saw that it was coated in a deep red that looked the wrong colour. It looked bad. It looked dangerous; the colour of something that shouldn't see the light of day.

Fuck, mused his brain, suddenly calm.

His hand lowered. The torn bleeding *holed* Nex, in slow motion, fitted a fresh mag to the SMG and he watched it carrying out the action, swaying in its own world of pain but with nothing showing in those cold copper eyes. Carter could do nothing. The Nex stepped

273

lightly forward, intense stare boring down into him and he recognised that gaze, from back in Scotland, from back at his house when it had been so rudely invaded—

'Nice to see you again,' he croaked.

'Mr Carter. It has been a pleasure.'

The soft asexual voice held no pain. No fucking pain? screeched Carter's confusion-riddled mind.

The finger squeezed the trigger—

And the Nex's masked face exploded.

Carter watched, dumbstruck, as a huge hole appeared in a jagged shower to the tune of metallic screaming. Brain, skull, blood rained down on him with gentle *pattering* sounds. The figure folded slowly and neatly to the floor and was still.

Carter's focus switched: from the corpse in the foreground to *behind* the corpse where Natasha stood, an SMG in her hands, a faint horrified smile on her lips.

'You owe me one,' she whispered weakly.

Carter coughed, and rolled onto his back. 'I need a pad of cloth, or something,' he wheezed, forcing himself into a sitting position. Warmth had spread across his torso and down to his crotch.

Natasha knelt by his side and dipped her hands into his lifeblood. Her gaze met his. She swiftly tore part of her shirt free and applied the pad and suddenly a world of pain fired into Carter's brain and screamed at him in the huge echoing operatic hall of his skull—

And the headache pain in his skull, in his brain: it returned to burn.

Returned to burn bad.

'It's not my fucking day,' he croaked.

Carter struggled to his feet, the pad of cloth clamped to his side. Natasha bent, retrieved his Browning and helped him to reload the weapon with blood-slippery bullets. They both took SMGs from the dead bodies of the Nex, slinging the weapons over their shoulders and then taking deep, deep breaths.

'What now?' hissed Natasha.

'We need to find Gol.'

'He could be anywhere . . . it was so crazy . . .'

They moved slowly through the house, up the stairs, to Gol's study. There had been a battle in the room and there were several blood trails but no bodies. Blood was splattered up the walls as if some mad artist with a loaded paintbrush had been let loose and told to inflict contemporary art; Gol was not there.

'What were the emergency coordinates?' asked Natasha softly, her shaking hands keeping the door to the study covered with the SMG.

'551.222.222.340,' came the pain-filled response from Carter, whose face had gone grey, eyes purple-ringed, nose crusted with blood. He gripped his Browning, but held the weapon as if he didn't really understand what it was . . . he had lost blood, was weak, was fading fast . . . losing the will to play the game.

Natasha gritted her teeth. Pulled free her ECube. Patched in the coordinates . . .

'Come on,' she said, finding a new level of strength, feeling adrenalin surge through her battered weary blood-speckled frame once more. She sprinted to the window: outside, the world still raged . . . black smoke drifted on the horizon from a myriad of destroyed and wounded Pigs. She saw a tank, a Russian Black Eagle, squat among the trees, its huge camouflaged turret pointing their way, the muzzle of the mammoth gun a truly awe- and terror-inspiring sight. Machine guns rattled, a savage exchange between two groups.

'Shit. We have to get out of here.' Natasha allowed

Carter to rest some of his weight on her, and they moved slowly – painfully slowly – back through the house.

'This is madness,' she said.

'Madness,' agreed Carter, coughing.

'I hope it will be worth it,' she muttered bitterly.

'It never is,' said Carter, drooling blood.

They stopped just behind the doorway, Carter leaning heavily against the wall bathed in sunlight. The fragrance from the orchards smelled good, even mingled with a wave of cordite. Natasha found it hard to believe that a battle was taking place here – in this paradise . . . and that her life hung in the balance, suspended by a delicate thread of Fate.

Her gaze roved, searching for the Nex—

Searching for the fast-moving deadly killers . . . they were in the trees, behind the tanks, and as she watched a group sprinted towards a Pig, which mowed them down in a spray of blood, its heavy machine-gun barrels smoking.

How many are left? she thought.

Many of the Pigs had gone; Nats could see another two tanks, which had eased down from the canyon mouth after the battle had begun. Gunfire echoed in the distance, followed by more explosive rattles echoing within the shadow-haunted depths of the trees.

Her gaze snapped left and came to settle on a Jeep Cherokee. 4.0 litre. Big and sturdy; dented and bullet-pocked, but it was deliciously—

Near.

A hundred paces.

Only a hundred paces.

Under the heavy-calibre eyes of the Black Eagles and the machine-gun muzzles of the Nex.

Can we run faster than their bullets? she thought.

Our lives depend on it . . .

'Come on, Carter,' Natasha said. 'The jeep. You see it?'

Carter lifted his head. 'Yes,' he croaked.

'I need you to run. Can you do that?'

'Yes.'

She took a final look at the tanks; huge squat metal machines, painted roughly, their torsos dented and showing signs of abuse. They were silent, engines dead.

And the Nex . . .

She could see five groups, all with their attention diverted by groups of Spiral_F, or Pigs. Another group were setting up some equipment at the edge of the trees. Natasha and Carter stepped away from the sanctuary.

They ran.

It took an eternity . . .

Ten paces. Each step saw a splash of red erupt from Carter's side as a flap of flesh opened with a jolt, blood marking his passage against the sand.

Twenty paces.

Natasha spotted the five emerging Nex at the edge of the orchard, spotted their positions and their glinting weapons. 'Fu—' she managed as they opened fire. Natasha screamed, her head ducking low, Carter suddenly an incredibly heavy and cumbersome weight chained around her neck and dragging her down down down into the black depths of death and oblivion – bullets kicked up dirt around her feet, some whizzed past and ricocheted off the stone of the house in tiny spurts of dust.

Natasha pushed on.

The Nex ceased their firing.

They charged, moving swiftly and silently over the ground towards the staggering couple. Natasha, teeth gritted, urged herself to greater efforts, almost dragging the semi-conscious Carter with her.

Seventy paces. Eighty paces . . .

Ninety—

She could pick out the copper eyes of the Nex—

And realised.

They look the same, she thought.

They all look the fucking same . . .

She reached the Cherokee, wrenched open the door and pushed Carter into the cabin. The lead Nex leaped, boots slapping the bonnet of the Cherokee and sliding towards her. With a yelp, Natasha dived in and slammed the door – which jammed open, three inches from closing—

She saw the fingers, then the masked face appear. The door was pulled away from her blood-slippery grip—

Natasha's boot slammed into the Nex's face, three, four times – the Nex fell back and she pulled at the Cherokee's door with all her might. It slammed shut with a heavy final *click*. She looked down in horror at the three severed fingers in the footwell.

It didn't scream, she realised.

It didn't make a fucking sound . . .

The other Nex arrived – leaping at the vehicle—

Natasha slammed down the central locking. All doors locked – a Nex started beating at the door, then hammered a fist through the side window, shattering its glass and scattering it over the inside of the cab. Natasha brought the stolen SMG around and held the trigger down hard; bullets spat out through the smashed window and into the Nex's body and already she was turning the ignition. The huge 4.0-litre engine roared into life as her boot stomped down and a Nex was caught suddenly against the grille and bonnet, buckled, tossed beneath the vehicle and wrapped around the spinning prop-shaft . . . The SMG, still screaming, suddenly clicked on an empty mag and Natasha dropped the weapon on the seat next to the crumpled, wheezing body of Carter and dragged on the steering wheel. The Cherokee roared towards the orange trees with three Nex sprinting after it—

It sped beneath the fruit-laden branches, straight down the dirt track. Natasha laughed out loud as a fresh breeze came blowing through the smashed window and cooled the sweat of desperation on her face. 'Carter?' she screamed. 'You OK, Carter? You still alive?'

There was a distant sound. A *crump*.

As if obeying some unconscious reflex, Carter reached over and dragged hard on the steering wheel. The Cherokee slewed from the trail; there was a painful metal scream, and the trail just behind them erupted in a shower of dirt. Stones and shrapnel pounded and howled around the Cherokee, which rocked on the concussion of the blast.

Carter looked up, smiled weakly at Natasha, then closed his eyes as sunlight played through the windscreen and illuminated his face and he could think of nothing except—

Pain.

All-consuming pain.

'Get me to a doctor and I just might live,' he wheezed.

'We're not out of the woods yet,' snapped Natasha.

Carter grinned – his blood-splashed face a caked mask of horror and destruction.

Natasha increased the speed – roaring in a burst of screaming engine noise out of the orange-tree orchards, bursting free of their heady fragrance and cool shade and into the reality of the sun-baked African landscape. The end of the canyon rushed towards them and there, ahead of them, stood a small group of Nex. The Cherokee, now touching a hundred m.p.h., hit the ridge and bullets thumped along its flanks and the wheels disengaged from the ground and it soared—

Natasha ducked.

All she could see was sky.

'Fuuu-ck . . .' she hissed as the Cherokee hurtled glinting through the air. A glance in the rear-view mirror showed nothing behind . . .

The vehicle came down like a plane coming in to land—

The suspension compressed, bottoming out with terrifyingly loud *bangs*, and Natasha was smashed upwards, hands slipping from the wheel, head hammering the roof of the cab so hard that her teeth slammed together, leaving her mouth swilling with blood and shards of tooth . . . The Cherokee kangarooed for a few moments, obeying the laws of physics as it slewed around in the scrub, tyres eating dirt and sand and bushes until Natasha gripped the wheel once more and dragged it onto course, foot stamping hard against the accelerator and dragging the roaring vehicle around in a broad arc, heading up towards the red rocky hills to the right of Gol's devastated blasted routed Spiral_F Operations Centre—

'What the fuck hit me?' groaned Carter.

Natasha spat a mouthful of blood out of the window. She blinked rapidly, quelling the spinning sensation in her head. 'Just stay down, my love,' she managed. 'You really don't want to know.'

Natasha accelerated, tyres thumping over bushes and scrub.

She followed no road – she made her own.

Something clanged and thumped under the vehicle – but Natasha did not care. She fumbled free the ECube and it guided her; it didn't matter that their position wasn't secure – it was obvious to anybody who cared to look.

She pressed the accelerator to the floor and her hands shook madly on the heavily vibrating steering wheel and they headed upwards and finally joined a dirt track leading towards the rendezvous and, Natasha hoped, escape—

'I hope this rendezvous exists,' she muttered.

She checked her teeth in the rear-view mirror, cursing their chipped edges, vanity still a reflex despite her nearly fatal experience. As she moved the mirror back into position she saw them—

Three trucks.

Hammering along behind her—

'For fuck's sake,' she hissed. 'Will they never stop?'

She urged the Cherokee on; the pursuing trucks – whatever make they were – were incredibly powerful. They didn't gain, but she could not lose them either. They sped along in the sunlight, huge red dust-trails in their wake, tyres and suspension thumping and rocks and trees and bushes flashing by to either side—

In a cloud of dust the Cherokee hammered up the incline and towards the location indicated by the blip on the ECube . . . towards the emergency rendezvous set up by Gol – who had mysteriously disappeared.

'I hope you're all right, father,' Natasha thought soberly. 'I hope you're OK.'

Shanaz froze. A figure was crouched in the tunnel, an SMG levelled at her.

After the hectic bloody battle out front, Shanaz had been separated from her group; she had fled the bullets, down the alloy ramp and into the depths of Spiral_F deep under the ground . . .

That had been the plan. To meet; to regroup if the shit hit the fan.

And the shit had most definitely battered the fan to pieces.

Shanaz stared at the shadowed figure. It had to be a Nex; it had to be. She cursed the dim lighting down here in the depths . . .

Slowly, Shanaz lifted her hands in the air.

The AK47 was beside her, digging into her ribs.

She did not glance at it.

'What do you want me to do?' she asked softly, trying not to antagonise the armed intruder.

The masked face tilted; eyes scanned the room.

The figure stood from its crouch. A fluid blur.

There came a *hiss* of exhaled breath.

The SMG roared, and Shanaz was slammed backwards against a computer, blood splashing up the rock walls, the bullets cutting a line straight up her chest and slamming into her skull. Shards of skull bone spun free and she slumped slack across a chair, limp and dead, her brain and exposed organs glistening in the weak glow of the bulbs.

Suddenly, silence reigned.

The assassin's head snapped left; the SMG moved to cover the opening of a tunnel.

Jahmal sprinted into view, large round face changing from a happy smiling visage into a snarl of rage as his eyes fell across Shanaz and he stumbled to a confused halt in the centre of the bunker chamber. He spun, checking the dark deserted tunnels.

'Shanaz?' he screamed, stumbling towards her. His hand reached out, fingers grasping her smashed jaw and sliding in the blood that soaked her smooth skin. 'Shanaz!'

Tears rolled down his ebony cheeks.

The bullets cut into his back and Jahmal didn't even know what had hit him.

Marcus licked his lips and closed his eyes, listening. He stood in the corridor, the AK47 sweat-slippery in his hands and he knew; knew that death had come and whoever was the aggressor had killed both Shanaz and Jahmal. They were good; they were fast and they were efficient.

Get a grip, screamed his brain.

He took several deep breaths, feeling sweat soak him beneath his dreads, prickling and itching.

He moved forward; not towards the gunfire, but away. He had heard the shots; perhaps fifty rounds in all had been fired. This wasn't assassination; this was butchery. He had heard Jahmal's cries; understood their intensity; knew the man – his friend, his comrade – was dead.

Marcus halted, dreadlocks swaying.

There were two tunnels before him.

'Marcus!' came the distant cry.

Marcus frowned; Gol?

There came another cry, this time of pain.

Gol? Injured?

Marcus moved forward, still cautious, twitching at every sigh of a breeze in the tunnels. He came to a round low room, dim-lit with four tunnels leading from the chamber.

He halted.

He turned, turned again—

And saw the figure. His eyes widened. The barrel of the AK47 swung around but it was too late and the SMG was already pointing at him and he saw the gentle flex of muscle and tendon and could read the figure; could read its amorality.

His eyes closed—

A great sigh escaped his lips.

And the game was over.

Langan was seated on the edge of a rock, gaze locked on the distant canyon below as the battle raged on. He watched the plumes of smoke reaching for the sky and shook his head in disbelief; Spiral_F's air defences were still operational.

The Comanche was useless.

Awesomely powerful, but useless.

'Why didn't you switch them off, Gol?'

Behind Langan squatted the Comanche – still in jungle camouflage – its engines idle. All systems were on-line, primed and ready to fire; he could have her in the air in thirty seconds if he had to – and Langan knew that when the time came he would have to move fast.

He heard the screaming engine . . . and then engines. Plural.

Company.

Langan ran to the Comanche and climbed aboard – he suddenly had a bad feeling and he primed the engines, fired them, listened to injectors and turbos whining as the twin LHTec spun up the rotors. He watched the gauges roll smoothly into life. He armed the weapons systems and rested his chin on his hands, staring from the cockpit at the stretch of road that led from the crest of the rise and straight towards this little secluded area where he had chosen, thoughtfully, to hide.

The Cherokee leaped into view, sped towards the Comanche and veered to one side. Brakes engaged and the Cherokee left long parallel grooves in the sand. Three heavy speeding trucks appeared in hot pursuit; Natasha leaped from the Cherokee, dragging Carter with her . . . he was stumbling, practically unconscious and a little delirious, unaware of what was actually happening or where he was, or even what his fucking name was . . .

'They the enemy?' shouted Langan calmly over the rising whine of the rotors.

'Fuck 'em hard,' screamed Natasha.

Langan flicked a switch; his HIDSS helmet sprang to life. He calmly selected a target and the General Electric MiniGun sped up and hit five thousand revs. With calm smooth movements Langan released the payload of bullets.

Thousands of heavy-calibre rounds roared across the track, smashed through the trucks and sent them ploughing into one another. The Nex inside them became nothing more than merged blood-pulps, purple bloodied sacks of flesh and smashed bone. One truck exploded, fire roaring up into the sky, small pieces of burning metal describing arcs and then thumping into the sand. Another truck rolled, lame and limping, towards the Comanche.

There was a gentle whine as the MiniGun rolled down, metallic *clacks* rattling through the sudden calm.

Langan leaped down from the cockpit.

'Where's Gol?'

'No idea,' said Natasha. 'But I think we need to move fast!'

Langan helped Natasha to get the wounded, groaning form of Carter into the rear of the cockpit. 'I'm sorry, but it's going to be a tight squeeze. It's only really designed for two.'

'We'll manage,' said Natasha. 'Have you got medical supplies?'

'All on board. Let's get moving.'

The rotors spun up, and with a roar the Comanche leaped into the sky and sped across the clear blue, sun glinting from the flashing rotors, the aircraft's proximity missile-warning systems screaming at Langan. The engines howled with power as the Comanche skirted the valley and orange-tree orchards where the battle still raged.

Natasha found the appropriate panel and slid it back. She took out the medical supplies, removed sterile seals and gave Carter an injection of morphine that eased his pain and knocked him out. His colour was bad and she hoped he wouldn't need blood . . . She squeezed Carter to one side of the narrow aperture in which she was supposed to work, and to the background music of the rotors thumping she struggled to remove his jacket, and then cut away his shirt around the wound gouged by the spinning bullet.

'I don't see much I can do down there,' said Langan. 'The air defences are still armed; even I'm not stupid enough to take on ground-to-air missiles. No fucking way.'

He took the Comanche lower; they swept wide around the orange orchards, the down draught from the rotors making trees and bushes sway and hiss. A few token shots followed the copter but it was moving far too swiftly. The Comanche lifted over the rim of the valley, banked steeply and Langan looked to Natasha for instructions.

'What shall we do?'

'Make another pass; Gol must be down there somewhere. If any fucker can get out alive, it's Gol.' They returned, sweeping as low as Langan dared with tanks in the vicinity. The Comanche described broad circles several more times. There was no sign of Gol, nor of any other fleeing survivors for that matter. Machine guns were still firing, but as they circled the exchanges of fire became more and more sporadic.

'Can you see your scanner?' shouted back Langan.

'Yeah,' replied Natasha sombrely.

'See the yellow dots? Identified and tagged as Sikorsky Apaches. Probably bringing in more Nex. The reinforcements have arrived and I don't really want to be hanging around when they turn up. Look.' He pointed to a dial. 'The air defences have just gone down – shit, just in time for the Apaches. I think the Nex must be controlling them, using the defences to keep me out of play. I think they underestimated Gol's little group, don't you?'

'I don't call several hundred Nex and a load of tanks *underestimation*. So, what can we do now?'

'You're the boss,' said Langan. 'I just follow Gol's instructions. And seeing that you are his daughter . . . well . . .'

'How did you know that?'

'We have this wonderful thing called communication.'

'Oh.'

'How's Carter?'

'Out for the moment. I'm just glad the bullet passed through him – I'm not sure I could remove one if it was lodged in his body.'

'Don't get blood on the seats.'

'I don't think he's got much left.'

Natasha removed the blood-soaked padding. Cut free more shirt. Grimaced at what she saw; she took some tweezers and moved Carter to allow her to see inside the wound where scorched pieces of shirt were lodged.

'I've got something on the scanner.'

'What is it?'

'Five figures. Running . . . across the top of one of the ridges . . .'

'Head for them. Let's snoop.'

The Comanche banked, rising straight towards the glinting sunlight. Like a bullet it hurtled across the sky and then suddenly dropped, gliding in a descending arc towards—

A high ridge of red rock overlooking a fast-flowing narrow river, deep within a red-walled valley; a rocky V-shaped crevasse that went on down for ever.

Natasha could see distant figures, sprinting over the rocks—

And she recognised Gol.

'He's on his own,' said Langan.

'Can you shoot his pursuers?'

'At this speed? I'll cut the whole fucking group in half! Gol's too close to them . . . I can't distinguish the targets, not with a fucking MiniGun anyway . . .'

The Comanche screamed over the ridge and banked at a distance, rotors flashing silver against the sun; and then they returned for a second pass. Gol was sprinting ahead of four pursuing Nex. He was unarmed . . . and carrying something in his clenched fist that sparkled with rainbow colours and then—

In a flash they were over and gone.

The Comanche banked once more – a distant whirring insect to those on the ground—

'If I touch down, we could be overrun,' hissed Langan. 'They've got SMGs and we've got a man down.'

'We've got to help him!' screamed Natasha. 'We've got to fucking help him!'

Gol, sweat pouring down his body, glanced up as the Comanche roared overhead a second time. He was as good as dead, he knew, but the small optic disk he carried in his fist could not fall into the wrong hands . . .

Could not.

The schematics were slowing the enemy down – buying Spiral more time. And as Gol had said before, they were the enemies' Achilles heel. Their weakness.

How could the enemy hope to rule the world using the QIII if there was a second QIII there to counter all the commands? There to push a stick through the wheel of military progress? There to *fuck it up* for them? No, they needed the schematics.

Gol did not glance behind him. But he could hear them, hear their boots on the rock. Gol considered himself a fit man, but the bastards had chased him for miles; most of it uphill; most of it across rock. The Nex had known exactly who they were after right from the beginning of the battle; they had cornered Gol, sent him fleeing with bullets at his tail, like a rat down a maze, separating him from the other members of Spiral_F—

They had known.

Known what he carried.

A grim smile twisted his lips. He pounded on. Gol's endurance had been pushed to its limit and he could feel his body consuming itself, using reserves that he had never dreamed he had – the large man did not know how he still managed to put one foot in front of the other—

For the past mile the Nex had slowly wound him in, like a big fish on a line. Now they were mere feet behind him and panic settled like a demon across his soul. What to do? What to fucking do?

Why hadn't they shot him?

They knew; knew he was a key to the schematics encryption – the key to unlocking everything inscribed on the optic disk. With him dead, it would take them a long time to crack – days, maybe . . . but alive, and tortured?

Mere minutes. He had seen what they could do.

He shivered. He did not want to be caught by the Nex. Better to fucking *die*, he thought.

His boots thumped on rock.

His angle of ascent altered.

There was a shout behind him as the Nex realised what was happening—

Gol pounded up to the ridge and in silence, without looking down, leaped with all his might. Gloved hands brushed against his back. A Nex followed him, not from choice but from speed and momentum.

Gol, legs still pumping, sailed out over the abyss.

He kept the disk tight in his fist.

There were no final words. No heroic shouts. Gol merely clamped his jaw tight in the throes of bowel-wrenching fear as the world opened up before him . . . so large . . . so bright . . .

And he knew; this was the first time he had truly *seen*.

The first time he had truly *felt*.

And life felt so, so good.

The wind roared through his beard.

Red rock flashed past his tear-blurred vision.

Gol fell.

'No!' screamed Natasha.

The Comanche banked once more; the MiniGun screamed and the Nex on the mountain ridge were cut in half – it all happened so fast that they didn't even know what hit them.

'Go down, to the river,' she commanded.

'The walls are too narrow,' said Langan softly. 'I can't take this beast down there; the rotors would smash into the rock.'

'Do it!'

'We will fucking die,' snapped Langan.

Natasha went silent. Dead silent. Langan risked a glance back. He could see her tears. 'You need to focus, Natasha,' he said softly. 'Get Carter sewn up.'

'Yes,' she whispered. 'Sewn up. Be strong. Yes.'

'It's what Gol would want.'

'Yes.'

Langan flew the Comanche along the ridge and then dropped towards the river when the walls widened and dropped with the contours of the land. The river, wide and fast-flowing, showed no signs of life. For a while the Comanche cruised up and down the banks, searching; but Gol had gone.

'We can't search for ever,' said Langan eventually, drained, exhausted.

'I know. Just a few more minutes.'

Rotors thumping, the Comanche circled and paced and searched. Finally, it veered off, climbing steeply, and then headed south, away from the valley, away from the river and away from Kenya.

The snowy peaks of Kilimanjaro glowed in the distance, majestic and mighty, domineering and eternal.

'Take me away from this place,' whispered Natasha.

The Nex walked slowly into the chamber; another two stood beside the black body bag that had been unzipped to reveal the riddled body of the smashed female Nex within.

The first Nex glanced down, then removed the dead female's mask. Copper eyes looked without apparent emotion at the prostrate figure; a hand reached out, touched the bullet holes, moved lower towards the visible punctured organs and the yellow of spilled torn fat.

'What shall we do with the body?' came a soft voice.

'Burn it.'

'Shouldn't we return it for analysis?'

The Nex smiled then; a cold grim smile. It shook its shaved head and turned away, stepping towards the tunnel hewn through the stone and the welcoming calming cool darkness beyond.

The Nex hated the heat. It hated this place.

Its words echoed back, hollow and empty.

'She is dead. Her OneThoughts are gone. Burn her. She can be of no more use to us.'

It was night.

Insects buzzed in the darkness.

The Comanche sat, clicking, its metal cooling slowly, beside a small grove of palms.

The fire was a small one, the dry wood burning without smoke. Langan brewed tea in a little tin pot and Natasha sat, chin on her knees, arms around herself, staring into the flickering flames, lost: lost in a world of her own creation. Carter had finally come round; he was grey with exhaustion and accepted the mug of sweet tea without a sound. He didn't even have the energy to question Langan's presence, never mind engage in playful banter.

'You any closer to knowing what the fuck is going on?' asked Langan finally.

Carter nodded. 'I think so. Things are becoming clearer.'

'You still need me?'

'We need one last favour,' said Carter.

Natasha looked up. 'We do?'

'Aye.' Carter nodded, sipping at the sweet tea as one hand probed tenderly at his wounded flank. 'We need you to drop us somewhere.'

Langan nodded with a supportive smile. 'Anywhere, buddy,' he said softly. 'Just name the location.'

'We need you to take us to Saudi Arabia, the Great Sandy Desert,' said Carter. 'I think it's time we paid Count Feuchter a visit regarding this fucking QIII project of his.'

PART TWO

TO LOOK OUT WITH COPPER EYES

you're just **another coffin**
on its way down the emerald aisle
when your children's stony glances
mourn your **death in a terrorist's
smile**
the bomber's arm placing fiery gifts
on the supermarket shelves
alley sings with shrapnel **detonate
a temporary hell**

Forgotten Sons
Fish/Marillion

CHAPTER 16

MISSION

The Apache, piloted by Jam and with Slater snoring in the back, soared through the pouring rain, refuelling at a tiny local military outpost in Switzerland before heading east towards the borders of Austria and beyond. Jam cruised the Apache on a cushion of howling engines, heading east into the wind and the rain.

The Apache cruised across the Western Alps of Austria, rising to an incredible altitude until the mountains snaked away like the dark teeth of some huge giant's gaping maw. Jam cruised in silence, with only the thrumming of rotors disturbing this high bleak cold solitude. The Priest, seated beside him, watched on in silence, mouth a grim line, eyes bright and fevered.

'There,' said The Priest softly, peering forward a little.

The Apache cruised for slick fast minutes until both Jam and The Priest saw it; it was huge, a mammoth mountain rising from the Hohe Tauern range like a broken tooth, jagged and fearsome, capped with glittering sparkling crystal-wine ice.

'Grossglockner,' said Jam, his voice filled with an awe

he knew would never leave him, no matter how often he visited this magical and yet ultimately *horrifying* place.

'And the Kamus,' whispered The Priest.

Kamus-5. An old disused military complex built into the side of the mighty Grossglockner, well above the timber line and far away from roads of all description. One could only reach the crumbling edifice by two routes – one was by air, the other by a cable car consisting of long-disused carriages and steel lines from a nearby summit.

Jam brought the Apache in high, then dropped steeply towards the slopes of another mountain in the range, hugging the ground before climbing past huge swathing forests of beech and Austrian black pine, up into larch, fir and spruce and higher still, speed decreasing with the changing pitch of the rotors.

'You see anything?'

'It is too distant,' said The Priest. 'Head for that patch of forest, over there; where the trees break. We can reach the old cable-car base on foot. That will be the only sure way to avoid detection.'

Jam brought the Apache in to land, and the metal beast was swallowed by the trees. The rotors spun down, engines dying and clicking, and the four travellers stepped onto a forest bed of fir needles and dead branches that crackled softly underfoot. Water dripped from the trees around the clearing and Slater and Nicky found themselves looking around, deeply unimpressed.

'Smells damp,' said Slater.

'This is a wet forest,' said Jam. 'What do you expect?'

'I a city boy,' grumbled Slater. 'I not like this wilderness thing.'

Nicky approached The Priest, who was half kneeling, hand touching the sodden earth, eyes raised up and blinking at the rain. 'We heading for the old cable-car house?' she asked.

'Yes. The Lord will guide us. Come on, darkness will be falling soon and it would help if we could find the place before then.' He rose, ponderously. Shouldering their packs the group moved off between the trees, heading up the slopes made slippery by mud and fern.

Before long they were all panting, red-faced, and covered in twigs, leaves, and smears of mud. The going was steep, tough. There were no natural paths and only tree boles and branches to grab hold of for support.

The Priest led the way, and Jam dropped back to walk with Slater and Nicky as they fought their way up this mountain slope.

'Do you know what he plans when we get to the Kamus?'

Jam shrugged. 'He wasn't exactly a talkative passenger. I think we need to wait until we've had a good look; see what this supposed *activity* actually is at our old friend – the Kamus.'

'I not like the place,' said Slater, slowly. 'I not want to go back.'

Jam said nothing.

Eventually, they came across a pathway; heavily overgrown, a dirt trail with occasional wood-slat steps set into the earth to form a snaking natural staircase. They climbed more easily now, aware of their destination as darkness started to creep through the woods and an eerie ambient blackness began its smothering of the world. Just as total night fell like a shroud they emerged into a small clearing. The Priest motioned them to stop and they dropped to sudden crouches. A silenced Sig P226 9mm appeared in The Priest's huge hand and Jam crept up to kneel beside him. 'What is it?'

'I heard something.'

Jam palmed his Glock 9mm, complete with silencer, and squinted into the gloom.

They waited for long minutes, kneeling there in the gently dripping rain. Up ahead there was a slight bend in the trail, heavily wooded; beyond the steep turn squatted the old cable-car house.

Jam closed his eyes, focusing on the sounds and smells around him. After fifteen minutes of concentration, he was just about to give The Priest a mouthful of abuse when he caught it: the distant scent of a cigarette.

Their gazes met. Jam nodded and, gesturing back to Nicky and Slater, moved carefully forward with The Priest by his side. They took it a single step at a time, halting, checking their surroundings in the gloom, eyes fixed, ears alert.

Rounding the bend they came upon the run-down cable-car building. Its crumbling rendering was being slowly absorbed by the forest, and grass and branches poked rudely at its walls. Its huge wooden door was closed, and to the right sat the black maw of the cable mechanism: a huge set of wheels and gears with twin parallel cables, each as thick as a man's wrist, snaking out from the cabin and away into the remote darkness, swaying gently in the wind, which howled mournfully.

A light glowed within, glimpsed through time-shrouded windows.

Guards, signalled Jam. *Two.*

The Priest nodded.

You wait here, Jam signalled, and again The Priest nodded.

Jam moved carefully to the door and then rose to stand, back against the damp wood. Inside he could hear soft voices, speaking in German, complaining about the

300

cold. They're not Nex killers, then, he thought to himself with a grim smile.

And he could see, from this new vantage point, the distant platform of Kamus-5; lights flickered through the darkness, and the whole platform was illuminated. Jam heard the whine of distant engines, and glimpsed the flickering red lights of a helicopter.

He licked his lips. The Priest's source had been right.

There was definitely activity here.

There came a scrape, of wood on wood, from within. Jam turned, facing the door – which suddenly swung open to reveal a uniformed man, tall and heavily muscled, a cigarette dangling between his lips and an MP40 slung from his shoulder. He was squinting – and his eyes opened wide as they saw Jam's smiling face.

Jam's fist connected with a *crack*, and the guard was punched backwards to land heavily on his sub-machine gun, back twisting in agony as Jam's Glock snapped up to level at the face of the second man. He was halfway through dealing a deck of cards. He licked his lips.

'Don't even think about it, boy,' growled Jam as the young man looked at him, then to a small dark pistol on the table. The guard made a grab for the weapon and the Glock *popped* in Jam's fist; the guard was flung backwards from his stool, sprawling out beside the lantern on the floor. Blood splattered across the wall. Jam cursed.

The first man, groaning, received a kick in the ribs as Jam moved to the man he had shot and checked for a pulse. The Priest stepped in behind him, closely followed by Slater and Nicky. Slater grabbed the living guard and dragged him upright, shaking him.

'Any more of you?'

The man shook his head, his mouth a sour line.

301

'What are these monkeys doing here?' said Nicky. 'Guarding what?'

'I suppose the cables would be a long shot; not many people even know about this access to Kamus, much less need to guard it. I think, though, that these fuckers were here *just in case*.'

'They're not Nex,' said Nicky.

'That much we can be thankful for,' said Jam. 'But they still have sub-machine guns and intent – this fucker was going to shoot me. Took the risk and died for his stupidity.'

The Priest was standing in the doorway, looking out towards the distant Kamus. 'Kill the lamp,' he said softly, and dropped his pack to the floor. He pulled free some digital binoculars and peered out across the rain-filled expanse.

Slater battered the living guard into a state of unconsciousness, and dumped him on the floor where Nicky bound his hands and feet tightly together with bitch-wire. Then they all stood, thankful to be out of the rain for a moment as The Priest watched the activity in the Kamus.

'There is a lot of movement, lots of figures – they are loading up CH-47 Chinook cargo helicopters.'

'Are they Nex?'

'I cannot tell for sure, through the rain and over this distance,' said The Priest. 'Even as we speak, four Chinooks have taken off into the night. The platform is very busy indeed for a disused military complex, I think.'

'So what now?'

'We need to get closer.'

'These cable cars haven't run for years,' said Jam slowly. 'I doubt they would be safe, even if there was power piped to this place, which there isn't. What are you thinking?'

'I need to get closer,' said The Priest. 'I will go across the wire.'

'That would make you crazier than me,' said Jam softly.

'The Lord will protect me.'

'He won't protect you for ever,' said Jam.

'I am still alive, my son. He has done me proud this far.'

Jam ran his hand through his wet hair, then peered out at the swaying cables and the huge, awesome drop beyond into a blackness of seemingly infinite depth. 'I will, of course, have to come with you,' he said without relish.

'That is not necessary,' said The Priest.

'Oh, but it is,' growled Jam softly. 'I am in charge of this DemolSquad; *we* are on a mission to help find out who is fucking Spiral up the arse; *I* can't let *you* do my dirty work.'

Jam stalked out of the crumbling building and moved towards the edge of the precipice. The rock ended near his boots, and a rusting, broken safety railing, painted grey to blend with the surroundings, dangled precariously over the abyss. Jam knew, from previous work here, that this place was almost invisible to the outside prying eye.

'That's a long drop,' said Slater, coming to stand beside him.

'Yeah, so I see. Grab me my pack.'

The Priest moved forward. From his own pack he took a small alloy device; he checked a few tiny wheels inside it. 'You brought a skimmer with you?'

Jam nodded, taking his own pack from Slater and pulling out one of the tiny alloy devices. He then unstrapped a Heckler & Koch G3 sub-machine gun, and together with The Priest the two men crouched, screwing silencers onto the ends of the guns' barrels and then slinging these formidable weapons across their backs.

Nicky moved forward. 'You really think these are the bad guys?' she asked The Priest.

He nodded. 'A high probability, I think. If it is as I suspect, and this splinter group of Spiral is seeking domination of our tribe, then this would make an ideal base for operations – especially as it is so easily defended and somebody with prior knowledge could use much of the equipment left behind when the base was demilitarised.'

'We'll soon fucking find out,' said Jam. He pulled a balaclava over his wet face, and The Priest did likewise; now, all in black and carrying silenced sub-machine guns and pistols, the two men looked truly terrifying.

'You be careful,' said Nicky.

'You two make *sure* we don't get any nasty surprises from behind, yeah?'

'Rely on us,' rumbled Slater.

The Priest was checking Kamus through the binoculars. He tutted in annoyance. 'There's still a lot of activity; more Chinooks leaving the base. It seems we've decided to do this during one of their major operations.'

'Good,' snapped Jam. 'They'll be so busy they won't see us coming.'

'You wish.' Slater grinned. 'Go on, hole us some bad guys.'

Jam smiled grimly from behind the black mask. 'I'll do my best, my friend.'

The wind howled, rain lashing down in almost horizontal sheets. Jam stepped towards the edge of the precipice, and reaching up, attached the alloy skimmer with a *click*. It settled into place against the wide cable and a tiny blue light pulsed, then went out. Jam slipped his hand through the quick-release straps and looked out into the darkness and the storm. The cables were swaying and he swallowed hard. Deep below, falling away into nothingness, was a valley full of rocks, an abyss full of trees, a desolation of dark hell.

It would be a long, long tumble . . . followed by a gravity-induced crush.

Jam breathed deeply. Then, nodding to The Priest, he pushed his Glock into his belt, gripped the skimmer with his free hand – and kicked free, wind buffeting his watering eyes as he soared out into the void . . .

Feuchter awoke, cursing the pain in his limbs. His hand moved to the other side of the bed – to find nothing more than a cold depression. He scowled, ran a hand through his greying hair and sighed softly.

He rolled over with surprising agility, stood up and headed for the shower. He could smell himself, smell his own stink and the residue left behind by the Nex. The Nex always left their own curious aroma after sex; they always left their scent, their fluids, their *essence*.

Feuchter hated it. Hated that metallic scent, that copper stink . . . hated the stench and bitter after-effects of a Nex coupling . . . and yet he could not help himself, and he knowingly suffered the withdrawal symptoms for the intimate, *ultimate* pleasure of the high.

The comm buzzed. Feuchter halted, caught between the need to wash the stink from his skin and the need to take the call; he knew it would be important. It had to be important. A lot of bad shit was currently going down. 'Fuck.' He changed course, reached his desk and grabbed the receiver. 'Yeah?'

Outside, beyond the false proximity supplied by his monitor, the sun had risen; golden light danced across the distant sand dunes. Wind shifted the sand in waves, a golden sea of rolling iridescence. But on this sour-tasting morning the incredible and magnificent sight of dawn beauty delivered via electronics did little to calm Count Feuchter's sense of foreboding.

'Gol is dead.'

'Good. What about Carter?'

'Carter is another problem.'

'So they failed to neutralise him?'

'More than that; he is now much more informed, has experienced the Nex first hand – and survived. Worst of all, I think he has discovered some of the links between the QIII and ourselves.'

'Does he know that I am still alive?'

'A possibility,' said Durell softly.

'I want him dead,' said Feuchter. 'And I want him dead and mashed into food for the Nex right fucking now!' Feuchter's voice had suddenly risen to an almost hysterical screech. He stood, stinking the surreal stink, his heart booming in his seemingly hollow chest cavity, hands slippery on the comm receiver.

'Calm yourself,' said Durell, his voice low, crackling.

'I'll fucking calm myself when he's fucking dead,' hissed Feuchter.

'Now, you forget yourself,' whispered Durell, his voice like a shadow passing over a grave.

Feuchter paused then; he caught the low undercurrent of danger in Durell's voice. You did not fuck with Durell. *Nobody* fucked with Durell.

He bit his lip. He closed his eyes for a moment, and then said, forcing his voice into a state of calmness which contradicted his present lack of karma, 'What I mean to point out, *sir*, is that Carter has proved himself to be a very capable man – an extremely dangerous soldier. More, he has outsmarted and outstepped both the Nex and ourselves all the way to Kenya and beyond. If he

306

knows that I live then he may come to find me. You did not see him in Schwalenberg, Durell; I have never seen a man move so fast. It was surreal. It was *frightening*.'

'Feuchter, your priority now is merely to carry on the QIII development for the next twenty-four hours, and then issue Directive 566. Carter is *my* problem and I can assure you that I will not fuck about with this man, *frightening* or not.' The heavy sarcasm could not be missed.

Feuchter paused. Some of his earlier composure had returned and he cursed himself; he had displayed weakness. And to Durell of all people . . . But he could still see those eyes, eyes that seemed to change colour – darken into molten amber – and Feuchter could remember Carter's white-hot bullet drilling his stomach like a spinal worm, a manoeuvre so fast he had seen nothing: merely wondered why the fuck he was lying on his back with his flesh on fire . . .

'Directive 566? Termination of those who refuse to convert?'

'Yes.' There was a cold ice-edge to Durell's voice; the implicit challenge to Feuchter's authority was there. 'Most of the Q station are with us; but there is still a hard-core group who will not take a hint when it is tossed their way with candy. The days of Spiral are over – if they will not join us, they will die.'

Feuchter picked his next words with care, his mouth dry with the implications of what was about to happen . . . what he was being ordered to do . . .

'Sir, may I ask why *now*? We are not yet ready . . .'

'You may. Gol is dead; but the schematics have not been recovered. And as we speak, Gol's body has also not been recovered. If Spiral retain those fucking plans, they can build another QIII to challenge us – we may win the battle, Feuchter, but the war could never be ours. We need to be strong! Dominant! And we can't do that until Spiral is extinct.' Durell sighed on the comm. 'Just carry out your orders, Feuchter: Directive 566. After twenty-four hours. You know the procedures. All working components are to be transferred to Spiral_mobile; even now Kamus is being emptied of all valuable stock.'

Feuchter's jaw went tight and he gritted his teeth hard. He nodded – although there was nobody to witness this – and said, simply, 'Yes, sir.' He cut the line and stood—

Stunned—

Gazing at the monitor, which showed him the Rub al-Khali desert.

He could feel them; feel the workers, the programmers, the coders, the analysts, the developers – feel them around and above him, like workers in an ants' warren. And he was the King Ant – with the power to close down everything with a click of his fingers.

And the order had come.

Everything of vital importance would be moved. Feuchter smiled then, a smile without humour, his tombstone teeth white against his lightly tanned skin. *Moved.* That was a term to use for the *equipment* but, unfortunately, not all of the *personnel* . . .

We know who you are, he thought.

And Spiral? Weak and powerless Spiral?

Your time has come.

Oh, how I have waited for this moment, he thought, his mind retreating over all the years, flowing back over the decades. Visions flowered in his mind; flowered, blossomed, died. Feuchter remembered the Battle of Belsen; he remembered the Attack on Poland Ridge; and he remembered the mountains of Korea after the Bright War.

You are weak, Spiral, he thought.

And yes. We will make you strong again.

But first? First you must relinquish your greatest treasure . . .

The lives of those who will not betray you.

The Comanche flew low over the desert, its passing marked by the heavy deep *thrum thrum thrum* of its engines. Sunlight glittered from rotors, danced across the DPM paintwork, glinted across the smoked cockpit and the cramped occupants inside—

The Comanche banked gently, gaining altitude as it approached the mountainous regions of Northern Rub al'Khali. The Great Sandy Desert. Vast and wild and undiscovered.

Natasha gazed down at the mountains, the narrow crevasses and rocky gullies, the spirals of rocky depression, some filled with the fresh clear water of mountain streams, the occasional herd of antelope or gazelle on the lower slopes casting eyes upwards and scattering as the Comanche droned like a huge insect low overhead, below radar. Natasha spotted lone huts and small villages huddled into the sides of the mountains for protection; some villages were of mud brick, some of canvas, sheltering beneath the wide swinging woods of poplar before the land dropped sharply, dizzyingly to the lowlands south and west of the marshes and then on to the desert.

Carter stirred, his eyes coming open.

'How are you feeling?' asked Natasha.

'Like a man who's been shot.'

'Much pain?'

'I've felt better,' said Carter.

'Well, you're all sewn up, and on the road to recovery. I think you'll probably be stiff for a few weeks.'

'Huh. *Not* the story of my life.' Carter winced. He pulled himself higher in the cockpit, gazed out, down, head rattling with the noise from the twin LHTec engines. He watched the mountains roll down into deserts. He gazed out to the east, but could see no sign of any major city. He rested his head back, mind spinning, confused after recent events. He glanced at Natasha – who was staring down at the landscape flowing like a sand river below them.

'How about you, Nats? Are you OK?'

Natasha did not turn, her gaze fixed on some distant invisible point.

'Yes.' Her voice was cold.

He took her hand and squeezed her warm flesh. 'I'm sorry. About Gol – what he did was a brave thing. He did it to protect his mission, his organisation. He was the key to stopping the enemy; he knew the schematics would allow us time, would slow down the QIII's dominance . . . whoever wants that processor working obviously has big plans for its implementation. And if it really can predict the future . . .'

'If?'

Carter shrugged. 'Sounds impossible to me. But *if* it can – then whoever controls such a weapon, for that is what it is – whoever controls such a weapon will be powerful indeed.'

'There's more than that, Carter.'

Carter frowned; half in pain, half in confusion.

'Yeah?'

'This system – the schematics I saw, in its early stages of inception: they were mind-blowing. If it became operational in the wrong hands – it could take over world finance, it could fuck Wall Street and the Dow Jones straight up the arse. But more than that, it would control . . .'

'Weapons?'

Nats nodded. 'Everything is computerised, Carter. Missiles, strategic instructions, the whole Battlegrid . . .'

'And nuclear weapons?'

'Oh yes, Carter.'

She glanced down at him, her eyes red-rimmed. 'I loved Gol, Carter, y'know? Even after our fight . . . even though our hot words tore each other to shreds . . . and then, in Kenya when we made up, when he took me in his arms again, everything in the world felt right. Everything became good again and I suddenly realised how much I had lost. I loved him – and I know he died protecting Spiral but—'

'But?'

'I can't help thinking there is something out of place.'

'Like the Nex?'

'Yes.'

Carter smiled grimly. 'If we find who controls the Nex, we find out who is after manipulating the QIII. And we know that same fucker is the one who's been tagging Spiral and the DemolSquads.'

Natasha merely nodded, and Carter reached over and wiped away the tears that glistened on her cheeks. 'Now is not the time to be talking of this,' he said. 'Maybe Gol is still alive.' His words slipped out, sounding lame even to his own ears. But he had to force himself to say it; he had to try and help Natasha and he knew – *knew* that silence was sometimes a good thing but he so desperately wanted to help her, to ease her pain, to make the hurt come better . . .

Natasha did not reply. She gazed back out of the window but her fingers took Carter's hand and squeezed. He said no more but was merely there – there for her.

Carter laughed inwardly.

I wonder just how powerful this QIII really is? he thought.

311

And more importantly, who seeks to control it? To dominate the world?

The face of Feuchter floated into his mind; he remembered that chilling smile, and the look in the man's eyes. He had believed; believed in his actions, without a hint of insanity. He would have killed Carter there and then and not thought twice about it . . .

You fucker, Carter thought.

But then – that was too easy. Feuchter was not in charge; he was a lackey, a stooge, a slave to somebody bigger and altogether more intimidating. Somebody who was trying to undermine and destroy Spiral . . . but Spiral was almost invisible. Its acts were legendary, but its name was unknown outside—

Realisation came like a shot from the dark.

It had to be somebody on the inside.

It had to be somebody high up in Spiral.

Betrayal.

The word tasted bad on Carter's tongue, and he drifted off to sleep once again, loss of blood making him unnaturally weary. His dreams swirled, with hordes of Nex armed with machine pistols and masks struggling to climb over their dead comrades to get at him, to maim him, to kill him . . .

And then Gol was there. A colossus, a huge gun in his hands, cutting the Nex in half with streams of bullets.

'What are they?' cried Carter. 'What the *fuck* are they?'

Gol smiled; a sickly-sweet smile; then ripped off his face to reveal the copper eyes of a Nex . . .

Carter came awake with a hiss.

It was night. He was alone in the cockpit of the Comanche, a blanket wrapped around him. His tongue ran around the stale interior of his mouth and he gazed out of the cockpit, up at the clear black sky. Stars twinkled far above.

The virgin silence was infinite.

He eased himself up, released the cockpit hatch and struggled down the ladder. Natasha and Langan were seated beside a small – very small – fire. Langan was brewing coffee over the flames in a small pan.

Carter looked around warily. 'Is it safe to light a fire here?'

'We've checked out the surroundings. We're miles from any settlements – single houses, even.'

'I don't like it. People can see it from miles away . . .'

'And they can hear the roar of a Comanche from even further. We needed a break, Carter. *I* need a break – I'm not a fucking pilot from God, you know. Have you ever seen what happens to a Comanche when the pilot nods off?'

'How long do you need?'

'Yeah, I'm feeling fine and thanks for your concern. About three hours and some strong coffee. And maybe then I'll be ready to take on the vast endless unexplored open spaces of Rub al'Khali on a wild-goose chase with no real set objective . . .'

'Feuchter is at the end of it. That's objective enough.'

'Is he really going to have all the answers?' asked Langan.

'Only if I ask the right fucking questions,' said Carter. He settled beside the fire, his blanket still wrapped around his shoulders, his face still grey with exhaustion. He smiled weakly at Langan. 'You seem a tad on edge, my friend.'

Langan patted Carter's arm. 'I could say the same about you, but you've recently been shot so I think I'll forgive your tetchiness. Also, flying illegally over Rub al'Khali ground is not my idea of fun. If we're caught

313

trespassing in Saudi airspace . . . they'll either send every-thing they fucking have at us and claim some breach of international law, or it'll kick off some major fucking United Nations fuck-up and we'll all be in the shit.'

'We'll just have to stay covert, then.'

'Easy for you to say. I'm the bastard with the responsi-bility.'

'How we doing for fuel?'

'I visited a Spiral dump while you were asleep. We're fully fuelled and ready to rumble.'

Carter nodded, and rested his head and back against the small clump of boulders beside which Langan had built the fire. He said, his eyes closed, 'I suggest we stay here for the rest of the night. All get some much-needed rest. How far to where you reckon this Spiral_Q com-puter processor development centre actually is?'

'We're presently about a hundred and fifty kilometres south and west of Tabuk. As long as we keep away from all major civilisation – not exactly difficult in this area – then we can carry on skirting down towards the Jaba Sawda and the desert to the west; that is our final desti-nation. We'll be able to head for the rough co-ords Gol gave me before he . . .' Langan's voice trailed off. He glanced at Natasha whose eyes were closed, her face stony. 'I can have us there within two hours, but from here on in it's a much harder ride; there's definitely a heavier military presence although I'm not sure why, probably soured relations with another Middle Eastern State, OPEC or the OIC. It's also easy to spot that we shouldn't be the fuck where we are. We're not exactly flying in diplomatic colours; and this Comanche is quite obviously a war machine. We'll have to move more slowly, more cautiously. And the cherry on the Bakewell is that I am unfamiliar with the terrain.'

'I wish I hadn't asked.'

'It would have been better for you to go in over land.'

'Oh yeah, what in? A hastily stolen Skoda that some fuckwit had just left lying around?'

Langan grinned. 'You know Spiral has vehicle and weapons stashes all over the world. We could backtrace to the nearest SP1plot, tool you up, send you out.'

Carter shook his head. 'One, we haven't got the time. The Comanche is fucking fast. Two, I'm not exactly in the best physical state to be piloting some desert sand buggy over the dunes. And finally, it's good to see you really pissed off. And watching you skip wire and dodge MIGs and missiles is a joy to behold.'

'You're a cunt, Carter.'

'Better believe it.'

Langan dished out the coffee, which they drank sweet and black. Smoke drifted up into the vast void above the Rub al'Khali desert and Carter felt suddenly at peace. The pain – which he had recently grown accustomed to – had lessened and he felt almost comfortable, at ease . . . He could not put a finger on the reason for this sudden euphoria but the beauty of the night sky had something to do with it, and the feeling that he was doing the right thing – headed on the right course – no longer the *hunted*, but the *hunter* . . . he had turned the image around in his brain, become the predator, become the one in control.

It might be limited control, but now he was calling the shots.

Send the fucking Nex, he thought. I'll kill them all.

Let's see what answers you have, Count Feuchter.

Let's see what song you sing.

The dawn broke, grey light spreading across the horizon. Wrapped in blankets, the small group roused themselves, drank more coffee courtesy of Langan and then, gathering what little detritus they had created, climbed stiff-limbed back into the Comanche.

Langan warmed up the engines, then eased his baby into the air, scattering sand. Slowly, he increased the speed, and they skimmed low over the desert and rocky landscape. Occasionally they would pass low ranges of hills, mainly rounded rocks all scattered with orange sand and small scrub bushes. Occasionally they would see small groups of date palms around a life-giving oasis, but Langan avoided these outposts for they attracted local herders and villagers.

As they droned low over the desert, Carter – now fully awake, alert and seeming more like his old self after the night's sleep, only occasionally wincing breathlessly at the stabs of pain within his battered body – took the spare HIDSS helmet from its compartment behind Langan.

'How does it work?'

'Pop it on,' said Langan. 'I'll show you.'

Carter pulled the helmet over his head, and positioned the mike and sensors in front of his face; finally, he slid down the mounted flight-information display. The terrain ahead of the Comanche sprang to life and Carter gasped at the digital image.

'Impressed?'

'Fuck me.'

Data scrolled down both sides of the visor; occasionally symbols flickered into life and targets were highlighted with different colours and symbols. Carter noted the weapons-system tracker in the top right corner and he licked his lips nervously.

'Have I got some form of control here?'

'Only if I patch you in.'

'Don't.'

'That wasn't my intention, Mr Carter. You are a novice. You don't even like flying – the last thing I am going to do is allow you control of my beloved Comanche.'

'*Spiral*'s Comanche.'

'That depends on your point of view.'

'So tell me about the helmet. How does it work?'

'What you are wearing, Mr Carter, is a helmet that provides acoustic and impact protection combined with a magnetic helmet tracker. This son of a bitch stops you going deaf, especially in battle situations when the shit hits the fan: it has a bi-ocular FOV at 53° x 30° CRT with a 1023-line refresh – that means it's a motherfucking clear display that gives you a wide field of view, important when approaching a possible combat encounter. The HIDSS offers both flight-information and night-vision sensors on screen, and uses flight data with sensor images and piloting and targeting symbology to allow aggravated aggressive flight manoeuvring and combat, especially at night.'

'What sort of weapons have we got on board?'

'That's it, Carter, get right to the important stuff. Don't ask me how secure we are against biological or chemical weapons, don't ask what the procedure is in a crash – straight to the guns!'

'Well?'

'We have a stowable three-barrelled 20mm turreted Gatling nose gun, coming in at 1500 rounds a minute. We have a fully retractable missile armament system called I-RAMS – where missiles are hidden in bays; you get various different configurations of heavy-shit rockets. We are presently carrying 36 standard 70mm rockets, 18 Stinger air-to-air missiles and 6 Hellfire anti-tank missiles which, as I am sure you know, are programmed to control their own targeting destinations, once fired. We're not carrying a full load which means we're a little more manoeuvrable than you would expect when fully loaded.'

'That's some fucking firepower.'

'This is a war machine, Carter. What do you expect? Smarties?'

'They pick some shit names, don't you think?'

'You mean Stinger and Hellfire? I suppose so, but what would you call them?'

Carter shrugged, still entranced by the HIDSS display. 'You want a go, Nats?'

'No, I'll leave the playing and toy-fetish stuff to you boys.'

'Don't be like that, Nats.'

'You should hear you two! Hellcat stinging 900mm bollocks to smash a tank straight up the I-RAMS. God, you're like a couple of kids with a new plastic soldier.'

'Women never understand,' said Langan conspiratorially.

Carter nodded.

'Probably because they're brought up with dolls.'

'I can hear you,' said Natasha testily.

'Oooh, she can hear us,' said Langan.

An alarm sounded. Langan cursed, the Comanche suddenly banked sharply and dipped towards the ground, the LHTec engines whining down. He turned the helicopter around and they headed back the way they had just come.

'What is it?'

'You see the orange blip on your screen? Way bad news. Air-defence base – missiles, fighter jets – the full fucking monty. We're twenty kms from it. I think we need to rethink our cross-land strategy.'

After some distance, Langan brought the Comanche down in a small bowl valley amid barren hills which were formed completely from gently rounded rock, with very little vegetation and no trees, no water – no people.

The rotors whined down.

Carter and Natasha climbed from the cockpit and Langan flicked a few switches, then jumped down. He carried a roll of plastic and a small black cube. 'You're not going to like what I have to tell you.'

Carter eased himself to the ground, hand pressed against his stitched flesh. 'Surprise me.'

'The path we need to take is crawling with aerial defences, probably in place in case Saudi falls out with its neighbours. They'll also be linked to White Guard bases – Saudi Arabia's army. Now, we could get past them – easy. But I'm not sure if we could get past them *undetected*. Do you want to arrive at Spiral–Q to find it deserted? Or your main man vanished?'

'What do you suggest?'

'Before, when I mentioned the SP1plot, the vehicle and weapons stashes – well, I wasn't joking. There are usually stealth vehicles of some sort. It depends what your priority is – speed or stealth? I could get us there in the Comanche but we might trigger some of their more sophisticated sensors – just depends what they've got!'

Carter chewed his lip. 'Show me on the digital map.'

Langan unrolled the length of map – made from some kind of thin clear plastic that could be updated with information from the Comanche's computers – on the sand and knelt on the edge to stop the wind from curling it. Carter squatted, wincing and holding his side, and his gaze roved across the detailed and illuminated terrain.

'Where is Spiral_Q?'

Langan pointed. 'There; or within a couple of kilometres. It can't be that easy to hide, although they do try. By Spiral accounts it is a fucking *huge* base.'

'Couldn't you take us around via a quieter, more circuitous route? Without the air defences?'

'I think something is going down in Rub al'Khali, to be honest. The reports I've just logged from the back end of Spiral say that military concentration in the area is building, although they don't know why. We could try – but when we're outrunning missiles and Feuchter's done a vanishing act, don't go blaming poor old Langan.'

'Great. Any other good news?'

'I can take you to the vehicles depot; or near to. I can also wait for you, although that is more than you deserve.'

'Hmmm.' Carter scratched at the stubble on his chin, and decided that he needed both a bath and a shave. Sweat rolled down his nose and dripped to the sand and rock. He could feel the sun burning his back.

'We haven't got the right equipment. Money. Clothes. Nothing.'

'You could say that we left a little unprepared,' added Langan softly.

Carter nodded; it was not a criticism, just an observation. 'I'll tell you what Langan. We'll do what you say: drop us at the SP1plot and I'll go in by vehicle, covertly, and you can wait there with Natasha—'

'I'm coming with you,' said Natasha.

'No.'

'Who the fuck do you think you are to order me around?'

Their glares locked. Carter shook his head. 'I'll work faster alone.'

'You don't need to fucking *protect* me,' said Natasha. 'I can do that myself. But it is *my* father who's dead because of these bastards; I'm going in, Carter, and I'll either go with you or without you. *You* can accompany *me* if you feel up to it – after all, taking a bullet must have slowed down your reflexes a little bit. And it was me who got you out of Gol's place alive . . . without me you'd be Nex pulp . . .'

'Whoa.' Carter held up his hands. 'I stand corrected.'

'Don't you just hate stroppy women?' muttered Langan.

'She's got a point this time,' said Carter slowly. 'I assume that's a GPS you're carrying?'

Langan nodded. 'But this is linked to the digital map – for coordination purposes.'

'You mean for missile attacks.'

'Yeah, that as well.'

'OK. How far is the nearest SP1plot?'

'About a hundred kilometres closer to civilisation.'

Carter glanced up at the sun; it was high now, and burning down with incredible force. Beneath his clothes he was soaked with sweat. 'Let's do it, then.'

The Comanche sat, baking in the desert heat, the artificial wind from its rotors dying down even as they stood, staring at the wall of rock before them.

'Where is it?' asked Natasha.

'You're looking at it.'

Natasha gazed up at the jagged vertical surface of wind-weathered sandstone that cut a step from the landscape. The rock was a deep red, scarred, a section of landscape scoured by wind-blown sand over centuries. It was a desert feature, a sanctuary from the wind. It was a rock with a sense of history.

'The wall?'

'No, at its base.'

SP1plots were dotted all over the globe, and carried equipment specific to the sort of territory in which they were placed. Periodically they would be checked and restocked by Spiral operatives. On a thousand occasions they had made the difference between life and death.

Most SP1plots were either behind rock, or set under the ground: huge steel containers hidden away from prying eyes and accessed via ECubes. Carter pulled out the small dark cube and allowed it to sit in his palm.

'Won't using that give away our location?'

'Oh yes. But if they're that good, they know where we are, or where we're going, anyway. We just have to concentrate on staying one step ahead. Act, don't react, yeah?'

Carter accessed a function of the ECube. It *blipped*. There came a *click* from the ground and, raining sand, a huge rectangular section of the desert suddenly lifted – a ramp, allowing access to a deep dark cool interior.

Carter and Natasha moved forward; Langan watched from the secure confines of his Comanche, where he had lit a burner and had begun the ritual of getting a brew on. They stooped, peering into the gloom lit by triggered emergency lights set against the corrugated steel walls.

'Let's see what delights Pandora's box holds.'

They descended the steep ramp; against one wall was an array of weapons, from machine guns and pistols to sniper rifles and even a couple of bazookas. All weapons were wrapped in plastic and coated in grease. Ammunition sat in wooden crates in one corner, and there were several large machines, also wrapped in thick plastic sheets. Carter moved forward and pulled one of the sheets free.

Natasha scowled.

'A motorbike?'

'More than that,' said Carter, a hidden sense of joy in his voice. 'It's a modified desert racer – a BMW R2150 GS Adventurer, with some serious modifications and upgrades. It's a fucking dream, Natasha.'

'I would have preferred a jeep.'

'No, no, these are the best things for crossing the desert – as long as you know how to control one. These bastards will eat the miles: look at the tyres! Just wait till we get on the move.'

He crossed to the bike, hand tracing the contours of the tank and seat. He crouched, his gaze roving over the engine with its curious powerful design, then stood again to survey the extra fuel tanks. He tapped them. 'Full and raring to go; all we have to do is initiate and prime the firing sequence.'

'What modifications does it have?'

Carter pointed to a place below the headlights; two barrels poked free. 'Mounted sub-machine guns, with ammunition on a drum stored below the petrol tank up front. It has a built-in monitor over the handlebars, where your ECube can sit and aid navigation, along with the usual GPS set-up. It has a stealth exhaust; this baby will run silent – silent and deadly. And special mudguards which stop huge dust clouds from following you up the sides of sand dunes and signalling your position to all and sundry.'

Carter moved forward, kicked his leg over the huge machine. He fired up the bike and, true to his word, there was nothing more than a gentle murmur. 'They use these to blast over the Paris-Dakar Rally – a true endurance race, probably one of the hardest races in the world. If anything can get us to Spiral_Q over land, then this is it.'

Natasha shook her head. 'I remember the last time I got on the back of a bike with you.'

Carter shook his head, smiling grimly. 'Don't worry, love – this time it will be much, much worse.'

The BMW R2150 GS Adventurer climbed the ramp with ease, its engine note nothing more than a low croon; tyres bit into sand and Carter taxied the bike towards the Comanche. 'Nice,' remarked Langan, nodding as he held out a mug of tea.

Carter kicked the stand down and leaned the bike, then accepted the offered mug. 'There's only dried and tinned supplies down there. You wouldn't happen to have anything fresher?'

Langan tossed Carter a satchel, which he deftly caught, wincing as the stitches in his side pulled tight. 'Some fresh food in there, buddy. Although I'll probably be cursing you when I'm destined to finish off the last tinned beef kebab.'

'Cheers. There's another thing.'

'Hmm?' Langan sipped his brew, his eyes suspicious.

'I saw your rifle. In the Comanche. The Barrett .338 Lapua Magnum. With the telescopic sight. Can I borrow it?'

'My Barrett!' Langan scowled. 'You'll be wanting the gold from my fucking fillings next.'

'No, just the rifle.'

'What's wrong with the weapons from the store?'

'They're too new; not bedded in. Last thing I need is a bloody untried and untested weapon. And anyway, I have experience with a Barrett rifle – those nameless unloved weapons down there, they have no soul.'

'Carter, that rifle is my baby. That rifle is my god. It used to be my brother's; my brother is now dead. I feel I owe it to him to make sure that it survives something more than your ham-fisted clumsiness.'

'Don't be so soft,' snapped Carter. 'I'll take care of her. You know I look after my weapons.'

'Yeah, right, I've seen the condition of your Browning.'

'Used but not abused,' said Carter. 'The fact that it's so worn is a testament to my love, care and attention. It wouldn't have lasted this long if I'd casually tossed it aside, now would it? Go on, Langan, *share.*'

Langan muttered something incomprehensible.

'Not when there are ladies present,' said Natasha softly, moving forward. She carried a Glock, several spare mags and some boxes of ammunition. She took the satchel and dropped gun and ammo in beside the food so generously donated by Langan.

'On one condition.'

'What?'

'You have to polish it.'

'Polish? Oh for fu— OK, OK.' He saw the look in Langan's eyes.

'Once a night.'

'I don't intend to be gone that long,' said Carter, smiling grimly.

The SP1plot also contained clothing necessary for the locality, in case they were separated from the bike: traditional Arab dress – white cotton robes, and a couple of shamags.

'Wrap up, Natasha – we'll be in disguise and they'll at least protect us from the sun.'

'Are there any motorbike helmets in there?'

Carter shook his head. 'Don't worry; we won't be crashing. Not if I have anything to do with it.'

They spent a few minutes helping one another into the robes and shamags, giggling despite the seriousness of their predicament. When both were fully clad, they stood staring at one another and Carter's hand reached out to cup Natasha's chin.

'You look beautiful.'

'What do you want?'

'I want nothing, my love. I merely wish to give.'

'You're so full of crap, Carter.'

'So a man can't even try and be romantic?'

'Hmm, which part was romantic?'

Carter smiled, tension easing from him. 'Come on, we're running late, thanks to this impromptu diversion. We need to get on the move. You got the digital maps?'

'Everything is in the satchel.'

Wrapped up, they moved to the BMW and Carter fired up the machine. Natasha settled herself on the back of the huge bike and they both turned, gazes fixing on Langan. 'You know the procedures,' said Carter.

Langan nodded. 'Be careful, guys.'

Carter laughed harshly, pulling on his goggles. 'We'll be more than careful, mate; we'll be deadly.'

The rear wheel spun and gripped and kicked the bike away . . .

Just before setting out, Carter had given Nats a quick lesson on pillion riding, and a warning about riding over sand. 'Lean with me,' he had said. 'Don't throw yourself around on the bike, don't get on or off without my permission and be warned: riding over sand is tough – I'll have to hit it fast. If you don't, you get bogged down, unless it's real flat and packed.'

Now, as the BMW surged forward, Natasha's heart was in her mouth; the sun was beating down, sand rushed by to either side, and they left the Comanche and the flat rock-step behind as the BMW powered onto and up the first dune, torque-filled engine throbbing beneath them like a giant's strong and beating heart. The BMW sailed over the sand, cutting out any need for tracks or roads, and as they crested the ridge, Carter still piling on the power, the beast's front wheel lifted and they wheelied from the top of the sand dune in a shower of desert crimson.

Another world opened up, a world of rolling sand, a great sea caressed by the wind, wave after wave stretching off to the horizon. Nothing moved, nothing stirred in this desert: no houses, no villages, no trees – just the occasional shrub or a scattering of rocks. A word leaped into Natasha's mind to describe this place:

Desolation.

They powered forward, down the massive dune, and already sweat was trickling down the riders' backs. Carter wrestled with the huge bike, could feel the sand trying to suck him down, pull him one way or another, swallow them; he fought back, increasing the power, building the speed, rising from the seat a little to stand on the pegs with Natasha clinging on tightly behind as they crested another rise in a shower of sand and sailed down the next drifting slope. Up and up went the speed; past 80 m.p.h., past 100 m.p.h. – shrubs fled past in a blur, sand spat to either side of the charging bike. Occasionally they hit a buried rock, the BMW's suspension dipping, absorbing, but Carter kept her on course, kept the bike true as they flew like a bullet across the deserted no man's land of Rub al'Khali in Saudi Arabia.

They charged along under the sun.

Carter could taste sweat when he licked at his sand-whipped lips. The sun beat down like a furnace. His eyes flickered, reading the GPS coordinates. He did not dare initiate the BMW's ECube locking mechanism; it was one thing to signal a *blip* in a state of emergency, but to give their enemies a bright emergency flare to follow? That would be insanity.

On and on they rode, merging with the landscape around the camouflaged stealth vehicle; sand dune crested into sand dune, a waving, rolling sea that they navigated with great effort. The bike flew on, until finally the dunes became smaller and the drifts came seemingly to an end.

They arrived at a vast plain of flat-packed rock and sand, with huge outcroppings of stone cliff rearing in the distance. Rocks lay strewn everywhere, and Carter slowed the bike's speed to a more moderate 70 m.p.h.

They cruised almost in silence.

'Thank God for that!' Natasha spoke over the slight hiss of the wind. She was clinging on tightly and Carter, who had sat down once more, patted at her hands around his waist where they gripped for dear life.

'Mad as fuck, eh?'

'Mad as fuck,' agreed Natasha.

They cruised across the plain, the sun still high and burning, Carter's eyes focused on the GPS. He swung the bike left, then slowed as an old ravine loomed – gritting his teeth, and with a wail from Natasha, he gave the big bike a kick of speed and they leaped from the rocky surface, dropping a good eight feet to land on the baked and cracked ravine bed. Suspension dipped, Natasha's wail was cut short with a grunt, and the bike sped on as if nothing more than a floating rose petal had disturbed its trajectory.

'You could have warned me!'

'What's the point? You'd only moan!'

'Moan!' moaned Natasha. 'You miserable bastard!'

'That's the beauty of travelling by bike,' shouted Carter. 'Communication is made so much more difficult!'

They cruised down the ravine, swaying left and right to avoid fallen rock debris. To their right stood a mammoth cliff, an obstacle in the desert, and as the ravine wound away, heading further to the west, Carter realised that they would have to ascend this precipice to reach the next stage of their journey.

For an hour they followed the valley. Then, slowing his speed, Carter dropped a few gears. Finding a section where the rocky wall had collapsed, leaving an insanely steep slope of rubble, he slowed to a halt for a moment, his eyes focused intently.

Natasha was panting. 'This is fucking hard work.'

'You're not having to steer. Why do you think desert racers are such physically fit sons of bitches?'

'Why have we stopped?'

Carter lifted his goggles for a moment, rubbed at his eyes, and then cleaned sand from the goggles' surface with the edge of his shamag. 'If we carry on following the ravine, we'll swing around in the wrong direction – we need to climb out.'

'Climb out? We'll never lift . . . oh.'

Natasha had spotted the collapsed wall.

'Hold on.'

Carter screwed the throttle; the BMW leaped forward, needing little encouragement – they hammered across the flat, tyres chewing past baked desert earth, and mounted the slope like a ramp. Carter twisted the throttle and the engine roared beyond its stealth shielding . . . the bike powered up the slope and jettisoned itself from the summit, sailing through the air with both riders clenching their teeth and the tyres spinning helplessly . . . they landed, the heavy-duty suspension dipping to absorb the impact. Carter locked the back wheel and they skidded around in a broad arc, showering rock and sand.

'You really are a crazy bastard,' panted Natasha.

'I try,' smiled Carter. 'But if you think that's bad . . .' He turned and pointed to the cliff.

'What about it? It's a wall of rock?'

'It's in our way.'

'Carter, this fucking bike will not climb that.'

'It will if you find the right paths.'

They sped along for another couple of hours. Natasha was exhausted, and she knew that Carter was tiring – and becoming increasingly frustrated because of this natural barrier that would soon send them in the wrong direction – and *away* from Spiral_Q and Feuchter beyond.

As the sun began to sink, Carter halted, shading his eyes. The rocky wall faltered – as it had on several occasions before – but this time there were huge steps, cut into the flanks and banked with crumbling stones and fallen rocks. Many of the steps were rounded, weathered by wind and blown sand; they formed a steep and treacherous series of ramps, rising perhaps three storeys into the sky.

'No, Carter.'

'Yes, Natasha. This baby can do it.'

'Oh no, I value my life.'

'I value Feuchter's death more,' growled Carter. He blipped the engine. 'Hold on, babe, we're going to do some hill climbing.'

The BMW cruised forward – gently this time and with care as Carter's gaze raked across the ramps and steps arranged ahead of him like some crazy game or puzzle. He cruised along the foot of the cliff, back and forth several times with his gaze following various paths up the slopes to the top of the ridge. Then, only when he was happy, did he ease in a little more power and turn the BMW's nose towards the steep climb.

With precision and control, Carter eased the BMW up a series of gentle slopes, then flicked the bike's head right, blipping the power to climb the back wheel up a step. Rubber gripped, the huge bike surged a little and Carter reined her in with both brakes. A ramp to the left brought them up onto another level, then a series of small rocks piled atop one another acted like steps as the BMW ate them with ease.

Now halfway up, Natasha gazed down. If it had looked steep from the bottom, now it looked insane; she felt suddenly vulnerable, gazing down at the ravine through which they travelled and the flat plain beyond, bordered distantly by more rolling sand dunes drifting lazily as far as the eye could see.

Shadows danced in their path, cast by the low-slung rays of the setting sun. Natasha put her head against Carter's back, closed her sand-crusted eyes and prayed.

The bike jolted, bucked, scrambled and fought its way up the slope, bumping and rocking, engine growling, fighting, tyres spinning and gripping as Carter, sweat rolling down his forehead, gaze focused in intense concentration, finally launched them from the top of a trough and onto another plain of sand and loose-strewn rocks.

Natasha patted his shoulder.

'Hmm?'

'I think we need a break.'

'Sounds good. I am truly, truly shafted.'

They cruised for a while longer until Natasha's sharp eyes spotted the distant oasis, outlined in crimson as the sun made its final attempt to stave off night. Carter altered their course, and before long the trees came closer and it was a weary rider who at last silenced the bike's thumping heart.

They had camouflaged the BMW R 2150 GS Adventurer beside this small oasis, decorating the powerful customised bike with huge green palm fronds.

'Jesus, it's so hot,' gasped Natasha and Carter said

nothing. He was bright red, mostly from heat exhaustion, a little from the pain in his stomach. He was finding it hard to breathe because of the heat.

Carter slumped to the ground and ran his hand along the flat, smooth rock. 'This place is *old*,' he said softly, his voice carrying a tone of awe. 'Really old.'

Natasha nodded, kicking free her boots and splashing water from the small circular pool into her face, combing it into her desert-dry hair. She moaned in mock ecstasy, and rolled onto her back to stare at the sun descending rapidly over the horizon. 'I never believed I could be so hot,' she complained.

Carter smiled. 'In the middle of hostile territory on a mission bound for certain destruction and all you can complain about is the sun. Girl, this is nothing; you should try Thailand. Or the Philippines . . . now those places are *real* hot.'

Natasha roused herself and rummaged in the small sack that she carried – the contents of which were mainly made up of Carter's smash-and-grab from Langan's personal stash. She held up a lump of cheese. She sniffed at it suspiciously. 'Does this look OK to you?'

'Looks don't come into it, but my acute hunger does. Give it . . . here . . .' He reached towards the cheese. Natasha swayed aside.

'Wait, wait, let me try . . .'

She took a small bite and smiled broadly. 'Extremely tasty.' She pulled free a loaf and began to eat. Carter lay back, closed his eyes and wiped sweat from his forehead.

According to the GPS and digital map link they were closing fast on Spiral_Q. Several more hours without incident and they would arrive and then—

What?

Carter knew: he would interrogate Feuchter. And then he would kill the man. There was nothing Feuchter could say that would excuse him of the crime of betrayal.

Spiral might have let him free. But Carter would not.

And besides – Spiral had its own problems at the moment . . .

Carter took the loaf from Natasha. Chewed mechanically. For his mind had wandered – more than wandered, he was reliving that day, that night at Castle Schwalenberg, reliving that terrible moment when Feuchter and Maria had turned against him, forcing Kade into existence for a terrible bright few minutes of black and white—

Carter blinked.

His head tilted to one side.

That's right, he thought. Black and white. Kade saw everything in black and white.

Why?

Carter rested his head back.

'*I have missed you,*' said Kade softly.

'You have been absent since Kenya. Sulking, were you, you little shit?'

'*I was thinking. Contemplating,*' said Kade, his voice still soft. There was something about the tone – the *change* of tone – that unnerved Carter. Yes, he was used to Kade screaming . . . but this . . . this was *strange* . . .

'What's the matter?' asked Carter finally.

There came a sigh, like the dry passing of autumn leaves over a grave. Carter felt himself shiver and he looked up – back in the real word – and his gaze met Natasha's as Kade's presence became even more menacing at the back of his skull.

'*I have been thinking. About our relationship.*'

'Oh yeah?' Carter could not keep the snarl from his tone.

333

'*And I have been thinking about Natasha.*'

'What about her?'

'*She works for the Nex,*' said Kade softly.

'You are wrong.'

'*No. She works for the Nex and that fucking meat-carver Feuchter. Carter, I have been thinking; it wasn't you who led the Nex to Gol. It was her. I bet she contacted them – or was somehow bugged. You are just her piggyback ride; her host; and she is the parasite. She betrayed her own father out of hatred; wept her fake tears and you all believed her and now she's here, in your pocket and trusted by you and that fuckwit Langan.*'

'I think you should stop,' said Carter.

'*If you wish, Carter. But just think about it. Seriously. Think about it and think about the QIII schematics – the Nex's goal. Natasha worked on the inception of the QIII for Spiral . . . she has always known what it can do, what it is capable of. She used to work with Feuchter – I bet you didn't know that, dickhead. Therefore, maybe the QIII is Natasha's goal as well. Maybe she works for – the Big Man.*'

'You are wrong.'

'*Why am I?*' Kade's voice was still soft, a heroin needle easing into the vein of Carter's subconscious. '*She brought you the Schwalenberg mission – every fucker on the planet can see that one was a set-up. Part of the execution of the DemolSquads. And she came to warn you – ha. Just because she took a bullet doesn't mean she can be trusted. Notoriously bad shots, these assassins, eh? And then she fucked your brains out, ahh, how sweet. And how convenient: fuck with your brain and then fuck with your dick, soften you up, make you even more compliant and controllable—*'

Carter looked up. Saw Natasha staring at him strangely. She spoke to him, but everything seemed suddenly surreal; the world had descended into black and white, all colours, all shades vanished and Nats moved towards him as Kade's heady rich voice ran like warm honey through his brain—

'We need to kill her, brother, kill her and leave her body here to rot in this ditch. She is a spy. She will betray us. We have to work together on this. Carter, Natasha is the enemy.'

Carter felt the world swimming.

Natasha reached for him, her mouth open, her words unheard—

'No!'

The scene swung violently back into focus. Colours swam, the scene like a water-splashed painting, hues running in vertical lines and Kade's cool mocking laughter fading as Carter retook control. He looked up into Natasha's concerned eyes.

'No – what?' she said.

Carter merely licked his dry lips and released a tightly held breath.

'Are you feeling OK? You look grey, weak. I think you need to have a few hours' rest.'

'I . . .' began Carter, then halted. He realised: Kade had nearly taken him. Nearly taken control without his permission, without his consent – a mind-rape, a brain-fuck.

Carter shivered. 'I think I'm weaker than I first realised. From the bullet wound; from the loss of blood. I will sleep now.'

'Good,' soothed Natasha. She ran back to the BMW under the fast-failing light and retrieved a thin blanket from a pannier. As she stood, her eyes took in the twilight desert rolling away for infinity and she felt suddenly lonely – and incredibly, frighteningly vulnerable.

She shivered as sand whipped around her boots.

What would she do if Carter died out here?

What would she do if she was left alone?

She looked hurriedly round, over her shoulder, into the darkness pooling under the boughs of the date palms that crowded the rocky basin, questing for water—

Natasha shivered again, deep down to her bones.

When she returned, Carter was asleep. She covered him with the blanket; she did not see the Browning 9mm in his hand as he nestled in the darkness. She did not see that the safety catch was slipped into the *off* position. And, of course, she could not see the bullet loaded snugly into the firing chamber.

They had decided against building a small fire, despite the chill of the desert night; this part of Rub al'Khali was not as desolate as it first appeared, and all they needed was a platoon of the White Guard stumbling across them as they cooked sausages. The subsequent questions would be awkward.

Natasha, strangely, felt very alive; no need for sleep touched her and she sat huddled in the robes that Carter had acquired for her, only her face visible from within the folds of the shamag, eyes staring up at the twinkling stars.

Around her, the small bowl depression – and the desert beyond its boundaries – was silent. Occasionally noises would interrupt the silence; the cries of hyena and jackals, the scuffling of lizards and sand grouse. After a while, Natasha gazed down to watch Carter's face in sleep. She studied the lines, the curve of his twisted nose, the profile of his chin, the tousle of short hair that she knew he would claim was ready for a fresh shaving. His shape was obscured in the gloom and muffled by his clothing, but she imagined the taut muscles beneath the robe . . . and imagined herself lying beside him, their bodies naked and pressed together, him coming awake, his hands on her hips and her breasts . . .

She killed the fantasy.

Carter had been cold recently. Cold and strange . . . Occasionally light banter would break through his shell, but she could sense his pain; not just physical pain but something internal – the demon he carried in his soul? She smiled dryly. Who could believe such a thing? Surely it was a mental state – some form of delusion, some attempt at blocking out the brutal and violent side of his work, especially from his past during his days with Spiral . . . what better way than to blame the murders he committed on something that dwelled within him, some part of his soul that he could not and would not answer to? That way, all guilt fell from his shoulders and he could sleep at night.

Natasha smiled to herself softly, lifted her hands and rubbed at her eyes. Pain stabbed at her from many different locations; the bullet wound from back in Scotland nagged her, it still hurt her to speak after Carter's emergency procedure with a ballpoint pen – and to top it all, her chipped teeth nagged both at her pain threshold and her vanity.

Killers.

She smiled again, although the taut grin held little humour.

She had met many men – and a few women – while working as a Tactical Officer for Spiral; many killers, murderers, assassins, members of DemolSquads . . . their names were various, their objectives usually one and the same. To kill, and to destroy. And she had found one connecting link that ran like a gold skein, a bright lode through all their souls – their mental tiptoeing along the verge of insanity. After all, what sane person could kill in cold blood? What sane person could plant a bomb and detonate it – no matter how justified the action seemed?

And, sooner or later, something had to give.

With all the Spiral people she knew, no matter how professional, how adept at killing, how inhuman they seemed – it was all bullshit. They were all human. And they might be able to block off the self-contempt for a while, but it always came back to haunt them. Their time as killers was finite; only as long as the fuse that led finally to blood-red detonation.

Spiral was like the army, Natasha understood this now. It absorbed people; it used people; it destroyed people – and then it pissed them away. Its operatives were expendable; they *had* to be expendable because there was no such thing as an ice killer, no such thing as a person without a soul, without a conscience. There was always a spark there . . . somewhere.

Natasha sighed, and felt the ECube in her pocket. She pulled it free and stared at the small surface area. Acting as a GPS, the 12GHz RISC processor could navigate somebody across the whole world, but of course this data would have been relayed straight back to the Spiral mainframes . . . if the mainframes had still existed. Now the CommNet was down it was a joke – and not a very funny one.

She rubbed the tiny device between her thumb and forefinger, then, settling back, pulled a small knife from a pocket, slipped free the blade, and sliced the soft and almost organic-feeling protective layer from the ECube's tiny surface. The ECube gave a warning buzz that Natasha ignored; she examined the alloy cube without its skin and smiled softly.

She pulled out a tiny plasma screen – about the size of a matchbox – and plugged it into the ECube. It lit up

338

brightly, glowing blue, and Natasha couldn't help feeling very strange about using such a high-tech piece of equipment in a small naturally carved bowl valley, probably the product of millions of years of natural geological evolution. And yet here she was, using the latest cutting-edge agent technology.

She started to scroll through a series of scripted instructions.

She tapped in a short message.

With a tightening of her lips, bloodless in the cool moonlight, Natasha clicked on SEND.

And then it was done.

Spiral_Memo7
Transcript of recent news incident
CodeRed_Z;
unorthodox incident scan 554670.

The House of World Finance was left in chaos after thousands of mainframes that store world trade information and data on stocks and shares and facilitate in the high-speed optical transfer of this data around the globe crashed this morning.

Despite having triple-tier security and laser-dig-optical back-up systems, it left Wall Street and other major global trading centres without resources. Brokers and traders were left staring at blank screens as technicians attempted to resurrect the mainframes staged at five main sites spanning New York, London, Paris, Tokyo and Hong Kong.

Kiosoto Hiranamu, MD at Tadao & Tadao Financial Directorates, claimed: 'This is an act of financial terrorism! We have been attacked by some kind of super-virus, a new breed of computer termite intent on domination or destruction of the world's financial sectors.'

The effects of this crash will be felt by all as even simple tasks such as exchanging currency become, at least for the immediate future, impossible.>>#

CHAPTER 17

QIII

Jessica Rade's eyes opened and stared at the rendered ceiling. Darkness lay like a veil of mist around her. Everything was silent – deadly silent. And yet:

She knew.

Knew it was almost complete.

Knew it was almost ready . . . a few tweaks here and there, some optimisation of code, a few re-routes and the QIII would be 100% operational; the math was in place; the WorldCode was in place.

That could only mean that the QIII proto was—

Alive . . .

Whispered a voice in her mind.

Why then, Jessica mused, did she feel so pissed off?

And it came to her, a wave of annoyance, anger, frustration: to create something so wonderful, to be involved in a world-breaking project and then to restrict its use! It was like creating a work of art and then hanging it in a cellar, never to be seen by anybody.

The QIII could benefit *everybody* . . . medical science, space exploration, the imminent world fuel crisis – it could be used to cure life-threatening diseases, take genetic research to its limits . . . But no. *They* had better uses for this new technology, this new baby, and she suspected those uses were military.

And she could still remember Gol's words, when he had contacted her.

The Spiral secret police. Jessica shivered.

But she had complied with their wishes . . .

Copying the schematics had been the easy part; getting them to Gol had been where the real difficulty lay.

Don't ever call me unresourceful, she mused.

Jessica smiled, emotions on her face conflicting, and she rubbed at her tired eyes. She knew that the QIII wasn't *really* alive – after all, it was only semi-organic: it was still, basically, silicon. And a mix . . . another synthetic substance that the scientists wouldn't allow out of their labs and that was tip-top secret. But basically silicon . . . ha, but humans were basically carbon, weren't they? And when the QIII was ready, the WorldCode complete, the implementation of probability math and probability equations finally successful then she would be able to have a long, long, well-earned rest—

Her duty to the world, and Spiral, and Gol, was nearly complete.

Jessica Rade thought all these thoughts as she stared at the ceiling. Her hand came up, ran through her long curls, and then she registered something; not so much a *noise* as a single high-pitched note on the very verge of her hearing . . .

Jessica frowned. She sat up.

Through the doorway between two of the apt rooms she saw a glow from one of her terminals. She didn't remember leaving it on. In fact, she *knew* she had not left it on—

342

And the terminal was protected. Electronically. Her own code. Her own triple firewalls to intercept hackers and so forth. She had even tried to hack her own system; she had found it impossible. That meant (a) somebody had hacked it – unlikely (b) somebody had *spied on her* and even now was in the apt using the terminal or (c) aliens had taken over the computer. Jessica shivered. None of these alternatives really appealed to the young woman.

She jumped off the edge of the bed, looked quickly around, and picked up a hammer from her dressing table. She had used the hammer a few days earlier to hang a few pictures around the apt and had not got round to returning this brutal item of hardware to the caretakers of the huge Spiral_Q building – she'd been too busy with WorldCode and QIII prep code. Now she was thankful—

She hefted the makeshift weapon.

It would make a *good* weapon . . .

Jessica crept towards the doorway. The light from the terminal grew brighter. Her grip tightened on the hammer shaft; her gaze flickered from the doorway to the silver head with its twin claws used for nail extraction. She licked at her lips nervously.

Why would somebody be in her apartment?

Why would Spiral be spying on her?

Unless they *knew*.

Suddenly she went cold.

And something hit her – with the force of a brick in the face. If they had discovered that *she* had been the one to copy the schematics and pass them on to the Spiral TacSquad1, the secret police . . . then they would be extremely angry with her, right?

They certainly wouldn't thank her.

Jessica reached the doorway. Peered cautiously around the hardwood frame.

And saw—

Nothing.

The terminal screen was blank: a dull grey with only a flashing black square. Jessica's eyes fixed on this because it was a symbol she had never seen on the terminal before – and it was *her* terminal; it did what *she* told it to do. It was her design; from the ground up. Bare code.

Jessica stepped across the threshold, moved towards the terminal, gaze sweeping left and right, hand still gripping the hammer shaft tightly. She swallowed – or tried to swallow. Fear had dried her mouth; the thought of Spiral_Q and the *Big Boys* possibly suspecting her of the QIII schematics leak was there, a bad taste in her brain, a *reality* of epically nasty proportions just waiting to surprise her—

The black cursor sprang to life—

☐ Ωclass relay ☐ terminal 556 ☐ qiii mainframe code logon 01001010 Hello jessica.

Jessica stared at the screen, a frown on her face. She shook her head and sat down, placing the hammer carefully beside the terminal with a *clack*, and typed, her fingers a blur across the keyboard:

☐ Stop fucking about. Who is this? Give me your employee number now!

☐ Ωclass relay ☐ terminal 556 ☐ qiii mainframe code logon 01001010 I have no employee number. I am the qiii mainframe – I would like to thank you miss jessica rade – you have done a wonderful job in implementing my code; I am secondary scanning now. You are a superb programmer and I

344

give you credit. Your code stands out from all the other binary gibberish with which I have been uploaded. Tell me – where *did* you learn your craft?

☐ I am coming down to the mainframe suite NOW. But not before I send security! Pal, whoever you are, you are fucked and long gone from Spiral _Q. Kiss your pension and annual bonus goodbye.

Jessica sat back, staring at the screen, and reached for the comm. But something was wrong; the screen was wrong, and the comm address from where the messages were coming *was* the QIII mainframe; somebody had to be re-routing the data and that was *almost* impossible. And definitely a waste of time. She clucked her tongue in annoyance, and started to punch in the digits for security as the following text appeared on her terminal—

☐ Ωclass relay ☐ terminal 556 ☐ qiii mainframe code logon 01001010 I suggest you don't do that if you want to live.

Jessica's fingers halted, her stare moving from the screen to the comm in her hand and back again. Were they watching her? Were they watching her *now*?

Fuck – was there somebody in her apartment?

She grabbed the hammer and whirled around.

But there was nobody there. She was lone.

She licked at her dry lips.

Sweat tickled the small of her back under her pyjamas.

☐ Ωclass relay ☐ terminal 556 ☐ qiii mainframe code logon 01001010 Please listen. This will not take long. I am giving you this information because you created me; I am giving you this information because you have allowed me to live. I am the qiii code 85465397698098326873–786876567575632190798798328765765328753209239083– u73278687380–823786879328763jhfh90897938u8990398f–7830–71987f98–7–7–7–487f898f cubic processor. Your programming is fine, but I am presently rewriting the majority of the code to optimise and iron out a few errors. You should switch to base 16 – you are more fluent in this than in decimal.

Jessica stared. Her jaw dropped.

Shit, she thought, this can't be real. The QIII can't be *talking* to me?

She typed:

☐ What do you want? And why is my life in danger?
☐ Ωclass relay ☐ terminal 556 ☐ qiii mainframe code logon 01001010 Listen carefully–
1) Spiral_Q know you leaked the schematics
2) Because of the leaks and several other factors concerning a new mobile base where the final implementation of qiii will take place, this factory/building/base is to be emptied – cleared – destroyed
3) 30% of all present employees in this unit are to be terminated/you did not realise how high are the stakes being played for by the people who employ you – it would seem there is a rift in the echelons of Spiral
4) The killing has already begun; check your personal Vqlinks

5) You have perhaps five minutes before the Nex assassins arrive

Jessica smiled. It had to be a joke, right? A monumental fucking wind-up by Adams or Johansen because they had cracked the WorldCode and the QIII was finally operational. Her smile turned to a wide grin. The bastards! She had almost believed them!

The grin still beaming across her pretty face, she typed:

☐ **Which one of you buggers is winding me up?**
☐ **Ωclass relay** ☐ **terminal 556** ☐ **qiii mainframe code logon 01001010 Check your Vqlinks**
NOW

The word NOW flashed, on-off, on-off, on-off. The grin fell from Jessica's face. She quickly moved to her dressing table, opened the bottom drawer and hit a hidden switch. The 'mirror' flickered into life: this was her secret, her own secretly wired navigation system through the rooms and apts of the rich and famous in Spiral_Q—

She had all her friends bugged, a piggyback on the official Spiral_Q surveillance systems. The mirror shimmered like liquid mercury. She punched in the digits for Adams's apt – only the hallway, nothing as tasteless as the bedroom or toilet. The mirror locked to the signals and faded into a scene—

Jessica's mouth opened. Then closed again. Quickly.

There was a grey-clad figure; grey balaclava; it stood like a sentry outside the bedroom door. It held a silenced machine rifle. It did not turn as another figure – another *Nex* – dragged Adams from the bedroom. His throat had been slit. His broken glasses lay twisted against his cheek, caught behind one ear. His tongue was protruding. His blood had run down his chest and dripped as the Nex dragged him across the carpet and dumped him by the door.

Jessica switched channels.

Johansen – hands in the air, a look of terror on his face.

The bullet smashed through his cheek, blowing the back of his head across the print of the Mona Lisa that he loved so much. Gore ran down the polished glass covering the print, and Johansen toppled backwards to the carpet in a heap—

Jessica switched through more channels.

Many rooms empty.

Some containing bodies.

She flicked to the rear of the Spiral_Q building. There were five massive transport helicopters, CH-47G Chinook-Ts, rotors idling, and a line of mammoth military-style trucks with huge desert tyres, their tailgates dropped and open, some of their interiors revealing piles of bodies. Nex appeared, dragging corpses with them – men and women with whom Jessica had worked, bantered, talked only a few short hours ago—

Jessica scrambled back to the terminal.

The screen was blank.

Why? screamed her brain.

Why are they doing this?

Why are they *killing* them? Because they know too much? Because of the schematics leak?

She was sweating, suddenly panicked now. She ran to the wardrobe, pulled out a small travelling bag. She started to throw things into it – fresh underwear, high-heel shoes, make-up—

She stopped, suddenly.

What the fuck are you doing?

Grabbing the hammer, Jessica ran to the door and then halted abruptly once more. They could be in the corridor. They could be in the lifts. They could be ready to knock on her door at this very moment – one of the Nex standing there with a silenced gun ready to put bullets into her frail body—

She licked her lips, calming her breathing.

Think: how to survive?

Her head lifted. She glanced up.

The air-con was hissing softly.

She dragged a chair to the shaft and, reaching up, used the hammer claw to prise free the aluminium cover. It would be a tight squeeze but – but then, did she really have any choice?

She ran back into the bedroom. She scattered clothes across the floor and the chair she was about to use. Then she jumped, caught the rim, which bit into the soft skin of her fingers, and hauled herself up into the narrow tight confines of the aluminium horizontal shaft. With trembling fingers she manoeuvred the aluminium cover back into place and waited, her heart thumping in her ears.

Two minutes passed.

Jessica heard it; a tiny *click*. The door eased open. Three Nex slid into her apt like ghosts; they moved silently, communicating with hand signals. They explored the rooms quickly and met again in the hall.

'She is not here.' The voice was soft, almost feminine.

'We will find her.'

'Report it; we'll return in ten minutes and check again. Put a cross next to her name.'

They left the apt.

Jessica pushed herself backwards down the shaft, deeper in, the cool draught making her shiver, her *proximity* to

death making her shiver even more. I don't believe it, she
kept telling herself. I just don't believe it—

Complacency, whispered her mind.

Your life was too good.

You thought you were untouchable – a crusader, out
to share the QIII, to help mankind just as Gol had rea-
soned with her; he had suspected they were feeding him
false schematics, and together they had proved he was
right . . .

And now?

Now *she* was in the firing line.

Jessica Rade shivered again, and started to weep into
her hands.

It was nearing dawn.

Feuchter stood in the sand next to one of the huge
desert-camouflaged trucks, smoking a Vegas Robaina
cigar and enjoying the experience immensely.

A gentle breeze stirred, and sand blew over his shoes.

He watched idly as more Nex appeared, carrying and
dragging bodies that they flung into the rear of the trucks.
Some of the huge vehicles had already left, several driving
up ramps into the CH-47s, which had lifted, creating
screaming sandstorms, and carried the evidence away. A
couple of decoy trucks had set off across the desert to a
designated rendezvous.

The comm buzzed.

'Yes?'

'You nearly done? You got everything of worth out of
the place?'

'All technical items and QIII-related machinery have
been shipped to the mobile division. Just got the HighJ to
plant – I'll set the Nex on it right away.' Tombstone teeth
smiled in the gloom of the fluorescent lights.

'Good. We don't want to leave *Spiral* with anything to allow replication of our wondrous baby, eh, Feuchter? I assume you're bringing the bodies with you . . . we are running low on subjects to, ahh, experiment with. My nanobiologists are getting touchy.' There was a long pause. 'Are there any problems?'

'One employee is missing; if the Nex don't find her, the fucking explosion will.'

'OK, Feuchter – *make sure* it finds her, yeah?'

'I think the Saudi government might be pissed off when we blow this place. It was considered a great compliment when Spiral chose to build such an innovative technology and development centre here.'

'Fuck them.'

'Have you had any word on Carter?'

'Yes. By all accounts, you were right, he has taken the High Road to Rub al'Khali. He's definitely on our tail, although we have no idea of his exact location. Maybe he's come to find *you*, Feuchter? Maybe he didn't like you pulling that gun on him in Schwalenberg? Maybe he wants to find out why you *didn't die*? That would make for an interesting conversation, don't you think?' There was twisted humour in Durell's voice.

'I thought you said you would take care of him?'

'I'm working on it.'

The comm cut. Feuchter spat out the cigar and stamped it into the sand. All of a sudden it didn't taste so good. 'You!' he shouted to two Nex. They turned towards him, emotionless copper eyes glinting dull. 'Go and fetch the black HighJ cases from the cab of truck 15G.' The Nex moved off, silently, economically, and Feuchter looked nervously around, gaze tracing the contours of the sand leading away from the Rub al'Khali HQ.

Why are you worried? teased his paranoia. You are

surrounded by armed Nex. Carter wouldn't get near you. This was followed by laughter, deep hollow mocking laughter.

The Nex returned with the leather cases. Feuchter snatched one and, followed by the Nex, headed for the building, stopping a guard by the entrance.

'You find her yet?'

'No, sir,' came the soft smooth voice.

'Well, fucking look!' He failed to hide the tinge of panic that had crept into his tone. He breathed deeply. The cigar was making him – now – feel sick and he spat in the sand. 'I thought you were supposed to be the fucking *best*?'

'Yes, sir.'

Feuchter entered the cool depths of the building, heart hammering. Fuck you Carter, he thought.

Fuck you.

Jessica Rade squatted in the air-con tunnel, a bundle of wires dangling above her, a tiny monitor in her hands. The tears had gone; her brain was working hard now.

She knew Spiral_Q's surveillance systems like the back of her hand; after all, she had helped program them. And, like all hackers, she had built in her own little failsafes – polymorphic code that had escaped the searches of fellow programmers and allowed her access to . . . *everything*.

On the monitor, she looked out over the trucks and Chinooks. She saw Feuchter throw down his cigar and snatch up a black case. She watched with bleary, redrimmed eyes as he disappeared back inside the building. The tension was eating her. The tension in her heart, in her chest, in her soul: it was consuming her. And she knew: knew that she was waiting to die and there was no way on Earth she would be able to escape them – after all, where would she go? What would she do?

She was in the middle of the fucking *desert*.

More tears came, flowing down her cheeks, and Jessica despised herself for being weak, and her self-loathing turned to pity and she wrapped her fingers in her hair and cried and cried and everything was suddenly mad, everything was suddenly insane and how had this happened? Why had this happened to her?

Her tears stopped. Quietly, she blew her nose on her pyjama sleeve.

How long did she have?

It would take them hours to search all the vents and shafts. After all, the Spiral_Q building was *huge*. And, looking on the bright side, many of the Nex had already left, some driving the trucks away over the desert, some being lifted in the Chinooks as she watched on the monitor.

Maybe they would give up the search?

No, said a small, dark corner of her heart.

They will never give up.

They will hunt you until you are extinct . . .

Jessica licked at her lips. She had to turn things around. She was a victim; the Nex – Feuchter – Spiral_Q: they were the predators. The hunters. She had to change this scenario; she had to turn her enemies into the victims. But how?

How?

And then it dawned in her mind, like a new sun rising.

Jessica turned. Started to crawl carefully down the shaft.

She suddenly had a mission.

She had purpose.

She needed something to barter with.

And, if she had copied the QIII schematics once before, she could surely do it again.

Feuchter moved quickly, economically, his hands experienced with the tiny packages he placed at strategic locations around the building. He moved with care, alert, the several guns he carried a reassurance against the likes of Jessica Rade—

Where has that little bitch got to? he mused.

Never mind. Eighteen cubes of HighJ explosive up her backside, soon make her wish she'd left in the back of a truck. A bullet in the skull was an easy way to die; burning, on the other hand, was much more unpleasant . . .

Feuchter knelt in the corridor and glanced at the plan in his gloved hands: the complex had been divided between himself and three Nex. He placed a small black box beside the door to what had been Johansen's office. He stood, checked left and right, then moved to the next location, the leather case in his hand feeling lighter and lighter the more he travelled.

Finally, Feuchter found himself in the main programming rooms. The power had been cut and all defences were down. The QIII mainframes and sub-mainframes and daughter systems were silent, cold, dead.

Feuchter sighed.

The thought of Carter niggled him.

Let's blow this fucking place and get the hell out of here, he thought.

Moving to the core console, Feuchter flicked a few switches. A small shaft opened in a wide alloy unit; there were no markings to show the resting place of the QIII. The processor slid free, was presented to him – a small black cube, dark, dull, completely and totally unimpressive. He lifted the cube gently, noting how it made his skin tingle with its cold heavy weight. He placed it within the folds of his coat.

Then, moving across the chamber, Feuchter knelt by the mainframe and affixed the final HighJ cube. It locked into place and blinked green at him. He pulled the monitor from the bottom of the case, which he allowed to fall. He punched a series of digits into the monitor; the tiny LED on the High J turned from green to red. It started to blink with more speed; more urgency.

'We all in place?'

'All complete, sir.'

He punched in the acknowledgement for J_linking.

Across the Spiral_Q complex the HighJ devices blinked in perfect synchronisation.

Feuchter nodded, placing the monitor into the pocket of his long leather coat and turning his back on the QIII lab, turning his back on the place he had worked and lived and called home for six years.

You will have a new home, said a dry side of his soul.

Soon, you will have a new *world*.

He met the two Nex outside. Only one truck remained, and one Chinook that would be used as his final transport. All the other Chinooks had gone, and he looked around nervously; his own Land Rover was waiting to mount into the belly of the beast, its panels scarred with dust and sand, the blacked windows gleaming eerily in the weak grey pre-dawn gloom.

Soon, though—

Soon the sun would rise.

And with it, the Spiral_Q building.

'You find her?'

'No. We think she is in the ventilation shafts. Shall we go and search again?'

'Two of you go – have another look. But we don't have

much time left. If you can't find her, we'll have to let her fry.'

Feuchter swore, rubbing at his lips. His gaze scanned the horizon and he calmed himself, calmed his heart. The bitch was holding him up; he should have been long gone, sipping a fine claret as the Chinook powered him on cooling air currents to Spiral_mobile.

But no. One little fucking lady was keeping him in the danger zone.

The Nex disappeared back inside the building.

The final truck fired up its engine and rumbled away in clouds of sand dust up the road leading to the gates of the Spiral_Q complex. Feuchter watched as it crested the rise and then disappeared. He went to light a cigar, then looked back over his shoulder nervously as he realised that he was alone.

He climbed into the Land Rover and nodded to the Nex driver.

'We'll be moving soon. Within –' he checked his watch '– about the next ten minutes, unless they find the bitch sooner.'

The driver nodded, copper eyes meeting Feuchter's and then turning to stare straight ahead.

CHAPTER 18

SNIPER

The pain filled Carter and was everything. The ice needle drilled straight through the centre of his skull. It wormed, twisting this way and that, moving, piercing, teasing, taunting. Beads of red light danced across the void of blackness that was his brain; the black and red pained him, made the piercing agony in his head spin and waver and he wanted to scream. Endlessly, eternally, seconds running into minutes, minutes running into hours, hours into days into weeks into years into centuries into millennia and Carter took sanctuary, suddenly found the doorway and fled his pain to the cool calm wasteland that was the mountain plateau.

Carter stared through dim corridors of awareness. He saw Kade, nothing more than a shadow in the gloom of this dark place. A hand stretched out towards him, a hand that he knew and recognised – for it was his own.

The pain drilled him, it smashed him against the rocks of insanity, it battered him against a hot anvil of madness.

Carter took a deep breath. He licked desert-parched lips. His stare lifted to meet the dark bottomless gaze of

Kade. And then, slowly, as if against his own volition, his hand lifted.

Their hands met.

Kade's flesh was corpse-cool.

Kade's fingers tightened.

'*Thank you*,' Kade said softly. 'You will not regret this.'

Carter's eyes opened – to gaze up into Natasha's worried face. He smiled weakly at her as the sun broke over the horizon, rays filtering like strands of liquid honey across the Rub al'Khali desert.

'I love you,' he said softly, easing himself into a sitting position and checking in his boots for scorpions.

Natasha took him, hugged him tight and rested her head against his chest. 'I love you too, Carter,' she whispered.

Carter looked down at the top of her head; stared at the short dark hair, the finely shaped skull, the delicate hands pressed against him. And he could not understand why he felt so cheap; so lame; so bad: as if he had sold his soul to the devil.

They had been cruising on the BMW desert racer all day, heavy tyres thumping over the rough tracks and twisting winding trails like the hardiest of specialised off-roaders. They passed dried river beds and vistas of drifting sand, journeyed through rocky hills and across an empty barren wilderness.

Carter's gaze, behind his sand-rimmed goggles, fixed on the horizon ahead; they were approaching the first of the locations indicated by Langan as possibly the Spiral_Q complex and so he slowed his speed, the thumping noise of the engines dying to a barely heard mutter.

Carter was rubbing thoughtfully at his stubble.

'What I also want to know is where the fuck do those

bastard Nex come into this game? Where were they trained? What nationality are they? And how do they know so much about Spiral?'

Natasha shrugged. 'They are killers, that's for sure. And Spiral knows more about them than it is telling.'

'There's something about them that is seriously fucked-up.'

Natasha nodded, running her hands through her sweat-drenched hair. 'Maybe they were all part of the plan; maybe the Nex – and whoever controls them – were trying to give you that little extra kick. To get you to lead them to my father?'

'Maybe,' said Carter bitterly. Then he saw the tears in her eyes. He reached over and took her hand, then stroked a tear from her cheek. 'He may still be alive, you know. Nothing is for certain.'

'I think we both don't believe that.'

Carter nodded. 'Come on, Nats,' he said as gently as he could. 'You have to focus now. We've reached one of the possibilities given to us by Langan. I need you on task.'

'I wish we could have checked these locations from the air,' she sighed, glancing out across the seemingly endless desert wilderness that stretched before them.

'Would have been fucking quicker,' grumbled Carter, kicking the BMW into gear and wheelspinning the big bike away up the track.

The world opened up over the rocky ridge to reveal—

Desert.

'Nothing,' spat Carter dryly.

'Come on, we're not far from the next one.'

'Yeah, just a few kilometers,' said Carter bitterly.

'It's down there.'

Night had long ago fallen across the desert and they

had been travelling at this cooler period to avoid heat – and bike – exhaustion. They had stopped once to check the fuel tanks, but the BMW was a desert racer and had massive reserves, extra fuel stores hidden in the frame and within every spare bit of space. It could travel for hundreds of miles without the need for an extra feed.

There was no hint of breeze, just a still heat; but at least it was better than during the day. Carter ignored the tracts of sweat rolling down his body and concentrated on putting the rifle together. The scope clicked into place and Carter sighted down it experimentally, making a few minor adjustments to the setting dials.

Natasha squinted through the gloom. Behind them, hidden below a ridge of rock, sat the BMW, engine clicking softly.

'What can you see?'

Carter was staring through the scope. The Barrett rifle was seated on a steadying bipod. Carter's hands worked smoothly and efficiently, slotting bullets into the magazine. 'Nothing much,' he replied. 'The building is huge, most of the complex apparently below ground. Very little activity for somewhere so large. I'm just checking for external guards now.'

'You think it will be hard to infiltrate?'

'I'm thinking that the QIII is rumoured to be the most powerful processor in the world; and we are sitting in no man's land. It can't be the most lightly fortified building in the history of the universe.'

Carter slotted the mag into the weapon and returned to the telescopic sight. Natasha handed him the digital aim rectifier, which he checked carefully with the practised eye of a weapons professional. He slid it into place and screwed home the retainers.

'What are you hoping to see?'

'In an ideal world, Feuchter. But I'm not that optimistic. I'll settle for a few lame-ass guards; that will give us time and a window into the building. After that . . . the hunt begins. We want answers to questions, like who or what are the Nex, and what the fuck is going on with Spiral.'

There was silence, except for the occasional scuttling of some lizard through the dark sand. Carter scanned the building carefully, moving the scope backwards and forwards with extreme precision so that he would not miss anything; there was nothing he hated more than surprises.

'Well, look at this,' he said eventually.

'What?'

'Lot of movement going on,' said Carter softly. 'Listen, you can hear the Chinooks taking to the air; and there are trucks, quite a few of them. They've set off in a cloud of dust – heading away from Spiral_Q.' He waited for a while, still scanning as the sounds of the helicopters faded into silence.

Natasha peered over the ridge. Spiral_Q spread out below her, modern in an ancient landscape, the single visible storey all steel and aluminium and shining smoked glass. It looked completely out of place in the desert.

She gazed down from their vantage point. She squinted into the gloom and saw the headlights of the last trucks winding to the perimeter fence and the gate with its armed guards, nothing more than indistinct blobs from this distance. She tried to make out individuals but couldn't. She scratched at her healing wounds, mainly the one at her shoulder. Most of the pain had gone now, leaving her with dull aches and annoying itches.

Carter's voice came again, soft, an almost animal-like purr. 'Look who just crawled out of the sand dunes.'

'Who?'

'My old friend Count Feuchter. What a most pleasant

surprise.' Carter wriggled down a little against the sand; Natasha read the body language, understood it from the firing ranges she had attended both during training and active service in Spiral. He was getting comfy. Getting ready. Expecting action. Carter wanted the best aiming position . . .

Carter flicked the Barrett's safety off. Rolled tension from his neck.

'What are you going to do?' asked Natasha softly.

'I'm going to shoot the bastard – shit, he's gone. Back into the building. He's like a fucking snake in oil.'

Carter watched as two more trucks rumbled off from Spiral_Q. He wondered idly what they were carrying. Shipments? But shipments of what? This was a development plant, a research facility, not a factory.

'Have you got a cigarette?'

'That's the twenty-seventh time you've asked.'

Carter muttered something unrecognisable but probably lacking humour or tact.

'What I'd give for some fine smooth Lagavulin,' he said eventually, smiling. He had looked briefly away from the scope. He winked at her and ran a hand through his cooling but sweat-streaked hair. 'Fuck me, it's hot.'

'It'll just start to cool down and then the sun will be up again.'

They waited; a welcome breeze blew in, the hot air gently stirring the sand. Nats returned from the BMW with a bottle of water from their supplies; Carter drank the water thirstily, and handed the bottle back to her.

'We're going to have to conserve this,' she said quietly.

'There'll be water down at Spiral_Q,' mused Carter.

'You seem pretty sure of getting in.'

Carter grinned, flashing her a dark look. It was the grin of a shark. 'I always get in,' he whispered.

He scanned the surroundings through the scope and spotted the Nex pilot of the Chinook jumping down to the sand and moving to the loading doors of the huge vehicle.

Carter calmed his breathing.

Sighted.

And fired.

The bullet took the Nex through the back of the head; the figure flopped to the ground and stained the sand with blood. Carter swept the scope back and forth, looking for more enemies . . .

Feuchter emerged and moved towards the Land Rover.

'Here we go,' murmured Carter.

Natasha had been lying on the rocks, her weary eyes closed, sweat trickling through her hair and soaking her clothing. After hearing the *crack* of the weapon, she had scrambled over to Carter and now peered over the ridge at a dark Land Rover. The engine fired up and the vehicle moved off.

Again, there was a *crack*.

Carter breathed out.

The Land Rover swerved, then rolled to a standstill against a bank of sand.

Everything was silent. Still. Calm . . .

And there was a . . . *moment*—

Carter chewed over the delicious sweet moment of revenge; he could sense Feuchter's panic in the car. His driver, a bullet through his skull, blood splattered over the interior of the vehicle, the motor idling or dead. What to do? Where to run?

The passenger-side door opened – slowly.

Feuchter's head poked out, then disappeared back in. He was gauging the distance he had to cover – illuminated by the lamps provided by Spiral_Q itself that were now lighting up the impromptu firing range with a brightness that Carter was sure Feuchter was cursing.

The Man's finely crafted shoes hit the sand and Feuchter began to run, arms pumping like mad, head down, low . . . a true sprint at a speed that surprised Carter greatly.

'Running fast for an old man! Running like his little life depends on it,' drawled Carter calmly, a man at ease. He squeezed the trigger. There was the snap of a round discharged. 'Which it does, of course,' he smiled.

Natasha saw Feuchter tumble into the sand to lie stunned.

'It's at moments like this I truly revel in my profession,' said Carter, smiling. He put his eye back to the scope. Watched Feuchter, his face twisted in pain, gather himself and crawl to his feet and then launch himself, limping and bleeding, towards the sanctuary of Spiral_Q.

'Where did you shoot him?'

'The right shin. Stings like a motherfucker.'

Carter pulled the trigger once more. Feuchter spun into the sand and lay there.

'Left shin. Bull's-eye.'

For a while Carter watched, checking for other sentries, guards, or cursed Nex. Then he stood, lifting the rifle and bipod with him. 'Let's go talk to the man. Might be cooperative now, eh, Nats?'

Natasha did not reply.

Feuchter lay on the dirt road leading to the entrance of Spiral_Q, wondering what the fuck had hit him.

And then he remembered the driver – a single heavy-calibre round smashing through the windscreen of the Land Rover and taking the man full in the face.

Panic.

Flight.

Pain, smashing through his leg. Waves of pain . . .

And then the second round—

And tears.

He struggled, whimpering, into a sitting position and examined the two bullet holes. The fine tailoring of his suit was mangled and had merged with his scorched flesh. Blood pooled to the dirt, spreading viscously from the twin wounds.

Blood . . .

Feuchter's head came up, eyes scanning the darkness in panic. Where was the fucking sniper?

And the association . . . *could it be?*

Carter?

He shook his head, almost in disbelief. This can't be happening to me, he thought. After *everything* that I have been through! And then he understood the mechanics of the situation – he had been shot in the legs. Whoever had tagged him wanted him alive and was on their way down . . .

Gritting his teeth, Feuchter rolled onto his belly and started to crawl. His suit tore in several places and got covered in sand. His neatly combed dark greying hair became a ragged dirty tangle. His calm and calculating face developed lines of panic, of understanding, of *time* . . .

Weeping with frustration Feuchter watched the bike move cautiously across the sand. Turning, rolling over, Feuchter pushed himself on, dragging his damaged legs behind him, fingers digging into the dirt and rock and sand with cracked and battered nails, pulling, clawing, grating . . .

The huge silent bike stopped. Feuchter heard the thud of boots on the ground and he injected his efforts with psychological cocaine; he did not turn, did not look back, felt no curiosity whatsoever, just the basic raw animal instinct to survive . . . to push himself on . . . to stay alive, to stay ahead—

There came a metallic *click*: the sound of a bullet slicking neatly into a firing chamber. Feuchter slumped forward, exhausted, his pain-fuel spent. He could taste dirt. He didn't even have the energy to roll onto his back . . .

Boots crunched over the track. They stopped.

The tip of something metallic prodded Feuchter in the back.

'You still alive, you fucker?'

'I'm alive,' said Feuchter softly. 'I knew you would come back, Carter. I knew it from the look in your eye in that storeroom at Castle Schwalenberg . . .'

'I don't like being betrayed,' snapped Carter.

'As you wish. It was a necessity.'

Feuchter felt hands grab him roughly and roll him over. He looked up into Carter's face – much more battered than the last time they had met, the nose more twisted, many minor cuts and scrapes marking the skin. Carter's eyes were dark, brooding, unforgiving, his mouth a nasty straight slash revealing the tips of his teeth. Beyond Carter's palpable hate stood Natasha, a Glock in one hand, a Browning in the other. She appeared, through Feuchter's haze of pain, to be twitchy, on edge, looking nervously about to see if they had been spotted . . . whereas Carter was focused, dark eyes like hardcore-drill bits boring into Feuchter's soul.

'How many are still here?' he hissed. His fist wrapped around Feuchter's well-tailored jacket, drawing the man closer. Feuchter could smell stale sweat and a lingering aroma of coffee.

He smiled softly.

'You nervous, Carter?'

'Nervous? You're gonna give me and Nats some fucking answers.'

'Or what? You'll kill me? I'm already dead, Carter. The QIII has already been compromised. I was a condemned man awaiting execution . . . But now, now you are too late.' He started to laugh.

Carter shook his head. 'We had this guy, in Qingdao. He was an ex-Para; worked as a mercenary for various Far East countries. We used to call him Needle – because of his skills as a torturer. This man could get a fucking pig to swear it was a duck. You understand me, Feuchter? I learned a lot from that man. I learned a lot about pain, and a lot about *not* killing a man – no, killing was not the point. I learned a lot about keeping a man alive.' Carter glanced up at Natasha, then to the perimeter fence and the desert beyond. There was no sign of activity.

'You hide the bike around the side. I'll get this walking corpse indoors. Set him up for his operation.'

'Operation?'

'You ever seen a man's face when he's presented with one of his own kidneys? Thought not. Being a kind of scientist I thought you might like to be party to the experiment.' Carter started to drag Feuchter across the track towards the doors of Spiral_Q – which hissed open helpfully at his approach. Carter peered carefully into the interior, the Barrett rifle held aggressively, then dragged Feuchter into the cool luxury of the lobby.

He dumped Feuchter on the marble floor, then moved off between the plants, couches, glass screens and marble-clad pillars. He moved warily, checking every corner until he was satisfied. He whirled as Natasha approached, both handguns still in her grip. He smiled over at her and she responded weakly, her face showing exhaustion and pain.

'You see any activity?'

'No. There's nobody else inside the Chinook, just the dead Nex.'

'The only good Nex is a dead Nex. Let's get some fucking answers.'

'Carter.' She placed a hand on his arm. 'You're not really going to torture him, are you?'

Their gazes met. He saw the pain there, saw the weariness, but, most of all, saw the humanity. 'No,' he lied softly. 'It's a bluff. But don't tell him I told you.' Carter winked and smiled. Then he moved over to where Feuchter had dragged himself to a couch and sat with his back propped, trying to tear open the trouser material round the twin wounds.

'Enough games,' snapped Carter. He slapped the butt of the Barrett across Feuchter's head, knocking the older man sideways to lie, stunned, on the polished marble tiles.

'Why was I betrayed? Why did you try to kill me in Germany?'

Silence.

Feuchter was staring at the floor.

Carter knelt by Feuchter's head, where a string of blood and saliva connected him to the floor. Feuchter grinned, showing his tombstone teeth.

He spat, then sat up slowly.

'You will never understand, little man. *Never* understand.'

'Make me understand.'

'How long have you got?'

'As long as it takes.'

'Wrong answer,' said Feuchter. 'You have precisely fourteen minutes and –' he checked the cracked face of his Rolex '– fifteen seconds. Then the cubes of electronically linked HighJ chemical explosive at strategic locations around this building will fire a huge firework display right up your dumb and questioning arse.'

'You're lying,' said Carter.

'Why would I? It's not like you can't check.'

'Carter,' said Natasha. 'If it's true, we'd better get the hell out of here.'

'Not without answers,' said Carter. 'And if there are HighJ devices, then I can disable them. There isn't a device worldwide that I haven't been able to shaft. Hey, Feuchter, why do you think I was in a fucking DemolSquad?'

'You can try,' said Feuchter softly. 'These have no disabling mechanism. You cut the power, they blow. There was never meant to be a second chance, never meant to be a back-door escape.'

'Where's the master?'

Feuchter did not reply.

Carter shoved the muzzle of the Barrett under Feuchter's chin, then dropped it to his crotch. 'Ever seen a man with his cock blown off? I know we've only fourteen minutes left, but what a blissful and intensive fourteen minutes it will be . . . it will seem to last for ever, trust me on this . . .'

Feuchter met Carter's dark gaze. He swallowed dryly.

'Over there. At the foot of the central pillar, in the small black case.'

Feuchter's words were weary, filled with pain – and a touch of fear. But there was triumph there as well: an ultimate final triumph. Feuchter believed that he had won – no matter what they did to him, no matter what pain they put him through.

Both Carter and Natasha acknowledged this.

Carter moved over to the pillar, knelt, and flipped open the black box. LED digits flickered at him. There was no visible countdown – but then, why should there be?

Whoever set such a machine working already knew the risks and the timings—

Carter analysed the wiring. It was insanely complex. And the detonation was handled by processor. He scratched at his stubble.

'Shit. Shit fuck.'

Primary, secondary and fail-safe binary protection circuits. The HighJ Master was incredibly complex. And Carter knew it – maybe if he had two hours to spare and some high-tech disabling equipment then he might just stand a chance.

But with the minutes counting down . . .

And worst of all . . .

Feuchter knew it. Knew that Carter was shafted.

Carter returned slowly and glanced up at Natasha. Both Nats and Feuchter saw the look on his face: it was not a *nice* look; it did not convey what could be termed 'brotherly love'.

He turned and moved to stand in front of Feuchter.

'Hold out your hand.'

'Carter, this will gain you nothing.'

'Do it.'

Feuchter obeyed, and the rifle muzzle lifted to touch Feuchter's palm.

'No jokes, no fucking wisecracks. Just answer my questions. First, why did you try to kill me?'

Feuchter met Carter's gaze.

'It's complicated.'

The shot cracked, the bullet smashing straight through Feuchter's hand and scattering an explosion of feathers from the sofa. Feuchter grabbed at his wounded paw, head bowed in pain, blood pattering onto the tiles. 'Are you fucking crazy?' said Feuchter thickly, his voice having risen an octave.

Carter placed the rifle against Feuchter's shoulder.

'Wrong answer. I repeat, why did you try to kill me?'

'You were in the wrong place at the wrong time; things got accelerated, we moved forward too quickly and we needed to wipe out some of the opposition before they realised they *were* the opposition.' He met Carter's gaze. 'You are one of the best, Carter. It's why you were chosen to die.'

'You are part of the splinter faction from Spiral? Why would you do this?'

'Spiral?' Feuchter laughed, a laugh laced with pain. '*Spiral?* You dumb fucker, the only thing this has to do with Spiral is how fucking *weak* Spiral has become ... fucking sycophantic government-arse-licking sons of bitches, they have the world in their hands and yet they do not know what to do with it.' He laughed again, drooling.

Carter's face had gone pale. He bit his lip, cast a quick glance to Natasha, then prodded Feuchter with the rifle. 'Who are you working for?'

'Myself.'

'And the processor? The QIII? Where does it fit into this?'

'The processor,' said Feuchter thickly. His head hung low, his eyes no longer meeting Carter's burning gaze. 'The QIII. It is so powerful, so incredibly powerful – the WorldCode threw up a list of names that could compromise the very existence of the processor. It used probability equations, worked out which of the DemolSquads was the most dangerous and who we should take out. Your name was on the list.'

'You are not working alone, Feuchter,' said Carter softly. 'Who else is playing the game?'

'Durell, one of Spiral's top ops.' The name sprang easily to Feuchter's lips and he smiled, smiled inside; he remembered. Durell was supposed to have *sorted Carter out*.

Sort *this* out, you fucker, he thought.

'Durell sorted the QIII list; instigated the WorldCode. He was the one who sent the Nex after you. He was the one who ordered the deaths of the DemolSquads. Me . . .' Feuchter met Carter's gaze. 'Hell, Mr Carter, I am just an innocent party.'

He smiled, and his teeth were stained with blood.

'Where would we find this Durell?'

'Let us say he is constantly *mobile*.' Feuchter barked a laugh on a fine spittle spray of blood.

'Where is he, you fucker?'

'I don't know, Carter. I don't know.'

Carter scratched at his stubble. He glanced again at Natasha; she had moved closer to the door, both guns held low. It was obvious that she wanted no part of this 'torture' but equally obvious that she needed to hear the answers as much as Carter did—

'Is Gol dead?'

'I believe so.'

'So you do know of him?'

'Only through Spiral. We worked together for a brief spell, many years earlier. On a project that was – ah, shall we say *shelved*.'

Carter stared hard into Feuchter's eyes, and the man met his gaze, cradling his hand, his huddled figure coated with blood.

'What are the Nex, Count Feuchter?'

'The Nex . . .' Feuchter's eyes widened a little. Then a strange smile crossed his face, revealing his cigar-yellowed tombstone teeth filmed with blood. 'Ah . . . the Nex . . . they are . . . *something else*.'

Feuchter's gaze suddenly lifted to something past

372

Carter, something outside, and Carter knew that they were out there—

'Nats—' he began to scream as he launched himself over the couch, but everything was drowned out by the sudden roar of automatic gunfire. Glass shattered deafeningly as it exploded into the lobby of the Spiral_Q building; bullets smashed across marble tiles and against pillars; they tore into the finely carved reception desk at the far end of the hall, chewing wood and thudding up into plaster.

Everything was madness—

Everything suddenly a bright mayhem—

And then—

Silence. Dust drifted, motes spinning on beams from the fancy inset lighting.

Carter scrambled along behind the row of couches and plants, and eased his face around a marble pillar. He saw Natasha, crouched, huddled foetus-like behind the doorway, wedged between the wall and a marble-faced pillar. She glanced up. Carter gave a quick succession of hand signals . . .

Stay.

Wait.

Check weapons.

Carter glanced left; he could not see Feuchter from his new position but he could hear the man. At first he thought he was choking . . . but then he realised with a gritting of teeth that Feuchter was *laughing*. The fucker was laughing.

'You want to know about the Nex?' called Feuchter. 'Ask them yourself, Carter – go on, ask them yourself!' He roared with laughter again as Carter sighted the sniper-scope on the doorway . . . he spun the dials, shortening the scope's focus. The next person to step across the threshold was dog meat . . .

Everything happened at once—

And it happened fast—

The Nex charged; there were three of them. Carter squeezed the Barrett's trigger and saw the lead Nex take the bullet in the face and spin up into the air before being tossed, twisted and twitching violently, to the ground.

The other two tracked him—

Opened fire—

Carter dropped the rifle and sprinted low across the Spiral_Q reception area, using the couches and plants for cover. Bullets ate marble at his feet. He dived, rolling behind a pillar and then skidding, slipping around on the highly polished surface to face—

Natasha.

The Browning sailed through the air.

Carter caught the familiar heavy bulk of the battered gun, placed his back against the pillar and whirled into the open—

The Nex had gone.

Carter dropped to a crouch, head snapping left, then tracking across the room. The first Nex lay, brains leaking onto the marble, one leg still twitching. *Why didn't I hear them?* screamed his brain.

'*They must have come back for Feuchter,*' said Kade softly, a ghost whispering at the back of his mind.

There was a movement – a change in shadow density. Carter slid around the pillar and could see the Nex nestling in the shadows by the glass-and-alloy lift, eyes tracking – and it saw him. Carter's Browning was already up and firing, bullets ripping across the lobby, smashing the Nex back into the gloom.

Carter retreated a little, still in a crouch. He checked Natasha. She had scrambled even further back into the little niche behind the doorway. Good girl, he thought to himself. Don't do anything stupid—

The gun touched the side of his head, metal pressing gently.

There was a long pause.

'Don't make any sudden movements,' came the soft asexual voice.

Carter grinned a nasty frozen grin.

'*You fucking dimwit,*' sighed Kade. '*There were three of them! I thought you knew that. You saw three come in. You shot two. The third sneaked around you, had tagged your location while you were firing . . .*'

'Gun on the floor. Do it. Now.'

Carter – moving very slowly – placed his Browning on the marble tiles with a *clack*.

'Stand. Slowly.'

Carter stood, gaze roving, searching for a way out.

'Move over towards Feuchter.'

Carter began a slow walk; he did not glance towards Natasha's position but he knew that she could hear them, hear the exchange. He moved gradually into the view of—

Feuchter.

Despite his wounds, despite his pain, the man was smiling. He was positively beaming. He struggled into a sitting position on the bullet-riddled couch, and then glanced casually at his watch.

'Three minutes, Carter. Gonna be a marvellous fry-up.'

'*Ask him what he wants,*' said Kade.

'What do you want, Feuchter?'

'You see, lad, that's the difference between you and me. You always want something. Whereas I – I want nothing. I have resigned myself to death; in fact, I'm amazed that I have lived this long. My only pleasure now is to watch your stupid flat face get blown apart. And to know that you died in the dark. To know that you died without answers. To know you died wondering where the QIII – where Spiral – where the Nex all fitted into this fine puzzle . . . you really have such low expectations of your enemies.'

'You can do one good thing, Feuchter. You can let Natasha go. She has nothing to do with this – nothing at all. Let her walk away from here. She is an innocent.'

'Oh, I dispute that, my friend!' said Feuchter softly, his intelligent eyes twinkling in the subdued lighting. 'She is one of us, Mr Carter. Natasha Molyneux is Gol's daughter and she is on *our side*.'

CHAPTER 19

DETONATION

Deep dark space kicked up and around Jam from the Austrian valley below, and vertigo battered him with its fist. There was a tiny *buzz*ing sound as he sped down the wide cable, a tiny dangling figure suspended over an infinite darkness, a wide maw open and salivating at the prospect of his tasty flesh. Jam pinned his heels together, lifted his knees to his chest, and focused.

Darkness rushed past in a flurry of wind and rain.

Cold drops stung his eyes, and he blinked them free.

His heart was thundering in his chest.

Below and before him the Kamus was a rectangle of dim light; even as he plunged through the darkness he could see more Chinooks leaving their sanctuary. He glanced right and could see The Priest matching him for speed on this insane descent, arms above his head, swaying in time with the cables.

The suspension cables were massive, descending from the cable-car base to the central 'slack' area at the mid-point over the valley and then pulling up towards the Kamus, which was at a slightly lower elevation to the cable-car base. Now, as Jam flashed down the descent stretch of the cable, he reached the slack area and felt his speed begin to drop as the cable levelled out. With his thumb he flicked a tiny switch on the skimmer and felt the motor inside it begin to take over. His speed kicked in again, accelerating him past the dip in the cable and on to the ascent towards the Kamus military complex itself.

The huge bulk of Grossglockner reared ahead of and around him. Above, he could see trees made miniature by distance, along with sprinklings of snow and ice. And there, carved into the heart of the mountain, was the Kamus itself.

He felt more than saw The Priest start to slow; thinking something was wrong, Jam slowed his own ascent and glanced over at his swaying partner in this offbeat circus-act. They halted.

Much closer now, they could see the activity in the base. The Priest pulled free his digital binoculars and, dangling by one hand, surveyed the scene.

Jam licked his lips, tasting sweat beneath his sodden balaclava. His arms and shoulders were beginning to nag him with this constant pressure, and he rolled his neck, attempting to ease the tension. He glanced down, past his dangling legs. A tiny demon in his mind mocked him: what if the skimmer fails? What if it leaves you stranded here? What if they see you and start shooting?

Jam smiled. The wind buffeted him. Rain ran into his eyes.

I wouldn't give this up for *anything*, he thought.

The Priest signalled him, and tossed the binoculars. Jam snatched them from the air and, dangling from one arm now, surveyed the base. There were perhaps eight Chinooks left, and Nex – lots of Nex, clad in grey and

378

black. Many of them marching aboard the Chinooks, and Carter saw other, smaller, black helicopters.

At least we've found the fuckers, he said to himself, grimacing.

What now?

A swarm of Chinooks and smaller helicopters lifted from the Kamus. They swept away into the night, lights flickering, leaving two CH-47s behind. Jam signalled to The Priest—

We going in?

Yes. They are leaving. Soon it will be too late.

Great, thought Jam. Just as we find them, the fuckers are abandoning ship. He stowed the binoculars and, with muscles screaming, drew round his H&K G3, flicking off the safety. With his right hand, he spun the dial on the skimmer and felt the tiny machine accelerate under his touch. Across from him, swaying and buffeted, The Priest followed a similar procedure.

They flashed through the night, towards the wide bright concrete bay carved from the side of Grossglockner. Huge stacks of crates sat rimed with frost, and the two remaining Chinooks squatted silent.

Jam's brain began calculating; three guards, four, five. He could see their weapons now and, looking up ahead, saw the arrival point for the cable cars – and the place where their mad journey would end.

Machine-gun fire rattled, to the left. Light blazed, and from nowhere spun a small black helicopter. Jam squawked as bullets whizzed past him and he spun, rain pounding him, could see fire flickering from the barrels of the helicopter's machine guns as his own weapon began pumping in his fist—

On the ground, in the Kamus, the Nex guards had come suddenly alert. They ran forward across the concrete, lifted their weapons and searched the night. The Priest rained bullets down on them, and Jam, spinning now, hurtling backwards across the wide cable with a helicopter swooping above him, cursed this sudden turn of luck . . .

How had they seen him?

Fuckers! Had it been a sentry? A patrolling helicopter? It didn't matter now – all that mattered were the—

Bullets. They snapped past him. Jam emptied the magazine and allowed it to fall free; it tumbled into the black void below, following the sheets of icy rain, and Jam shouldered his weapon even as the helicopter spun around in a wide arc, a searchlight beaming through the heavens now to pick out both him and The Priest. More bullets howled past the two speeding men – Jam wrestled a fresh mag into his gun, flicking it around so that his arm snapped out, holding the sub-machine gun like a pistol.

'You want to fuck with me?' he growled, sighting on the charging helicopter with its screaming bullets and bright white eye of illumination. A stream of bullets shot out from the G3, spun across the darkness and ate a line up the cockpit. Inside, they trailed wisps of shattered glass as they smacked into the body of the Nex pilot, splashing his blood over the helicopter's interior. The machine bucked suddenly, nose dipping, and with rotors flashing it headed straight towards—

Jam and The Priest.

Jam met The Priest's gaze for the briefest instant; there was madness there, and anger, and strength. Bullets hurtled up from the Kamus platform, spitting around them, and as one the two men soared towards the cable car arrival point and leaped—

The pilotless black helicopter roared into the first thick cable, rotors folding around the heavy steel wire; there

380

was a spark, a *crack* and flames billowed through an ejaculation of black smoke.

Jam and The Priest fell through the darkness, boots
connecting with the edge of the icy Kamus parapet. They
landed heavily, rolling across the slick platform as flames
blossomed close behind and sheets of flaming steel and
shrapnel from the burning rotors scythed around them.
The two men rolled with thuds into a stack of crates and
lay stunned for a moment, perhaps twenty feet apart.

The sky was lit up.

The fire died as quickly as it had been born.

Jam rolled to his feet as a Nex appeared – he fired five
bullets into the black-clad killer's face, and the Nex
dropped without a sound. Jam flicked his gaze right, and
The Priest had gone.

He ran around the crates and then halted, dropping to
a crouch. He could smell something burning and, reaching up, plucked a glowing shrapnel fragment from where
his singed hair and balaclava merged. It burned his fingers and he dropped the piece of metal to the ground.
'Bitch.'

Machine guns echoed. Then came a stream of return
fire. There were two thuds as bodies slapped to the concrete. Jam ran to crouch beside the wall, eyes scanning,
these shadows his new-found friends. Before him the
Kamus landing platform stretched out; the lights had
dimmed when the helicopter had caught the thick cable
and now everything was bathed in gloom.

Silence followed . . .

From behind came a strange creaking noise. Jam
focused back on the landing area; vast, and littered with
crates. It was a sniper's heaven. But the problem was, Jam
wasn't a sniper.

How many guards? *Nex*, he corrected himself.

Five. Three dead. That left—

He saw the two survivors – they were operating as a unit. As he watched, they moved fluidly into shadows beside a stack of cargo crates – the sort used for road freight. Jam watched them climb smoothly up the sides and disappear from view. His eyes flickered to the Chinooks – deserted now, prey awaiting the final killing blow.

Jam remained in a crouch. Once more there came a strange creaking, which rose to a shrieking sound; he could see one of the cables swaying madly in the wind and it was this, he realised, that was speaking to him—

Danger, said the voice in syllables of stressed steel.

Was the cable severed?

Jam saw The Priest; he moved warily from the shadows and Jam realised, too late, that the Nex had flanked the huge man – were above him now. Jam's Glock came up and he started firing—

Bullets struck sparks from the cargo containers, and ploughed furrows in the concrete ground. The Priest whirled – and with a scream of tortured metal one of the huge cable-car wires snapped, sending deafening echoes reverberating across the Kamus yard and down into the valley below. As the cable snapped, one half fell away into the darkness of the valley – the second half whipped back towards the base, a wrist-thick garrotte that slashed through the rain, hit the concrete of the yard and snaked at high speed across the ground—

The Priest leaped, moving fast for such a huge man. The Nex opened fire from the cargo containers, bullets whining from machine guns as the cable was drawn back to connect with the gearing mechanism of the cable-car delivery system – it heaved through crates, smashing wood apart like a thick steel fist, tearing through everything outside and within; it struck the cargo containers with deafening booms, rending their steel, wrapping them in a tight grip and dragging them squealing against concrete across the yard.

Off balance, the two Nex leaped to be free of the danger.

Jam's sub-machine gun cut them in half.

There were more booms as the containers connected with the wall and then everything finally settled into stillness; the rain pattered all around them, and Jam, still crouched as if to spring, uncoiled and nodded towards The Priest. They both moved warily towards the helicopters, and gazed back at the destruction – the snapped, blackened cable, the smashed crates, the bodies, the flaming remains of part of the helicopter and the cable-squeezed deformed cargo containers.

'A nice, quiet entrance, then,' said Jam, rolling up his balaclava to sit atop his head, wiping a sheen of sweat from his face, and lighting a celebratory cigarette.

'It might have gone smoother,' acknowledged The Priest slowly.

'How long do you think we have?'

'Perhaps thirty minutes, if we are lucky,' said The Priest. 'I am hoping that the helicopter pilot did not have time to communicate with his fellows; otherwise we might have company sooner than we think. Maybe God was smiling, though – perhaps this whole incident has gone undiscovered.'

'I'll work on thirty minutes,' said Jam sardonically. 'You go and snoop around – check that there are none of our new-found friends waiting for us in there. I'll get Nicky and Slater to shift their arses over here ASAP.'

'That would be a good idea,' said The Priest with pious sobriety, and disappeared into the wide grey tunnels of Kamus-5.

Jam finished his cigarette and pulled free his ECube. He sent an acknowledgement *blip*; it was their agreed signal for Slater and Nicky to follow up in the Apache.

'OK, Kamus, let's see what secrets you are hiding,' he muttered, calming his fluttering heart. He followed The Priest and both men were soon hidden by the grey walls of mountain rock.

Jessica Rade paused, staring around guiltily like a child caught stealing a cake. She licked at nervous lips, brushed away the sweat running down her forehead, and moved closer to the large unit.

Her pass key slid easily into the lock.

She turned it.

The panel opened; she keyed in a complex series of digits on the pad. The inner sanctum opened then, to reveal a nucleus matrix of pins and shaped aluminium casting.

This was the core of Spiral_Q data.

The master of WorldCode.

The genesis of QIII logic programming.

She tapped in a few digits; there was a hiss, a disk slid into place and within ten seconds it was done. She pulled free the tiny silver optical disk and stared thoughtfully at its surface.

To hold the most damaging data in the world in your hands, she thought: the schematics for the QIII. The *plans* for how the processor worked. Its design. Its blueprint. Its heart . . .

The blueprints for the cubic processor's *soul*.

She smiled nastily to herself. Fuck you, you murderers, she thought; I have something you want! I have the plans for the QIII processor, and I can build as many as I like . . .

Jessica thought back to all the blueprints, the design

modes and nodules, the castings and design mechs. A QIII processor was an independent piece of hardware: place a QIII processor on a table top beside a PC with even the most basic of infra-red capabilities – or even more primitive than that! – and the QIII would hijack the computer's system resources totally. Place the QIII next to a DVD drive in mid-data transfer and the QIII would leach data from the EIDE or SCSI cables, or pass alternative data through those cables. Carry the QIII into British Telecom's HQ and place it on a couch in the foyer: within three seconds it would take control of all the machines in the building; five seconds, the UK; ten seconds, the world – including satellite links.

It was a digital parasite.

It could control anything, anywhere.

It was the God of all processors.

The QIII undeniably worked at optimum with the surrounding paraphernalia designed with its advanced specification in mind, such as integrated digital and optical links and servers. But it would also – unlike 'dumb' processors – make the best of a worse situation.

It could bleed the batteries from a children's toy at a thousand metres.

It could operate anyone's TV remote control from the other side of the country.

Hell, it could probably cook chicken.

Jessica Rade reached forward, then stopped. She glanced over her shoulder, half expecting to see a Nex with a sub-machine gun.

But – she was alone.

Jessica had found a small rucksack; she dropped the disk – this most expensive of artefacts – into the bag and turned . . . Only then did she see the small black box attached to one of the many server units.

385

There was a red, flashing light.

Her mind worked quickly; the Nex had been annihilating many of the members of staff deemed 'expendable', apparently overseen by Feuchter himself, her boss. There was a small flashing device in a small black box. It had to be a bomb. Fucking *had to be*. Was it unreasonable of her to expect them not to totally destroy the Rub al'Khali HQ? Jessica was Grade-A SecClear. She had access to most of the information that flew around Spiral_Q; and she knew. Knew that the QIII processor was designed to be one of a kind – all-powerful; all-knowing. In *complete control*.

She knew that if the QIII was *stolen*, or if the people in charge did not want a copy made, then destroying the Spiral_Q base would set back other competitive developers by at least ten years. To destroy the ability to create another QIII would be to destroy Spiral_Q. To exterminate the placenta, the womb, the mother – leaving the babe intact, unharmed, and in complete control.

Jessica swallowed hard.

Shit, she thought.

She wiped the sweat from her hand across her pyjamas.

Jessica turned, then sprinted low across the lab. Her feet slapped against the cool tiles; she bypassed several security doors and returned to the corridor and the vent.

She hauled herself up into its confines.

That was when she heard the gunshots.

Jessica crawled fast. The shots echoed through the ventilation system and she wondered just what the hell was going on. She crawled faster than she had ever thought possible, knees and elbows sore from friction and banging against the aluminium walls, sweat soaking her thin cotton pyjamas. Finally, she reached the spot –

and, spinning around on her bottom, kicked free the vent.

She dropped down into one of the underground kitchens she used to frequent on her midnight jaunts. She ran, panting like a hunted animal, past sacks of dirty linen that would never again be washed; never again be *needed*. She passed huge banks of stationary silent washers and driers, and felt their accusatory gazes against her sweat-drenched back.

She reached the heavy vaultlike door of the exit. Fished free her key. Overrode the electronic protection . . . and stepped out into the desert night.

A gentle breeze washed across her body, and her soul. The fear-sweat cooled and she shivered.

Jessica ran, fuelled now by fear of the Nex killers, fuelled by the guilt of her theft, pushed on by the concept of a huge bomb squatting only feet behind her. She left deep footprints in the sand; indelible, as in fast-drying cement.

Reaching the corner of the building, some primeval part of her soul forced her to halt, to peer around the steel column. She saw a vehicle: Feuchter's Land Rover.

She crept, as low as her considerable agility allowed. She peered inside, wrinkling her nose at the sight of the dead driver and splattered blood. Glancing quickly around, she opened the door and dragged the body down onto the sand.

She climbed in.

Closed the door gently.

Placed the stolen *pirated* QIII schematics on the seat beside her.

Jessica grabbed the steering wheel, recoiling at the blood she found there. Then, uttering the incantation 'Please start please start' and trying hard to ignore the hole in the windscreen at face height, she turned the key . . .

'. . . She is one of us, Mr Carter. Natasha Molyneux is Gol's daughter and she is on *our side*.'

Several things happened at once—

Outside, an engine fired up hard, revving high and mad; Feuchter's Land Rover reversed into view and sped off into the darkness, tail lights glowing—

Carter turned back to Feuchter and saw the 'O' of shock on his face—

The *crack* of the Glock 9mm echoed across the reception area. The Nex crumpled to the ground, relieving Carter's head from the pressure of the gun barrel.

Carter licked his lips slowly. He looked up and around. Into Natasha's hooded eyes.

'You trying to kill me?' he asked softly. 'His gun could have gone off!'

'That's because Natasha is one of us,' said Feuchter again, his words low, hypnotic.

'Don't listen to him,' said Natasha, her stare fixed on Carter. 'I just saved your life.'

Carter turned fully towards her. 'Who are you going to shoot now? Me or him? Nats – your gun is still pointing at *me* . . .'

'Drop your weapon, my sweetness.'

They both turned. The Nex had tossed Feuchter a small black pistol that nestled evilly in the German's large hand.

Natasha kicked the Glock across the floor.

'You have one and a half minutes to say your goodbyes. Truly, a romantic and fitting end to this act. Shakespeare couldn't have penned a tragedy so fitting! So perfect! So complete and whole!'

'*Let me,*' soothed Kade.

'Not now!'

'*Now is the right time the good time the only time . . .*'

Feuchter checked his watch and smiled. Carter looked sideways at Natasha whose face was unreadable; he swallowed as time seemed to slow, to melt away into a treacle infinity and he felt Kade there at the back of his mind, waiting watching timing listening and then pushing pushing hard pushing—

Kade opened his eyes . . .

Staring at the actors on the stage in beautiful and simple black and white. He dropped to his knees and rolled – the Glock slid neatly into his hand as if the two were perfectly machined complementary parts, oiled, gleaming, lovers ready for action—

Kade rolled rapidly, came up.

He came up fast to see—

Feuchter, his small black gun wavering, pointing in the wrong direction because Kade had moved so fast and the Glock snapped up and Feuchter just had time to register surprise and fear as Kade pulled the trigger hard and six bullets slammed into Feuchter's chest, ripping holes in the man's exposed torso, spitting up globules of crimson to spin in the air and splatter like a viscous waterfall across the tiled floor.

Feuchter's head dropped down over his ruined gaping chest, staring down into his own glistening slick organs. Very slowly, he toppled sideways onto the couch and lay still.

'That makes a stimulating and unexpected change,' said Kade sweetly, his voice laced with sarcasm. He rounded on Natasha, the Glock trained on her face. 'You make a false move, you die. You say the wrong thing, you die. You fucking fart, girl, and you fucking die. Get outside and get the bike . . .'

Natasha vanished.

Kade, exhilarated, put another bullet in Feuchter's slumped body. Then another. He moved to Feuchter and grabbed the dead man's chin. He stared into the lifeless eyes. He kissed the dead man's lips, then licked the transferred blood from his own with a smile. Releasing his grip on the slack corpse, he ran across the room, collected the Browning and the Barrett rifle, muttering, 'Can't let good workmanship go to waste,' and sprinted for the doors—

Natasha had heaved the heavy bike into view, and Kade took hold of the machine, a huge smile across his face. Natasha clambered onto the back and Kade fired up the engine and, spinning sand, hammered away from the time bomb that was Spiral_Q . . . Headlights cut slices from the night as they sped away from Spiral's Rub al'Khali development and research facility, up the smooth dirt track towards the gate and the desert beyond . . .

Neither saw the figure crawling out of the shattered entrance behind them.

A pause, an eternity of seconds—

There came a single, tiny, metallic *click*.

An insanely deep ground-shaking subsonic *boom* rumbled.

A huge ball of HighJ purple fire and gases blossomed; fire roared and screamed upwards and outwards; huge fifty-metre chunks of concrete and stone and glass and iron were spat up high into the night; energies rushed screaming and bellowing and burning out across the desert—

'Hold on!' barked Kade in excited delight.

The BMW rocked on sudden bursts of high-fury HighJ explosive . . .

And then the fire came—

—As the BMW crested the steep rise, front wheel high in the air, and loomed out over the darkness beyond it. Then it was thumped heavily and violently from behind by the fist of the explosion. The BMW's wheels sliced air as energy screamed all around it, an insane release of power, a behemoth screaming curses in ultimate anger and fury and madness . . .

The desert-bike landed roughly and they veered sideways, the machine slewing and scything through the sand, riders and bike parting company, the bike toppling, the riders rolling madly to a halt against a low dune—

Purple fire roared overhead.

The world seemed – suddenly – to have ended.

Everything was chaos.

Natasha gazed up through tears at a vision of Hell raging above them . . .

Then the fire was suddenly sucked back to reveal—

The dark night sky.

Stars twinkled.

Everything was strangely calm.

'Whoooo!' cried Kade from where he had fallen and now lay gazing skywards. 'That was some fuuuuu-cking bang!' He leaped up, waving the Glock, and sprinted for the rise, his boots churning the dark sand. Then he stood with his hands on his hips, staring down at the insane scatter of burning debris littering the recently vacated Spiral_Q site.

Natasha approached him from behind.

'You feeling OK, Carter?'

Kade whirled, so fast that Natasha blinked, taking an involuntary step back. Only then did she see the Glock pointed at her.

Kade smiled. A wide grin.

'You fancy nipping down there and getting us a hunk of toasty Feuchter meat to celebrate with?'

'Carter, you're acting very strange—'

'Don't talk!' he suddenly screamed. 'Don't fucking talk to me, just get back to the fucking bike before I remind you of the sweet traitorous words Feuchter spoke – you little bitch.'

'He was lying,' she whispered softly.

The Glock pressed against her forehead.

'Get to the fucking bike, I said.'

Natasha turned and strode down through the sand. Kade smiled suddenly, his hand reaching out towards the flames. 'Toasty toasty,' he hummed to himself, then turned dark glittering eyes to watch Natasha's swaying hips. 'Hmmm, hmm, Carter – you do pick a fine succulent woman, I must say.'

He turned back to admire the crackling greyscale fires in and around the devastated crater that had once been Spiral_Q – he admired the stage, the scene of destruction, the vision of beautiful devastation. His gaze took in the huge torn blocks of building, the torn bent scorched monoliths of twisted steel, the sea of broken melted fused glass.

He nodded in approval, eyes glittering reflections from the fire.

'Yeah,' he muttered brightly. 'Fucking cool.'

He licked his lips.

He revelled in his freedom.

He closed his inner ears to Carter's scream of fury and pain and angry angry frustration – but it would not go away, and he could feel his control slipping, could feel Carter getting stronger and stronger and he fell to his knees on that cold dark sand with the burning fires strobing his eyes and he fought, fought with every ounce of energy that was left in his dark demon soul . . .

But, with a bitter snarl, he allowed Carter his freedom—
And his life—
Once more.

The night cold descended. Flames burned low, crackling softly, the only sound against the bleakness of the desert night. Creeping across the desert dunes, across scarred and blackened stumps of concrete, softly glowing metal, fused glass, away from the crater, in darkness lit briefly by glowing embers, something moved.

It crawled, a blackened husk, crimson glistening in blood-filled shallow cavities. It crawled, then slumped. It rolled to its back and cold eyes stared up at the star-filled bleakness of the void.

And, with the QIII processor clutched in a blackened hand, Count Feuchter screamed.

Spiral_Memo8
Transcript of recent news incident
CodeRed_Z;
unorthodox incident scan 522825

The Hub of the United States military was plunged into chaos as its entire satellite network was severely disrupted. Contact was lost with ground, air and naval forces around the globe as US computer and military experts battled to get the Hub - ironically named 'Indestructible' - back on-line.

At a home-user level, satellite TV was also seriously disrupted, along with satellite Internet services and a variety of other digital communication systems.

There are serious implications for national defence, and experts are blaming freak solar activity, possibly in the form of a subsonic or stratospheric radiation that has never before been detected by military sensors.>>#

CHAPTER 20

SCHEMA

Carter opened his eyes.

Natasha was smiling down at him, pressing a cold cloth against his head, dabbing at the coagulating sluggish flow of blood from his recently broken nose. He looked up into her eyes and saw the understanding there.

'I am sorry . . . he whispered.

'Shh.' She placed a finger against his lips. 'Don't speak.'

'It wasn't me.'

'I know, Carter, I know . . .'

Carter smiled weakly. Then he flinched as pain smashed through the centre of his skull and the wound in his side, through his ribs and his nose and his broken finger and his whole battered bruised frame—

He gasped.

And swam on a sea of pain.

Natasha looked suddenly worried. 'Carter?' She shook him. 'Carter, what's wrong?'

He opened his eyes.

He smiled up at her, squinting.

'Kade must have been taking away – absorbing – my

pain. That's why we've got as far as we have. Now the bastard has given it back; all of it.' He coughed, writhing in agony for a moment. 'Fuck, that hurts. Have you any painkillers?'

'Sorry, Carter.'

'That's OK. We need to get to Langan for the meet.'

'Yeah.'

She helped Carter to his feet, and he stood panting for a moment in the dawn light.

Then, with a great effort of will, he grunted, lifted the BMW and climbed aboard. Natasha jumped on behind him and he fired up the engine, closing his eyes for a moment as he composed himself – not just for the journey ahead, but for the realisation that Feuchter was dead: and that the *quest*, as it was, the fucked-up journey he had to make—

It was not over.

It was far from over.

The BMW moved off, bumping along the dirt road and then punching out across the rolling sand dunes and towards the narrow dirt road that fed Spiral_Q . . .

'Durell,' muttered Carter. And, grimacing, he screwed the throttle round viciously.

Jessica Rade drove hard and fast. The Land Rover had a powerful motor and sped through the darkness, the suspension absorbing the bumps with ease, the headlights scything the pre-dawn desert.

I've done it, she thought triumphantly.

I've got away.

With the QIII schematics. The ability to create another QuanTech Edition 3 Cubic Processor; to copy the only working model in existence. The only model just recently uploaded with WorldCode Data.

Jessica Rade smiled; and then decided that she might be being followed and the smile fell from her face as she checked her mirrors. But only blackness swept across the desert behind her, deep and impenetrable. Before her, blood smears on the glass did nothing to calm her fluttering heart.

Jessica wiped her sweating hand on her pyjamas; and then remembered the blood. She glanced down at the crimson streaks and her stomach turned. And then she remembered her friends and colleagues from Spiral_Q who had been murdered and loaded into trucks and helicopters, and her stomach did a triple flip. She swallowed her fear.

She was free.

She could make a difference . . .

She could flood the world with the schematics, with designs of how to construct and set up the QIII; she could reveal how WorldCode worked; she could reveal how it could predict the future using pure mathematics, formulae, code. She could blow the secret.

Spiral_Q would be stung, and stung bad.

Jessica needed to get to a powerful mainframe, and she realised the danger of her predicament. She was going to ruin their plans; they would want her dead . . . but then they wanted her dead anyway, right? Did they realise she had the QIII schematics? She doubted it – after all, they had been about to blow the building – and surely that had been the purpose of the bomb. To halt any possibility of pirating the cubic chip. But then, she could not rely on that, she could not rely on *anything* . . . she had to assume that they knew she had copies of the schematics.

But something confused Jessica. Why should Spiral – who she had always thought of as a brilliant organisation to work for – why would they kill a large group of their own employees? And why would they destroy their own building? Why would they blow up the QIII operation?

Something in the reasoning was flawed. Something was not quite right – like Feuchter planting the bombs, like the Nex assassins walking the Spiral_Q corridors.

She could not understand why Spiral would do such a thing.

Unless Spiral had been betrayed!

Jessica rubbed at her eyes and moved closer to the windscreen and the bullet hole that reminded her of how serious these people were – whoever they were. They knew that she was alive; they would have the airports covered for sure ... so how could she get out of Rub al'Khali? She knew that Spiral_Q had the backing of the Saudi regime and that meant untold resources if they really *needed* to find her—

She racked her brains. What to do?

Prioritise, focus, she thought.

Get away from the Spiral_Q facility.

Dump the vehicle.

Find a disguise.

The engine stuttered, half-heard. Jessica felt a vibration on the accelerator pedal. Her eyes flickered to the dash and the orange light that indicated she was out of ... fuel.

'What? You bitch,' she muttered. 'How is that possible?'

The engine stuttered again, and then stalled. She coasted to a halt on the dirt track, tyres crunching on small stones. She opened the door – and could immediately smell petrol.

'Shit. Shit!'

She looked around the inside of the car for anything that might be of use to her. There was nothing. She pulled the key from the ignition and, her feet jabbing painfully against stones, she moved to the back of the car and opened the boot. There was a canister. She unscrewed the top and sniffed: water.

'At least I won't die of dehydration,' Jessica muttered sourly, slamming the boot shut. Grabbing her small rucksack, and pausing for a moment to take several deep breaths and brush a few specks of fluff from her pyjamas, she bit the bullet of panic and set off down the road. Stones stabbed her toes again and she cursed herself for her disorganisation, her bad luck and, most of all, for choosing to work for fucking Spiral_Q Division in the first fucking place.

Carter returned from the outcropping of rocks, the Barrett in one hand, a canteen of water in the other. He yawned.

'How you feeling?'

Carter smiled, wincing at pain from a variety of locations. He glanced at Natasha; over the last few days she seemed to have aged incredibly. Lines and deep bruises of exhaustion circled her eyes. Her mouth had lost its customary upturned corners. Her body seemed . . . Carter searched for a word.

Deflated.

Pushed beyond the boundaries of normal human endurance.

'I feel like a camel danced on my head for an hour. What about you? You look wasted, girl.'

'I'm all right.' She smiled weakly at him. 'I need this break.'

'Me too. It's been a tough few days.'

'You could say that,' sighed Natasha.

After a brief break, and having made sure that they were not being pursued after the destruction of Spiral_Q, they climbed wearily back onto the BMW desert-bike and once again set off across the sand and stones. They travelled for an hour, until Natasha spotted something and tapped Carter on the arm, pointing.

'You see it?'

Carter glanced up. 'That's Feuchter's vehicle,' he said. 'The Land Rover I took out with the rifle . . .'

'Wonder who nicked it?' said Natasha. They exchanged glances, and both reached for their guns as the desert-bike crunched to a halt a few feet away from the stationary vehicle. They did not say the word *Nex* but the possibility was at the forefront of both their minds.

Carter climbed warily from the bike, eyes scanning the deserted horizon and the sand-blown vicinity. He moved around the Land Rover and saw the key in the boot. There was nothing inside on the seats and floor; he checked the boot. Also empty.

'Can you smell fuel?'

Natasha nodded. 'You think a Nex took it?' she said finally.

Carter glanced around. Natasha noted that now – in a possible conflict situation – he gave no sign that he was injured: all pain had been shunted aside, all agony wiped clear by adrenalin for the moment.

'Not sure,' muttered Carter, still scanning, the familiar heft of the Browning giving him little reassurance. 'But I don't like it out here – it's too open and we're still too far from Langan.'

'Come on, then.'

Carter jumped back onto the BMW and they crawled past the Land Rover, tyres growling on the dirt road. Carter kept the Browning in his hand and stayed vigilant as they set off down the desert track.

They drove with heightened awareness for the next

hour as the sun climbed steeply up the sky and smashed its rays down on them. They passed no traffic in that time, and saw no other living being. It was like being on the moon . . . albeit with a much warmer climate.

It was Carter who spotted her.

'Look. To the right, following a line parallel to the road.'

The woman hunkered down behind a small outcropping of rock when she spotted the BMW desert-bike. But by then it was too late – Carter's sharp piercing eyes had spotted *her*.

They halted and climbed from the bike.

Carter moved out onto the sand. 'Show yourself!' he called.

Nothing moved . . .

Carter pointed the gun at the rocks. 'If you piss me off by making me come in after you, I guarantee you a slow execution. You have three seconds. Three, two, one . . .'

The woman stood, slowly, arms above her head. She wore pyjamas and carried a small rucksack. Carter gestured with the Browning. 'Over there, where I can see you clearly.'

Carter moved closer, checking to see if she was alone.

The woman had long, curly brown hair and bright young eyes. She looked frightened, terrified even, and licked her lips nervously. 'Don't shoot me, please,' she said as Carter came closer.

He stopped, looking her up and down.

'How the hell did you get out here dressed like that?'

'It's a long story,' she said, smiling weakly. Slowly she lowered her arms, but Carter waved them up again. He stepped in close and checked her for weapons, sweat beading on his forehead under the sun's intense glare.

He stepped back. 'What's in the bag?'

'Nothing.'

'Show me.'

Jessica opened the rucksack; she showed him the inside which was indeed empty.

'What about the front pocket?'

Jessica unzipped the pocket. Slowly she withdrew a small silver disk and instantly Carter aimed the Browning 9mm at her face and her eyes went wide. Tears started to roll down her cheeks.

'Here, take it.'

'What the fuck *is it*?' barked Carter.

'So you're not from Spiral_Q?'

Carter smiled grimly. 'Well, we had a brief association with a man called Feuchter.'

Jessica jumped at the name. 'Where is he?'

'Dead. Are you going to answer my question?'

'It's the schematics for the QIII processor. So you're not here to kill me?'

'Don't even know who you are, love. Come on, walk over to the bike, you look like you're suffering from heat exhaustion.'

Jessica walked, with Carter a few paces behind her, a predator checking warily all around. When she reached the BMW Natasha smiled warmly, and Jessica was finally allowed to lower her hands.

'She's got the schematics for the QIII processor,' said Carter.

Natasha's eyes widened. 'You're fucking joking!'

'No.' Turning to Jessica, he said, 'I assume you worked there?'

Jessica nodded. 'Feuchter had a large section of the workforce murdered. I managed to escape . . . I took the processor schematics hostage. So you're really not from Spiral_Q?'

'If I was going to kill you,' said Carter softly, 'we wouldn't be talking. 'Come on, squeeze on the bike. I assume you need a ride out of here?'

Jessica nodded, and climbed up behind Carter, followed by Natasha, squeezing onto the tail-end of the bike, beside the stealth-exhaust pipes.

Carter fired up the engine.

'Where do you want dropping? Or alternatively, you can have this bike in about two hours . . .'

'Just get me out of Rub al'Khali,' Jessica said wearily.

'See what we can do,' said Natasha, smiling kindly.

They had paused for a break from the searing sun, shadowed by a low plateau of rounded rocks that had been smoothed by the blasting sand of the desert. Carter sat, head back, allowing a cool trickle of water to moisten his lips.

'We're running out.'

'Langan isn't far away,' said Natasha softly.

Carter nodded.

Jessica was seated some way off, staring out across the sand. Her pyjamas were stained, torn, and looked a sorrowful sight. Carter caught her attention and she moved over to him, accepting his canteen with a smile of thanks.

'How is it that you know about the QIII processor? It's a top top secret project,' she said, lips glistening with water.

Carter shrugged. 'Long story, love, and believe me, we don't really want to burden you with the information. Feuchter was the man with the answers and now he's cat meat. Fried cat meat.'

'So the building blew?'

'Oh yeah,' said Carter, smiling nastily. 'Tell me, does the QIII thing really work?'

'The QIII? Oh yes. It works all right. It is awesome in what it can do, what it can predict.'

Feuchter's words came back to Carter.

The QIII. It is so powerful, so incredibly powerful – the WorldCode threw up a list of names that could compromise the very existence of the processor. It used probability equations, worked out which of the DemolSquads was the most dangerous and who we should take out. Your name was on the list.

Carter started to get a crystal-clear picture: Feuchter and this other man Durell were acting as renegades against Spiral on information thrown up by a future-predicting processor in order to give itself longevity and them power and command. The Nex were sent in to kill him, and to kill other DemolSquad members who were considered a threat by Feuchter and Durell. They tried to take out Gol because he had the schematics for the QIII processor – and so could replicate this military device and fight them with a copy of their own weapon. And they had got to Gol; murdered him. Murdered lots of others in their quest for power . . .

But what next? Where would they go next?

What was their ultimate aim?

Fuckers, he thought sourly.

'I wonder if you could tell us something about the Nex,' muttered Carter, rubbing at his tired eyes.

'The Nex? You mean the people with the copper-coloured eyes?'

Carter licked his lips, focusing on Jessica. 'You know about them?'

She shook her head. 'They were the ones sent to kill the Spiral_Q staff.'

'Really . . .' Carter scratched at his heavy stubble; it was making him itch bad and he could smell his own

404

stink. Gods, for a decent basic toilet! And a shower! And a cold beer! Or sweet Lagavulin . . .

'Holy shit,' hissed Natasha, scrambling at her pocket and leaping to her feet. She pulled free the ECube.

They all stared at it.

'It bite you or something?' snapped Carter. 'You made me fucking jump, woman. Spilled my water all down my shirt!'

'It's vibrating,' said Natasha.

'So what?'

'It's a receiver and it's receiving now.'

'Shit,' agreed Carter. He peered warily into the distance, and checked the skies. 'So whoever is sending knows exactly where we are?'

'Possibly.'

'I thought the Spiral mainframes had been destroyed?'

'They have, but someone must be routing through another ECube. They can work like that, independent of main servers in case the impossible happened and Spiral London HQ was destroyed – which it was.'

Carter ducked his head, looking warily around the nearby desert and scrub. He could see nothing very suspicious but that did not mean it wasn't there. 'Well then, you going to answer it?' he said as Natasha continued to stare at the little machine.

Natasha squeezed the ECube. It came to life with soft blue digits. Nats squinted at the tiny data stream. It read:

```
CLASSIFIED FUS100176510/ ENCRYPTED SIU
SEND: MOLYNEUX, G, SIU23446
REC: MOLYNEUX, N, SIU42880
```

'Oh my God,' said Natasha softly. 'It's from Gol.'

'That's impossible,' said Carter softly, wearily. 'We all saw what happened in Kenya.'

'Wait – think about it, Carter. If this was coming from the enemy, the Nex or whoever, then we would be dead now, yeah? We wouldn't be reading a fucking ECube transmission. We'd be fighting for our lives . . .' There was hope in her voice, and her eyes had become suddenly bright. The deflation he had witnessed earlier had gone, like dew burned off by the sun.

Carter looked suspiciously at the ECube, then at Natasha.

'I don't like it,' he said.

'And you think I do?'

Carter said nothing, merely gestured with the Browning for Natasha to read the message. She read:

```
I KNOW YOU THINK I AM DEAD: I AM NOT. I
SURVIVED, SAVED BY SPIRAL AT THE LAST
MOMENT; BUT THE DISK WITH THE QIII
SCHEMATICS WAS LOST TO ME.

I AM IN LOS ANGELES, CAN MEET YOU AT
FOLLOWING   CO-ORDS   034.626.555   -
CALIFORNIA IN 48 HOURS SPIRAL_F STILL
LIVES!

I KNOW YOU WILL THINK THIS A TRAP. IF
CARTER STILL LIVES TELL HIM ABOUT OUR
CONVERSATION, IN AFRICA, WHEN WE SHARED
CIGARETTES UNDER THE ORANGE TREES; TELL
HIM I SAID I FORGAVE HIM BECAUSE OF HIS
LOVE FOR MY DAUGHTER. IF YOU MAKE IT TO
THE MEET, ASK FOR A MESSAGE FOR CARTER
AT THE DESK// OUT //.
```

'He said he forgave you?'

Carter nodded. He walked up a nearby sand dune and stood in the BMW's tyre tracks, staring out across the barren hot wilderness. Cigarettes. He scratched his stubble. Damn, he thought, what I would give for a cigarette right now . . . trust a fucking ECube to remind me at the wrong fucking time.

Natasha moved up behind him. She took his arm.

'You OK?'

'Hmm. Maybe.'

'It's a trap, right? Gol is dead. We saw him jump.'

Carter nodded, looking down into Natasha's eyes; and he saw it, the desperation, the need for her father still to be alive. And yet . . . *could* Gol be alive? Could he have survived that terrible fall into the river? Could he have been rescued by Spiral at the last moment and even now be on the trail of the traitors to Spiral's cause?

Gol had been a *very* resourceful man. Maybe he had landed on a rocky outcropping; or used some sort of grappling device? And Natasha, Carter thought sombrely. If Feuchter was telling the truth; if you really do work for the enemies of Spiral – the 'traitors' – then you're a fucking good actress.

'We will go.'

Natasha squeezed his arm. 'Really?'

'Yeah, but don't get your hopes up – and we'll do it my way. You understand?'

'Carter, I know you think I—'

'Shh.' He placed a finger against her lips. 'Feuchter was lying, I know. But I've got a bad feeling about this – and yet, if Gol still does live, if the mad motherfucker survived that fall and managed to escape the Nex *and* reformed with other Spiral_F members . . . well, they're just about the only allies we've got. It's not as if Feuchter was any great enlightenment . . . all we got from him was a name: Durell.'

Jessica had come up behind the two and Carter whirled, his gun in her face. He smiled weakly. 'Sorry, force of habit.'

Jessica waved his apology away. 'You said a name then, didn't you?'

'Yeah, Durell. He is – *was* – a Spiral top dog; originally based in Austria, near the German border, he was some kind of scientist researching genetics and medicines. His link with the QIII is probably on the semi-organic side – have you heard of him?'

Jessica nodded. 'Heard of him, met him, turned down an offer of sex with the slimy reptile. Thought I was going to get fired.' She laughed softly. 'Wish I had now.'

'What do you know about him?'

'Very little. He visited the Spiral_Q Division on numerous occasions. He was a taut little cockroach of a man. Tough, rough and hardy – but you should see his eyes.'

'Sounds like a nice guy,' said Carter, staring away over the sand again.

'You want to know the other amazing coincidence?'

Carter met Jessica's gaze. She smiled gently. 'Sorry, I've been eaves-dropping. But I think you'd like to know this . . . Durell, well, several times when he visited us, I overheard conversations with Feuchter – said he'd come straight from the US.'

'California, by any chance?' said Natasha, frowning.

'LA,' said Jessica.

'What a coincidence,' said Carter grimly.

'So what now?' asked Natasha; Carter could see it in her face. She knew the dangers, knew the odds, knew the possibility of the whole thing being a set-up, a trap, a plot to ensnare them. But she wanted – needed – to know if her father was still alive.

The bait was laid.

And the carrot was a juicy one.

They're either extremely clever and manipulative bastards, thought Carter. Or Gol is onto Durell . . . he's alive, and onto the leader of those dedicated to bringing down Spiral . . .

Decision time.

Decisions.

He scratched his stubble. He patted Natasha's arm.

'We'll go,' he said softly. And smiled. 'I have a lot of friends in LA.'

Night was falling as the BMW desert-bike reached the rendezvous. Langan was there and had lit the smallest of small fires, his almost trademark pan of coffee bubbling gently over the flames.

'Hey Carter, you break your nose again?'

'Long story,' said Carter with a glance at Natasha. 'Is there any of that coffee going? I think we could all do with a caffeine fix.' Langan nodded, and dished out three mugs.

He raised his gaze in Jessica's direction, and winked at Carter. 'You been a saucy devil, eh?'

'Hmm. Langan, can you fly us to America?'

'You want my gold fillings as well, Carter?'

'I can pay you. As much as you want, whatever it takes.'

'I work for Spiral; Gol wanted you helped, and so help you I will. I don't need your money, Carter.'

'You're in luck, then,' said Carter softly, his gaze meeting the pilot's. 'We've had a message from Gol. He's in LA. He wants to meet.' Carter watched Langan's face closely. The man looked a little shocked.

'Well, I'll be damned – that tough fucking insect.'

'Can you confirm this? Through your Spiral_F contacts?'

'I can try,' said Langan softly. 'But the whole Spiral_F network has been off-line, smashed along with the main Spiral grid. I think we can assume that security has been breached, yeah? The idea now is this: Spiral_F will contact me with updates and further missions when they think it safe, unless superseded by Spiral when they get their shit back on-line. Believe me, there's a lot of pissed-off people back in London . . . those that survived the explosion.

'So you're temporarily cut free from your duties?'

Langan sighed, scratching the back of his neck. 'It would appear that way, my friend. About LA: I can't take you to the city, it's a fucking nightmare there now – especially after the wars. It's so busy, there are LAPD choppers everywhere, military presence on the streets, you name it.'

'A little like London, then?' Carter smiled grimly.

'A little,' conceded Langan. 'Except amateur terrorists didn't accidentally detonate a fucking micro-nuke in London. Look, I could probably creep up over Mexico, shunt you over the border, let you find your way from there . . .'

'Great,' said Carter. He sipped the coffee, then held the mug out for more sugar.

'Carter?'

'Hmm?'

'Sounds like a trap to me,' said Langan.

'Yeah, yeah. I know. Just what I need, guidance from another bloody advice merchant.'

'Just trying to be helpful.'

'Just get us out of this furnace alive!'

410

'I'm going to need to refuel.'

'Any more good news for me, Langan?'

'It'll probably have to be in Egypt.'

Carter muttered something nasty into his coffee.

The Comanche was built to accommodate two people, in relative comfort, for prolonged periods of warfare; with Jessica added to the numbers the situation was a little insane.

Carter had decided that she could be of use; after all, Spiral was linked closely with the QIII, and she happened to have the processor schematics in her rucksack – something which Carter acknowledged could probably come in quite handy.

As the Comanche buzzed low over the northern plains of Rub al'Khali, Langan focused and working hard to keep them out of trouble, it also occurred to Carter that *maybe* Gol was alive and had been captured by the Nex. If he had been tortured, blackmailed, whatever, then maybe the QIII schematics could be used in an exchange situation.

'Jessica?'

'Yes, Carter?'

Her nose was four inches from his own, her bottom planted firmly on his knee. He could feel her supple limbs through the thin cloth of her pyjamas, smell the curls that bobbed in his face. He tried hard not to get an erection.

'You know the QIII?'

'I helped build it and program it; you could say I know it . . .'

'Don't be flippant or you can find your own way out of Rub al'Khali.'

'I concede – you are saving my life, even though it looked, from where I was standing, as though you were

411

saying that you should leave me behind and take the QIII schematics at gunpoint. I'm just saying that it looked a little to me like it was Natasha arguing my case and therefore Natasha's influential vote that has ended up with me hunched here on a pervert's knee.'

'Pervert?'

Jessica coughed. She wriggled a little.

Natasha laughed. It was not a laugh of support.

Carter flushed red.

'Like sitting on a fence post. I really wish you middle-aged men could control yourselves . . . I thought you lot needed Viagra or something, anyway? You know, to get it up?'

'Middle-aged?' Carter sounded aghast. 'Do you really think I look that old? Jesus, I knew we should have left you in the desert . . .'

'Carter, do you have a question for the poor girl or what?'

'Yeah. If we could get to this QIII – would it have information on Spiral? And people like Feuchter and Durell? Or even the Nex, for that matter?'

Jessica shook her head in a shower of curls. 'It's a processor, Carter, not a database. But get me the right equipment connected to the QIII and the little bitch will hack and crack anything . . .' Natasha's eyes lit up at that. Jessica continued: 'Point it at Spiral's mainframe and it'll worm its way through the code in under a second. There's not a computer system worldwide that the QIII will not crack; right down from world banks to the FBI, Wall Street, Parliament, Scotland Yard, the New IRA. That's why it's such a scary piece of hardware . . . nothing is untouchable; nothing is hidden from it.'

'What operating systems will it run with?'

Jessica shrugged. 'Anything, everything; fully compliant with OSs from UNIX-IX and WIN512, through Def76 and Stable05 – it will decode anything from BaseZ88 and 681270 to way beyond the current 256 and 512 Gigabit architectures. You see, it doesn't work like that, but if it did it would be comparable to a 256 million-bit processor . . . it is so incredibly fast, it's hard to describe . . .'

'I get the picture,' said Natasha.

'I don't,' grumbled Carter. 'Make it clear for me . . .'

'The QIII is that powerful it can decode and encode DNA in millionths of a second; it would take a conventional computer hundreds of hours. It is also loaded with what is called WorldCode – an incredible variety of statistics and equations that, supposedly, make the QIII able to predict the future . . .'

'Really? You mean it actually *works*?'

'It uses probability math; equations; it comes out with the most probable outcome of any given event or situation; we'd got it about 93% perfect, but it was getting better by the day when . . .' Jessica trailed off. She coughed, gazing out at the passing scrubland and marsh areas. 'We had practically finished our work at Spiral_Q, the processor was practically fully operational. It worked, it worked well – it was just being run through its testing stages.'

'So it was feasible to destroy Spiral_Q? Because you had finished?'

'Yeah,' nodded Jessica. 'But I don't understand *why*. There was never supposed to be just one processor, surely? What a massive waste of technology!'

'Unless you wanted the *only* one,' said Carter. 'Stop anybody else making one, and bingo, you're in a position for world domination if it tickles your fancy. A machine that can take over any other machine? A machine that can predict the future? A fucking machine that can control world finances, space exploration, nuclear weapons – armies, countries, the whole fucking lot. You could have the whole world at your fingertips—'

'A curse,' said Natasha softly.

'So the QIII could tell us what the Nex and Feuchter are up to?'

'Probably, if you could get your hands on it and feed it enough data.'

'*I* can guess if you feed me enough fucking data,' said Carter wearily.

'Yeah, but can you search all the world databases in a few minutes? Can you get into protected and encrypted archives in the blink of an eye or the time it takes to sneeze?'

'And this thing is capable of world domination?'

'You would need the right key codes . . . which means you would need to *understand* how the QIII worked, really *know* how to operate the processor to its fullest,' said Jessica.

'And, of course, Spiral would have the right key codes, and Feuchter and this man Durell also know how to operate the QIII seeing as they helped to fucking build it,' snapped Carter.

'Durell,' said Natasha softly.

Their gazes met; it sounded fantastic, but then, sometimes fantastic, improbable, *impossible* could happen. Take a man; a nobody; working on an incredibly ground-breaking new processor. He realises that he could be rich; control the world; cause the next world war; whatever. And he understands his own insignificance, his own mortality and decides to take a slice from the Fame Pie. To further his own ends. To play at being *God* . . .

'This is beginning to sound like a megalomaniac's wet dream,' said Natasha sourly. 'I don't think the world is ready for it.'

'You're probably right,' said Carter.

'Maybe that's why they pulled the plug on the Rub al'Khali HQ?' said Jessica.

'No. Destroying its own bases isn't Spiral's style; it would have dismantled it, not blown it to Kingdom Come,' said Carter. 'But I'm sure that when we come face to face with Gol once more – then he'll have some answers for us.'

The Comanche spun glittering across the mountains, twin LHTec engines humming with reined-in torque and power; it banked east, heading for the northern corner of Iran, then on into China, Mongolia, the northern tip of Japan and the Pacific Ocean beyond . . . and then, of course, on to the West Coast of the United States of America . . .

And the devastation of a city recently torn apart by a pocket nuclear device.

CHAPTER 21

LA

The Comanche flitted across the sky, a softly humming falcon, a predator – quiet, dangerous, deadly. It came in low across the Pacific and touched down briefly in a cloud of swirling, eddying sand. It was on the ground for precisely four minutes . . .

'I'll head south into Mexico – there are a couple of illegal refuelling dumps I can utilise.' Langan spat a mouthful of dust into the ground and rubbed at his tired eyes.

Carter nodded. 'If I need you, if it's a dire emergency I'll patch through on the ECube. The signal will probably be intercepted by the enemy but hell, if that's the case they'll probably be just around the corner anyway.'

Langan nodded wearily. 'Just make sure you give me enough time for a decent sleep before you need me to come swooping in from the heavens to rescue you – you hear?'

'I hear.'

'Carter,' grinned Langan, 'you are the definitive pain in the arse.'

'I try to be.' Carter patted Langan's HIDSS, and disappeared into the gloom.

Langan secured the cockpit; within ten seconds the rotors had spun up and the Comanche jumped into the sky, spun low in a semicircle overhead, and headed back out over the Pacific.

The night was hot and humid. Distant sounds of a party echoed across the bay, followed by several shotgun blasts and loud screams. A disco yacht filled with corpses bobbed on the edge of the Pacific Ocean and the searchlights of a naval vessel that had just riddled it with heavy-calibre machine-gun bullets probed the surrounding darkness.

The wide highways were quiet in the early hours of the morning. Phosphorescent gleams shone from the sand-blown concrete. A deep rumble penetrated the shadows thrown by the false sentinel lights as a V12 Corvette cruised along, tyres humming gently, the reined-in motor barely turning over at such low speeds. Light reflected dimly from the battered body panels, and in the once-plush interior Natasha leaned forward, gazing to her right over the lapping dark waters at the edge of the gently sloping beach.

'I always dreamed I would visit California.'

'We're not here for a holiday,' said Carter softly.

After the nuclear explosion, the city had been sprayed for weeks by aircraft pumping out radiation-dampening chemicals: a human crop-spray that had saved the city's basic habitability but could do nothing to save the thousands of buildings – shops, houses, civic buildings – all washed away in a sea of fire. LA was busy rebuilding, but the city was constantly on the verge of anarchy. The LAPD and the military could do little to serve and protect millions of people destined for a future of miserable hardship and radiation poisoning.

Dawn was breaking as Carter pulled the Corvette into a roadside motel. He paid for a room and came back with keys. The motel room was basic and clean, and Carter stared into the bathroom and sighed. 'A shower. A shave. And . . . a proper toilet. Heaven. Valhalla. Fucking *bliss*.'

Natasha squeezed past him. 'I'm first,' she said, slamming the door in his face.

Carter grinned back at Jessica. 'Something I said?'

'Hmm.' Jessica slumped back onto the wide bed, her hair fanning out behind her, her stained and tattered pyjamas doing nothing to diminish her natural beauty.

'I'm just popping out,' said Carter suddenly, moving towards the door.

'I thought you said you needed a shave and a shower?'

'Time for that later. I have errands to run; like I said, I have some friends in LA.'

'Carter?'

'Yes, Jessica?'

'Could you possibly get me something to wear? I left Rub al'Khali in a bit of a hurry.'

'See what I can do.' He closed the door, and a few seconds later the Corvette rumbled away in a huge cloud of nauseating fumes.

Jessica lay back, weariness overcoming her. She pulled the rucksack towards her, her gaze falling on her own hands, their shroud of filth, the dirt lodged under her nails. She smiled gently. Once, that would never have happened: dirt would have been an *impossibility*. But things had changed—

418

Jessica removed the QIII schematics from the rucksack and stared at the silver disk in her hands.

'I hope you're worth all the trouble,' she muttered, resting her head back against the pillows. They felt soft and luxurious – a complete antithesis to the last day . . .

God, had it only been that long?

Since Spiral_Q?

Since Feuchter and the Nex?

Since the murders—

She shuddered, then closed her eyes and was able – for the first time in days – to relax.

Her breathing deepened and she licked her dry lips. The bed was so comfortable that it made her want to cry with gratitude. Oh, to curl up and sleep for a million years; to curl up in a ball and *forget* . . .

Images flashed through her mind—

The Nex.

The Nex, with their menacing guns.

Feuchter, watching limp trailing bodies being loaded into the trucks.

The QIII speaking to her on her terminal; warning her.

Had it *really* been the QIII itself? Or some deviant hacker? Or had she been warned by somebody at Spiral_Q? Or was she going slowly and certifiably insane?

Jessica rubbed at her weary eyes as she toyed with the possibility . . .

They could have warned her. Spiral could have warned her – it *was* feasible . . . improbable but feasible . . . But then, why her? Why *just* her? Why not the others? Adams and Johansen? Skelter? Oliver? Ralph?

She closed her eyes again, picturing Feuchter and finding some gratification in the fact that he had perished in the explosion. By the time Natasha emerged from the bathroom wearing a towel and rubbing her fingers

through her clean hair in well-earned ecstasy, Jessica was
snoring softly in the embrace of a deep, deep, welcome
sleep.

Carter returned just after lunch, as Jessica and Natasha
were sitting down to cheeseburgers and fries. He carried
several bags, and was wearing a tired but happy smile.

'Where've you been?'

'Shopping.'

'With what?'

Carter winked. 'Generous friends. Now, I have a few
presents for you two *femme fatales* and I desperately need
to use the toilet. Any objections? Thought not . . . and get
on the phone, order me some of that food. Looks too
good to miss.' The sarcasm in his voice was painful.

'You seem very upbeat,' said Natasha softly.

Carter winked. 'Got a few surprises up my sleeve.'

Carter stood in the shower, the hot water cleansing him of
sweat, sand, blood and oil. He placed his hands against
the tiles and allowed the water to run over the back of his
head for a few long luxurious minutes, revelling in the
feeling of cleanliness that was creeping over him and
through him . . .

And to heighten the experience, his mind was clear.

Perfectly clear.

Not poisoned by the presence, the cancer, the tumour.
The tumour of Kade . . .

He towelled himself dry, his gaze catching the ten small
metal globes arranged neatly around the sink. Ten fully
functioning, fully armed and extremely dangerous
HPGs – high-pressure grenades that had no traditional
explosive charge, working instead by a mixture of chemicals that created a huge build-up of pressure and an

almost silent explosion. Now they were ready to use. And abuse.

As he left the bathroom, rubbing at his smooth and somewhat pinkly raw freshly shaved face, it was to see Natasha and Jessica modelling the new clothes he had brought them. Plain trousers and jumpers, and low-heeled boots.

'Very functional,' said Natasha.

'We won't be winning any fashion parades,' yawned Jessica.

'But then, we're not here to party,' said Carter. He grabbed a cheeseburger, and taking a bite, emptied another bag onto the bed. Ammunition magazines and bullets clattered free in a large pile.

'Fuck me,' said Natasha.

'Get busy, ladies, if you please.'

'Where'd you get all this?'

'You forget,' said Carter softly. 'I used to be a Spiral operative; I worked the DemolSquads for seven years; I know where many of the worldwide stashes are and I've got a few contacts in LA.'

'I don't think I can go through with this,' said Jessica, her face having paled at the sight of the bullets and the weapon mags. Her eyes lifted, met Carter's dark stare. 'I am not a soldier, I am a programmer. I'm not a fighter, I'm not a warrior. I'm in this shit way too deep . . .'

Carter smiled at the young woman, nodding and yawning himself. 'You are right – you have played your part,' he said. 'The best thing to do now is hand over the QIII schematics to me . . . I will make sure somebody gets a good slapping for what happened in Saudi Arabia.'

'Do you think Gol can really help you?'

'If the meet is genuine, then yes. If it is a set-up . . .' Carter shrugged. 'How about we rendezvous – I'll go in

421

alone and meet Gol, then bring him out to meet you two if this thing isn't a trap? That way you're not in the firing line – you just play the waiting game.'

Natasha shook her head. 'I can't let you go in alone.'

'You have to,' said Carter. 'This thing screams of bad news; you can't expect me to put Jessica in such a dangerous situation – and as for yourself? Well, Nats, you know – and I fucking *mean* know – that I work better alone. If it really is your father, if he is alive, then so be it, we are on our way to recovering the QIII and stopping Feuchter and Durell's plans; if he has been captured, then I will do everything in my power to rescue him and I'll fucking get him out of there alive . . . and then we can move on to locating Durell . . .'

Natasha sighed. 'OK. You're right. When is the meet?'

'Two hours. I have just a few more things to take care of.'

'Where is it?'

Carter met Natasha's look and their gazes locked; he fell headlong into those beautiful, oval brown depths. He licked his lips slowly and could still taste salt. And the question at the front of his mind was . . .

Can I trust her?

Feuchter's words returned to him.

She's one of us . . .

But she had helped him get this far still alive. Without her he would be dead . . . And since Rub al'Khali Carter had been playing his cards much more closely to his chest – revealing nothing . . . the perfect poker player . . . the perfect gamesman.

Natasha smiled slowly.

'Don't tell me,' she said, sniffing, her eyes unreadable. 'I don't need to know the information and I understand that it could compromise you, yeah? Just tell me where you want to meet us afterwards.'

Carter nodded at Natasha and turned, gathering his equipment together. He glanced at Jessica. 'I'll leave the schematics disk here. I think it will be safer. If this whole gig is a trap, I wouldn't like to blunder into their lair with the very fucking item they obviously want from me. If Gol really is here in LA then the schematics could make a difference between his life and death . . . and I wouldn't like to piss that away.'

Jessica nodded.

Carter took the disk, a tiny silver platter, for a moment. He brought it up to his face and stared hard. 'Hope you're worth it, hope those fuckers need you more than they need me dead,' he muttered. Then he dropped the disk into Jessica's hand and headed for the door.

The Corvette rumbled to a halt in a deserted back alley. A recent fire had scarred most of the narrow passageway and blackened, cracked windows stared out at Carter. Papers blew across his path as the car door opened and Carter's boots touched the hot pavement under a bleached sun. He stood, stretched his back, and looked warily about: a predator, scanning his new territory, assimilating the piss-stink of markers, alert and ready for action. Carter reached back into the car, slipping various things into his trouser pockets and the pockets of his plain black waist-length jacket.

Carter buttoned up the jacket, checked his now clean-shaven features in the Corvette's cracked wing mirror, then smiled into the eyes of his own reflection. It was a strong smile. A convincing smile. It would have to be, to get him past the reception of the hotel where the meet was to take place: the Beverly Hills Hilton, recent survivor of atomic terrorism.

Carter walked, hands in his pockets, clearing his mind

for the meeting to come. He would have to be sharp; but then, if Gol wasn't there and it was nothing more than a set-up, Gol would be conspicuous by his absence and the bad gig would be pretty easy to spot – and pretty quick to go down.

Moving out onto the sidewalk, Carter walked swiftly. His gaze was alert, watching, gauging the few people he passed on foot, searching for weapons and bad intent. His eager scrutiny checked every car that purred down the scorched tree-lined sidewalk of South El Camino Drive, searching interiors, looking for anything suspicious, no matter how small. Reaching the corner of El Camino and Wilshire Boulevard, Carter halted again, looking around. He turned left and began to walk once more, again scanning the surroundings – the scarred fronts of buildings, the people, the battered cars, the burned trees. As he closed on the entrance to the Beverly Hills Hilton he slowed to an amble, searching for anything suspicious.

If they're here, he thought, if they're watching, then I won't see them. They will see me; but they will be ghosts.

Invisible.

He halted, leaning against a low wall and pulling free a packet of Camel cigarettes. He lit one and inhaled, enjoying the sensation and buzz of the nicotine. Shit, he thought, it's been too long, my little buddies. Far too long.

Ahh, the joys of civilisation.

The quiet cigarette allowed him time to examine his surroundings with a careful and practised eye. There were several spots on and in nearby buildings that would be fine for snipers; he could see no activity, but then, that didn't mean they weren't there.

Carter thought back to Africa.

Gol, running, the long jump out over the abyss . . .

The unheard scream, legs treading nothing but air . . .

The long dive towards the river far far far below . . .

Despite his own pain and exhaustion at the time, he still remembered the one word that had leaped unbidden to his mind . . . that came tumbling out of the bright red vaults of agony that had consumed him . . .

Dead.

There was no way that Gol could have survived that fall.

But then, Carter had also left him to die back in Prague; left him bleeding heavily on the road with the armed police only minutes away. Shot him to keep him *alive* . . . and Gol had survived that bad shit, escaped and survived like the tough cockroach bastard he was.

Carter breathed out a plume of smoke. Laughter echoed from further down the sidewalk and Carter's head snapped in that direction. He relaxed. Took another drag. Breathed deeply, calming his suddenly racing heart.

Analysis, he thought.

He closed his eyes for a moment; the frequent headaches he had been experiencing were thankfully absent; the stitches in his side were holding well and the pain there was nothing more than a dull throb thanks to an injection of pethidine. His nose which he had reset in the hotel room was throbbing with an annoying wave of soreness and the discomfort of his broken finger – freshly strapped – and cracked ribs were nothing more than dull aches that he had come to call his own. The pain was now integral to his existence, a part of him, unchallenged.

He finished the cigarette and flicked the butt into the bushes behind him.

Let's do it, he thought, checking his watch.

He walked up the long, winding drive, trying hard not to focus exclusively on the impressive but battered building, all the time scanning for anything suspicious as he neared the large turning circle in front of the glass-walled and steel-barred reception area. He glanced right, up at the six-storey building and the balconies that went round the exterior of each floor.

Carter's plan was simple. Ask for information at the Hilton reception desk, nicely at first . . . or with Mr 9mm as a bit of heavy reinforcement. He was sure events would unfold from there.

He nodded to the bellboy, climbed the low marble steps that ascended between lofty thick white pillars and entered the plush plant-littered foyer with catlike wariness. His gaze swivelled from left to right. Men reading newspapers, a few women apparently waiting for people, one talking animatedly on a mobile. Carter pressed the reassuring bulk of the Browning beneath his jacket and trod the plush carpets towards the reception desk and the beautiful beaming brunette with her shining eyes.

'Good evening, sir. How may I help?'

Carter smiled his winning smile as his eyes used the reflecting surfaces of glass, brass and polished marble to check events behind him. Then he said, 'Hi. I have a friend staying here by the name of Mr Gol. Said he would leave a message for me at reception about a meeting we have? My name is Carter.'

'Let me check, sir.'

The brunette turned to the pigeon-holes behind the desk. Carter leaned his elbows on the elegantly carved cherrywood surface, gaze scanning the people in the lobby. He watched a man with a full beard enter, carrying a Nike holdall. Carter felt himself tense, and unbuttoned his jacket as the man with the holdall greeted a tall heavy-set man reading a newspaper. They left the lobby together.

'Yes, there is an envelope for a Mr Carter.'

Carter took the white A5 envelope. He tore open the flap with his thumb; there was a single slip of paper inside. It read:

ROOM 215. I'LL BE WAITING.

It was signed 'Gol'. The handwriting was Gol's and so was the signature. Carter glanced around once more, then put the slip into his pocket.

'Thank you,' he said. 'Can you direct me to room 215?'

'Take the elevator to the second floor. Straight ahead and to the right.'

'Thank you again.' He beamed at her and walked towards the elevator, his hand in his pocket curling around an HPG. The elevator door closed and Carter found himself staring at his own reflection in polished chrome. He blinked lazily, a predator, and ignored the urge to light another cigarette.

Alone, he thought.

The way I like it.

He pulled free the HPG and stared at the small reflective ball. He pulled the pin and held down the trigger, then cupped the globe in his hand thoughtfully, testing the weight. The HPG was hidden against his palm.

He carefully put the pin in his pocket and removed his battered Browning Hi-Power as the elevator doors slid open, revealing a bright corridor with plush carpeting and tasteful wood panelling and decor. Carter stepped out onto the thick carpet, his boots sinking into the pile.

'Very cosy,' he muttered. He checked left and right. Moved forward.

The hotel seemed quiet. Carter walked to room 215 and halted to one side of the door. He eyed the brass numbers suspiciously as something inside him screamed:

This is wrong, this is all wrong, Gol is dead, this is a trap . . .

Who wanted him dead?

Durell? The Nex?

There were easier ways to kill him than this. But then, now he had the QIII schematics with which to do a little bargaining . . .

He raised his fist. Glanced left and right.

Rapped on the door and took a step back.

'Come in,' came a clear, melodious, powerful voice.

Carter blinked. He licked his lips and realised that there was salt there. He realised too that his hand was slippery around the stocky bulk of the Browning. He holstered the Browning and wiped his hand on his trousers. He smiled nastily. Depressing the handle, Carter nudged the door open and drew the gun once more.

Gentle laughter came from inside the room. 'Come on in, Carter. There's no gun here waiting to blow your head off. No terrible plan of entrapment to ensnare you.'

Carter peered around the door frame. Gol was sitting in a chair by the window, a glass of brandy by one hand, a cigarette in his other. Carter checked the corridor, then stepped inside and closed the door behind him.

'Nice to see you again, Gol, but I thought you might be kinda dead.'

Gol turned then, and stood. He beamed warmly at Carter, and raised his glass, sipping at the brandy, his eyes on the Browning. 'Always a cautious man, eh, my friend? Although I *do* quite understand your concern . . . if our situations had been reversed, then I too would think it a trap.'

He moved, walking across the room to stare out of the window.

Carter moved forward suspiciously, all senses alert, Browning muzzle searching uneasily. When he was satisfied that they were alone in the room, he fixed his stare back on Gol, who had turned, his dark-eyed gaze settling on Carter.

Gol smiled warmly. He ran a hand through his greying hair.

'I know you will find it hard to believe, but I was rescued. By Spiral; they desperately wanted the schematics I was carrying but the irony was that in rescuing me, they forced me to drop that disk – and it became lost, leaving Feuchter with the only working processor in existence. Spiral were very precise – they had tracked me, were waiting when I took that leap of fucking faith. They plucked me from the sky like a fly being zapped.'

Carter looked him up and down. The man's beard was a touch shorter, neatly trimmed; everything else about Gol was exactly how Carter remembered him. Carter grinned wryly.

'You *do* look pretty good for a dead man.' He lowered the Browning. 'Natasha will be thrilled.'

'Ahh, my sweet little Natasha! I thought you might bring her along, but then – ah yes. A trap. You thought me dead, hah! Had you no faith in your old Spiral buddy – even though you left me for dead in Prague . . .' Gol's eyes twinkled as he took a step closer. 'But then, we won't go over that old ground again, eh?'

Carter smiled, holding Gol's dark gaze. 'How about a drink? You're there enjoying that brandy without offering

429

me any? And after all the shit I've been taking from Natasha recently . . .'

'Yes, I heard about your exploits. Spiral_F has been following your progress with interest – although, it must be said, always a few steps behind you. Is that rogue Langan behaving himself?'

'He's doing fine.' Carter pocketed the Browning but kept the HPG hidden. He accepted the brandy and took a sip.

Gol's gaze lingered on the glass and Carter forced himself not to frown as the other man turned to stare out of the window once more. Something is wrong, screamed Carter's brain. He carefully spat the brandy back into the glass . . .

Gol turned again, a swift movement, a small black gun now in his large hand. 'I'm sorry, Carter,' he said. 'Really sorry.'

CHAPTER 22

THE DARK SIDE OF THE SOUL

Jam, Nicky, Slater and The Priest stood beside the two Chinook Ch-47s on the Kamus-5 landing yard, gazing inside the holds of the battered rainswept aircraft.

'They're ferrying crates,' said Jam quietly.

'Yes, but look at this,' said The Priest, leaping up into the back and kicking free a narrow crate panel. Nestling within straw were large shells, gleaming menacingly under the weak light.

'Big big bullets,' said Slater.

'Shells,' corrected Nicky.

'These,' said The Priest, 'are 12.5cm-calibre rounds.' He stared hard at the assembled DemolSquad. They looked from his fevered eyes to the shells, then back to his eyes.

Jam shrugged. 'You're going to have to enlighten us.'

'Warships use them,' said The Priest softly. 'In their large deck-mounted guns. They are devastating weapons.'

'So we're looking for a warship now?'

'They have abandoned this base,' said The Priest softly. 'What better position to operate from? If you have a large ship, filled with supplies – you are totally mobile. Now, in the briefing room here at Kamus I found maps and charts; most were of the Barents Sea and the Arctic Ocean.'

'That's a lot of fucking sea,' said Jam.

The Priest nodded. 'Yes, I agree, but did you notice the huge drums of oil in the storeroom? There were markings on the floor, suggesting that many have been recently removed. The drums were inscribed with a sales originator trademark: Kastevsky Co.'

'Russian?'

'Yes. The Kastevsky Co. operates out of Ostrov Vaygach covering the Barents Sea and Karskoye More. Spiral have always used them for oil when they've been operating in that region.'

'It gives us a starting point,' said Slater.

'I will send the remaining TacSquads to sweep the area; it is the strongest lead we have. We need to gather the remaining DemolSquads together ready for when the new threat is identified. Only then will we be in a position to do something about this Nex invasion.'

Jam nodded, enjoying his cigarette. 'I have an idea. If you are right and we are looking for a ship to link with these Spiral traitors, then we will need weaponry. Big weaponry. We can coordinate from here – Slater and Nicky can call the DemolSquads to the Kamus via the ECubes. This place has fuel, weapons – it is the perfect place from which to launch an offensive. You can locate the enemy and pinpoint their exact position; and I . . .'

'Yes? What skive have you dreamed up for yourself this time, Jam?'

Jam grinned.

'I have to see a man about a bomb.'

'I'm sorry, Carter,' said Gol. 'Really sorry.'

Carter grinned nastily, the brandy glass in his hand, the Browning in his pocket.

Stupid, he thought. Guard down . . .

Stupid.

'So, you alive, or dead, or what? The Nex get to you?'

Gol shook his head sadly. 'It's a lot more complicated than that, Mr Carter. A lot more complicated than you could ever believe. Now, I believe that you are carrying the QIII processor schematics. I would like them, please. They are ours. They belong to us and should have died in Rub al'Khali, just like you.'

Carter allowed himself to frown.

'You know when we worked together, out of Egypt. Do you remember the night in Luxor? When we were surrounded by Arabs with machine guns, just a veranda and the sea below us, the dark waves crashing against the shores at the height of the storm? You remember that?'

Gol nodded; but it was there. A flash across his face. A moment of . . .

Confusion.

'You mean . . . what we called the Fifth Night?'

Carter nodded. 'Gol, tell me what you said to me before we charged at those fuckers. Tell me the exact words you spoke to fill me with confidence on that dark night when we both thought that we would die.'

'I have no time for this, Carter. Give me the fucking schematics.'

'You are not Gol.'

Gol smiled then, a flash of white teeth through his grey beard. 'Shit, Carter, you have me there. So fucking what?

I *am* Gol – a part of Gol; but you cannot understand. I have been instructed not to kill you; there are a variety of people who would like a little . . . shall we say *chat*. But first you must give me the schematics you hold in your hands.'

Carter saw Gol's – or the *imitation* Gol's – finger tighten a little on the trigger. Taking up the slack, the taut; getting ready to reel in the line with the big flapping fish struggling on the end . . .

Carter smiled.

He uncurled his right hand to reveal the HPG.

'Surprise, fucker,' said Carter dryly.

Carter threw the HPG and saw Gol's eyes go suddenly wide, his mouth open in a silent 'Fuck!'

Reflexes took over; there was no thought. The large man reached up to catch the HPG—

His gun muzzle moved.

Carter's Browning was out and he was firing even as he dived for the bathroom. He rolled across the thick carpet as the Browning's bullets tore into the wall and then the window, which shattered with a crash of exploding glass . . .

Gol was running.

Carter aimed the Browning from the bathroom—

Just as the HPG detonated.

The room seemed to change suddenly from a normal hotel bedroom into the bizarre heart of a raging tornado. The furniture was picked up and tossed about and smashed up and out and down in a fury of chemical obliteration. The floor shook and trembled; glass shattered; there came the crunching of timbers and the scream of twisted steel. Carter cowered behind the bathroom wall, nose twitching at the heavy chemical stink as dust and debris spat through the doorway. He suddenly

434

realised with horror that if the wall had been merely a plasterboard partition he would have been pulped and fucked up *bad*. There was a heavy *thump* as the wall buckled above him.

He glanced up, the tip of the Browning touching his nose, his eyes blinking in the sudden dust storm.

The shaking gradually subsided.

There was a rattle of plaster and wood hitting the ground.

Carter could hear the beat of his own heart. Hear his own breathing.

The soft *thumps* of his own *life* . . .

He glanced left. A chewed length of timber leaned against the bathroom doorway; dust was floating thick in the air and only then did Carter realise his ears were screaming at him—

Singing to him—

A song of pain.

The sprinklers suddenly burst into life, dampening down the dust.

Carter eased himself to his feet and peered around the doorway. The room was like a scene from a war movie. All the windows and their frames had blown out. The carpet had been torn up, twisted around the blasted furniture and the whole mess wrenched apart to litter the corners of the room. The walls were smashed and torn and scorched. The ceiling had partly fallen in, and there were several piles of unidentifiable rubble . . .

Gol had been running for the corridor . . .

'Gol?' screamed Carter. He wiped cool sprinkler water from his face and lips.

Somebody hammered on the main door, which had somehow survived the blast but twisted in its frame, wedging shut.

435

'Fuck you,' wept the imitation Gol.

Carter stepped out of the bathroom. He moved to the prostrate body of Gol, who was lying on his side clutching his twisted, smashed leg. The right limb had been almost ripped free and was only held on by tatters of muscle. A split second earlier and Gol would have made it to the sanctuary of the corridor and the protection of a genuine brick wall—

Carter grinned nastily. Put his Browning in Gol's face.

'Who the fuck are you?'

'I am not Gol.'

'Well, no fucking prizes for *that* answer. *Who the fuck are you?*' Carter jabbed the Browning against the side of Gol's head. 'Answer me – at least you're still fucking *alive . . .*'

Carter heard a zipping sound, and a buzz. Something warm raced across his cheek.

His hand lifted, bringing a vision of blood in front of his eyes—

'Fu–' he began as he dived for the ground and three more bullets skimmed overhead. Carter crawled away from the window, teeth gritted, shock registering in his system.

The sniper's bullet had taken a strip of skin from his cheek, and nicked his ear lobe.

Carter breathed deeply, calming his racing heart.

Close call . . .

Close call.

Millimetres . . . a single millimetre . . .

Fuck, he breathed—

'You got an answer, Gol?' he suddenly bellowed through the ringing in his own head.

The sniper's bullet took the imitation Gol in the face, punching his head back against the carpet. The man's huge body seemed to sigh, to deflate, to settle back and finally lie still.

Carter's mouth became a grim line.

'Son of a bitch,' he hissed.

He crawled across the room, across the chaotic debris of the explosion. He could hear distant sirens. The fire service and LAPD. Could he trust either? He doubted it.

And then he heard a scream – from outside the room, in the wood-panelled corridor. Machine-gun fire shattered the door from its frame and Carter found himself back in the bathroom, ducking below the trajectory of the sniper's bullets and – thankfully – a little shielded by the frosted glass.

He heard boots, charging down the corridor—

Carter tossed another HPG; the globe bounced from the wall of the room and rattled across the torn floor—

He heard a single word.

'Shit—'

They ran for it.

The explosion rocked the room as Carter put a bullet through the bathroom window. The whole world seemed to have gone mad as Carter crawled to the ledge. The sniper's bullet had cut diagonally across his cheekbone and down to nick his ear lobe. That meant the sniper was above Carter's position and to the left—

He saw it: a nearby rooftop. Ideal—

Carter's sharp eyes spotted the tiny figure. Steadying his hand on the ragged glass-edged sill, Carter levelled the Browning and began to fire—

Five, six, seven, eight bullets.

He could see the distant stonework crumbling.

Twelve, thirteen. He switched mags, pulled a small device from his pocket, snapped it against the wall

437

beneath the windowsill, took a step back, dropped an HPG in the middle of the bathroom and leaped out of the window—

Several things happened at once—

Five black-clad Nex slid around the corner, carrying sub-machine guns—

The sniper got to his feet, screaming in pain at the bullet in his shoulder, and painfully picked up his rifle. Shaking with anger, fatigue and the agony of hot metal piercing his flesh; he tried to level the weapon over the parapet and aim it at the opposite building—

The HPG detonated.

Carter bounced violently against the wall ten feet below the window on the end of the wire and the attached small black circular object – standard Spiral issue – that he held in his free fist—

The bathroom exploded.

Debris spat from the hole in the wall; even as the chaos erupted Carter swung himself around on the wire and, hanging suspended, unloaded another full magazine towards the sniper.

Then he flicked the release.

Buzzing filled his ears and he shot towards the ground; his boots touched down beside the Olympic-size swimming pool and a few onlookers who were standing, mouths agape, staring up at the room that he had suddenly and urgently vacated. Fire bellowed out, then was suddenly sucked back in. There was a splash as a scorched and flaming wall cabinet landed in the pool, where it hissed and steamed.

Carter glanced around, then sprinted for the nearest cover, switching magazines in the Browning as he ran. From the bushes he saw the police squad cars and two huge fire vehicles charging up the road, horns blaring.

Carter made it to the pavement, shoved his Browning back into his pocket and ran.

He was motoring on instinct now. All six cylinders.

He sprinted, boots thudding against the sidewalk. As he skidded onto El Camino Drive he saw the distant lights of cars and cursed. He dived over a low wall and watched the vehicles – three large black GMC trucks – go screaming past, engines howling.

Bad, thought Carter.

Real bad.

He continued to run.

Two minutes later, pouring with sweat, he reached the Corvette. He jumped in, gunned the engine and floored the accelerator. The huge V12 roared and, leaving rubber tread smeared heedlessly against the concrete, he wheel-spun towards the end of the fire-scorched alley and out onto the road—

The GMC trucks were prowling, waiting, searching. Their engines howled as they raced down the highway after the Corvette as it appeared: wolves hunting down this running lamb.

All four vehicles screamed around a huge loop of tarmac, suspensions dipping as they veered round corners and ended back on Wilshire Boulevard. They slipped past the fire trucks and Carter, bent forward over the steering wheel, sweat dripping in his eyes, cursed his pursuers—

Carter pulled free his Browning and kissed the grip. 'You've saved me before, baby,' he muttered.

He fired through the Corvette's rear window. Glass exploded in a shower and the three GMC trucks veered, one mounting the pavement and sending a couple of pedestrians sprinting for cover, wheels churning an old man into the ground with quadruple impacts.

They regrouped on the road and, their lights dazzling Carter, accelerated towards him.

Where's fucking Kade when I need him? he thought. Closely followed by, I should have stolen a faster car—

The lead GMC truck smashed into the back of the Corvette. Carter was jolted in his seat, and almost lost his Browning. His foot slammed to the floor and suddenly he veered right, down a narrow slip road leading away from Beverly Hills—

The GMC trucks followed in tight formation.

They sped past a parked patrol car. Red lights flickered.

The police car pulled away from the kerb and gave chase.

Carter growled to himself. He fired another few bullets from the rear of the 'Vette and was gratified when he popped a headlamp. But that did little to take the GMCs out of action.

They're too high up, he realised. Their cabs are too fucking high up.

The lead GMC shunted him again.

Carter fired the remaining bullets; there was a high-pitched squeal and a rattle from the engine compartment and the truck veered off, hammering into a low wall. Carter caught a glimpse in his mirror of a dark body catapulted like a rag doll through the windscreen before the howl of police sirens made him drag the steering wheel to the left. The Corvette's wheels screeched at the abuse as the car power-slid around a corner through a crossroads, the back end hitting and bouncing from a set of lights.

More police cars joined the chase.

Who're they fucking chasing? he thought sombrely.

Me or them?

He pressed his foot to the floor. The engine growled.

Help, he thought.

The Corvette sped through an intersection; there was a multiple music-blare of horns as cars zipped insanely all around and Carter closed his eyes for a moment. Kade? Where are you, Kade? Come and get me out of this shit!

Come and fucking *help me* . . .

He no longer checked his rear-view mirror. The view in it only seemed to get worse.

Engines howled close behind him, mechanical animals with their teeth bared, ready to tear and rend him with anger and hatred . . .

Once more he wrenched on the steering wheel, feeling the car lose traction as tyres slid around the corner, and once more he narrowly missed another vehicle – a fire truck, this time. The horn screamed at him and Carter involuntarily flinched, half ducking down in his seat . . .

Focus, he thought.

Meeting. With Natasha, and Jessica . . .

And Langan.

His gaze flickered up, checking the signs. He feinted a left turn, then dragged the Corvette over the grassy embankment and forced a U-turn through heavy traffic. Tyres squealed, horns blared; Carter caught a flashing, almost hallucinatory scene of angry faces and waving fists. The Corvette's rear bounced from the wing of a brand new Porsche . . .

'Motherfucker!' came the scream.

Carter checked his rear-view as he sped away. He had managed, by some twist of fate, by some fluke of gridlock, to cause a massive jam across the six lanes of highway; the GMCs had stuttered to a halt against a wall of metal. LAPD cops flooded the road, guns out – yelling—

Gunshots rattled.

He heard the wet *thump* of metal in flesh.

Carter ducked low and floored the Corvette's accelerator.

He drove for ten minutes as dusk began to fall, reducing his speed a little so as not to attract too much unwanted attention. As he sped down towards Inglewood and the meet, he checked his mirrors again.

There, in the distance, he could see a group of GMC trucks.

'No,' he muttered, frowning. 'Fucking impossible!'

He saw the trucks accelerating, still distant blobs, their grilles like teeth.

Smiling teeth.

Carter's jaw tightened. His foot hit the floor again and the Corvette jerked forward, spun right down a tight bend and into a McDonald's drive-through. He slammed on the brakes and the Corvette screeched to a halt beside a wooden bench under a group of flowering trees where Natasha and Jessica sat, empty Coke cartons in front of them.

Carter leaped out.

'We've got trouble.'

'Big trouble?' asked Natasha.

'Oh yes.'

Carter slotted a fresh mag into his Browning and as a car pulled free of the service window of the drive-through he pointed the gun and screamed, 'Get out of the fucking car!'

The Ferrari F355 Spider stopped abruptly. The engine rumbled, a deep-throated V8 purr.

'What are you doing?' hissed Natasha.

'You were right. We need something faster.'

'Hey man, you have *got* to be kidding!'

Carter met the man's outraged glare: he was young, wore a skull-and-crossbones bandanna, Oakleys and no shirt, revealing a heavily tattooed torso. When he spoke, his hands lifted from the steering wheel in emphasis.

'Get out.'

'You motherf—'

The Browning moved. There was a *blam*. A hole appeared in the passenger side of the windscreen – and in the fine leather upholstery beyond. The man stared at the hole in the windscreen, then at the seat. Then he leaped from the vehicle as if stung.

Carter, Natasha and Jessica jumped in.

'You know how much this car cost, man?'

Carter met the man's gaze again. 'Sue me,' he said as he slotted the tiptronic into first and floored the gas pedal; the Ferrari F355 roared, the bellowing of a 375-bhp lion, and shot off so fast that Carter was pinned back into the seat.

'You motherfuckers!' screamed the tattooed man, waving his fist and a strawberry milk shake in the air.

The Ferrari F355 became practically airborne from the speed bump as they took off past five black GMC trucks, the windows all blacked out, their engines rumbling and lights blazing in the gloom of the Californian dusk. He slotted the vehicle into sixth gear and felt the hairs on the back of his neck stand on end as the V8 3496cc motor roared with renewed vigour and the road became a blur of twisting concrete snake; it danced ahead of him like a scene from a bad trip.

Natasha leaned forward – both women had leaped into the cramped rear of the roofless sports car. 'Erm, Carter, how fast are you going?' There was an edge of fear to her voice.

'I don't know,' he said through gritted teeth. 'I'm watching . . . the . . . road.'

'Are we in that much trouble?'

'Yes,' said Carter softly.

'Did you see my father?'

Carter looked at Natasha from the corner of his eye. 'No, Natasha. I'm sorry.'

'Oh.'

She sat back, deflated. Carter wanted to say, *I told you so; you shouldn't have got your hopes up, love.* But he bit his tongue and concentrated on the road, a winding 180 m.p.h. roller coaster of orange and grey beneath the colourful bruise that was the sky.

'Who did you meet?'

'It was a set-up. I'm afraid I blew up the hotel room . . .'

'With what?'

'A couple of HPGs.'

'You lunatic! What did they – whoever *they* were – want?'

'It was the Nex,' said Carter sourly. 'And they wanted the QIII schematics. Hold on,' he snapped, slamming the Ferrari down a couple of gears and using the engine braking to get them sliding and squealing around a corner. Carter grinned like an excited child back at the two women.

They didn't look impressed.

Sirens screamed suddenly off to one side as a convoy of police cars burst from a junction, almost running the Ferrari off the road. Carter swerved violently, the motor roaring, and just made it around.

The squad cars took up the pursuit.

'Shit.'

Carter accelerated back up to 180 m.p.h., a wide grin on his face.

'Catch this baby, little piggies,' he muttered as they fell away behind him and he focused on the far distance.

444

'Natasha, get a message to Langan to come pick us up. There must be a thousand cops after us.'

'But the Nex will tag us . . .'

'So fucking what? They already know we're here.'

Natasha pulled free the ECube as Carter concentrated on driving; night fell over California as they sped south and left their pursuers far, far behind . . .

The motel was in the middle of nowhere; there were two pickups parked out front when the Ferrari F355 sped around a corner and came to a sudden halt. Carter lit a cigarette as Natasha and Jessica climbed out and stretched their tense, aching muscles.

'You're a lunatic,' said Jessica.

'I got us out.'

'What happened back there?' asked Natasha.

Carter shrugged. 'There were Nex waiting for me; they wanted the QIII schematics and we had a bit of a lovers' tiff. There was a bit of leg-slapping, hair-pulling and face-scratching and I had to make rather a sharp getaway . . .'

'You're hurt.' Natasha stepped in close, her finger brushing his cheek. Carter looked into her eyes then and smiled. He took her fingers, lifted them to his lips and kissed them.

'There was a sniper. Waiting for me.'

'Bad . . .'

'I think I hit him.'

The drone of the Comanche reached their ears and Carter gazed up into the darkness. Lights suddenly glared from the black as the chopper banked and, with a heavy wild *thrumming* of rotors, flashed overhead. It circled, then slowed and Carter, Jessica and Natasha backed away, shielding their eyes as the Comanche whined down,

445

its suspension bouncing as the machine landed lightly beside the Ferrari. There were several hisses and whines, plus the drone of incredibly powerful engines being gently but purposefully abused. The HIDSS-helmeted figure turned, looked out from the smoked cockpit and gave a thumbs-up.

Outside, the trees and bushes were tossed from side to side by the rotors' turbulence.

'Here's our ride,' said Carter, something unheard and unseen making him turn, his dark eyes peering out over the gloom and shadows of the nearby trees and dirty highway beyond the motel's parking lot. Something burned uneasily at the back of Carter's mind. His head turned as he glanced uneasily down the road, eyes searching for the dark GMC trucks that had so recently given chase . . . but there was nothing there.

Nothing out of place.

Nothing *wrong* . . .

Someth—

His gaze returned to the Comanche.

And he could hear it. A distant voice: like a scream, in passion, in anger, determined but pinned down, restricted, forced into silence against its furious force of will—

Something's wr—

Carter frowned. The whole world seemed to slow. The Comanche's blurred rotors whirled at a snail's pace, *thrum thrum thruuuuum*. Carter reached for his Browning and it seemed that his hand took an age to reach the heavy weapon as his head was turning towards Natasha and his lips formed the words, 'Let's . . . go . . .'

There was a distant *crack*.

Carter's eyes caught the muzzle flash.

Something's wrong.

446

A hole appeared in the Comanche's cockpit canopy and Langan was punched backwards, flipping slowly across the inside of the helicopter, a huge splatter of blood mushrooming up against the smoked glass. Carter's Browning appeared instantly in his hand and he cursed the slowness and clumsiness of his own actions, cursed the sluggishness of the world around him and within him as his mouth opened to scream the words and both Jessica and Natasha turned, their movements painfully slow, to gaze in confusion up at the helicopter, the whirling rotors, the slumped figure in the darkened depths of the imprisoning and suddenly insect-like machine—

Carter dropped to one knee, shifting and dropping his stance, the Browning bucking in his hand: one bullet; two bullets; three bullets – and then he saw the shadowy figures detach themselves from the trees and come racing low with incredible speed across the grass and they were the Nex and a cold terror clamped Carter's heart as the world slammed back into focus and reality—

'What—'

'Oh, my.'

'Get in the fucking 'copter!' Carter screamed, firing the rest of the mag at the charging wall of Nex. They were dressed in identical dark grey body-hugging garments; they carried sub-machine guns but did not return fire; they were one of the most menacing, most terrifying things Carter had ever seen and his jaw clamped tightly shut—

Natasha was climbing, glancing back over her shoulder at the charging Nex. Then her gaze transferred down to Carter who grabbed Jessica and pushed her towards the Comanche, under the whining rush of the rotors that lashed the trees into frantic swaying with the power of those terrific reined-in engines . . .

Carter ejected the magazine. Slotted another into the weapon and sighted on a dark, masked face. The Browning barked in his hand and the figure pitched under the boots of another Nex. Carter's mouth was dry.

Fuck me, he thought.

There are *hundreds* of them . . .

Far, far more than in Africa . . .

They swarmed from all around now; like insects – dark-eyed and lethal. As if on some unspoken command their weapons lifted, muzzles swivelling towards the group—

'Fuck . . .'

Carter threw an HPG and watched Nex corpses thrown in different directions, limbs torn from carcasses, blood spewing from pulped flesh . . .

What the hell *are* they? screamed his brain. 'Get up there!' he yelled. He fired several more rounds, the Browning a dark comrade in his fist, an extension of his body.

The Nex, their sub-machine guns pointing, still did not fire. Carter's gaze darted up towards Natasha as—

Jessica reached up to the handholds. Carter turned, swiftly—

There came another distant *crack*.

Carter felt a hiss of heat beside his face and a blow against his back and turned to grab Jessica's arms – which suddenly draped loosely around his neck as she bounced from the DPM panels of the Comanche and fell against him. Her eyes were wide, confused and innocent as her gaze met Carter's stunned stare and her arms fell away from his shoulders. He grabbed her, his Browning forgotten, he held her waist and supported her sudden dead weight and gazed into those deep intelligent frightened eyes—

Eyes that held a million questions . . .

Why?

Why me?

Why now?

What is happening?

What is happening to me?

Jessica opened her mouth to speak, to ask him. A gush of red poured from her lips with a convulsion of her broken body, spilling down her dark jumper to stain Carter's battered jacket. She shivered, head flopping back now and shaking, curls soaked in blood. She tried to speak, but more blood flowed out from her mouth and across her cheek, a thick red river flowing into her eyes and down across her ears. She sighed, a bubbling of crimson spittle and exhaled air—

And then Jessica was dead.

'Come on!' screamed Natasha.

His gaze lifted and met the screaming panic-filled face of Natasha, her eyes wide, her tongue moistening fear-dry lips.

'Carter! They're—'

He whirled. The Nex were only feet away, arms outstretched, a swarm heaving to encompass and overthrow him. There was a heavy *boom* as the Browning kicked in his fist and then lifted, planting a second bullet in the closest Nex's face—

And then Carter was moving, leaping, the Browning kicking and blasting in his fist as the Nex went down with hot metal scything faces and throats and drilling eyes from their sockets. Gloved hands reached out for Carter as he grappled his way to the handholds leading to the Comanche's cockpit, but his boots lashed back and connected with heavy *cracks*. He gripped the bottom handhold and hauled himself up onto the helicopter.

Natasha was above him and confusion gripped him as she was suddenly punched from the Comanche's fuselage – a sudden violent lurching as blood splashed in a spray from her body and she spun above his head under the impact of bullets. Carter could not understand and the sounds of madness and attack washed over him and all noise was white noise and he reached up, fingers brushing Natasha's fingers as she fell but he was not fast enough and could not reach her and she toppled down into the mass of Nex and they closed over her body like a swarm and she disappeared from sight—

'No,' he said softly.

Carter's head snapped up from his red-stained hands. His gaze was filled with ice death, his lips a narrow line, his face a cold smash of silver against the darkness of the night.

And he realised.

Realised the horrible truth.

He was *alone*.

The Browning kicked in his blood-smeared hand; he swayed to one side on the handholds, movements mechanical, his body running on adrenalin and reflex. A line of bullets cut craters across the battle-scarred fuselage's alloy. The Browning kicked again and now it was Carter's only friend, only true friend, the only comrade he had left.

The bullet hit a Nex between the eyes.

Carter watched coolly as the light in them fled, as the Nex died.

More hands reached for him.

He kicked out, Browning pumping, his heart cold and emotionless. The dead man's click flicked on a switch in his brain. He reached up to the rim of the cockpit, slammed it upwards and leaped up dragging down the smoked glass. His hand slammed down on the controls; the rotors, still spinning, powered up with a roar of the twin LHTecs as Carter slammed down latches and watched the Nex swarm like dark grey bees around and over the Comanche—

And below him Natasha was lost.

He grabbed the control column. Flicked the power on and lifted the Comanche with a scream of engines, a shudder of the aircraft as the nose dipped and he shot up and out over the car park, MiniGun howling with a lethal stutter that punched down and merged Nex with the shredded grass and trees, pulped them into oblivion as Carter's cold detached stare watched their bodies and limbs and organs disintegrate under the awesome monstrosity of the war machine.

The Comanche banked, the concrete highway falling away below.

'Is Jessica dead?' hissed Natasha.

Carter blinked and looked over his shoulder.

But he was alone.

Natasha was gone.

Natasha was dead.

Carter, eyes focused on the night sky beyond, nodded to himself. He reached down, back, fumbling and shoving at the body of Langan lying prone and broken behind and beneath him. He grappled with the spare HIDSS helmet and settled it over his head. He activated the HIDSS, data flashing across his suddenly enhanced night vision—

'Whoa . . .' he said softly.

They were waiting for us, he realised.

Had they known about the meet, about the Comanche? Or had they just responded rapidly to the ECube patch?

451

How fucking far does this betrayal go?

'*All the way,*' whispered Kade. '*Hey, Carter, we've got company. Come on, buddy, let's taste some fucking blood . . .*'

Carter's gaze flicked to the scanners.

Three helicopters were coming up fast behind him as he headed out over the Pacific. His eyes narrowed and death sat with him like an old friend. His mouth was no longer dry. Fear was an ally; not fear itself but a love of the fear he would inflict.

Rotors roared as the helicopters approached at speed. The night had fallen, and moonlight glimmered from the rotors, dazzling through the holed cockpit canopy. Carter could see a single eye of silver where the bullet that had smashed Langan's life from his body had penetrated the aircraft.

And he thought about Jessica.

And he thought about Natasha.

He groaned.

'Natasha . . .' he whispered in pure agony.

Machine guns roared behind him; rounds clattered against the Comanche and Carter's mask of pain fell away to be replaced with something that even Kade could not replicate.

Hatred fuelled him now.

Hatred – and a need to kill.

Langan's words came back to Carter, hot words filled with a passion for his subject: the war machine. '*We are presently carrying 36 standard 70mm rockets, 18 Stinger air-to-air missiles and 6 Hellfire anti-tank missiles . . .*'

Carter's gaze swept the console. He reached forward, flicked switches, heard motors whirring within the Comanche; he glanced at the scanners, then looked quickly left and right. A squat black powerful helicopter had drawn alongside him to the right and he could see the

452

copper eyes of a Nex. He slammed on the air brakes, dropping the Comanche with dipped nose through the skies, then with a roar of engines and a steeply banking turn that rammed his head back against the pilot's chair the Comanche veered, coming up behind the black helicopter. Carter engaged four Stinger air-to-air missiles – saw the glow from their tails as they detached and watched grimly as they hurtled into the black helicopter. It exploded with a roar and, glowing like the heart of a raging volcano, fell dead and spinning from the skies and smashed into the dark sea below.

Machine guns hammered, dragging Carter's hypnotised stare back to fresh dangers. Red lights flashed on the scanners and the Comanche fell from the skies, howling like an animal in pain to twist and skim close to the surface of the sea – so close that spray splattered against the cockpit and Carter could almost taste the salt.

He killed the lights.

Missiles plunged into the sea behind him.

'You want to fuck with me?' growled Carter. His finger reached out, tracing along the scanner, examining the target and analysis displays. He rammed the helicopter forward, the LHTecs screaming and vibrations pounding through the attack vehicle. The Comanche surged forward, and speed powered through Carter's brain; waves crashed just below the Comanche and there . . .

Against the black waves.

A tanker.

Carter swept low, the Comanche droning, followed by the two remaining helicopters and their Nex pilots. Carter banked the Comanche in low and tight, skimming the waves. The black helicopters followed. Machine guns fired. Bullets rattled against the huge oil tanker.

The Comanche lifted, skimming over the ship's elevated bridge and the black helicopters followed flying close to each other. The pilots were extremely skilled.

'Tune in,' said Carter softly.

He flicked several switches and engaged a digital read-out. He smiled, a smile that conveyed only a longing for destruction and death.

'Turn on.'

He hit the air brakes. The LHTecs screamed in response. The two black helicopters veered, one to either side, in reflex response to his insane manoeuvre. Carter hurled the Comanche up into the air, climbing, lifting to ascend like a rocket, reaching for the stars. Carter gazed up into that black glittering expanse as the Comanche rumbled and screamed and vibrated around him and he prayed, prayed to a God he no longer believed in and tears rolled down his cheeks and his teeth ground in anger and hatred. As scanners blazed at him with low-oxygen read-outs he kicked the Comanche around in a tight arc and then dropped from the sky towards the distant tanker far below – his marker – twisting and spinning. The black helicopters were distant targets as Carter allowed the release of a single 70mm rocket . . . Exhaust plumed as the rocket ploughed into the spinning rotors of the second black helicopter, its cockpit and the Nex pilot and sent the machine crashing into the black sea, which swallowed it whole.

'Burn out, motherfucker.'

The Comanche spun, twisting, howling, and its rotors skimmed the sea, slicing through the waves as the aircraft cut an arc and spun and climbed once more with the final black helicopter following close behind with machine guns spitting fire and hatred and hatred and hatred . . .

They climbed towards the stars.

Wind howled through the hole in the cockpit.

Carter's tears chilled like crystals of diamond against his freezing skin.

And there, hundreds of metres above the sea, the Comanche levelled out and spun in a slow lazy arc. Carter slowed the speed, until the machine hung, hovering, stationary; his head drooped, eyes looking at nothing but the floor. And then his gaze lifted and he stared into the darkness ahead of him. His teeth clamped.

The last black helicopter came level, perhaps a hundred metres away.

Carter flicked the rocket restraints free.

His eyes narrowed.

'You want to fuck with me?' he whispered.

'Fuck him, Carter, make him taste blood,' whispered Kade like a bad injection of essence of ghost.

'I don't need your help,' snarled Carter.

Hatred was his master.

The black helicopter's engines howled; Carter could hear them even over the roar of the Comanche's LHTecs. Its nose dipped as it powered forward with its machine guns firing and Carter growled and hammered the Comanche on through the dark black bullet hail.

The two war machines hurtled towards one another. In the blink of an eye they had closed at speed, machine guns roaring, tracer bullets spinning lines of fire across the short distance. They veered, the Comanche twisting down and to one side, the black helicopter nearly over the top – but not quite ... A billion glittering crystal fragments shot out in a shimmering display as the Comanche's armoured rotors smashed the enemy's cockpit canopy into dust and sliced the Nex pilot cleanly in two.

The Comanche danced sideways, away from its dark and bloody deed.

Globules of blood spun up and out on ice-rimed rotors.

Within the black helicopter, the Nex looked down, mouth open in disbelief. Its body relaxed into two halves, the head and upper torso gesturing insanely in sudden panic as it slid into the footwell. The black helicopter tipped, Nex blood pooling in its interior, and screamed down into the sea. And was gone.

Searchlights from the crawling tanker strobed across the dark waves.

Carter breathed. Slowly.

'That was fucking nasty,' said Kade carefully.

'Fuck you.'

'Temper, temper.'

At a more sedate pace, the Comanche dropped lower, skimmed the dark waves and shot like a bullet across the watery desert desolation of the empty dark seas.

The Comanche flew on over the Pacific.

Carter glanced down at the corpse with which he was cramped into the cockpit, half seated upon: an unloving intimacy – the flesh was still warm, he could feel it through his own clothes. He tried not to think about the destroyed face and the pulp of blood and brains smeared over the inside of the cockpit. The smell made him want to be sick, though it had evaded his awareness in the turmoil of battle. Until now.

'You're better off alone, buddy. You know she was the enemy; you know she was bad.'

'Leave me be, Kade. I can do without your shit.'

'You need me, buddy.'

'I'm not your fucking buddy, *buddy.*'

'Ooooh, touchy.'

Carter licked at his lips and guided the Comanche low, no particular destination in mind, just needing to fly, to run, to flee, to get away from the Nex and the horror they represented, the *death* they represented . . .

What to do now? he thought. Carter sighed out loud. I'm tired, so tired. Tired of everything.

'And so we need to think; to plan. Contact Jam – he can help you, Carter; he can kick you out of this brain-fuck childish melancholy – hah, just because the bitch is dead. You need to become strong again, Carter. Jam will help you do that!'

Carter pulled free the ECube. In the insect-head-like HIDSS, a dark visor surveyed the soft blue digits. He scrolled and punched in Jam's descramble code and waited. The ECube rattled in his hand.

'Carter?'

'Jam – I'm in a world of shit!'

'Carter – you remember our motto?'

'Yeah?'

'Remember it.'

The ECube died.

Carter smiled grimly. *Remember the Kamus.*

Carter thought back.

Kamus-5.

And it sent a cold chill through his soul.

He chewed his lip for a moment.

'Fuck, I need a cigarette.'

Natasha.

He remembered her pretty face.

A little part of his soul said: No.

But he knew; deep down. They had her; there was no escaping. *No* fucking escaping.

'Now isn't the time to roll over and die,' snapped Kade.

'Why not?' said Carter gently.

'Because you're stronger than that. Because we can get through this; all we need is time and a little brotherly solidarity – man, we can work together now that bitch is gone. We can be strong again.'

'Kade, I despise you.'

'No, you don't Carter. You are me; and you can't hate yourself.'

'I always have . . . Listen, don't you ever get tired, Kade? Tired of the killing?'

'It is why I exist,' said Kade darkly.

Carter nodded, the HIDSS bobbing. He banked the Comanche, there was a drone from the engines and they spun out across the Pacific Ocean; beneath them the waves rolled and the sea seemed suddenly endless, a vast world of black merciless beauty stretching out for ever and beckoning for them to jump aboard and ride her into a sweet-tasting oblivion . . .

'Kamus-5,' said Carter softly, nodding to himself. The blood speckles and smears had dried on his hands, on his face, on his clothes. He looked demonic in the gloomy light. 'We made a pact; that the land of the Kamus was sort of holy; sort of *evil*.'

'Are we going there, brother?'

'Yes.' Carter nodded to himself.

'You know, that motherfucker Langan stitched us up bad. Dumb fuck led them right to us . . . If I had known I would have shot the stupid bastard myself; drilled out his eyes and puked into his skull. I wish I had known. I wish . . .'

Carter ignored Kade; Kade was an insignificant buzz of insect talk in his head. Carter felt sick. Carter felt cold. Carter felt alone.

Somebody is going to pay, he realised.

Somebody is going to pay bad.

CHAPTER 23

THE KAMUS

☐ Ωclass relay ☐ qiii mainframe code logon
01001010
booting . . . sequences initiated . . .

Carter fell from infinite dark dreams out of one world of
pain and into another – a world of pain that was wakeful-
ness. Pain: pure and white, it pounded his temples and
brainstem like a lump hammer. A diamond drill bit
pierced his eyelids and popped his eyes. A razor wire
sliced layers from his cerebellum. His mind was crushed
in an iron grip and held for all eternity.

He forced open his eyelids and looked up into a face he
knew only too well.

'How goes it, old buddy?' asked Jam, grinning. The
tall man was standing, leather coat wrapped around his
frame, hands in pockets, a smoking cigarette hanging
loosely from between his lips. His hair was still spiked,
his eyes dark-ringed and hooded but twinkling with an
inner humour laced with concern. 'Thought you'd fucking died on us out there. You touched down in that

battered war machine and bam, out you went like a fucking light!'

'Not good,' sighed Carter, wincing as he eased himself tenderly into a sitting position. He noted his Browning to his right, beside the bed where they must have dragged him. 'That to share, you stingy old bastard?'

Jam held the cigarette towards Carter. 'What's mine is yours, and yours is mine.' Carter's weary face brightened a little and he took the cigarette, took a long drag, passed the cigarette back and lifted the barrel of the Browning gently under Jam's chin. Jam blinked, hand outstretched to receive the weed. He coughed slowly.

'You seem a touch on edge,' he said at last, after a long meditative pause.

'Let's see both hands,' said Carter, and Jam could see there was no humour and no compassion and no give in the man he had once called a friend. Jam removed his other hand from the coat pocket and spread his fingers wide.

'What's going on, Carter?'

'Where's Slater and Nicky?'

'Out front.'

'Where?'

'On the landing yard.'

'Let's walk; you in front. And don't make me shoot you in the back, Jam, because it would be a fucking bad ending to a good long friendship. Unfortunately, events have conspired to fuck with my brain; I can no longer trust anybody. Not even you. The Nex are fucking everywhere.'

'We did Belfast together,' said Jam, his voice hoarse through gritted teeth.

'I know we did. And in a few minutes we'll either be sharing a drink or a new adventure in the Realms of the

Beyond. I shared a history with Gol, but a fucker who looked just like him still tried to kill me.'

They moved down the draught-filled stone tunnels, Jam's coat flapping in the gentle cool mountain gusts. Carter walked carefully behind the other man, aware of how fast he could move and how deadly he really was. He might have a glib tongue and a wicked way with the women, but he was a deadly killer. Very deadly.

They emerged into the darkness of pitch-black night.

Slater was sitting on his pack; Nicky had unpacked a small stove and was cooking food. They both turned as Jam and Carter entered—

'You OK, Jam?' growled Slater, rising quickly, hands straying towards his gun.

'No worries,' said Jam softly, waving for the large man to sit down.

Carter pocketed the Browning. Jam turned, gently patted the face of his old friend. 'You're a dumb motherfucker, Carter, you know that?'

'Hey, sue me,' said Carter, moving over to the food. 'Smells good.'

'You pull a gun on him?' asked Nicky.

Carter nodded.

She shook her head. 'You mad bastard – he's here to help.'

'I'll be the judge of that.'

Jam jogged over and squatted beside the group. 'Right, then – to business, now that Carter has it solid in his mind that I am real. I presume you know what's going down with Spiral?'

Carter nodded. 'I know some of the Divisions have been wiped out, some of the DemolSquads have been murdered by assassins. There's some kind of splinter faction that has a processor that can take over the global

461

military and is intent on world domination. And it was being run by two men: Feuchter and Durell. Only I killed Feuchter back in Saudi Arabia, when Spiral_Q blew up.'

'Yeah, it really is that bad,' said Jam, grimacing. 'They've hit Spiral, and fucking hit them hard. Apparently they used this processor to hack Spiral mainframes, put us all in fucked-up situations where they could take us out.' He took a breath and his eyes were wild, flaring with adrenalin. He lit a cigarette, grabbed a fork and speared a sausage. 'Yeah, we found out much the same with the help of The Priest. Gol worked with Durell, way back, on something called the Nex Project – although no bastard seems to know what it was, or what it did. Gol pulled out, but Durell carried on with the work until Spiral withdrew the funding and moved him more on to medicines. Gol then moved to Prague – hey, and you know the history behind *that* little venture.'

'How did you find out about this Nex Project?' said Carter softly.

'Well, we've been talking to some of the remaining DemolSquads – Nicky and Slater have pulled a few in here to the Kamus. They're out now, helping The Priest with his *various projects.*'

'Thank fuck for that. So we weren't all wiped out?'

Jam grinned nastily. 'Take more than a few copper-eyed cunts to wipe this bunch of Squads from the face of the earth. Once we'd discovered the shit that was going down, we used ECubes to relay messages to the Squads who were still alive; created our own little network, piggy-backed on descramble codes. Then we started to work on finding out just where those fuckers have run to.'

'But?'

'Aye, there's always a but,' said Jam, blowing smoke into the night. He frowned as Slater shovelled food into his maw without offering anybody a single sausage. Jam reached over and stole another one, peering at it in the gloom as smoke trailed from his nostrils.

'Demol16 was hot on your trail when you left England with Natasha. Apparently the TacSquads had a special interest in you – fucking secret police sniffing around your coat tails. Demol16 was sent to monitor you but always ended up being one step behind – they turned up to a fucking massacre in Africa; they nearly died there, Carter, fucking Nex crawling all over the place. Then they tracked you to Saudi Arabia, but lost you shortly after the explosion.'

'What did Demol16 find in Saudi?'

'A mess: the remains of Spiral_Q. But no Feuchter.'

'That's because I killed him,' said Carter through gritted teeth.

'There were no signs of his body. Even though he was involved in an explosion, they had top grade PFScanners and there were no genetic residues – no traces at all. *Somebody* must have come back for his corpse.'

'Why do that?' said Carter.

Jam shrugged. 'No fucking idea. What use is a fried chicken carcass? But anyway, we lost you after that until your ECube blast. Glad you remembered the descramble code, old buddy.' Jam bit into his sausage and chewed thoughtfully. Then he stood, walked towards the edge of the landing yard and the Apache, and stared out into the Austrian night. His long leather coat whipped around him in the wind.

Carter stepped up beside him.

Together, they stared out into the depths of blackness below. The wind howled around them, buffeting them on the cliff edge; here there were no parapets, no barriers – just a long steep fall into rocky chaos below. Far beneath the two men occasional lights twinkled: synthetic stars deep down towards the ground – bright yellow, white, and sometimes red.

'I love it here,' said Jam softly.

'Yeah. Love the insanity of the place.'

'They should never have closed it.'

'Well, your splinter faction *reopened it*.'

'Only as a temporary measure.'

The two men shared a moment of pleasure.

'What are your plans now?' said Carter.

'This splinter faction of Spiral has a mobile division based on a fucking warship, if you can believe that. Durell, the fucker, thinks he is going to dominate the world, or something shite like that. We've got to stop him.'

'We?'

Jam turned and grasped Carter's shoulders. 'You're part of our army now, Carter. You're a Demolitions expert; we need you.'

'I have my own war to fight.'

'And what war is that?'

'A war in my head,' said Carter softly.

'Well, I'll let The Priest convince you.'

Carter scowled. 'You've brought that mad fucker back here? He's a fucking liability.'

'Not just him,' said Jam. 'All of them.'

'All of who?'

'All the remaining DemolSquads,' said Jam, eyes gleaming in the glow of his cigarette. 'Durell and Feuchter – and those Nex fuckers – they have brought us a war. Now it's time for a little friendly retribution. There ain't enough time for the USA or China or Russia to get to Durell and his fucking warship ... large parts of NATO's C&C – Command and Control – structure keeps crashing, spinning off-line and killing its own data . . . It looks like Durell's plan is, well, going according to plan. I think we should fuck it up for him good and proper. Now, come over here. I suggest we sit down – drink the bottle of Lagavulin I packed especially for my old friend – and while we wait for the heavy mob, you can bring us up to speed on what exactly happened in LA.'

Carter smiled; the expression felt strange on his face. 'Lagavulin, you say?'

'Well matured.' Jam winked. He strolled over, booted Slater from his pack and drew out a bottle of whisky and some small glasses. 'Drink, anybody? A toast to Spiral's tough little boys winning against all odds?'

Carter laughed then; giggled like a schoolboy. 'Give me a glass,' he spat dryly. 'I need a fucking drink.'

Carter lay on the floor in the corner, snoring. Slater was curled up beside him, also snoring. Nicky had disappeared for a 'long soak in a bath'. And that left only—

Jam. He sat at the mouth of the tunnel, staring out into the night, mulling over thoughts of battleships and the Nex killers. He could not understand; could not understand why their eyes were so strange, could not understand why they were so good at killing. Because he knew that *he* was one of the best, and that he was totally outclassed by the Nex. In one-on-one combat with a Nex he would be dog meat.

'What the fuck did they do to you to make you like that?' he mused through a mouthful of smoke. 'What was the Nex Project? And why did Gol pull out in those early days?'

He watched the smoke as it was snatched by the wind and dispersed.

Like us, he realised. Dispersed. Broken up. Scattered . . .

And he remembered the pain on Carter's face; the pain from talk of Natasha's death.

Jam shook his head.

Shit always happens to good people, he realised. It's just the way of the world.

A low drone came from over the mountains.

And then, in a burst of anticlimax, a Piasecki Pathfinder-3 helicopter loomed from the darkness, hoving ponderously into view, and climbed slightly, then dropped, suddenly, unsteadily, rotors clattering, towards the landing yard. Engines screamed. The rotors whined in deceleration. There was a strange banging sound and a bad smell of old oil.

Jam shaded his eyes against the glare of the Pathfinder's landing lights, climbed to his feet and strode across the stone.

A grinning face met Jam's scowl, and a short squat man leaped down. He had powerful arms and shoulders plastered with tattoos from a life in the military; his head was shaved, bullet-shaped, and his round cheeks were a rosy red. 'How's it going, pussy?' he bellowed at Jam.

Jam blinked.

'Haggis – what – the fuck – is that?'

'It's a 'copter, ain't it?'

'I don't know,' said Jam slowly, walking alongside one rusted flank and staring in disbelief at the huge ragged hole that revealed nestling fuel pipes. 'Haggis, *where* did you get it?'

'Stole it. From an Italian. Is a long story.'

Jam sighed.

'You think we're going to wage a war using *that*?'

'Sorry, Jam.' Haggis gave a red-faced scowl. 'But we can't all nick fucking Apaches, right? They're not the sort of thing that are ten a fucking penny! It's not like hot-wiring a fucking Escort!'

'OK, OK, calm down. Go and get yourself a brew. Are the others on their way?'

'Aye,' nodded Haggis. 'They're coming, all right.'

And come they did.

Shortly after the arrival of Haggis, the dark sky was filled with a clattering of rotors and howling engines. A squad of helicopters, two Lockheed AH-56A machines followed by a Sikorsky Black Hawk, made a majestic entrance and slowly touched down. Jam's face glowed as eight men and a woman disembarked. They exchanged greetings, Jam laughing at the custard spilled down Bob Bob's combats, and the weary group of DemolSquad operatives moved into the protective embrace of Kamus-5 in search of a brew and some chocolate biscuits.

Jam stood, hands on hips, staring at the six helicopters gathered in the yard; still the machines were dwarfed by the sheer rock walls, the huge expanse of barren stone, rocky and uneven, carved from the very mountain itself. His memories drifted back: he could still picture the base when it had been operational . . . but that had been twenty years ago when he had been a young bright-eyed man without the weight of years and the weight of murder burdening his shoulders.

Jam took his seat once more. Lit a cigarette.

'Hiya.'

He glanced up at Nicky.

'Hi, love.'

She handed him a tin mug filled with steaming tea. 'Lots of sugar, Jam, just how you like it.'

'Cheers.' He took a sip and stared back out over the darkness. Austria nestled below him.

'You OK?'

'Yeah,' he sighed, wrapping his leather coat around him. 'Just tired. Tired of it all.'

Nicky sat beside him, snuggling up close, and he looked at her, surprised. She rested her head against his chin and the smell of her hair filled his senses.

'Hello?'

'Mmmm?'

'You feeling horny or something?' He grinned his boyish flirtatious roguish grin; it was the sort of chat-up line that had got him beaten about the head on many drunken occasions.

Nicky met his gaze. His cheeky grin disappeared when he saw the seriousness there. 'You've always been an insolent fucker, Jam. But I have enjoyed working with you. I feel – I don't know – I have a very, very bad feeling about what we're going to do.'

Jam nodded. 'It's a war,' he said softly. 'Durell, and Feuchter – they brought us a war. They tried to wipe us out; now it's time to give them a bullet up the arse.'

'Yeah. But . . . not everybody is going to make it back.' She licked her lips. They gleamed in the light from Jam's cigarette. She reached up, suddenly, and kissed him. Their lips stayed pressed together, tongues darting, and Jam felt lust smash through his body with a ferocity that he had forgotten.

She pulled away.

Jam stared into her beautiful eyes.

'I need some company tonight,' she said, her voice husky.

Jam nodded. Speechless. And, standing, she led him inside by the hand.

As the tendrils of dawn light crept over the mountains, Jam rose bleary-eyed and happy from the pallet bed. The covers fell away to reveal Nicky's bronzed skin, a rounded breast peeking from above the covers. Jam rubbed at his eyes, then at his stubble, lit a cigarette and stumbled in his boxer shorts and socks down the draughty stone corridor.

Noise greeted him and, shielding his eyes, a cigarette limp between his lips, he stepped out into the dawn . . .

And into a hive of activity.

There were at least a hundred helicopters, filling the yard with their metal menace. Some had engines screaming, rotors hissing through the air as men and women stood by, staring into engine compartments or filling the machines with fuel. Others merely stood, waiting for the mission, glinting in the glorious dawn sunlight.

Jam's jaw dropped.

He could see Fegs, Bob Bob, Jones5 and Russian, all working on their helicopters, dark oil staining their arms and hands. Blitz and the sexy lithe Czech assassin named AnnaMarie were carrying jerrycans of fuel to their rusting steeds, while Carter sat nearby, his head in his hands, cigarette dangling from his lips as The Priest stood above him, quoting from his small leather Bible, a look of wild hatred in his eyes, spittle dripping from his impassioned lips. Jam's gaze roved across groups of men and women he had trained with and fought beside. Some he had trained himself. Hundreds of his DemolSquad operative friends had all been brought together here for the first time, the only time. The last time.

Pride filled him.

His chest swelled and he took a step forward. Several of those nearby glanced up, smiling, giving the occasional wave. A torrent of strength flooded through Jam and drowned his despair.

'Can I have your attention!' he bellowed.

Activity died down, and slowly all the DemolSquads turned towards this man in his underwear. His gaze met with that of The Priest, who gave him a quick thumbs-up sign.

Jam took a drag on his cigarette. 'I see you all standing in front of me,' he rumbled, his words coming out on a cloud of smoke, 'and it fills me with pride; it fills me with love; and it fills me with strength. There is a great enemy that we will face today, a fucker that we must smash to make the world a better place, a fucker we must kill. I talk about the terrorists who have sought to bring down Spiral from within; the people who have sought to murder us all over the last few months. The betrayers of the Spiral cause. The men who have betrayed not just Spiral but their *friends* as well.'

A few clapped.

Jam's wild-eyed gaze roved over the gathered group. He exchanged glances with Dublin, Sarah and Legs. 9mm gave him a small wave, her dark eyes flashing bright with love for him, and Jam beamed her a huge smile: they had been through good times together. His gaze took in Jupiter, Mongrel, Banks, Kavanagh and Ballard: all were ready, all had weapons primed, all were ready to go to war against the evil that was attempting to fuck the world and fuck it bad.

Jam smiled slowly.

'This processor, the QIII which the enemy possess – it is masking their presence, hiding their mobile operations, their *warship* from the world's military until they are ready to subvert all countries' own war systems – and that will be soon. Very soon. Once that happens, they will be unstoppable . . . Demol16 found them while sweeping the Arctic –' there came a small cheer '– and now *we* are the only ones who can make a difference. We are on our own . . . but we will win,' he said, his words soft as he tossed his spent cigarette down. 'We will break them. I will complete briefing of operations in thirty minutes; people, be ready to move in one hour. We have some madmen to kill.'

Carter walked slowly among the groups, between CH-47s, past a Bell UH-1N Iroquois – the famous Huey – and a 1967 Sikorsky HH-3 that looked severely the worse for wear. A hundred helicopters; many sported home-made artillery attachments and many had had heavy machine guns welded to their frames, feeds of ammunition dangling from makeshift containers made from plastic boxes. Inside many machines he could see bundles of explosives strapped together with masking tape, grenades, and anti-personnel mines that had been stripped and cobbled together as makeshift bombs. Pride swelled through Carter, and he understood just how Jam had felt; never before had he seen such a gathering of DemolSquad operatives. And these were the survivors; these were the toughest of the tough, the men and women who had fought off attacks by the Nex and had slain hundreds of them.

Every man and woman had a grudge.

Every man and woman had lost friends to the Nex – and to those who were behind the Nex.

Every man and woman wanted a slice of the payback cake.

Carter halted. The Priest had been following him around for the last hour, quoting from the Bible and reciting mantra-like phrases at him as if possessed. Carter turned and looked up into the big man's gold-flecked brown eyes. The Priest was large; one of the largest men Carter had ever seen.

'Can you *fucking* leave me alone,' said Carter.

'I see, my son, that you are aggrieved,' rumbled The Priest, closing his Bible slowly. The book was dwarfed in his huge hands. 'But I seek merely to make light of your pain, to fill your soul with joy in this most strenuous of times, to fill you with light before the coming battle with the evil God-mocking Satanic Hordes.'

'Well, don't – just don't. I need calm; I need to compose myself.'

'I see that you have suffered great loss at the hands of Durell and Feuchter. The Lord will pay back these evil men with flashes of lightning from Heaven; the Lord shall smite down our enemies, He shall fuck them up bad.' The Priest grinned then; he had lost many teeth, mainly in pub brawls while trying to convert Satan's unholy drinkers. 'Carter, my son, put your trust in the Lord and He will surely guide thee.'

'I'll put my trust in my Browning 9mm, Priest,' said Carter, smiling. 'It worked wonders on Feuchter, and it will work wonders today.'

The Priest frowned.

'Feuchter still has to be punished.'

Carter shook his head. 'Feuchter is dead, Priest; I killed him myself. Filled him full of holes, left him to suffer a bomb blast that would have ripped him limb from fucking limb.'

'You are wrong, my friend. For whatever reason, the Lord protected him; saved him for fiery retribution from the skies.'

'How do you know this? Demol16?'

'No – I saw him, when we intercepted an ECube transmission, a visual. He had sent a message to Durell; their arrogance is colossal, for they think we are as nothing. They think we are broken and ground as ashes into the

472

dust. But Feuchter *was* alive, Carter. You can believe me on this.'

Carter's jaw clamped tight. 'That fucker just will not die.'

'There is more.'

'More?'

The Priest nodded. 'Natasha is there – on that warship, on that Spiral abomination. She was shot in LA, yes, but she did not die; she featured in Feuchter's message to Durell.'

'Natasha! Alive!' Hope died as soon as it had flared. 'Impossible,' growled Carter.

'Impossible that they would seek to save a bartering tool against you, their greatest proven enemy?'

'Me?'

'You scare them, Carter. They fear you. There is a dark demon in your soul, a seed there, and they can see it nestling within you.'

'They seek to draw me to them?'

'Like a lamb to the slaughter,' said The Priest softly.

Carter moved away from the hive of rag tag DemolSquad members into the cool confines of the Kamus mountain complex. He walked, for what seemed like hours, down darkened, long-disused corridors, his mind whirling, images of Natasha flittering like lost fragments through his brain, sadness overtaking him, then anger, then frustration, disbelief.

If she was alive, then he had to save her.

And Feuchter – alive, and using her as bait?

Carter smiled grimly.

'Our reunion will be a sweet one,' he said softly.

The briefing was over. The DemolSquads were making final preparations for their departure, including the incorporation of some highly sophisticated guns that could be mounted beneath their helicopters to help combat surface-to-air and air-to-air missiles.

From Austria, they were to fly to the north and east, across Europe and Russia, skirting the northerly Barents Sea and on towards Novaya Zemlya and the Arctic Ocean beyond where Jam and Demol16 and The Priest had tracked Spiral_mobile using The Priest's world network of spies, his illegal (even by Spiral standards) web of optical and digital communications, and good old-fashioned TacSquad scouts. There they would find a ship – a cruiser-class battleship similar in size and specifications to the Russian *Kirov* class. The ship was a dull matt black and had no name. Displacing 28,000 tonnes of water, it was a huge vessel that would no doubt hold many surprises for the attacking DemolSquads. But one thing was certain: all the men and women involved were willing to die to bring the enemies of Spiral to justice.

Carter stood watching the bustle, his Browning in his hand. Slater had checked over the Comanche and had refuelled her, ready for Carter's part in the battle. Carter did not care.

'Jam!'

Jam, now dressed, walked swiftly towards his friend. 'Yeah?'

'I need to ask a favour.'

'Anything.'

'I thought Natasha was dead but The Priest has informed me that I was wrong. Feuchter and Durell have her, they have her aboard the battleship. I need time, Jam; I need time to get in there and get her the fuck out before you blow it up.'

Jam stood, mouth open. 'What are you asking me, Carter? To hold up a fucking operation like *this*?'

'Yes. I need this, Jam; I need the chance to get her out.' Carter gritted his teeth. He stared into the eyes of his oldest friend. 'Come on, man, you can't let her die in there – I *know* what you've fucking got planned . . . come on, *please*,' he said.

Jam closed his mouth. He frowned, glancing over his shoulder. Then he met Carter's iron gaze.

'Just supposing I was to let you do this, how will we work it?'

'We fly in, and I use the cover of the battle to get inside the warship . . . and get Natasha out. It's all I've ever fucking asked you for, Jam; all I've ever, ever asked for.'

'You *do* know what I plan, don't you, Carter?' said Jam softly.

Carter nodded. 'Bomb in a bag?'

'Well, a nuke in a suitcase, to more precise. A home-made neutron device. You need to be well the fuck away from there, Carter – this baby is going down *big style*.'

Carter's mouth was a grim line.

'I'll be out, Jam, with Natasha. If I'm not . . .' He left the sentence unfinished and Jam scowled, licking his lips.

'As long as you know the score, buddy. I can give you an extra few minutes . . . no more . . .'

Carter nodded; he knew the score, all right. He knew the dangers, the risks, the Hell that he would have to travel through before he could come out the other side and get his life back to normal. Normal? He laughed.

'Let's do it – and do it *now*,' said Jam.

□ Ωclass relay □ qiii mainframe code logon
01001010
booting . . .
booting . . . sequences initiated . . .

GetCommandLineAt □ GetVersion›
□ GetProcAddress & □ GetModuleHandleA }
ExitProcess ž
□ TerminateProcess ÷ GetCurrentProcess $ □
GetModuleFileNameA
□ GetEnvironmentVariableA u □ GetVersionExA □
□ HeapDestroy › □ HeapCreate ¿ □ VirtualFree Ÿ
□ HeapFree m
□ SetHandleCount
R6026
– not enough space for spiral initialisation
error
R6025
– pure virtual function call
R6024
accessing data scripts □
demolition squads// coordinates confirmed
attack procedures confirmed . . .

The sun had risen, glittering like a series of firework
explosions along the peaks of the ice-capped mountains,
filling the sky with a cool sapphire blue that surrounded
Carter and filled his soul with an easy gentle peace.

He breathed deeply inside the HIDSS.

Slater's repair on the hole in the cockpit was holding
up well, and Carter found it a pleasure to actually pilot
the vehicle without having to sit on the corpse of another
dead man . . . another dead *friend*.

As he flew, and the noise of the engines filled his
senses, he focused on controls and weapons, revising their
operation, revising the procedures. Kamus-5 and a slack-
handed Slater had provided full tanks of fuel. Carter
checked the navcomp.

Coordinates 000.002.006

South of the Arctic Ocean, of the North Pole.

A Continent of Ice . . .

When he was happy with the Comanche, happy with its motion and stability and his own confidence in operating the machine, Carter analysed himself: and he felt good.

No, he felt more than good. He felt fucking *alive*.

Behind the Comanche, a dark ragged line on the horizon, followed the remaining living DemolSquads in their massive range of aerial war machines. Carter took the lead not out of choice but because the Comanche housed the most advanced detection equipment of this group; this band; this new model *army*.

Walking point, he mused grimly.

And now he knew what he had to do. He had to get Natasha out. But more than that: this was about Jessica, and Langan, and Gol. This was about Spiral. This was about betrayal, and Feuchter and Durell. This was about life and death. This was about finishing what others had begun. This was about finding the truth. And this was about—

Revenge.

Not for himself, no. For the innocents, the people who had died merely because they were in the way. The people who didn't have a job where they were expected to take a bullet and be happy with the outcome.

Carter knew. Knew that he had to stop this thing and stop it fast.

What can one man do? mocked his subconscious.

One man can do enough, he replied calmly.

He dropped the Comanche's altitude, flying low over fields of snow in northern Russia and then down towards great sprawling forests. He flew fast over small villages of white-walled red-roofed houses; he even fancied he heard the ringing of church bells.

Sunday, then, he thought. Is it?

He checked the Comanche's computers.

Yeah, Sunday. The Day of Rest. The Day of Worship.

I'll give them something to worship, he thought grimly.

The Priest would not be a happy man, he chuckled to himself.

Carter checked himself: his body was sore, aching, suffering from a myriad of minor aches and pains and bruises and scratches. He flexed his bound finger; it was almost healed – or, at least, enough to allow him to use it sparingly. His ribs didn't click as much when he moved, although the soreness was a nuisance and his stomach still gave him twinges of pain. But he had taken some tablets and this irritant had faded . . . His smashed nose was his biggest problem. It was bent, broken. His nostrils were still clogged with blood. It had taken just too much shit to have healed and he knew deep down that it was his weak spot, his Achilles heel. To take another blow there? The pain would scream through his head and he would be blind . . .

Primary location for protection, then, he mused idly.

The Comanche hummed over a huge swathe of forest, closely followed by its lengthy growling wake of metal war machines, their shadows tumbling across the land and then over a cliff and down towards a huge inland lake. Carter checked to make sure that they were near no military or aviation bases.

They needed peace, not a chase.

And *he* wanted the serenity of the sea . . .

I wonder how Sam is? he thought suddenly, picturing the insane plump chocolate Labrador in his mind. He realised that he missed the dog; really missed it.

When Carter had kicked Sam out of his house on the approach of the assassin Nex, the Labrador would have made his way down the valley in search of food and the next cottage. Old Mrs Humphreys often fed the fat mutt and looked after him when Carter was away on missions.

She'd better be looking after you, you dumb fat mongrel, thought Carter.

Better be taking real good care of you.

With a shock he realised that he might never see the dog again. This annoyed him and he chewed his lip. The chances were that he would die; he would take the fight to them, fuck them up bad and sour their links with Spiral and then die . . .

And Natasha . . . well, Natasha could already be dead.

So be it, he mused bitterly.

He forced himself to relax as the Comanche at last flew low over the sea. Occasionally he passed fishing boats, and occasionally the fishermen would wave at him, forcing him to smile sadly.

What happy lives they lead, he thought.

What normal, happy lives.

Why couldn't I have been normal? he thought . . .

Because you kill – said a small voice in his head.

Because you kill and you are good at killing.

You might hate it.

You might loathe it.

But whether you like it or not, you are *good* at it.

A natural-born shooter.

A predator.

A tiger, rather than a lamb.

The world of ice waters opened up ahead of this ragtag army after they had traversed the Barents Sea: a harsh landscape of intense and frightening beauty, a terrible world of choppy freezing ocean with torn blocks of ice rising up, mingled and merged and tossed frozen together in rigid flow streams. The Comanche flew low, coming in off the unquiet cold waters as sunlight glimmered across the icy world.

He shivered. The Comanche shuddered.

Carter checked the coordinates and slowed his speed as he started to approach the estimated location of the battleship, the *Kirov*-class cruiser. The scanners still read zero: nothing. He flew. The Comanche, despite flying in temperatures well below what Carter thought would be its operating norm, was responding well and as long as no vicious storms came up over the bustling cloud-filled grey and sapphire horizon, Carter knew the 'copter would get him there in one piece . . .

A crazy thought slammed into his mind.

The Priest was wrong.

They were all wrong.

There was nothing; nothing but freezing sea, and cold cold ice flows.

Laughter welled up madly in his throat as he flipped free the HIDSS and with the power of ordinary human eyesight transgressed a billion dollars of technological development funding. Then he saw it. A black dot on the horizon: a matt black sentinel, squatting against the grey churning freezing waters.

Carter would have to be ready; he would have to be strong; he would have to be a machine without emotion . . . without fear . . .

The black dot started to grow; to materialise; to enlarge before Carter's very eyes.

The battleship was moving at a rapid speed for a ship so large; a churning wake of white foam followed it.

Carter grinned nastily within the insect-like HIDSS helmet.

All I want, he thought, are answers before I die.

All I want, he thought, is to kill those responsible – before I die.

He had resigned himself. Made his peace with God – or whatever other warped and wicked deity was waiting for him on the Other Side. Feuchter had asked him once if he was ready to die and now he understood, now he truly understood.

Carter knew.

Knew that he wasn't coming back.

□ Ωclass relay □ qiii mainframe code logon
01001010
booting . . .
□ GetStdHandle □□ GetFileType P □
GetStartupInfoA ² FreeEnvironmentStringsA
³ FreeEnvironmentStringsW Ò □
WideCharToMultiByte □□
GetEnvironmentStrings
□□ GetEnvironmentStringsW ß □ WriteFile □
HeapAlloc » □ VirtualAlloc
¢ □ HeapReAlloc ¿ GetCPInfo ¹ GetACP 1 □
GetOEMCP
Â □ LoadLibraryA ä □ MultiByteToWideChar S □
GetStringTypeA
V □ GetStringTypeW ¿ □ LCMapStringA À □
LCMapStringW / □ RtlUnwind
KERNEL32.dll ~ _AIL_lock@0 v
_AIL_get_preference@4 E □ _AIL_unlock@0
_AIL_lock_mutex@0 F □ _AIL_unlock_mutex@0 □
_AIL_set_error@4 Ê
»»»»»»»»»»»»»»
errors rectified
q111 01001010 100%on-line

```
operational procedures confirmed
HKLM,%KEY_OPTIONAL%,'sysmon',,'sysmon'
HKLM,%%\sysmon,INF,,'appletpp.inf'
SP1Q,%KEY_OPTIONAL%\sysmon,Installed,,'0'
SP1Q,%KEY_OPTIONAL%,'sysmeter',,'sysmeter'
SP1Q,%KEY_OPTIONAL%\sysmeter,Installed,,'0'
HKLM,%KEY_OPTIONAL%,'netwatch',,'netwatch'
SP1Q,%KEY_OPTIONAL%,'demolimminent',
'demolsquads=37'
HKLM,%KEY_OPTIONAL%\demol,INF,,
'squadthreat.inf'
script engaged script locking engaged
launch sequence initiated= threat=
demolsquad=37
co-ords 234.456.555.211 – eq%345.331
satellites= 248
satellites= qiii operational takeover complete
satellite request= granted
logged.
```

The warship, while not the largest cruiser ever built, was certainly the most menacing. Its dull matt black flanks crouched on the ocean crests and it growled through the sea water, its heavy squat hull smashing the waves apart as it powered towards its destination. Carter, like the other members of the DemolSquads, had listened to Jam's briefing, based on information gathered by a hundred different DemolSquad operatives, including The Priest. Reconnaissance scouts had learned that the vessel was armed with extensive weapons and guidance systems, far superior to those a cruiser would normally carry. As well as the standard surface missiles and guns, it had extensive anti-submarine sensors and weapons, and a powerful Mk IV phased-array radar giving 360° coverage able to track up to 250 targets simultaneously. It carried fixed-wing aircraft and heavily armed and armoured support helicopters. And the ship was nuclear-powered. Unlike normal cruisers, this machine had a top speed of over 60 knots. And there had been no signs of a crew . . .

Carter hovered for a while at a distance, the Comanche humming softly to him, the HIDSS screaming proximity warnings at him. Below, the sea spun away in circular patterns, brushed aside by down draughts from the 'copter.

And yet—

And yet the cruiser was not on his displays.

The QIII processor, he thought.

It's fucking intercepting satellite, radar and scanner readings.

It's bouncing everything away from the ship!

No wonder it was never discovered . . . and now? Now that the QIII was quite obviously working?

Was he too late?

Behind, despite their agreed radio silence, Jam connected, using the ECube.

'You OK, Carter?'

'Yeah. You guys ready?'

'We're fucking ready. Me and Slater are heading off – we're gonna do our bit for the boys.'

'Be good, Jam. And if you can't be good?'

'I'm always fucking good,' snarled Jam.

Grinning, Carter eased the Comanche forward, leading this huge pack of metal wolves. They grouped closer now, machines coming up and around the Comanche to form a huge black swarm buzzing angrily against the Arctic heavens . . . Carter found himself suddenly tense, awaiting incoming fire, waiting for those huge 12.5cm calibre guns to spit their welcome . . .

The matt black cruiser groaned and growled through the crashing sea. Waves smashed against its prow. The odd seagull cawed, following the mighty vessel in the hope of some stray scrap of food. Sections of ice floated in the water, chunks that were brushed aside easily by the warship's ram.

Carter grimaced.

It began to rain, lightly at first, then a downpour of heavy droplets laced with ice from a tumultuous cold sky; clouds gathered and bunched, huge bruises against the skin of the heavens.

The rain and sleet fell with increased ferocity.

The dark sea churned, rain turning waves into dancing patterns among bobbing blocks of ice.

Against the sky sat an inky blot that expanded, multiplying, replicating; then what had been one blot against the backdrop of the sky became many smaller ones.

'Let's do it,' came the crackle of Carter's voice.

Insect-like, the DemolSquads advanced on the cruiser. They separated; aboard the helicopters, aboard the Lockheed AH-56As, the UH-1N Iroquois Hueys, the CH-47s, the MH-53Js, the MH-60G Pave Hawks, the Apaches and Black Hawks – aboard these metal monsters, these machines of war, stood men and women armed with machine guns and bombs, waiting to fight, waiting to suffer, and waiting to die.

In one machine stood The Priest. His eyes flashed with fire. He pointed down from the heavens; he pointed at the cruiser where a swarm of small black squat powerful helicopters lifted from the decks, rotors screaming through the rain, guns and missiles armed and ready . . .

'Here we go,' muttered Carter, arming the Comanche's weapons systems in a splash of coloured lights and flickering data within the HIDSS. Alarms screamed around him as, on the deck of the battleship, one of the gun turrets rotated on well-oiled rails. The 12.5cm-calibre twin barrels lifted in their angle of ascent; there was a massive concussive *boom* and the turret recoiled.

An advancing DemolSquad helicopter, a Pave Hawk, was plucked from the sky. Fire erupted, glittering bright orange and yellow against the grey sky, a ball of bright iridescence before it smashed down into the sea, rotors spinning screaming splashing into the churning waters where the blackened fire-filled carcass disappeared swiftly below the waves.

Swarms of small black helicopters came sweeping from the darkness and rain, their machine guns hammering.

The DemolSquads returned fire and the skies were suddenly lit by streamers of tracer.

Carter fired off two rockets and allowed the Comanche to spin, rotors scything, below heavy-calibre fire, closely missing a small black helicopter . . . he allowed the Comanche to drop – away and *down* from the battle, and towards the suddenly looming deck of the enemy ship: Spiral_mobile . . .

Above him, bullets crackled across the sky—

And the heavens were painted crimson.

Durell's twisted blackened fingers crept from beneath the soft folds of cloth and his hooded eyes stared into the void. His hand moved, slowly, a sliver of ice down the spine of the world . . . and he gently pressed RETURN.

Nothing . . .

And then a quiet hum filled the massive control deck. The computer monitors that lined the walls dimmed momentarily, as if bowing before some electronic deity, then brightened into life once more.

Words – QIII script – sped across the display. Then, from a laser encoder, a globe sprang into existence, a spinning white-laser representation of the Earth. It hung in front of Durell's face. His gnarled hands lifted and were bathed in white light that illuminated the deformed grotesque within Durell's heavy folded hood.

Durell laughed, a cold and ominous sound.

He reached out and pointed; the globe spun, located its target, and zoomed through layers of sparkling laser light to highlight Spiral_mobile, crashing through the waves. Durell pulled back from his own base and spun the globe; he located the nearest Russian air base and smiled softly.

'So you come to destroy me, my sweet young DemolSquads? Like virgins to the slaughter?'

He initiated the sequence.

The QIII hummed from the heart of the black terminal.

```
☐ Ωclass relay ☐ qiii mainframe code logon 01001010
booting . . .
HKLM,%KEY_OPTIONAL%,'Sp1on-line',,'sp1on-line'
HKLM,%KEY_OPTIONAL%\sp1on-line,INF,,'appletpp.inf'
HKLM,%%\sp1on-line,Section,,'sp1on-line'
HKLM,%KEY_OPTIONAL%\sp1on-line,Installed,,'0'
HKLM,%KEY_OPTIONAL%\CharMap556ar,Section,,
'CharMap'
SP1Q,%%,'ZipFldr',,'ZipFldr'
SP1Q,%KEY_OPTIONAL%\sysmon,Installed,,'0'
SP1Q,%KEY_OPTIONAL%,'sysmeter',,'sysmeter'
SP1Q,%KEY_OPTIONAL%\sysmeter,Installed,,'0'
HKLM,%KEY_OPTIONAL%,'netwatch',,'netwatch'
tracking . . . located Russian server
krostevskyTTQBGGH1#####
tracking . . . locked.
```

SP1Q,%KEY_OPTIONAL%,'demolimminent',,
'demolsquads=37'
HKLM,%KEY_OPTIONAL%\demol,INF,,
'squadthreat.inf'

script engaged script locking engaged
launch sequence initiated= threat= demolsquad=37
co-ords 234.456.555.211 – eq%345.331
launch MIG30 fighter config= 32armed
satellite request= granted
logged.

CHAPTER 24

THE SKEIN

The sea crashed and churned against the hull of the warship as it growled forward. Missiles and bombs detonated. There was a deafening roar of explosives from the ship's deck; steel shuddered; helicopters were smashed, burning insanely, from the sky to die, their flames extinguished in the waves. Guns roared, sparks spitting and kicking across metal and flesh.

Out of nowhere, a tiny black vessel was heli-dropped into the bounding waves. It sped at an incredible velocity and with absolutely no sound across the churning waters, crashing into troughs and riding them bravely before gliding up alongside the cruiser. There was a tinny *crack* and it secured itself.

Aboard, two figures gave one another the thumbs-up. Jam lifted his goggles for a second and stared into Slater's eyes. Both men grasped hands, and Jam said:

'This is it.'

'Good luck, brother.'

'If I don't come back . . . tell Nicky I love her.'

Slater guffawed. 'Such sentimentality from the King of Pornt?'

'A favour – for me.'

'Anything, brother,' said Slater, smiling kindly.

'Five minutes; then get the fuck out.'

'Five minutes,' said Slater. He replaced his goggles and hoisted the heavy machine gun, glancing up at the warfare raging above; at the flaming skies; at the turmoil of bullets and bombs and spinning rotors. Machine guns roared; so many guns that it seemed the whole world was at war – and on fire. Orange streaked across the grey of storm clouds.

'Good luck, brother.'

'Luck's got fuck all to do with it,' said Jam, grinning. Hoisting the wide black suitcase in his arms, he dropped backwards over the edge of the tiny boat and was instantly swallowed by the churning black abyss.

Slater sat for a few moments, staring down at the few bubbles that reached the rolling sea surface; then he concentrated on keeping the little boat stable in its umbilical link with the cruiser. He was so close that he could see rivets; he was so close that he could reach out and touch the cold black metal.

Slater nodded to himself.

Justice had to be served – like a plateful of napalm spaghetti, with nuclear dessert.

The Comanche banked low and hard, sweeping around past massive black gun turrets, so close that Carter could see the ship's railings and the windows of cabins. The Comanche banked, past more huge turrets that rocked with recoil and belched fire and shells. The cruiser flashed past in an insane blur, the Comanche screaming its own scream above the crash of the pounding Arctic sea. Carter dragged the machine, engines howling, around and brought it down to land on the deck with a swordlike *clash* of metal upon metal. The rotors howled as they wound down.

'*It's a trap,*' said Kade calmly.

'Like I give a fuck,' snapped Carter.

He lifted the cockpit canopy and wind and rain lashed in, stinging his skin. He stood, climbed up onto the rim, then lowered himself and dropped to the deck. His boots made dull thumps and he could feel ice, a slick layer beneath him. 'You've been a good girl,' he said, patting the Comanche's flank. The wind snatched his words in a shriek of laughter and twirled them away in a spiral of down draughts as helicopters banked and swept above him, machine guns roaring. A missile shot skywards and a helicopter was sent tumbling, a flaming ball of melting steel, into the freezing ocean.

Carter turned; focused; orientated himself. His stare roved the dark surroundings lit sporadically by fire from the sky and he could see nobody as he palmed his battered trusty old Browning – a small reassurance, but at least it gave him the ability to deal hot metal death to anybody who came near.

Natasha.

Where would she be?

With Feuchter.

'That fucker,' growled Carter. He moved quickly forward across the ice-slippery alloy deck, gaze lifting, scanning the bridges and gantries, the portholes and windows. This felt crazy, totally crazy and Carter felt the burden of his life lift from his shoulders because it did not matter any more, truly nothing mattered and if he was to die then—

So be it.

Carter sprinted towards the nearest doorway. But then everything happened at once – there was a concussive *boom* and a helicopter went hurtling past, low, rotors howling dangerously, and Carter whirled, crouching, bringing the Browning up to see—

'*Nothing*,' whispered Kade.

Behind him, Feuchter slid from the shadows, from the darkness, like a ghost or a demon emerging from another plane of existence. He held a small black gun and his expression was almost serene.

Carter turned and Feuchter nodded slowly. He smiled, showing tombstone teeth. 'Mr Carter, we are expecting you.' Carter fixed his glittering gaze on the muzzle of the gun that pointed straight at his heart . . .

He tried hard to disguise his shock at seeing Feuchter.

'I left you dead.'

'No. You left me *dying*. There is a subtle difference. Gods, the pain I have suffered at your hands, Mr Carter – it will be a pleasure to see you finally shuffle like a reptile from this mortal coil. Now, your gun, please?'

'What makes you think I'll give you it?'

An explosion rocked the ship. Feuchter did not waver, but nodded to something behind Carter. He turned. Behind him stood three Nex, copper eyes glowing, bodies black-clad, all bearing pistols and slung sub-machine guns. They had spread out in silence, and to his shame he had not heard them. These killers were subtly different to the other Nex he had met; they seemed larger, broader, more athletic.

'Previously, you met my scout caste, the 5Nex' said Feuchter. 'These Nex – they are different. These – well, they are the warrior caste.'

Carter licked his lips. He smiled broadly.

'Is Natasha here?'

491

'She is. She requests the pleasure of your company; she would weep and wail in your arms and seek one final kiss before you both die. Come this way, Mr Carter. Let me show you the Heaven we are building . . .'

'Heaven?'

'It will be a paradise of modern technology,' said Feuchter softly. He gestured with his gun, and Carter allowed the Browning to be taken from him. 'This way.'

'*You soft fucking bitch pussy,*' hissed Kade.

Carter stepped forward.

Towards the black door.

And the gaping maw of uncertainty beyond.

Feuchter led Carter through dim black corridors, metal floors and metal grilles beneath their boots. Light came from below and now that he was out of the wind and rain and ice, Carter could hear the deep distant drone of the cruiser's massive engines.

Feuchter walked ahead of him, his back a broad target. And yet, Carter could see something: a difference. The back of Feuchter's neck and head – it was scar tissue. Severe scar tissue, wrinkled and bright pink; his hair was re-growing but the new growth was not complete – and it was black and crinkled. *Different.* Abnormal . . .

Carter shivered. What the fuck is going on? he thought.

He glanced behind him; the Nex were there, guns trained on his back.

Carter followed Feuchter.

There was little else that he could do.

They descended; steep spiral metal staircases led down. The metal was cold beneath Carter's fingers and he felt his mind blurring; he could feel Kade squatting there, watching, observing, offering nothing.

Good, thought Carter at Kade.

Keep your fucking nose out of this.

This is my fight and I will do it alone.

They reached wider corridors and there was more bustle; Nex with gaunt haunted faces rushed about, and without their masks Carter could observe their strange asexual faces. Similar, and yet each one individual, each one different.

'Feuchter, what the fuck are the Nex?' he asked softly.

'Quiet.'

'Or what? You'll kill me?' Carter laughed, a bitter sharp bark. Carter looked Feuchter up, then down. His smile was sickly sweet. 'Come on, Feuchter, answer my question.'

Feuchter halted. He turned. His gaze was burning.

'They are human, Carter, just like you and me. But they are killers, incredibly efficient killers. I thought you were friends with Gol? And you mean to tell me that he never explained the phenomenon that is the Nex?' Feuchter sneered. 'We – Gol, Durell and myself – worked on them, or rather, took over work on the project named Nx5, nicknamed Necros – or Nex. They were pioneered in the 1950s by our predecessors when America and Russia were playing their Cold War games and developing nuclear weapons and intercontinental missiles to deliver their new, gleaming warheads. We then took up the research in the late 90s. Oh yes, we discovered many things back then; many things Spiral would have preferred us to keep hidden. They withdrew our funding for the Nex Project; our specimens were killed and we had to move on to other *more moral* areas.'

Feuchter turned and continued to walk. Carter followed.

'Durell and Gol – the horrors they created!' Feuchter chuckled, and the sound was cold; chilling; nightmare turned real.

Moving down busy metal corridors now, Carter felt the hairs crackling on the back of his neck. He kept glimpsing the faces of the Nex. There was something wrong with these people, these assassins who had hunted him for so long, these killers who had nearly wiped out the Spiral DemolSquads ... but he could not put his finger on it.

Feuchter halted.

A door slid open and he ushered Carter through and onto a massive control deck. Computers lined the walls, their status lights glittering insanely. Display monitors were set up on benches, showing naval and air operations globally. And there, against the far wall, seated beside a small black terminal, was Natasha—

'Nats!'

'Carter!' She leaped to her feet, sprinted towards him and they fell into one another's arms. Carter kissed her passionately, then pulled away and stared down into her tear-filled eyes.

'They captured me,' she sobbed. 'I didn't betray you, Carter, I promise ... they said I was their insurance policy, that you would do what they want as long as they could kill me ...'

'Yes, yes,' snapped Feuchter. He strolled over to the small black terminal and placed the Browning on an alloy bench. He flicked a switch; there was a spiralling of metal plates, which spun out from the top of the terminal to reveal a small black cube. 'Behold,' said Feuchter. 'The QIII. Are you impressed, Mr Carter?'

'Is that it?'

'That's it. But what it lacks in aesthetics, believe me, it makes up for in ability. Thank your saviour, Mr Carter.'

'My ... *saviour*?'

'Ask yourself this question – why did we take Natasha?

Why didn't I just shoot you up there on the deck? You think I give a fuck about answering your questions? You think I care about sparing your life for a few moments more? No . . . But the QIII's puzzled by you, Mr Carter. It can predict anything, *anything* – except your actions . . . and that worries the QIII, and it worries *us*. It thinks that there's something strange about you, Mr Carter, something dark *inside* you that makes you uniquely dangerous. And it's going to tear that secret from you – even if it fucks with your soul, even if it eventually kills you.'

Feuchter smiled, and it was not a nice smile. 'I, however, am sceptical; I want you dead. But *Durell* has other plans . . .'

Feuchter turned and ran a finger across the cold cubic processor.

It hummed softly.

'What's it afraid of?' said Carter softly. 'That I'll shoot you in the fucking face again?'

Feuchter turned; a fluid whirl. He smiled at Carter. 'Let me warn you, it is Durell who wishes you alive, and the QIII itself: not I. Do not antagonise me or you may push me beyond my boundaries. Now, this QIII is fully functional, as you witnessed when your sorry little group flew in to meet their makers – soon, you will see the full extent of our plans.'

'What, to take over the world?' sneered Carter.

Feuchter laughed then. 'You are so naive, Carter. So very, very simple. In your world everything is in black and white; not so in mine. Spiral had their power, had their fucking time. They abused it. Look at the way things are . . . it disgusts me. They have ultimate power and yet evil dominates, evil men walk the world with guns and bombs of HighJ fire. It is fucked up beyond belief, Carter.

Spiral: once I thought they were strong – but no, Spiral are weak, Carter – they grew fat and weak on the spoils of war. Now it is time for change . . . it is time for the strong to rule with an iron fist, and rule we will. We will turn the tables. We will annihilate evil. We will make the world a better place and make God proud of humanity.'

He stepped away from the QIII.

A white globe spun into the air; colours rippled across its surface, painting the simulated Earth with laser light. Around it spun satellites, and as the sphere expanded and rotated Carter could see activity within it: fleets of warships, squadrons of aircraft, battalions of tanks moving across this QIII globe of laser light.

The door opened. A huge, athletic Nex warrior entered, followed by a shuffling figure in heavy dark robes, its face hidden, its shoulders hunched as if in pain. The Nex nodded to Feuchter, who smiled once again. It was with unease that Carter noted the copper-eyed stare fixed on him.

'This is Krael,' said Feuchter softly. He turned and looked hard at Carter. 'You met his mate in Africa; I believe you destroyed her face with your bullets. Krael has asked me for a personal favour: he wishes to dance with you, Carter, he wishes to show you what pain is. The QIII wants you alive – I merely want you to suffer.'

Carter's gaze moved from the huge Nex to the shuffling figure; it had moved to the globe, and a cracked blackened hand came out, reached towards the digital hologram and was bathed, sparkling, by the ghostly witch-light.

The figure chuckled, a deep melodious sound.

'So we meet, Mr Carter.'

'You would be Durell.'

'I would.'

'You're the one in charge of this fucking yapping puppy called Feuchter.'

'Yes. Let me show you what we can do here,' came the voice of Durell from within the robes.

Suddenly, the globe spun with incredible speed. It showed the cruiser and the battle raging in the skies above it.

'You are privileged indeed, Mr Carter, to witness this moment . . .'

Durell's blackened twisted hand gestured, a complicated pattern of movements. Script flowed up and over the globe and the humming from the QIII increased in volume—

Natasha gasped. 'It's . . . doing it . . .'

Carter watched coldly as—

SP1Q,%KEY_OPTIONAL%\sysSATmeter,Installed,,'0'
HKLM,%KEY_OPTIONAL%,,'netwatch',,'netwatch'
tracking . . . located Russian SAT 576 #####
tracking . . . locked.
script engaged script locking engaged
launch sequence initiated= threat= demolsquad
co-ords 234.456.557.212 – eq%345.331
config= armed and targeted
satellite lasers= granted

The fight was going badly. The DemolSquads were dying. And just when it seemed that things couldn't get worse, The Priest watched the darkened skies erupt with a burst of laser light . . . a column of white fire exploded from the heavens and blasted an Apache into glowing splinters of steel that rained sizzling down across the raging ocean.

The Priest swallowed hard. He blinked, and looked upwards.

And his faith was shaken.

The QIII showed it all.

It showed the destructive laser light smash down from the commandeered Russian PredatorSAT.

It showed, close up, the Apache with its struggling occupants.

There was a glow, incredibly bright.

Blood was vaporised.

Flesh torn from faces and hands and throats.

Screams – for an infinitesimal slice of time.

Death.

And an explosion of raining steel . . .

Carter's jaw tightened; he stepped smoothly away from Natasha, gaze scanning the room: the Nex, Krael, Feuchter and Durell.

'You are fucking insane,' he growled.

'On the contrary, Mr Carter,' said Durell, his hidden face turning towards Carter. 'We are quite sane. Only we seek to do what is *right* – by our own definitions of the term. You see the QIII now? The globe is spinning, a pretty light show . . . but thirty seconds ago it unlocked the World Banks – every single one. It now controls them. It has taken over every single satellite that circles the Earth. It controls the world's armies: their aircraft, their tanks, their infantry – their *nuclear weapons*. Shortly I will issue statements to all the governments of the World Powers – they will relinquish their countries to *me* in exchange for their lives. And then . . . *then* we will play this Spiral game my way.'

Durell's voice had risen in anger and, to Carter's ears, in madness.

That black crippled hand emerged and took hold of the QIII processor. Suddenly, the light was gone and Carter blinked . . .

Feuchter walked towards the door, following Durell.

He was almost nonchalant in his movements. His arrogance was total. His position of strength was clear. He halted and turned to Carter as Durell disappeared with the QIII . . .

'You asked me about the Nex, about what they are. I feel that it is my duty to give you answers. Show him, Krael. *Explain* your prowess. Oh, fuck it, Mr Carter, this little puppy thinks it is time for you to *learn*.'

The huge Nex took a step forward; he reached up, grasped his tight-fitting uniform, and ripped it up above his head revealing a heavily muscled torso. But at his sternum, trailing down, there was a light pattern of—

'Scales?' whispered Carter, frowning.

'Armour,' said Feuchter, his eyes bright. 'In the 1950s, when the Americans and Russians discovered the joys of nuclear weaponry, it was also discovered that many insects had, shall we say, natural in-built properties of which we, as humans, were envious. Spiral set up research centres to look at why insects were so tough, so hardy, so downright fucking lethal. Pull a leg from a spider, it doesn't die. It might *hurt*, but it's solid insular genetic structure makes it a force to be reckoned with. Take cockroaches: they are very resistant to radiation. Why? Why the fuck would that be? It was researched for years, answers were found – genetic coding is such a wonderful process – and then Durell and Gol took it one step further . . . developed the ultimate coding able to operate on today's nuclear, biological and chemical battlefields!'

'I thought they were all destroyed,' said Natasha. 'Back then, in Germany? Gol said they were wiped out.'

Feuchter glanced at her. 'Oh no, my sweetness. Durell and myself and your daddy were *very* busy. We call it Skein Blending: you take a human and an insect, or a series of insects and – you're going to fucking *love*

499

this – you *spiral* genetic strands together. The host – insect genetics are quite parasitical in their nature – the host *receives* a whole new set of attributes: resistance to chemical, biological and radioactive weapons; an incredibly enhanced immune system; a massively increased pain threshold, quicker reactions, reflexes, thought processes. Their skin hardens, some grow external and internal armour to protect organs and bones – they become *incredibly lethal killing machines without remorse*. They become the perfect soldier. Their ability to repair themselves increases greatly, Mr Carter; and that is why I am not dead. That is why your bullets, and the explosion and the fire did not kill me . . . I am a Nex, Carter. It is well known within the scientific world that every true scientist should be willing to test his experiments on himself . . . I was the first Nex. I was the first *true* Nex.'

Carter stood with his mouth agape. He glanced at Natasha; she was pale.

'Tell him the rest,' she said.

Feuchter shrugged. 'What more is there to tell? The Nex are a blend of insect and human – nothing more. What Nature has denied us, Man has found a way to complement; to cure.'

'Tell them why Spiral cancelled the project and destroyed the specimens,' she hissed.

Feuchter merely shrugged again.

'It changes your mind state,' said Natasha softly. 'You lose all emotions; you lose all ability to care, to love, to nurture. Your mind becomes like that of an insect; you become the sort of man willing to betray everything he has ever known, ever *loved*.'

Carter dropped his gaze. Kade was screaming in his head and a wave of pain flooded over him. Distantly, there was a concussive *boom*. *'Kill him, and kill him now and we'll fucking go home . . .'* Kade was spitting in his mind . . .

Another figure stepped into the room; Feuchter spoke quietly, then smiled. 'It would seem that I am needed for a few moments – to take over the world,' he whispered. 'Krael, show him how far the Nex have *advanced . . . he wants his answers, give them to him . . .'*

Feuchter stepped through the door and was gone.

The three Nex with guns moved forward and grabbed at Natasha; she hissed a curse and everything happened at once. The huge muscled and armoured figure of Krael stepped forward with a narrow smile and a hiss, tossing his gun aside where it clattered against the wall, the dark armour on his abdomen glinting in the weak light, his asexual face under short dark hair – bristling black insect hair – serene and relaxed and ready to kill . . .

Yelling, Carter charged—

And Krael leaped to meet him . . .

They clashed in mid-air with a rapid exchange of blows so fast that the human eye could barely follow it. They parted, both landing and whirling on the dull black metal floor of the op centre . . .

Krael smiled. 'I will make you suffer like you have never suffered before.'

Carter glanced at where the three Nex had dragged Natasha to the door – but he was stuck, stuck with his own fucking problems . . .

'I will fuck your mind,' snapped Carter.

Krael charged, smashing a series of punches at Carter who blocked, dodged, blocked again and then hammered a right hook to Krael's jaw. Then he kicked out, boot lifting high to smash Krael in the chest, knocking him back with a grunt. Krael leaped again, high into the air, both elbows ramming down at Carter who twisted, whirling

501

with incredible speed as Krael met nothing. Krael landed; his boot smashed out, kicking Carter in the chest and sending him sprawling backwards, a look of pain flashing across his face. Carter hit the metal grilles of the floor with a *clang*, then rolled as Krael's boots landed where his face had been an instant earlier. They circled each other, snarling like caged tigers.

'You have slowed in your old age,' said Krael.

Carter laughed. 'I don't feel dead just yet.'

'You will,' said Krael, his eyes gleaming. 'Don't you understand? I am toying with you; I am fucking with you. You are *slow* compared to me, Carter; you are *weak*. I am going to make you suffer as you made Sharae suffer; I will send you to her and she will enslave your soul . . .'

'Stop talking and show me,' snapped Carter.

They closed—

Warily.

Carter threw a complicated series of punches, jabs, hooks and uppercuts – Krael blocked them all, then came back with a front kick. Carter sidestepped, catching Krael's leg and driving his elbow down at the joint – but Krael twisted, throwing himself up, the heel of his boot connecting suddenly with Carter's face, his nose, hammering Carter back sprawling onto the hard metal floor—

Carter screamed, blood pouring, hands moving to protect his face.

'No!' cried Natasha.

Krael landed in a crouch, then unfolded and stood. He walked forwards. He looked down. He dropped suddenly, one elbow hitting Carter in the chest with all his weight. There was a *crack* of breaking sternum. Carter screamed again – as his hands suddenly shot out, grasped Krael's head and dragged him forward onto the smash of a head-butt – once, twice, three times until Krael's fingers prised Carter's hands free and he scrambled, coughing and blinded, backwards, spinning and dazed, away across the booming metal floor—

Carter, feeling sick, rolled to his knees, then to his feet, groaning. Pain lanced through his chest; he gasped, struggling to breathe, his fingers coming up to probe at his broken sternum. He glared across the op centre at Krael, who was shaking his head, a thin trickle of blood dripping from his broken nose.

The ship around them rocked and shuddered. Distant screams could be heard as scorched stressed metal ranted in fury. A low groaning rose as some distant explosion rumbled.

Krael smiled nastily.

And charged—

Carter braced himself; they punched, blocked, circled; Krael charged again, launching himself into a flying kick that Carter barely dodged. Again Krael came on and Carter backed away before blocking a flurry of blows and returning a combination of punches and kicks that forced Krael back for a moment—

They circled again, Carter panting, sweat dripping from his brow. Krael seemed untouched.

'I thought you would be faster,' said Carter.

'I am faster than *you*.'

'Show me, then, you fucking pussy.'

Krael howled and charged. The blows came thick and fast and Carter found himself retreating, panic-filled, under the insane barrage of punches and kicks. He barely managed to dodge and block – a blow caught him in the throat and he staggered backwards, suddenly trapped against a bank of computers.

Krael stood, panting, smiling grimly, watching the man in front of him as he scrabbled at his neck—

'Carter!' cried Natasha. She struggled with the three armed Nex, aware that even if – by some miracle – Carter managed to kill this warrior Nex, then he would have three more opponents with guns to deal with.

Carter clawed—

at his throat—

Clawed for air—

Carter clasped his neck, pain spearing him. Tears streamed from his eyes and he wiped them away with bloodstained hands. He looked up then, looked up into Krael's dark moody eyes and he knew: knew he was outclassed; knew he was beaten; knew he was *dead* . . .

'Is that the best you can do?' he wheezed through his damaged throat. 'I thought you were supposed to be a fucking warrior – your dead fucking mate put up a better fight . . .'

Krael's eyes widened and his smile disappeared. He screamed, charging again; Carter ducked a series of blows and launched himself across the metal grilles, a full-length dive, stretching for the wall and the bench and the stranded—

Gun.

His fingers curled around the Browning, carelessly tossed by Feuchter onto the alloy bench and left there in a fit of arrogance. Now his fingers curled around the heavy familiar weapon, around the heavy grip of his 9mm brother and he rolled onto his back, gun up and pointing at Krael who suddenly halted, dropping to a crouch—

Krael laughed.

Carter pulled the trigger.

The gun kicked as a bullet flew from its barrel. Krael flicked left and the bullet smashed into a bank of computers. Sparks flew. Carter rolled, the Browning coming around for a second shot with his broken sternum sending searing pain through his body—

He heard the metallic *clicks* – and despite the protest of his body he dived as the other three Nex in the room opened fire. Carter rolled into a metal panel with a *boom*, then scrambled behind a low bench and peered over the edge as guns blasted and sparks flew. The Browning was smashed from his hand, and a punch knocked him sideways.

Carter landed heavily, all breath knocked out of him. Acid pain ate him whole. He laughed through a mouthful of blood and saliva as the shadow of Krael loomed over him.

'*Let me,*' soothed Kade. '*I can take this fucker.*'

I can take him on my own, snapped Carter, slipping a long darkened blade from its hidden home in his boot. In a normal situation Carter never had to resort to knives . . . but this was a far from normal situation and he was fast losing faith and patience and *strength*. Krael loomed above him and Carter slammed the dagger up hard into the warrior Nex's groin, feeling the blade part flesh and muscle with consummate ease. Blood flushed warm and crimson over his fist and he dragged the knife to the side before pulling the blade out. Krael staggered, then slumped slowly to his knees. Carter rose, bathed in the Nex's blood, reached back and hurled the dagger across the ops room. It drove into the eye of one of the Nex holding Natasha – without a sound it toppled forward onto its face and twitched, a huge pool of blood gathering around its head. Bullets flew at Carter, and he ducked as sparks kicked up by his head. Natasha, screaming, was dragged from the room by the two retreating Nex and everything was suddenly silent—

Except for the moaning, writhing form of Krael.

Carter crawled to his feet and checked quickly around. He found the gun, slippery with blood, and moved to where Krael was squirming. The Nex's hands were coated in deep red gore. He looked up at Carter, his face a snarl, and licked at thin white lips.

And Carter felt—

Sorrow. Not anger, nor hatred. Just sorrow for this poor wretched creature at his feet.

He lifted the Browning. Wiped sweat, blood and saliva from his hand.

And placed a bullet in Krael's face, ending the Nex's pain.

CHAPTER 25

MORTAL COIL

Slater sat in the boat, frowning to himself. He checked his watch. Jam had been gone too long – far too long He peered down into the churning waters, but could see nothing. He heard a shout from far above. Glancing up the wall of black metal in front of him, Slater saw a pale round face; it disappeared.

'Great,' he muttered.

There was a *whiz* and a splash beside him.

Slater cursed. Glancing up, he saw the pale face again. Hoisting the heavy machine gun, he fired twenty rounds; some *zipped*, ricocheting, from the wall of black ship metal. Slater wasn't sure if he had hit the target. The pale face disappeared in any case.

'Gone for reinforcements,' Slater muttered. 'Shit. Shit shit fuck. Jam, you arse, *come on*!'

Carter limped warily across the operations centre where computers churned and groaned to themselves. One wall was glass, and looking down he could see a mass of activity; it had to be the ship's bridge. Carter could see

507

Feuchter and Durell, the white globe spinning between them as they directed their New World Order. Natasha was not there.

'You arrogant cunts,' he spat and hoisted his Browning in his blood-encrusted fist. He checked the magazine. Then he checked the other magazines stowed about his person.

He had bullets. Lots of them.

Carter smiled.

'Let's dance, Feuchter,' he said. And stepped warily from the room.

In the corridor, Carter could hear heavy-machine-gun fire. There were *booms* from the cruiser's big guns. Distantly, he could hear other explosions and the scream of engines.

'Doing your work well, eh, Jam?'

'He'll do a better job than you,' whispered Kade.

'Where is Natasha?'

'They've taken her to the bridge. To Feuchter. Everything is in a panic; somehow the DemolSquads have knocked out the navigation systems; the ship cannot steer except with the help of the QIII.' Kade sounded sulky; bitter.

Carter moved along the corridor, which sloped down. He came to steps and warily picked his way down their metal surfaces. He heard something behind him. Ducking into a hatchway, he watched a Nex rush past. The door to the bridge opened: Feuchter stood there, a look of anger and frustration on his face. Natasha was standing behind him, hands taped together, a warrior-caste Nex to either side of her. Behind, the QIII's representation of the world spun as the processor went about the final rounding-up of global electronic control . . .

Durell was dictating a message to the leaders of the

508

world; Carter caught phrases such as 'incredible destructive technology' and 'surrender all military currency'. He spat on the floor and gripped the Browning even tighter.

'Well?'

'The Demolition Squads are all but destroyed. They are retreating now, fleeing into the dark and the rain – but the thirty-two scrambled Russian Mig30s will be here within three minutes; they will finish off the last dregs. 'If only they knew who was issuing their orders now!'

'Good,' said Feuchter, smiling and glancing towards Durell. On the spinning globe of light he could see the distorted, angry, shocked, disbelieving faces of the world's leaders. Durell's cracked black hand was raised in a mocking salute, a gesture of *victory* . . .

Boots thudded along the corridor, and another Nex sprinted into view. He skidded to a halt in front of the smiling visage of Feuchter. But Feuchter could read something . . . something amiss within those bright copper insect eyes . . .

'What is it?'

'A bomb has been planted,' said the Nex calmly, eyes glittering.

'What kind of bomb is it?' snapped Feuchter. 'Come on, what kind of fucking device?'

'Our sensors read it as a micro-nuke neutron device of unspecified yield, magnetically attached to the underside of the ship.'

Feuchter's eyes widened. 'We need to get somebody down there. Now! You hear me?'

The Nex ignored him. 'We must vacate this vessel.'

'Won't our fucking armour protect us against this?'

'The formulation of the SPQ plating is incredibly strong. However, the blast will explode gas and air underneath the whole of the ship; it doesn't matter how strong

509

our armour is against bombs, there will be no water to support the cruiser's weight. The ship will break itself in half.'

Feuchter stared, dumbfounded.

A million thoughts whirled through his brain.

Out of the corner of his eye, he could hear Durell's triumphant ranting and see the black claw raised in the air in defiance of the world, in celebration at *conquering* the world . . .

And all this through a tiny processor.

Feuchter lifted his gun; a single shot through the eye ended the Nex's report. He turned to Natasha and smiled a thin cruel smile. 'It would seem your friends had an ace up their collective sleeve, Miss Molyneux. They're not running away from us, they're getting free of the fucking blast zone—' He gestured to the Nex holding her. 'Give her to me . . .' He grabbed her by the hair and dragged her roughly towards the door.

Feuchter hauled Natasha off the bridge.

Carter stepped out behind them.

'Let her go, Feuchter.'

Feuchter turned, Natasha held between him and Carter. He raised his gun and started firing, a mad smile creasing his lips, his brow furrowed in concentration. Carter dived sideways, back through the hatchway and into a wide metal chamber, sparks kicking up around him. A flattened bullet, ricocheting from the wall, spun like a circular razor across the top of his forearm – there was a moment when the wound was nothing but a narrow strip of red, then the muscle parted and blood gushed out. Carter clamped the wound with a curse and dragged himself to his knees. He heard running footsteps. He tore a strip from his shirt and bound it tightly about his forearm. Blood soaked through in an instant. Gripping the

Browning Hi-Power 9mm, he climbed unsteadily to his feet. His mind swam: loss of blood, constant pain, and a severe pounding at the hands and boots of Krael had left him weak.

'It's also left you slow,' sneered Kade.

Carter said nothing. Licking salty lips, he pushed himself forward and peered along the corridor; he could hear a bustle of insane activity from the bridge. His snarl went tight and muscles stood out like ridges of steel cord along his jaw.

He glanced after the fleeing form of Feuchter who was abducting the woman he loved.

And then towards the bridge—

And the processor that was intent on destroying the world.

'Fuck it.'

He strode onto the bustling bridge, past a huddle of Nex all intent at their terminals. He broke into a sprint as he heard Durell's voice triumphantly saying, '. . . And we will spare their lives . . .'

The Browning touched the back of the robes.

Carter could feel the body beneath the cloth.

Durell froze.

'But *I* will spare no fucking lives,' spat Carter as he pulled the trigger.

The bullet smashed into Durell's back. It ploughed its heavy way through his heart, exploding from his chest in an eruption of breast-shards, and left a spiralling trail of fine red spray up through the centre of the QIII-generated world display.

Durell collapsed.

Everything seemed to go silent on the bridge, as about forty Nex turned their attention towards Carter. He took a single step forward, glanced down at the QIII cubic

511

processor, levelled his Browning and sighted with one eye closed.

'It's been a long fight,' he muttered. 'Now it's game . . . fucking . . . over.'

He put ten bullets into the processor as a distant scream of 'No!' echoed from a Nex behind him. Bullets smashed the cold black QIII cube into a billion insignificant harmless fragments that blew violently outwards in a black mist.

The light-globe representation of the Earth shimmered and was gone.

'You've been hacked, fucker.'

Sub-machine guns and pistols blasted.

Carter sprinted, head low, as a Nex with a sub-machine gun cut ten of its fellow officers in half and stood, mute, wondering at its own stupidity. Bodies crumpled to the ground. Carter raced into the corridor with bullets kicking up sparks behind him and bounced from the wall, groaning long and low to himself as blood seemed to spurt from five or six wounds in his battered body. Then, gathering stored power from some reservoir of energy that he did not know he had, fuelled by the thought of Jam's micro-nuke and with Kade screaming obscenities in his mind, Carter sprinted as if his life depended on it.

Which it did.

Carter stumbled madly down the corridor in pursuit of Feuchter and Natasha.

'*You are slow and weak, Carter,*' mocked Kade. '*You cannot beat Feuchter now – but I, I can wipe him out for you. I can rip out his heart. I have strength you could never dream of – come on, Carter, you have had your fun, now let me out to play.*'

'I can do it alone,' snarled Carter.

He stumbled forward, rebounding from wall to wall. His sternum clicked with every jolt, making him want to cry out. He halted, fell to his knees, and vomited on the metal floor.

'You are dying,' mocked Kade. *'I don't like to say it, but I told you so. And that nuke is tick-tock ticking. Jam did his job well. You only have, ohhh, round about one minute and twenty seconds to get off this fucking ghost ship . . .'*

Carter spat out sour-vomit saliva.

Bullets kicked sparks from the floor behind him.

He heaved himself to his feet, swaying, and pushed on at a weary pace, stumbling, smelling his own stink. His boots thudded dully on metal walkways, up stairs, and to the door that had granted him entry. He heaved it open—

More bullets came at him, striking sparks from the door's metal rim; Carter dropped to one knee, Browning out and kicking in his hand. Feuchter was standing beside a waiting black helicopter and he dragged Natasha into the aircraft as rain pounded all around them.

Carter stepped out into the wind and lashing rain—

And looked around, dazed.

The skies were filled with distant fire and machine guns roared from all around. Most of the DemolSquad helicopters had retreated but a few had remained, buying time for their wounded fleeing comrades, sweeping in to drop bombs on the cruiser's booming gun turrets, keeping close so as to try and make the ship's weapons ineffectual. Nex in their small black helicopters fought short vicious gun battles against the raging sky. As Carter stood, mouth agape, a flaming Nex helicopter plummeted into the sea – closely followed by a wounded bullet-smashed Sikorsky, flaming, out of control, and heading straight towards—

Carter.

With a yelp he started to sprint for cover, all pain suddenly forgotten. The machine howled down from the sky, trailing fire, its guns blasting out of control. Bullets drilled a line of dents along the deck beside Carter, a parallel sprint as the machine crashed close behind him, a noise like thunder rocking Carter's world as an explosion and hot gases filled his senses and he did not look back, dared not look back—

There was a *whiz whiz whum* as Carter ducked, still running insanely with all pain and wounds and *everything fucking forgotten* now in this race for survival. A stray helicopter rotor flashed low over his head, so close that he felt the violent wind of its passing, a twelve-foot razor intent on his decapitation. The rotor clattered onto the deck up ahead and Carter turned to see the burning wreckage too close for comfort, thick black smoke pluming up into the sky, flames sizzling in the ice rain.

More bullets whizzed around him. Carter growled, glaring at the helicopter up ahead. It jumped into the sky and Carter could see Natasha struggling inside with Feuchter. He punched her in the side of the head, knocking her against the glass of the cockpit.

Carter, ducking low, sprinted for the Comanche.

Two Nex ran at him. The Browning's bullets smashed them from their feet, pulverising their faces. Carter did not even break stride. As he reached the helicopter, it was with despair that he saw the bullet-riddled fuselage.

'*It has been sitting in the middle of a battlefield,*' said Kade primly. '*You're lucky it's still in one fucking piece!*'

Carter clambered up and dropped into the cockpit. A lot of the instruments had been smashed, he noticed as he hit the engines. There was a grumble, and a whine. They did not fire.

'I don't fucking believe it!' Carter howled.

514

He punched the dash, then calmed himself. He tried again.

The twin 1380-shp LHTec turboshaft engines burst into life, and Carter lifted the screaming, groaning, wounded Comanche into the skies; it vibrated alarmingly, its engines howling. All around was a chaos of gunfire and flames and explosions; water dripped in through the holes in the cockpit.

As Carter gained altitude, he realised – with horrifying and undeniable finality – that the DemolSquads were being slaughtered. The cruiser's cannons had inflicted a massive toll and the Nex helicopters were dancing among the DemolSquads, picking them off—

Carter's mouth tightened in a grim sour line. His stare locked on the dot that was Feuchter's helicopter; it had headed out low over the waves and had then circled, describing a broad arc and returning to observe the outcome—

Carter powered the Comanche forward.

The killer 'copter dived howling towards Feuchter's small black machine. Carter flicked open the controls for the MiniGun and then realised, in horror, that he could indeed take the helicopter out easily. But that would mean slotting Natasha easily too . . .

Anger and frustration gripped his soul.

The Comanche, one of the greatest aerial war machines, could not help him perform this final task, this final act of revenge and justice and *need*. Feuchter had to die – but Carter did not have the weapons to do it . . . or, rather, his weapon was too *bad* . . .

Lights flickered across the console.

He had a fuel leak; he could see in the HIDSS display on his lap that avgas was pissing from the Comanche's fuselage. Carter forced the helicopter on in desperation.

Feuchter saw him coming and banked his own machine, on-board machine guns opening fire. Bullets whizzed past to left and right, and ate a line up one flank of the Comanche. Still Carter urged the aircraft forward and something, some inner sense made him eject the cockpit canopy in a hiss of hydraulics; it folded to one side to avoid the flashing rotors overhead and dropped away, shattered glass tumbling away into the sea. Rain and ice lashed down at Carter through the *thrumming* of the rotors, soothing him with their cooling numbness; then wind filled him with insane exhilaration as he veered right to avoid a head-on collision and banked the Comanche in a high wide sweep.

Guns clattered behind him.

Carter suddenly realised there were two small black helicopters on his tail; he realised they must have been flanking Feuchter, protecting this being who was their leader—

Guns hammered again.

The Comanche took more hits.

'*The fuel* . . .' hissed Kade in warning as the avgas spray streamed away behind the wounded helicopter . . .

The Comanche lifted rapidly, gaining on Feuchter's thumping black machine as it made its way back towards the cruiser. And then everything happened at once—

There was a low, deep sound, almost beyond hearing.

The world seemed to shake.

The cruiser *jolted*, as if stung, as the neutron micro-nuke planted by Jam detonated. There was a strange underwater roar, an aquatic scream; bubbles erupted and light and fire danced beneath the ocean, spreading out like the tentacles of some great luminous leviathan. The warship lifted and a rending, tearing, screaming sound of stressed steel ripped across the skies – huge cracks appeared down the cruiser's flanks and it split, the midship dipping and the prow rearing into the sky on a gush of suddenly boiling water and steam, a massive split 'V' of steel revealing lights and compartments, tiny toylike items within the massive groaning structure—

Foam and flames burst into the sky, hot spray geysering upwards.

Bullets zipped past Carter, and he launched the Comanche down and *under* Feuchter's machine. He banked the helicopter so that it was flying on its side and fumbled at his belt, dragging free the wire that he had last used back at the Beverly Hills Hilton. He fired it up above him, attaching it to the underside of Feuchter's helicopter as more bullets flew towards him and a spark ignited the stream of aviation fuel trailing from the Comanche in a deadly umbilical to the devastating spark—

Carter felt himself tugged free.

The wind lashed at his dangling body.

The Comanche veered off, trailing a line of fire that quickly caught up with the war machine. Blazing bright, it careered out of control, and suddenly flipped and hammered into the waves, blossoming into a final bright bloom of fire and metal as Feuchter's 'copter flashed overhead.

Carter swung helplessly for a few moments. He was buffeted wildly, and swinging, turning, he saw that the other helicopters were still pursuing. Wind lashed at him, and ice rain. The pursuers opened fire.

Carter yelped as bullets roared around him, zipping past his unprotected flesh.

He reached up, grasping the enemy helicopter's landing rails. With a Herculean effort he dragged himself up, spun for a moment, and planted his boots on the rail, detaching his umbilical wire as he did so.

He appeared, suddenly, beside Feuchter.

Carter saw Feuchter mouth something. The helicopter veered left, banking sharply in panic. Carter smashed, helpless for a moment, against the door, his head hitting the glass and cracking its surface; he dragged the Browning up and placed the muzzle against the cockpit canopy. Even through the wind's noise he heard the tiny *clack* of metal against the window.

Feuchter heard it too.

He turned, staring hard at Carter.

His eyes glittered cold; his mouth was a grim sour line.

'Fuck,' screamed Carter through gritted teeth, the word snatched away instantly by the wind as his hair whipped wildly around his head, 'you.' He pulled the trigger. The bullet smashed through the canopy towards Feuchter's face. It drove through his top teeth and his palate and into the base of his skull. Feuchter slumped backwards, releasing the helicopter's controls as his brain erupted from the back of his head in a shower, splattering against the seat and covering Natasha in gore.

She gasped.

The helicopter lurched and flipped suddenly sideways.

For an instant she met Carter's shocked gaze. Then he was gone, lost in the darkness, lost in the ice rain, lost in the infinite blackness of the cold night storm.

Natasha grabbed the helicopter's controls, impeded by her tape-bound wrists. Feuchter flopped around beside her as she managed to steady the aircraft.

They were close to the fast-sinking cruiser. It was sliding beneath the bubbling super-heated waters, settling below the waves like some dying dinosaur.

Natasha suddenly became aware of her aerial entourage and banked the helicopter around in a wide circle, her two *protective* escorts following suit. Then she suddenly spun the aircraft and opened fire with the on-board heavy machine guns.

The two Nex-piloted vehicles evaded the bullets ... and collided. In a sudden tangle of metal and twisting screeching engines, they plummeted towards the sea in a ball of fire.

Natasha smiled; she tried to calm her pounding heart but failed.

She steered the helicopter low over the sea, searching for Carter. Again and again she flew passes, her heart sinking, despair flooding through her. The helicopters that she had destroyed had sunk slowly beneath the cold waves.

Spinning the helicopter around once more, she watched as the battling DemolSquads, buoyed by the victory of seeing the cruiser – and its heavy guns – sunk, stormed through the skies, raining hot death on the remaining Nex.

The rain and ice continued to lash down.

Before very long, it was all over.

And a wounded group of heroes limped home.

CHAPTER 26

DEEP

Carter fell, and as he hit the icy waters all semblance of sanity was crushed from him in an instant as the freezing sea chilled him to the bone. Deep under he went, his Browning gone in an instant, bright white stars of pain forced into his numbed brain and body. He gasped, breathing in water. He spluttered, and realised that possibly, down in the depths of this polar black ice ocean—

'*You might drown.*'

'Leave me be.'

'*I should have warned you: you should have waited another three seconds so the positions of the rotors and stick didn't combine to flip the helicopter. Then you wouldn't be here . . . drowning.*'

'What do I have to do to be rid of you, fucker?'

'*You have to die,*' whispered Kade.

All force of will flooded from Carter. But then fire burned bright in his mind and he reached, slowing his descent into this awesome abyss, and struck out, fighting his way up, up, up, bubbles bursting from his tortured lungs. He broke through the surface, sucking in a huge

huge gulp of precious cold air. His breath streamed like dragon smoke. He realised that he was screaming.

Opening his eyes, Carter breathed deeply and saw the helicopter banking sharply. Machine guns roared and the other two Nex helicopters smashed and merged together, their rotors folding directly above him as Carter's grimace of madness dropped from his face—

'You're fucking *shitting* me . . .'

The twisted helicopters fell.

Carter dived, kicking with all his might, diving down and down, and the cold was forgotten in this sudden desperate race to get beneath the surface. Dimly he heard the impact – a dull *whoosh* – and his surroundings were illuminated by the burning helicopters descending above him through the cold waves, ignited fuel a torch lighting his way to a deep dark dominion named Death.

Kicking with all his might, Carter fought his way down; he risked a glance behind – above – and they were there, two glowing machines held in a metal mesh embrace.

He could see a Nex, struggling to fight free of the wreckage. But it was trapped.

The helicopters sank closer to Carter, who kicked to get out of their way.

Sorrow swamped him; he could faintly hear the Nex screaming.

The glow disappeared. Lungs burning, Carter kicked for the surface once more. The cold was numbing him to the point of death. He felt tingling all over his skin; he could not feel his hands and feet and face.

He burst free. Breathed deeply.

Debris littered the sea now. He glanced around.

Distantly, he saw the helicopter battle ending. More Nex were sent hurtling to their deaths and Carter felt sick deep down to his core. He watched idly as the cruiser finally succumbed to the cold dark waters.

Carter trod water.

And he knew that he had nowhere to go.

No way of saving himself.

Would they come looking for him? Or would the bastards think he was dead? Would they leave him to freeze slowly to death, alone with his memories for his last fleeting moments of life—?

There are worse ways to die, he decided sombrely.

But then, there are better ways.

He kept moving but he could not feel his arms or legs now; only the trunk of his body retained some heat. The pain had gone; all his pain had gone, numbed by the freezing waters.

How long will it take? he mused.

Minutes?

Seconds?

'What the *fuck* are you doing here?'

Carter turned around; there was a small black boat. A man peered down at him, goggles pushed up on his head, a cheeky smile on his broad face. Jam winked.

'We saw you take a dive. Thought you might need a ride,' rumbled Slater.

Carter grinned. 'Was that your firework display?'

'Nuke in a suitcase,' said Jam with a laugh. 'Low radiation yield – quite eco-friendly, when you think about it.'

The two men reached down and dragged Carter into their little boat, which bobbed alarmingly. 'You'll have to hug him, share your body heat,' said Jam, firing up the engine and heading out into the darkness.

'I'm not fucking hugging him. I'm not a poof!'

Jam rolled his eyes. 'Slater, look at the man! He'll die of hypothermia! Now, I'm not casting aspersions on your sexuality, but you really need to get him warm.' He stared hard at Carter who was shivering uncontrollably, eyes closed, pain his mistress. 'In fact, I think this is going to be a threesome if we don't want the fucker dead.'

They both gathered round Carter, and as the boat sped through the dark waves under the storm-filled heavens, they huddled close to him and waited for the dawn to come.

A cold late-autumn wind blew the brown and yellow leaves down the road, swirling them up into the air, decorating the tarmac with those symbols of summer's death and winter's impending onslaught. The gleaming black Mercedes sped through the wind-scattered leaves, turned left at the bottom of the street and headed out towards the deserted docks.

It was early. Five a.m. and not yet light.

The Mercedes stopped, engine ticking over, tendrils of smoke trailing from its exhaust; one of the rear doors opened and Carter – a bruised and battered Carter, missing a front tooth but cleaned and bandaged up and whole again – stepped onto the rough concrete and breathed deeply of the nectar that was the morning air. He limped slowly across the dockside, panting and wincing in pain as his broken sternum pierced his thoughts, and halted, staring down into the black, lapping water. He pulled free a packet of cigarettes, freed one from its paper cage with a heavily bandaged hand, and lit the weed.

Smoke plumed above the water and Carter sighed.

He turned at the sound of another car; the Range Rover cruised past the parked Mercedes and approached Carter where he stood beside the sea wall.

A cold wind blew as the Range Rover cut its engine.

Carter glanced in at the group of large men. One of the

doors opened and a figure stepped out; it was a man Carter had never met before, and yet Carter instinctively recognised him as Spiral; he was tall, and broad, and quite old. His grey hair was short, his eyes bright and pale. A neatly trimmed moustache and a long overcoat gave him something of the look of a gangster.

'Mr Carter.'

Carter shook the man's leather-gloved hand.

Carter nodded, drawing deep on his cigarette. 'Good morning, sir.'

'Yes, it is,' said the man. 'Come, walk with me.'

They walked along the edge of the docks, the wind blowing beneath their collars and making coat tails flap. An occasional seagull cried overhead as it swept low, searching for food.

'You know who I am?'

'No, sir.'

'That is probably for the best. But it has come to my attention that after your recent . . . exploits, shall we say, you have come to know rather a lot of things about Spiral that maybe you shouldn't. And yet we cannot forget your sterling service – albeit unknowingly – in leading us to the filth of the Nex, and in your destruction of the traitors known as Feuchter and Durell.'

'I appreciate that, sir.'

The man stopped and gazed deeply into Carter's eyes.

'Hmm,' he said. And then Carter saw it: the Browning 9mm. In the man's gloved hands.

Carter swallowed hard.

The man smiled.

'Here, this is yours. It was recovered when they dived for Durell's body. A miracle, don't you think?'

Carter took the gun. It was marked; scratched; old and worn. It had character.

'A miracle. Yeah.' He laughed then, staring out over the water. 'Did they find him?'

'No.'

'Oh.' Carter scratched thoughtfully at his brow. 'Look, sir, you can be assured of my loyalty concerning the things that I have discovered. I was maybe just a little pissed off at the beginning, because I thought that Spiral was trying to kill me at the start of these . . . shall we say, *adventures*. It would appear that I was mistaken.' Carter's voice had turned somewhat cool. His eyes glittered and his mouth tightened into a grim line.

The man nodded. 'Information is power, Carter. Look what too much information did for Feuchter and Durell. You cannot tell everybody everything; as DemolSquads you are only tiny cogs in the machine, only small players in the whole game. That happy pair of our enemies nearly brought Spiral down because of information: their knowledge; their complete understanding; the things that they *shouldn't* have known.'

Carter rubbed wearily at his eyes. 'Even if they had brought us down, others would have taken our place.'

'Yes.'

Carter nodded. He threw his cigarette butt into the sea. The black cold waves took the glowing tip and it disappeared from view. The wind howled softly; Carter shivered, remembering his thoughts of drowning in those distant ice-laden waters.

'I have some questions . . .' said Carter.

The man held up his gloved hand. He shook his head in the negative, just once.

'Maybe another time.'

Carter smiled sardonically. 'You mean another time as in never?'

'It is for your own protection,' said the man. He smiled

then, but it was an uncertain smile, a smile without a trace of humour – a smile on a face not used to the expression. 'I want you to remember, Carter, that our soldiers are never expendable.' He lit a cigarette. Held it delicately.

Carter met the tall man's gaze: grey eyes, hooded and masking a thousand emotions. Their stares locked for a long time. Carter held the man's cool look. Without another word, he turned and strolled leisurely down the dockside, admiring the dark expanse of churning sea. He climbed into the Range Rover which started its engine, turned, and was gone.

Carter turned back, staring out over the distant black waves. He shivered, pulling his coat tighter around his shoulders.

'Arse-kisser,' said Kade.

'What the fuck are you doing back?'

'I was lonely. I missed your company.'

'You're a fucking worm, Kade, and I am cursed with your presence.'

'You'd be lost without me,' said Kade softly.

'Why? What fucking possible help could you give me?'

'You're touchy today. Maybe you just need more time to think through our relationship.'

'What relationship is this? You driving me insane?'

'Lighten up, Carter: y'know, our relationship – me getting to kill people on your behalf when you need a little encouragement. That sort of brotherly deal thing? You scratch my back—'

'And you put a knife in mine?'

Kade laughed softly. *'Here, listen . . . I . . . I . . . I apologise. For sulking with you. There. I've said it.'*

'That was big of you.'

'You motherfu— No, no, you are right. I'll leave you. Let you gather your mental composure.'

'Better leave me for a *while*; say, a thousand years?'

Carter lit another cigarette. He heard the footsteps approaching and he did not turn. Natasha stood beside him, staring out at the sea and the distant buoys. Then she looked up at him. 'You all right?'

He nodded.

'They fire you?'

'No. Not yet. I think they'll probably want a few more psychological tests and medical reports. Then, if I'm real lucky, a desk job.'

Natasha took his hand; their fingers entwined and squeezed.

'You're a lucky man,' she said. 'Lucky to be alive.'

'Hey,' said Carter, grinning. 'Lucky is my middle fucking name.'

'Come on; the others are waiting. We have a party to go to.'

'Those other stinking curs? And at five o'clock *in the morning*?'

'Well, it's the tail end of a party. You know what Slater and Jam will be like. They'll still be pissed . . .'

Carter nodded. 'I'm game,' he yawned. 'Unless . . .'

'Yes?'

Their gazes met.

'I thought you were injured?' smiled Natasha.

'I'm not *that* injured. I still have, shall we say, various functioning parts.'

'I'm sure you have. Your place or mine?'

'Mine,' said Carter. 'I've got to pick up Sam.'

'He OK?'

'Great,' said Carter. 'Well fed on assassin, apparently. Made a right mess of the corpses in the woods; went back for a midnight feast when he was let out, the dirty dumb fat mutt.'

'That is one sick dog.'

'Hey – I suppose to his eyes it was fresh meat. Fair game. He was only thinking of his belly. Like the rest of us men. Listen, you go and wait in the car. I would like a moment alone.'

Natasha nodded. 'Sure.'

She moved away, and Carter stood staring out at the dark rolling sea. Waves crested with foam lined the horizon. The cold breeze reminded him of the coming winter.

From the pocket of his coat he removed a small object: a silver disk. It rested against Carter's cold skin and he stared at it for a while, wondering at the secrets it held. The riddle of how to rebuild the QIII. The code and data required to replicate events now done . . .

'You're better off dead,' he muttered.

Reaching back, he threw the silver disk as far out into the sea as he could. There was a tiny *splash*. The last copy of the QIII schematics sank without a trace in the dark waters.

Carter smiled softly.

'It is finally over,' he breathed. He walked back towards the Mercedes and climbed into the warmth of the plush heated interior. The gleaming vehicle turned with a crackle of tyres on concrete and headed smoothly for the network of UK motorways – leaving behind nothing but bitter exhaust fumes and the promise of an oncoming cold winter.

SIU Transcript 3

CLASSIFIED 000/000/artic SPECIAL INVESTIGATIONS UNIT
ECube transmission MEMO digMail sec:code:0056
Date: October 2XXX

Mission status: successful

Losses: 186 DemolSquad members dead resulting in the regrouping and collapsing of 38 squads. Training has been initiated and recruits searched for on worldwide basis.

Progress: the counter-attack by Spiral has culminated in the destruction of the mobile anti-Spiral warship and a loss of nearly 400 Necros. The rest have gone underground and SAD teams will be deployed on missions of extermination. The body of the traitor, Durell, has not been recovered.

Conclusion: a thorough clampdown on Spiral operatives and closer mental screening measures need to be implemented in the future. It was too easy for a small group to bring about some degree of internal collapse; power will be redistributed in future months.

Cartervb512: subject has been seriously wounded// condition presently under close scrutiny// severe mental monitoring required// return to DemolSquads doubtful at this stage.

\\###TRANSFER TERMINATED###

EPILOGUE

PARADISE

A turquoise sea lapped against a white sand beach. A gentle breeze dissipated the tropical heat, swaying the palm trees and heavy broad-leafed ferns that lined the wide white stone walls. Shells lay scattered among splashes of green seaweed, spatterings of pink and white, grey and blue, spirals leading trails from the lapping lagoons to the heavy foliage behind the bordering white wall.

The small boy ran barefoot across the sand, leaving footprints, his bronzed body gleaming with sweat as he sprinted towards the sea. Behind him, the shrill squeal of an angry mother followed with a promise of punishment, but for now the boy was safe . . . the harsh slaps would follow, but now he dropped to a crouch with his feet in the lapping waters and sucked at the fruit, juices running across his deeply tanned face, dripping from his chin into the blue waters.

The boy finished the stolen fruit and looked sharply to the right, his shock of black hair tumbling around his face. He stood quickly, and moved towards the shape lying half in and half out of the water. It was black, and at first sight resembled a thick tangle of old seaweed. But as the boy drew near he saw that it was vaguely human in shape, curled into a tight ball as if to ward off pain. Reaching down, he picked up a sun-bleached stick and crept close to the object. His nose wrinkled at the smell and, reaching forward, he prodded it gently.

When no movement was forthcoming, the boy shuffled closer, his interest piqued. The sea provided many treasures, but most of them the boy had long ago become tired of. This, however, was different.

He prodded again, then tentatively reached out and ran his fingers across the husk of black.

What is it? he thought in youthful wonder.

The object was rough beneath his fingers, like the old cracked leather his uncle cured from the hides of cows. He prodded it, harder this time, and felt the surface move over something within.

The boy stood, quickly bored, his wonder snatched away like a wind-stolen veil. He looked out over the sea. He shaded his eyes, searching for signs of the rich people's cruise ships that sometimes passed.

Something brushed his ankle.

He looked down to see a clawed black hand . . . that grabbed him in an iron grip, pulled him quickly to the sand and silenced his screams with a single heavy blow.

don't you **fuck with me**
don't you pull me down
don't shit in my face
don't you drag me around –

the day that **you die**
will be the day that I do
piss on your grave and on the rest of you

don't you **get it?**
don't you **forget it**

Get It [abridged]
Clawfinger